This one's for Duncan:

The start of a new world,
for the start of a new life.

Late, though, as always.

Thank you for London and Paris.
And I'm sorry about Boston.

WHEN AM I? AND WHERE?

Evayne a'Nolan looked into the seer's ball. Mists caught the sun's rays and turned silver. She gazed into them, waiting for the visions.

At first all she saw was the faire itself. Then, recognizing the uniforms of the Hunter Lords and their huntbrothers, she knew she was in Breodanir, and as her vision scanned further, she realized she was near the Sacred Wood, the King's Forest.

When?

The mists rolled again. There! Stephen of Elseth was with Gilliam. She thought they might be fourteen or fifteen. Certainly, they were not the men she had met years ago.

The mists shifted once more, but not at her bidding. White light sparked like lightning across the clouds. Then, suddenly, the mists flew apart. At the heart of the ball, creeping through the undergrowth, was a shadowy figure, a young woman with dark, wild hair. *It can't be time yet,* Evayne thought. *In the now, Gilliam of Elseth is too young.* But the ball never lied, and she knew her task was urgent by the color and immediacy of the vision. She had to do something for or about the wild girl. But what?

She almost set the ball aside, but some instinct held her back. Because of this she was prepared for the second vision—and the second vision explained the first too clearly.

A tall, lean figure ran, catlike, through the forest. Suddenly it paused to stand and test the air with a flick of a sliver-thin tongue. Its eyes were obsidian, its teeth long and sharp. *Demon-kin!*

Securing the ball in her robes, Evayne a'Nolan, seer, mage, and historian, began to run. . . .

CHAPTER ONE

25th day of Corvil, 396 AA
King's City, Breodanir

A near-skeletal boy peered out from around a shadowed corner. His face was the color of winter; white, muddied by the dark hollows of wide eyes. Those eyes examined the thin crowd in the lower city streets.

Only one there caught his attention—a man dressed in audacious furs and bangles, with a thick, new purse attached to his wrist and a belt heavy with winter supplies girding him round his midsection. His cap alone would fetch a good price and guarantee food and shelter besides.

The boy was hungry and tired. That he was cold as well had ceased to bother him; the winter had been harsh enough that the icy bite of nearing spring felt something akin to warm. It had been a very bad season.

It would be worse still if he didn't go back to the den armed with some display of money or barter goods. Marcus, self-proclaimed den leader, had already made that perfectly clear; the bruises still showed on the boy's face. Fear set him to shivering and the cold joined in. A ragged cough that would not be ignored scraped at his throat. He needed a warm place to stay, and soon. Twice this winter he had seen cold kill.

The rich man stopped every so often to tsk-tsk at the state of the buildings. His purse bounced and jangled, even at this distance. The young boy swallowed nervously. He would have already made his mark, but for the dogs. Not even the most ignorant of children could claim not to know what their presence meant.

One of these dogs stayed at its master's heels, lifting

its proud, wide head. Its eyes, circled on both sides by patches of black, darted back and forth, but it didn't stray far. The other dog, a bitch by the look of it, was a little more testy, but its fur was clean and it was an almost even gray. Its low-throated growl could be heard when anyone approached. These were no city dogs, rough and mangy after winter's scavenging. They were obviously well fed—on what, the boy didn't care to speculate. But their jaws, their teeth . . .

Stephen, the boy thought to himself, as his hands shook, *he's a Hunter Lord. Find someone else.*

But he'd looked; Luck knew it well and had obviously seen fit to curse him. There was no one else that was even likely, and if he waited in the shadows like a dithering rat, he'd lose his entrance ticket and—he coughed, retching—any chance for a meal this day.

Hunger and cold decided him. He moved forward, his worn shoes squelching in the slush. Thin shoulders came up, as did his chin. Seen this way, he was a stick of a lad, but not uncomely, and not particularly dangerous. Only poor—and that, in the King's City, was danger enough.

Soredon, Lord Elseth, smiled softly at the sound of light steps. It was about time; how long did the urchin think to keep him out in this dismal weather? Corvil was a chill month; one to be avoided if at all possible.

Maritt growled and began to swivel her head. Her jaws were open, and her teeth, cleaner than the snow, were also whiter.

Easy, easy, Maritt. Stay at heel. Stay calm.

She heard his Hunter's command and shifted on her hind legs. Her growl didn't really diminish, and Soredon sighed, shaking the purse he carried with renewed vigor in an attempt to drown out Maritt's voice. It was his own fault, and he knew it. Maritt was his prize bitch, and he coddled her overmuch.

Ah, well. At least Corwel was behaving. Absently, he dropped one gloved hand to rest upon the alaunt's broad head. Corwel was young yet, but still the best dog that Elseth had ever produced. He tousled those flopped ears with genuine pride and pleasure.

Good. The boy was behind him, sauntering gently forward. Lord Elseth carefully positioned his broad back and began the inner search for the Hunter's trance. He was experienced enough to have earned the rank of Master Hunter at the King's pleasure. The trance came quickly and easily, fitting him better than these awkward, fine clothes. The crisp bite of the air grew keener still; the colors of the street faded into sharp, clean outlines. Everywhere, life ground to a slower, subtler movement.

He reached out from the trance, found Maritt's eyes, and looked carefully through them, feeling the background thrum of her deep-throated growl as if it came from his own chest.

The boy approached his back slowly. Through Maritt's vision, he examined the young thief. The boy was all bones and sallow skin, with a thatch of pale hair that might be paler still when less filthy. Lack of height and weight made his age hard to guess, but Lord Elseth was certain he was somewhere between seven and nine. A good age; one that suited the Hunter Lord's purpose fully. But would the little thief continue to linger in the half-melted, filthy snow, or would he at last make his move?

Please, Lady Luck, smile on me now. I've seen enough of your frowns for this ten-day.

Her answer was beneficent and sudden.

The boy darted, like a pale shadow, flickering at his side. He saw the gray flash of what once might have passed for a dagger and lifted his wrist in a snap of motion, carrying the purse strings easily out of the boy's reach. His turn was so smooth and deft that the child's knife didn't have time to stop its motion.

With a smile that was all white teeth, Lord Elseth grabbed the boy's wrist and hauled him off his feet.

"What have we here?"

He'd moved so quickly that Stephen still wasn't sure when the broad, fur-covered back had suddenly changed into the man's front—but he didn't like it. Thievery had its own penalty in the King's City—and the punishment was far worse when the victim was one of the Hunter Lords or Ladies. Hunger and fear were forgotten now, as was breathing; he saw instead the shadow of the knife at his thumbs. If he'd had the chance, he might have taken a swing with his dagger—but it was the dagger hand that the Lord held, and the Lord showed no signs of loosing his grip.

He swallowed a deep breath, lost it to coughing, and choked. His wrist was firmly trapped in the larger man's hand. *Think, damn it. Think.* He cleared his throat. "You've got no call to hold me, sir. I was just—"

"I know well what you were doing, whelp. And it has its price. Come along; your thieving days are over."

Stephen struggled as the tips of his toes brushed the ground. He kicked out with his feet and found the ribs of the large black-and-white dog. It snarled and snapped to the side, avoiding its target by turning at the last second.

"That's enough," Lord Elseth said, his voice remarkably similar in tone to that of the dog's. "You will *be still.*"

Gulping, Stephen nodded, and found the flat of his feet. What he did next was born of instinct and terror—but it was also unexpected. His small jaw found the inside of the Hunter Lord's wrist and clamped down.

The Hunter Lord cursed and pulled back, and for a moment, Stephen was free. It was all that he needed. He had had to become good at running. In a blur he was gone into the sanctuary of the alleyways and warrens that he knew so well.

Blood dripped down to the snow, mingling with dirt and water to become another murky patch of ground. Soredon smiled and shook his head. He bound his wrist carefully; it took him only seconds.

"Well, Corwel, Maritt. What shall we do?"

Maritt was straining at the invisible leash that held her at his side.

Lord Elseth reached down. From the left side of his belt, he lifted a silver-mouthed horn. He held it to his lips, feeling the chill press of metal and the thrum of the silent demands the dogs made. Ah, he had chosen well, even though it had taken too much time. The child had spirit and not a little cunning.

The long, loud lowing of the horn announced the Hunt

in the King's City. Twice it blew long, and a third time, short. Corwel waited until the last note had died and then placed his nose to the ground. His tail, short and stumpy though it was, began to crisscross the air.

"Yes, Corwel. Find him."

Stephen heard the horn. It cut across the sound of his feet and the horrible rasp of his breath. He had not heard its like before, but now that he had he would never forget it.

They followed by scent. He knew this because he always remembered the old stories, even when he no longer believed in them. He hoped that this part, at least, was true; nothing else had been.

Hunter dogs ran fast, and they were smarter than most normal dogs, but Stephen was certain he knew these alleys and buildings better than they knew their kennels and forests. His life depended on it.

His breath was quick and sharp with cold. He wanted to look over his shoulder, but he knew it would slow him down; that much he'd learned over the last year of running.

Please, Lady, smile. Let it work. I'll make my offerings. Please.

He made a sharp right past the building that was called the Stonemason's, cutting it close enough that he could use the wall as a balance while he pivoted.

If the dogs followed by scent, he was going to give them something to smell.

Soredon ran, keeping pace with his dogs. He was deep into the Hunter's trance and running came easily to him now. The boy, like any animal that knew it was being pursued, didn't flee along a straight path. It was another good sign; fear didn't make the boy stupid.

There was no question at all in Lord Elseth's mind that the boy was afraid.

Stephen lost time to the doubled doors of Benny's Tavern; they were tall and heavy enough to take the damage of a good sized brawl. His hands were shaking because he'd balled them into fists that were too tight, but he still managed to pull the doors open. Sunlight streamed in at his back, making a silhouette of his height and girth.

"Hey!"

He wasn't allowed into the tavern, but he moved quickly enough so that no one had time to stop him as he rushed into—and through—the sparse crowd. It was early yet, but lunch would soon be served, and the regular patrons had already filled the air with a steady stream of smoke, sweat, and salty language.

"HEY, YOU! STOP!" The bartender's bellow carried with an ease that spoke of too much experience. Next would come the slam of the wooden countertop as it was raised too quickly, and the heavy-soled tread of a large, angry man.

Stephen missed it all. He bolted past the last of the bar's patrons and into the kitchens. If the smell of this place didn't stymie the dogs, nothing would. It probably wasn't cleaned more than twice a year, and at that, only when Benny's mother visited.

The kitchens, of course, weren't empty.

"Hey!"

Stephen dodged a ladle—Benny's wife wasn't quite as slow and large as Benny was—ducked under the lunge of Benny's oldest son, and avoided sliding on a piece of something that had probably once been bread. He didn't even pause at the woodstove, although he almost smiled at the fleeting warmth.

The kitchen door exited into another alley. Stephen managed to yank it open and get through it before Benny's son caught up with him. Then his feet hit the snow and his lungs filled with clean, cold air.

Let them figure that out.

He had no intention of waiting to see whether or not they could. He ran.

Lord Elseth rarely cursed; his Lady found vulgar language ignorant and acutely embarrassing—and she exacted a high price for the latter. Nonetheless, he had just enough time to do so before his dogs leaped up at the closed doors of the tavern, growling.

Through the trance, the boy's scent passed from Corwel to Lord Elseth; it was strong and distinct. *Corwel, Maritt—away from the door. Come.*

Corwel obeyed gracefully, Maritt with a growl. But they both came to stand by his side, fur bristling, eyes trained on the closed doors.

Stay.

With a grimace of distaste, Lord Elseth pulled open a single door, and attempted to blend into the ambience of Benny's Tavern. Silence radiated outward from him like a wave as each and every patron in the large, beamed room stopped to stare at this newest customer.

"Good day to you, sir," Benny said. His voice, pitched out of long habit to travel over a crowded, noisy room, was uncomfortably loud. He ran out from behind the counter, wiping his hands almost fastidiously on his large, heavy apron. "Is there anything at all that I can do for you?"

Soredon was a tall man; Benny was short and somewhat rounder. It was not because of height alone that Lord Elseth looked down. "Yes." He reached into the pouch that jangled so obviously at his belt and pulled out a gold coin that bore the impression of a stag's antlers astride the King's Crown.

Benny reached for it, and Soredon snapped his open hand into a large, gloved fist. "I'm following a young thief. Slip of a boy, pale hair. I believe he came in here."

"Couldn't have," Benny said promptly. "No kids're allowed." He looked pointedly at the gloved hand.

Soredon growled. It was a feral sound, not a human one, and Benny took a step back as he realized—for the first time—that he faced a Hunter Lord.

"Uh, that is, no kids can come in and stay, your lordship." The bartender ran a hand over his forehead and tried not to look at the fist that held a small fortune. "He ran out through the kitchen."

"Good." Lord Elseth opened his palm and tossed the coin into the air.

Benny was still scrabbling for it when the dogs came in through the door Soredon held open.

* * *

Stephen ran, holding his side as the cramps started. Let Luck only smile, and he'd never thieve again. He thought, for a moment, that she'd heard his prayers and had chosen to grant them. For a moment. Then a new sound started, worse than the horn. The dogs were baying.

He thought of their teeth, and had no doubt as to which would give first: his skin or their jaws. The alleys that towered above him in faceless, near windowless walls, became distant, unfriendly terrain. He searched in vain for stairs, for anything that would take his feet off the ground and give the dogs another pause.

The baying grew louder and closer, filling his ears completely, obscuring his shallow breaths. He bounded around a corner, sliding in the muddied snow. His hands scraped a wall and came away splinter-filled and bleeding as he continued to run.

The alleys opened up as he crossed a deserted street. Buildings flashed by, and he recognized them: The Tern, its board flapping in the breeze; the butchers', the one baker's. He hesitated a moment in front of the butchers' and caught a glimpse of the bitch as she rounded the corner down the street.

There was only one place to go. His teeth bit through his lower lip as he put on a burst of speed—probably the last that was left him. The fear of the dogs was greater than the fear of Marcus and his retribution.

There. Ahead, in a nook that the restructuring a century ago had created, stood the door to the den. As always, it was closed. He ran at it full tilt, skidding at the last moment to give a first knock with his entire body.

A flap of wood, at an eye level that cleared his head by at least a foot, scraped open. Above the bridge of an oft broken nose, two dark eyes squinted in the sunlight.

"Marcus, it's me! Let me in!" Stephen began to bang frantically at the wood; the dogs were closing fast.

"What've you brought for me?"

"Marcus, please! I need to get in—they're coming!"

The flap shut. Stephen stood in the silence for a heartbeat before the dogs started again. He was shaking and gasping as he looked from side to side. There wasn't any place else to run; the den had been chosen because it stood in the middle of an alley that had no escape to either side.

He lifted his hand to strike again, and then let it drop. Steadying himself, he turned, his dagger shaking as much as his thin arms did. He would have to face them. Maybe, if he was careful, he could injure the dogs enough to get away.

The large black and white bounded around the corner and lifted its broad, triangular head. It came to a stop but didn't take its eyes from its quarry. At its heels came the bitch. The Hunter Lord could not be far behind.

If he'd had food, he might have tried to bribe the dogs, or at least distract them. It was an idea. But he wouldn't be in this situation if he'd had anything to eat, and he suspected that the dogs ate well enough so they wouldn't even look at the scraps he could throw them.

He crouched, holding the knife out as if it were a shield. Why hadn't the dogs come forward?

As if in answer, the Hunter Lord joined them, following the same trail that both Stephen and the dogs had left in their hurried race through the snow; he wasn't even breathing heavily. His cap was gone now, although he didn't appear to be carrying it. All he held in his hand was the horn that had sounded the chase. The dogs moved apart, and he came to stand between them, placing one hand on either of their heads. The bitch bridled at the feel of the hard, cold horn but stayed her ground anyway.

Everywhere there was silence.

Stephen met the eyes of the Hunter Lord; they were brown to his blue, and narrowed as if in thought. He waited, wordless, until the waiting itself was as fine a torture as the running had been.

"Don't—don't you move!" He waved his dagger, swordlike, through the air in front of his face. "I'm telling you, stay where you are! I don't want to hurt you!"

"Oh, indeed," the Lord replied. "I can assure you, my boy, that you needn't fear that. And I have no wish to harm you; you've led a fine chase. Better than I would have guessed. Come. Cease this nonsense. We have far to go." The hand that wore the thick, cloth gauntlet rose. "Come."

Stephen backed into the door, shaking his head firmly from side to side. How stupid did this Hunter Lord think he was? "I ain't going nowhere. Go away, or I'll have to use this." He waved the knife wildly, loosing a startled cry as the door gave way behind him.

Before he could react, he was jerked off the ground by the back of his collar. His dagger went tumbling into the snow. He didn't have to look back to know who held him.

"Well, fine sir," Marcus said, raising Stephen higher. "It seems that you've had trouble in our fair city streets."

"Let the boy go," the Hunter Lord replied. "I have no business with you."

"Don't you just?" Marcus looked down at Stephen, noted the creeping purple tinge to his skin, and slammed him to his feet. "Well, I've got your thief, at no small risk to myself. I think that's worth something." The convivial smile Marcus wore was so out of place on his face that the Hunter Lord couldn't even manage a similar expression. Lip curling, he said, "Let the boy go."

"Not from around here, are you?"

"No." The one word made clear what the Lord thought of that.

"Well, maybe I'll explain a few rules of the King's City. This," he shook Stephen, who was too stunned to struggle, "is a thief."

"I'm aware of that."

"I," once again he used Stephen as punctuation, "am the man who caught him."

The black and white answered with a low, warning growl.

"In my books that makes me the one who gets the reward. But I ain't a greedy man. I'll share it with you."

"Marcus—please. . . ." Stephen's voice was a rasping choke.

"Shut up." No openhanded slap, this. When Marcus' hand drew back, it was bloodied.

Lord Elseth stared hard at Marcus for a moment. When he moved his mouth, it formed no words, and the lift of his lips was no smile. "Corwel." The Lord took a step back. "Yours."

He lifted the horn to his lips.

The dogs sprang, their feet covering the short distance as if they needed no ground to run on. Marcus' eyes grew wide, and with a loud cry, he threw Stephen at them. He ran into the old building, yelling as if they had already reached him.

Corwel's voice joined his in the music of hunter and hunted. Without pause, he followed through the open door.

The Hunter Lord ignored the sounds that came out of the building. Quietly, he walked over to the huddled bundle of youth that lay at Maritt's feet.

No, Maritt, he sent softly. *Go and join Corwel.*

She needed no other word. Like the breeze, she passed them by, leaving almost no trace.

The Lord knelt, unmindful of the snow that immediately began to melt into his knees. He reached out with one large hand, saw the horn that it held, and stopped to return it to his belt.

Stephen was too tired, too weak, to offer any more resistance. He lay on his side, his face covered by hands that showed red. What Marcus had done had taken the last of his spirit and guttered it. It had been stupid to come here. But even if Marcus wouldn't let him in, he didn't have to—didn't have to . . .

Lord Elseth reached down gently and drew Stephen's hands away from his face. "Come, boy. Let me see it."

His lips were already swelling. Very gingerly, Lord Elseth probed at the bruised jaw. Stephen gasped.

"It may be dislocated. Can you walk?"

Nodding, Stephen tried to rise. His eyes were dark, their blue lost, as he glanced furtively up at the larger man.

"We don't go to the Justice-born, lad. We go to the Mother-born. There's a temple not far from the lower city. I'll make the offering." Lord Elseth rose and put his hands under Stephen's arms. He set the boy on his feet, saw that he wobbled dangerously, and lifted him up instead.

The child weighed almost nothing.

"Boy?"

Stephen shook his head, flailing weakly, although he had almost no strength for it. Then he sank into the furs that surrounded the Lord. They were soft, and so very, very warm.

"Dogs?" He muttered, an edge of fear in the solitary word. His lids were already too heavy and he missed the expression on the Hunter Lord's face, which was just as well.

"They'll be along soon. When they've finished here."

The silver mists rolled in over the scene like fog across the lowlands. She sat in an inn half a continent away, in Everani, a fishing village downcoast of Averalaan, her palms cupped around a glowing, crystalline sphere.

At her back, she heard the whispers: *seer-born.* She did not disillusion them; it gave her privacy for the moment, and besides, it was not altogether untrue. But she was more, and different, than simply talent-born.

Stephen of Elseth, she thought, as she pushed strands of hair back into the privacy of her hood. *You're so young. We don't meet yet.* But she knew where she was, and more important, knew *when* she was.

The mists obscured the young boy completely before she looked away. She was Evayne a'Nolan, and quite alone. She straightened her shoulders, took a deep breath, and rose. It was time for work now, not for dalliance, and she had lost precious minutes watching.

And remembering.

CHAPTER TWO

The broad-shouldered, auburn-haired noble who rode beside the Hunter Lord was not in a good mood. He spoke gently enough to Stephen, but every time he turned his attention to the lord, his lips whitened around the edges. The Hunter Lord was also angry.

Stephen did his best to shrink into the saddle and avoid the notice of either of the two large men. It was hard; his legs ached, first from walking and then from riding. Horses had been, at best, a thing to dream about until three days ago. Now, they were incredibly wide, large, and frightening animals that he could, just barely, sit astride.

The dogs were still the dogs, and if the bitch looked up and growled periodically, she was a good few feet out of range. When the Hunter Lord wasn't looking, he took the opportunity to sneer at her.

He'd been fed, clothed in warm furs, and given a real bed to sleep in as they'd traveled along the road to Mother only knew where. But his own mother had told him once that they fed sheep and cows before they slaughtered them, too.

He stared at his breath as it misted.

The red-haired man in gray and green glowered at his Hunter.

"Let it be, Norn," Lord Soredon said, his voice low and grating.

Norn of Elseth snorted.

Late snow fell in a thick, wet blanket that made travel difficult. Inns were cold and not well provisioned to deal with a Hunter Lord's disgruntled dogs, and Lord Elseth was never capable of dealing with ruffled innkeepers. In fact, Norn thought, as he walked his horse around a particularly tricky bridge—which had iced in the evening and was only visible at all because he knew the roads here well—Soredon wasn't capable of dealing with people. Period.

As a prime example, he took the waif who had walked, or ridden, listlessly between them for the better part of the journey. Fright was still upon him and he answered any question with a monosyllable or a silent nod. His winter legs had finally given out two days ago, and he rode now on the packhorse. The four-legged one. Of course the horses couldn't be further burdened down, not with Lady Elseth's commands for purchases in the King's City, and Soredon, stubborn idiot that he was, had refused to take a proper wagon. Norn, huntbrother to Lord Elseth, carried one half of the boy's weight in goods, and Soredon, grumbling, took the rest.

An argument was brewing between the two men, but Norn didn't wish to have it out in front of the boy. The boy was just too vulnerable and too isolated to have to deal with the tempers of the nobility. And Norn didn't trust him not to try to effect some sort of escape during such an argument, which would probably kill him in the end.

Norn glanced over his broad shoulder, shifting so the pack frame didn't block his sight. Stephen sat sidesaddle across the horse, clutching at the braided manes for dear life. They had had a coat and mittens for him, but the latter he'd removed when he'd been deposited on the beast. His fingers were reddened by cold; Norn feared the bite of frost there.

He exhaled a fine, billowing mist and looked at the sun's crisp shadows. Soon, he was certain, they would see the village that sprawled around the manor grounds. And once the boy was safely inside, he had a word or two to say to Soredon.

In winter, the light was gone too early from the sky. For the villagers and the farmers, dinner was an afternoon affair. The cost of tallow and wick was high enough that they were perfectly happy to see their hours dictated by the sun. Solstice had passed, and the day was lengthening. Enough so that the Lady Elseth, along with her two small children, took dinner amid the fading pinks that showed through the towering bay window that was the manor's pride.

A fire burned merrily against the two walls, and servants busied themselves tending to it; it was warmer here than in their quarters. All was as it should be in the manor of Elseth.

"Lady."

Elsabet looked up from her plate as the door opened and the keykeeper walked in. Boredan was an older man; the oldest of those who served the Hunter Lord. He wore his age as he did his fine, tailored robes: perfectly.

It was unusual for him to interrupt the Lady Elseth at her dinner, and she rose at once, fearing some accident or mishap. "Boredan?"

"My apologies for interrupting your repast, Lady." He gave a low bow. "It appears that the Lord and his huntbrother are home."

"Already? We weren't expecting them for at least three ... Where are they?"

"If I should be so bold as to hazard a guess, I would say in the kennels, Lady. They have, however, left a guest, and Norn was most insistent that he be attended to."

"Father's home?" The older of the two children leaped out of his chair, food forgotten. His linen napkin tumbled to the floor, a crumb-covered, gravy-stained heap.

"Gilliam."

"But—but Father's—"

"Father is busy." Her tone made it clear that she was in no mood to indulge him.

He sat, disgruntled.

"Maribelle, do remember how you were taught to use a fork." Lady Elseth carefully pushed her chair in, folded her napkin, which was spotless, and left it on the table. "Why don't I see to the guest?"

"It would be appreciated, Lady."

She was certain of it. "Boredan, I know you're very busy, but do you think you could stay with the children?"

Boredan nodded as Gilliam rolled his eyes in despair. Mother was bad enough, but no one else in the house compared to the keykeeper for strictness of manners and demands on behavior.

"Most certainly. It looks as if Master Gilliam has forgotten everything I've taught him about dining habits."

She could hear the shouting before she reached the wide, grand hall that opened out from the vestibule. The words were muffled by distance, and the voices were raised so much that she couldn't distinguish them, which was for the better. On the other hand, the manor had been quiet since her Lord and his huntbrother had left. This would give the servants at least a three-day's worth of amusement.

And it was good that somebody was going to be amused by it. Certainly, from the set of lines in her otherwise smooth forehead, and the faint creases around her thinned lips, it was clear that she was not.

Now, Elsabet, she told herself. *I'm certain things could be worse.* She stopped in the hall, found it empty, and saw that both sets of doors were firmly closed. The shouting, obviously, carried through them. Biting her lip, she reminded herself not to think that in the future—it invariably turned out to prove true.

So annoyed was she that she walked to the door and tested the handle with a sharp yank before she saw the guest that the keykeeper had spoken of. He sat, his knees curled beneath his chin, against the banister of the stairs. His eyes were wide and ringed with the dark of sleeplessness or illness, and his clothing . . . best not to think about the dreadful state of that. Yet even though it was oversized and quite thick, she could see that he was mostly skin and bones; his cheeks were sunken, his fingers almost skeletal.

She knew why he had been brought here, and what he would become. It was quite clear that he did not.

If she had been angry before, it was forgotten; she was furious now. That two grown men couldn't set aside their differences for long enough to see to a cold, starving boy. . . .

The child looked up to meet her eyes. His knees came down, and he straightened up, away from the banister. His effort to be more alert only made him seem more frail.

"Hello," Lady Elseth said softly. "I see that you've been left quite alone."

He nodded, not daring words in front of so grand a Lady. She couldn't see her reflection in the dark of his eyes, but she knew that he was well aware of the contrast her fine dinner clothing made with his winter wear.

"You must be starving. And cold."

He nodded again.

"Well, come then. You are a guest in our house, and I won't do our hospitality a disservice by leaving you here any longer." She held out a hand and he stared at it as if it were a weapon. There was no mistaking the fear that lurked beneath the wary surface of his eyes.

In all, it was probably a good thing that Norn and Soredon were outside. Had her Hunter Lord of a husband been within the walls, and within her reach, Lady Elseth might have killed him. In an instant, she forgave Norn— for she knew them well enough to understand the nature of their dispute after having met the boy.

"Come," she said again. "There is no fire here, and no food. I shall see that you have rooms set aside for you, but dinner is already served." She made her voice softer still, and lowered her hand gently, capturing the blue of his eyes with the hazel of hers. "Don't you want to eat?"

She saw him struggle with hunger and fear, and was thankful that hunger won out; it was a near thing. He stepped forward and she began to move toward the dining room, taking great care not to crowd him.

He didn't know what to think of the Lady. He was certain he had never seen anyone so lovely—she looked as if she'd stepped out of a story just to meet him. Her dress was so fine and so long, the skirts full and rustling, the sleeves soft and draped. Her hair was darker than his, and pulled back from her face to fall in curls at the nape of her neck. Her eyes were hazel, not as cold as blue or gray. She seemed friendly.

He looked away from her, disgusted at himself. Stories. At his age.

"Come and sit here. Boredan, this is . . ."

"Stephen."

"Stephen. I'm Elsabet, and this is my daughter, Maribelle."

Maribelle looked up and sniffed, but Stephen couldn't be angry; she was almost a baby. Her face was still sort of fat and chubby, and her hair, like her mother's, fell long at the back, but in finer, softer ringlets.

"This is Gilliam, my son."

Gilliam made to rise, and no one stopped him. He looked Stephen up and down and then shrugged, his young lips turning up in a curl that reminded everyone of his father.

"Gilliam!"

"Pleased to meet you."

Stephen didn't bother to answer. This Lord's son was his own age at least, and probably thought too much of himself, given the way he'd answered. Well, fine clothes didn't make a person—his mother used to tell him that—and this Gilliam wasn't so much bigger than he.

"Why don't you take that seat, Stephen. The servants will bring dinner in a moment, and I shall join you when they arrive. I have a few things to attend to first, but I hope you won't hold that against our hospitality." Lady Elseth smiled, nodded, and turned almost in one motion. She was used to being obeyed, and even though her voice was friendly and warm, Stephen heard the command in it.

He paused to watch her retreating back. She couldn't be real, but just the same, she reminded him of old words and voices that he could barely put faces to.

"Are you going to stare, or are you going to eat?"

"Master Gilliam."

"I was just asking." Gilliam picked up his fork and began to cut away at the meat on his plate.

Meat. Something white nestled underneath a blanket of gravy, and something green sat beside it, untouched.

Stephen looked self-consciously at his clothing and then straightened out. He'd be damned if that boy would make him feel uncomfortable. "I'm going to eat," he replied curtly, pulling the chair out.

"Aintcha gonna change?"

"Maribelle."

"Well," the child said, tilting her head to one side and looking seriously at Boredan. "Ma always makes *me* change."

"Yes, and your Lady mother also tells you that you mustn't question guests."

She shrugged and faced Stephen. "Want my peas?"

"No, he doesn't," Boredan said, quite severely. "You do. Please, Master Stephen."

Master?

Servants came into the hall carrying trays and plates and an endless amount of food. They began to serve Stephen at Boredan's curt nod as Stephen stared. Still, it was obvious that the food was meant for him, so he didn't bother to ask. He was hungry.

Into his third mouthful of meat, he froze at the sound of Gilliam's unwelcome snicker.

"Don't you even know how to use a fork?"

The fork, curled in his left hand, stopped moving as Stephen stared down at it, embarrassed in spite of his best intentions.

"Master Gilliam, it isn't an art that you are a master of yourself. Your manners, if you please." The last three words were as pointed and cold as any that Stephen had ever heard.

Gilliam's cheeks purpled in a flush, but he doggedly continued. "Well, why don't you tell *him* how to eat?"

"Because *he* is a guest. *You* are a rude little boy."

Stephen waited until just the right moment. Boredan's attention was still upon the Lord's son, but the Lord's son was glaring at him. He smiled, stuck out his tongue, and bent down to his food.

He decided right there that he hated Gilliam. But not enough that he wouldn't eat at the table with him.

* * *

"What do you mean, you didn't even ask?"

Soredon rolled his eyes, "Elsa, don't you think we might—"

"Don't change the subject."

He could tell by the familiar flash of her eyes that he wasn't about to enter his domicile without satisfying her anger. He might be cold, hungry, and already bone-weary with arguing, but it wouldn't likely budge her an inch from her place in front of the doors.

And Norn, curse him, wasn't being much help at all. He stood to the side, his arms crossing his broad chest, his mouth turned down in a frown that had only half the severity of hers.

"I didn't have time to ask."

"You had time to *hunt him* in the King's own city and you didn't have time to ask?"

"Elsa, I—"

"He thinks he's here for some sort of punishment, no doubt. The boy's positively terrified!"

"Before you get carried away with motherly sentiment, do remember that he was trying to rob me."

If she'd had an ounce of common blood, she would have spit. Instead, the line of her usually full lips disappeared further into the white set of her mouth. The stone that framed her was less hard and cold than she. Certainly less dangerous.

"Why wouldn't he try? He's cold, he's probably starving, and you were dangling enough money to feed him for a few years."

"What does it matter? The boy's here, he'll have better clothing, enough food, and any education you can force on him. Let's just drop it, shall we?"

"The 'boy,' as you call him, is here, but he doesn't have to stay if he doesn't choose to. Don't forget it."

"Elsa, the dogs have just been bedded down, and I'd like the chance to do the same. We've been traveling hard these last few days just to reach home."

"I should feel sorry for you, is that it? You're used to hard travel. The boy isn't."

"Elsabet," Norn said quietly.

She met his eyes, and he shook his head in response, mouthing a silent *later* that Soredon couldn't see.

Still she hesitated another moment before stepping out of the way. Soredon heaved a grateful sigh and inched past her.

"If we have another son, Soredon, I will never trust you to find a huntbrother for him. Is that clear?"

"Perfectly.

"Good."

"Oh, Elsabet?"

"What?"

"I missed you, too."

She didn't even bother to answer as he opened the door and walked through it. "And what are you smiling at?" But part of her anger was stemmed, and Norn didn't feel any sting in the words.

"You, Lady." He shook his head. "If the boy makes the choice and the vow, he'll be blessed in you. He couldn't ask for a better mother." He walked over and put an arm around her shoulders to shield her from the night's chill. "I think it will be fine. I had a similar experience with Soredon's father, after all." He felt her shoulders relax slowly. "It's the Elseth way. I don't know why they choose among the young thieves in the King's City; the Valentin custom of choosing local orphans seems much more intelligent."

"They enjoy the challenge of catching a likely thief, I suppose," Elsa answered as she walked with Norn to the door. "Or they like hunting in the King's City." She lowered her head, briefly, to his shoulder. "My husband has the best huntbrother in the kingdom of Breodanir, so I shouldn't argue with Elseth custom." Her lips grew thin as she raised her face. "Only with the execution of that custom."

"Elsa," Norn said, pulling against her arm. "It's cold. Shall we enter?"

She linked an arm with his and shook her head again, struggling free of temper. "Sometimes I think huntbrothers are more of a blessing to us than the Hunters we marry. But next time, Norn, keep a better eye on him. I am trusting you, after all, with my family's name."

* * *

He had a bed. A real one, with tall, thick posts and a headboard that disappeared into curtains. Those curtains were deep green—Hunter colors—with tasseled edges of harvest gold.

Better, he had pillows. Three, all thick and soft and fluffy. At the table by his bed, someone had left some sort of clothing, all neatly folded into a careful pile. He had enough food in his stomach to last days, he had a fire in the grate that was burning merrily, and the comforter that he sank into was at least as good as the pillows.

He was in the Heavens, he was certain of it. Either that, or he was about to embark on a journey to the Hells proper, and this was the price that they offered him. He didn't much care.

Not until the knock came at the door. He leaped to his feet and jumped away from the bed, glancing around the room for some place to hide. They must have realized that they'd made a mistake, sending him here. At least he hadn't touched the clothing.

"Hello?"

He recognized the voice. It was the huntbrother's. Norn's.

"Hello, Stephen. I've ordered a bath for you. Do you mind if I come in?"

Yes. He thought it, but the wariness hadn't left him at all, so he said, "No."

The door opened and Norn, carrying a small lamp, walked over the well-lit threshold. "Ah, I see you won't be needing this." The wick flickered and went out in the noisy gust of his breath. He stepped out of the way, and three people carrying a large tub entered in his wake. They put the tub down in the room's center and disappeared, only to return with buckets that appeared to be steaming.

Stephen didn't much hold with bathing and water—especially not in the winter. He eyed the servants with a suspicion that bordered on fear.

"It's a bath, boy," Norn chuckled. "You're not afraid of it, are you?"

"No," Stephen answered. The word was far more resolute than his face. "It's just water."

"And a good deal of soap, which you could use. Ah, Terril, that's quite enough of the hot for the moment."

Terril, a dark-haired younger man, nodded briskly, although he seemed dubious. He stepped aside and looked at Stephen.

Stephen stared back.

Norn cleared his throat. "Stephen, you're supposed to sit *in* the tub."

Stephen still hesitated.

"And you're to give your clothing to the servants. They'll see to its cleaning."

"I'm supposed to get undressed in front of everybody?"

"That's the way it's normally done. Come on, boy. There aren't any women about."

Gritting his teeth, Stephen submitted himself to the first bath of the year. He was fine; he didn't even yowl when his feet hit the water that he was certain would boil flesh.

The servants were gone, and Stephen sat on the side of his bed—his, as Norn had assured him—in the soft flannel of newly acquired nightclothes. He couldn't stop touching them, and occasionally his hands would fall to the comforter as if to make sure it was real.

Norn didn't miss any of this as he sat in the room's sole chair. Cleaned up, the boy looked much less like a street orphan—a little food and a little sleep, and no doubt the child would begin to look human.

"Well, Stephen, what do you think of our home?"

"You live here?"

"Yes.

"My apologies for the way you were found. We were overdue and Soredon was anxious to return home." It was a lie, but a harmless one. "It's Master Gilliam's birthday in two short months, you see."

That didn't mean much to Stephen, as was obvious by his lack of response, so Norn found another tack.

"Do you enjoy living in the streets of the King's City?"

Stephen's shrug was answer enough.

"Would you like to return to them?"

"Why're you asking?"

"Because you don't have to." Ah, now he could see the suspicion that had dogged the boy for the entirety of their journey. It was natural enough; hadn't he been suspicious when he'd first come to the manor? "Do you know what a huntbrother is?"

"Maybe."

"Because," Norn continued, as if Stephen hadn't replied, "if you so choose, you could be one."

"I ain't Hunter-born."

"No. Neither am I." Norn edged closer. "None of the huntbrothers are."

Stephen looked at Norn's fine clothing with obvious skepticism. But he was interested, that was clear.

"This would be your room. You would eat at the Lord's table, wear clothing as good as this, and take lessons. No one would expect you to thieve just to have a place to stay in the winter. No dens would try to kill you or force you to join. You wouldn't have to worry about running with, or from, a street pack."

Stephen's hands drummed the side of his bed as he stared past Norn's shoulders. Reflected firelight flickered in his eyes as if trapped there. It was warm here, and the food, like the Lady, had been something out of story or dream. It was almost too good to be true, and anything like that had its price.

"What do I have to do?"

"Perform the duties of a huntbrother."

It was a trick. Stephen was certain of it; Norn was a huntbrother. "Why me? Why not a real brother?"

"Stephen, no huntbrother is Hunter-born. No huntbrother is noble-born. Don't you know any of your stories?"

"Stories are for kids," Stephen replied, sullen at the implication that he was stupid.

"Not all stories are," Norn said softly, remembering another time, a different boy. He shook himself as the silence lengthened, and then continued. "Hunter Lords are like Lord Elseth—closer to their dogs and their hunts than they are to their people. Huntbrothers are supposed to balance that; to remind them of the rest of humanity."

Stephen nodded in quick agreement. "Why do we need 'em anyway?" he asked, warming to the subject. "Why're they worth more than the rest of us?"

"You don't know your history," was Norn's quiet reply. "And I don't have the time to teach you everything you'd need to know. But let me tell you quickly about the Betrayer, the Doomed King."

In spite of himself, Stephen leaned forward intently.

"You know that to kill your parents is a crime against the Mother," Norn said softly.

Stephen nodded. Everyone knew that.

"Over fifty years ago, the King of that time—the current King's grandfather—was challenged by his son, Prince Aered, to a duel in the Hunter's see. The King's Queen, Leofwyn, stood by her son, and the King's Priest stood by the Prince as well.

"Under the eyes of the Hunter God, Prince Aered killed his father, and saved all of Breodanir in the doing. But the Prince had still committed a crime in the eyes of the Mother, and he died after only a short reign."

"What do you mean saved Breodanir?"

Stories are for children, Norn wanted to say—but he knew that the time for teasing Stephen, if there ever was one, would come much later. "The King whom we do not name was a weak-willed man who wanted to please too many people. He made his court of foreign men and women, not the Breodani, and he belittled his Hunters.

"These foreign lords and ladies felt our customs barbaric and foolish, and over the years they convinced the King that they were right. Do you know what the Sacred Hunt is?"

Stephen flushed. "Everyone knows that!"

"And?"

"Once a year the King and all of the nobles go into the royal forests and call a hunt. And once a year, one of the nobles dies. Always."

"Yes," Norn said quietly, seeing the question in Stephen's eyes. "It's true. Always. The Hunter Lord, or huntbrother, is taken by the Hunter's Death—the Hunter

God made flesh. It's a gruesome death, Stephen. The death we all fear." He shivered even as he spoke, and then shook himself again. "Where was I? Ah, yes.

"The Doomed King did not call the Sacred Hunt as it had always been called. The Hunter Lords pleaded with him, as did their Ladies, the Priests, and even the Queen— but to no avail. He was tired, he told them, of being laughed at by greater men than they, and the foolish custom of the Hunt would end with him.

"But the Sacred Hunt is called for a reason, Stephen, even if you do not believe in it. The Hunter God made his covenant with the Hunter-born: that he would help them hunt and feed his people every day of the year; that crops would be bountiful and game plentiful; that the forests and fields would be green and grow well. But in return for this, the Hunter Lords and their huntbrothers must, one day a year, allow the God *His* Hunt.

"After the first year with no Hunt, the crops failed, and the game became scarce. The King's fine foreigners said that this was coincidence, but the Breodani knew better and they redoubled their efforts to reach their King.

"He was a weak man, as I've said, and having made a mistake, he would not acknowledge it for fear of seeming weak. So the next year, he again refused to call the Hunt."

"Why didn't another noble call it?"

"Because," Norn said quietly, "only the King can call the Sacred Hunt; it is part of our covenant with God. Now, save your questions and let me finish.

"Each noble must keep granaries full in case of drought or a very bad harvest. The second year emptied the last of the granaries, and people began to starve. Without the Sacred Hunt, the lands became parched and dry. The crops did not take at all.

"The King's oldest son, Prince Aered, knew that the Breodani could not survive a third such year. In anger and sorrow he took counsel with the Queen and the King's Priest.

" 'The Sacred Hunt *must* be called,' he told them both, and they both agreed. All of them knew what this meant, because only a King can call the Sacred Hunt. The Priest prayed to the Hunter God, as did the Prince, and the next day, the Prince killed his father in combat, by the grace of the God, and became King.

"He called the Hunt, and we knew the wrath of the Hunter God betrayed. Two-thirds of our number perished that day." Norn was silent again, contemplating deaths he had been too young to witness, but could imagine just the same. "But that year the harvest was the richest it had been in ten, and the hunting, for those of the Hunter Lords who still remained, was also good.

"This is why we need Hunter Lords, Stephen."

"Then what are huntbrothers good for?"

"Huntbrothers?" Norn cleared his throat. "They must be both protectors and friends to their Hunters. They must train in all things to do with the Hunt, and hunt by their Hunters' sides in the Sacred Hunt, dying if that is the will of the Hunter God. They must become well schooled and must deal with the Ladies and their laws.

"We are the common people whom the Hunters are supposed to protect and feed, Stephen—and our very presence, as decreed by the God, is meant to remind them of that, so that they never misuse the powers that God has granted them."

Stephen was silent; Norn wasn't certain that he understood all that had been said. But he'd understood enough of it.

"If you can vow that you will do all of this, you will be accepted as huntbrother. You will live with our family, and become Stephen of Elseth."

Oh, yes, it was a trick. Had to be. But Stephen's hands were sinking into soft down, and the warmth of the fire was pulling his eyelids down. Why shouldn't he say yes? Even if he didn't like the stupid boy, why shouldn't he lie? He could take the oath and pretend—and he'd have all this for his own. If he'd been born to the right person, he'd have had it anyway.

But Norn's words about the Hunter's Death had been true: Stephen could tell that Norn was afraid of it. "Are they afraid of this Hunter's Death?" he asked, before he could stop himself.

"No," Norn replied. "The Hunter Lords are not. But

they die it, just the same. I've seen it, Stephen," he added in a somber voice.

Stephen waited for Norn to continue, but the older man would not speak further. They were quiet for a few moments. *What difference does it make? I can die of cold or hunger, or I can take a chance that I might die once a year.*

"Yeah. I could do that."

"You'll take the huntbrother's vow?"

"Didn't I just say yes?"

"Then I will inform Lady Elseth."

Stephen froze, and his fingers became fists. "Tell the—the Lady?"

"Yes. It was she who provided the choice of room and clothing. I think she'll be quite pleased at your decision." Norn rose then, and made his way to the door.

Stephen wanted to stop him. He opened his mouth, and shut it forcefully enough that his teeth snapped. He didn't mind lying to Norn, and he especially thought he'd enjoy lying to the Lord's son—but the Lady was a different matter. She was—she must be—really nice. Special. And he wasn't certain that he wanted to lie to her.

His face hardened and he was disgusted at himself again. So what if she was special? She was a Hunter's Lady, after all. She'd had an easy life.

Even so, he was glad that he wasn't going to be the one to deliver the lie.

"Stephen?" Norn said, his hand on the door frame.

"What?"

"I hated Soredon when I first met him." That, and Norn's chuckle, lingered in the room long after he'd left. Norn was no fool, after all.

Four days into his stay at Elseth Manor, Stephen silently cursed his decision. If it hadn't been winter, he'd have taken the road back to the King's City on a minute's notice.

Oh, the food was everything that the first dinner had promised, and there was always a fire in the grate as proof against the cold. He'd clothing to spare, although where it came from he didn't know, and Lady Elseth was like a walking miracle. Better than that, Lord Elseth was never really home, except at dinner for one evening, and Norn was often out with him. The servants didn't even seem to notice that he'd grown up in the streets, and they were always polite, even when he was deliberately rude. After the first week, he stopped trying to provoke them out of frustration and shame.

No one pried into his past with unwanted questions, so he didn't have to tell them about the last year of his life. Didn't have to remember in detail the start of it: Three days alone in the small room he'd shared with his mother, after which he fully realized that he was alone. He didn't know what happened to her body; he didn't want to know. He didn't tell them about how he'd learned to steal things, about how many times he'd almost been caught, about how many packs he'd had to run from. He was alone here without being lonely, and he almost liked it.

The manor house was wonderful. It was so big and grand, he could get lost forever in it. The servants' wing was bigger than the den had been, and even their rooms were fine in comparison with what he'd lived in for most of his life.

He didn't even hate the lessons as much as he'd thought he would. Hours spent sitting in front of a rectangular slate with a piece of chalk while some "lessonsmaster," as Lady Elseth had called him, droned on and on actually became interesting. And he could put up with Maribelle, who followed him around every minute he wasn't busy, babbling at him and spilling things on his clothing.

What he hated was Master Gilliam.

"I don't have all day, Stephen." Just at the moment, said Master was trying to look down his broad nose. "Are you coming or not?" The side door that led to the outside from the empty kitchen let a draught of cold air into the room.

Stephen locked his eyes into place so they wouldn't roll. Unfortunately, his jaw also locked, making his smile more rigid than usual.

"Well?"

"It's sort of cold, don't you think?"

Gilliam snorted. "I don't care if it's cold. The kennels

aren't." His brown eyes narrowed, and he drew himself
up to his full height in unconscious imitation of his father.
It wasn't very impressive. "Besides, you're the huntbrother; you have to follow. And I say we're going."

And that was that.

It isn't worth it, Stephen thought, as he took deliberate
steps into the snow and the wind. *Food and a home isn't
worth this.*

No? His breath came out in clouds that wreathed his
thin cheeks; his cheeks grew pink under winter's weaken-
ing fingers. The sky was bright, the sun blazing, and both
conspired to cast his shadow forward in a long, thin line.
He walked it, delicately balancing between two bad
choices.

He swallowed and started to jog. The kennels, as
Gilliam said, were warm. He had almost decided again,
but biting back the words that anger gave him was difficult.

The kennel opened up around him. It was the longest
building Stephen thought he had ever seen, and it was
dark. It smelled of wood and straw and dogs. In both
stone—stone, of all things!—walls, the east and west, two
large fires burned merrily. The heat of their light put the
house fires to shame. The north and south walls were
wood, but not the dovetailed, clumsy work of many of the
poorer shacks he'd seen in his life. Whole families in the
King's City would be proud to call this home. And what
lived in it? Dogs.

There were, at the moment, twelve here; the others
were in their runs. Gilliam called them six couple, and
Stephen had learned that a couple was just another word
for a leash that held two dogs. Each of these dogs had a
heavy, oaken bed, with boards carved out in the simple
stark letters of their names. Stephen couldn't read them
yet, although it would be one of his duties. He didn't
need to. These dogs lived like kings. They even had a
second story in the kennel which was built solely to give
them more protection from the cold.

Well, at least they didn't have mattresses, and the blankets on them were rough wool, not down. Straw sur-

rounded them, and Gilliam had told him a huntbrother's
duty was to see to its turning at least once a day.

Closest to the west wall was the grandest of beds, and
in it, head perched on two crossed paws, lay Corwel, the
leader of the pack. Both eyes were patched black, and the
rest of his face was white, but his eyes, where they caught
the fire, were a peculiar red shade.

Stephen thought it suited well; these dogs, the Hells
would be proud to own.

As if hearing this, Corwel raised his massive head and
opened his jaws, displaying his teeth as if they were regalia. Stephen flung himself back, coming to rest in time to
feel foolish: the dog was only yawning. He smiled nervously, but stayed where he was.

Corwel sat up, shrugging the blanket off. He bounded
to the floor, shook himself, stretched, and then padded
forward, head up.

Lady Luck wasn't frowning, she was shouting in anger.

If he could have run, he would have—but his legs
didn't remember how. He opened his mouth and didn't
recognize the squawking that came out.

Corwel's jaws opened suddenly, closing on a snap that
seemed to break the air. He jumped forward, forelegs extended, and caught Stephen's jacket in his teeth, bearing
him to the floor.

Stephen screamed.

Corwel barked.

Five sleepy dogs suddenly joined him in a hideous cacophony of sound. But worse than that was the sound of
laughter. Master Gilliam's.

"You idiot!" He was bent over, as if laughter were a
burden that was heavy. "You should see your face! What
did you think he was going to do? Eat you?"

Corwel's tongue, wet and decidedly smelly, washed
over Stephen's face.

"Maybe you're too stupid to be my huntbrother."

"I'm not too stupid," Stephen said, giving Corwel a vi-
cious shove. He rose, straightening out his clothing. "I'm
too *smart*." And on that last word, he lashed out, his thin
fist all sharp knuckles.

* * *

"Mommy! Mommy! The dogs're barking!" Maribelle skidded to a halt around the corner, slipped on the carpet, and rolled knees over head, sending her carefully starched skirts into a wrinkled blue spray.

Lady Elseth rose immediately from the long chair, her lips turning ever so slightly in a delicate frown. "The dogs?"

The discovery was too important to be forgotten in tears, and Maribelle hastily pulled herself to her feet, any scratch or injury ignored. "Barking and barking."

"Oh, dear. Where is your father?"

"Don't know."

Norn, who had been sitting beside Lady Elseth while she practiced her stitches, rose also. "He's at his letters. Lord Poreval requested his presence on a Hunt in a two-month."

"Well, I hate to interrupt him," Elsabet said softly, "but this might be important." Her regret was completely genuine; it was nigh impossible to get Soredon to sit down with quill and ink, even when the correspondence related to the one true love of his life: The Hunt. And a two-month meant boar or bear, so it was a more serious business.

"Maribelle, why don't you wait here while I find your father."

Norn followed his Lady out of the sitting room. He could tell by her gait that she was worried; the dogs seldom barked for no reason. To be truthful, he was slightly worried himself.

They walked the halls to Soredon's study, and Lady Elseth knocked firmly at the door before entering. It was habit; Soredon rarely paid attention to formality, and was never insulted when one just walked into his chambers. That was, when he noticed the interruption at all.

True to form, he sat facing the window, his eyes captured by the winter world outside and its dreams of coming spring. Winter was not the best hunting season, but it was a fact of life, and Soredon never railed against the inevitable.

"Soredon," Lady Elseth said softly. She, too, knew better than to wait for his notice.

"Hmmmm?" He turned, and his eyes brightened on seeing her. "Elsa." He pushed the parchment aside and stood, thankful for the excuse to leave it.

"Maribelle says the dogs are barking. Can you see to them?"

He was up in an instant. Household squabbles and small emergencies couldn't command his attention or concern—but the dogs were his domain alone, and Gods help any who troubled or injured them. He was halfway out the study door when he paused.

"Where is Gilliam?"

Lady Elseth's brow creased in mild concern. Her brief shake of the head answered the question.

Her husband stopped inches away from her hands. He closed his eyes, pulled his chin up, and looked into the distance of eyelids and darkness.

Norn recognized the Hunter's trance at once. He, too, became silent and intent as he watched the blank lines of Soredon's face. He could see the subtle shift of lips and eyes that spoke of contact. He was, even bounded by walls and windows, with his hunting pack.

The contact lasted for seconds. It was over before the Hunter Lord opened his eyes and brought himself back to his study.

"Well?" Norn said softly.

Lord Elseth turned to him and smiled. The surface of the smile broke, and laughter welled up from beneath it.

"In the kennels," he said, as he managed to fit the words between breaths. "With Stephen." The laughter ended, leaving affection and memory in its wake.

Norn's expression lost its worry, and he shook his head wryly. "He's not as patient as I was. This is what, four days? Five?"

"If I might interrupt this?"

They both turned to stare at Lady Elseth, losing the privacy of their moment.

"Elsa?"

"What is going on in the kennels?"

"Stephen and Gilliam are at fist play."

"I see."

"Elsabet, where are you going?"

"To the kennels."

"Wait a moment, then. You know the dogs don't like—"

"I don't care what they like," she said icily. Nonetheless, she stopped.

"You're learning too much from Boredan," Soredon said, shaking his head in mock disapproval. "Why don't I go to the kennels and bring them."

"Why don't you?"

"Norn."

"With you," was the swift reply. Norn, brave and steadfast as he was, had no wish to be left behind with Lady Elseth's decidedly ill humor.

"And gentlemen?"

They turned warily.

"If you can stop congratulating yourselves for the Mother only knows what, you can bring both boys to me." Fist play indeed.

Silver mist obscured the reminiscing grins of Lord Elseth and his huntbrother, leeching them of color and warmth until they looked like ghosts within the confines of the sphere.

Evayne a'Nolan had been a young woman when she first walked the Hunter's wood—the King's Forest, as the Breodani called it. That was years past; more years than she cared to remember, although she was not, by the standards of the empire of Essalieyan, old now.

She shook her head softly and put aside her seer's ball, folding it into sleeves of midnight blue until its glow could no longer be seen or felt.

Gilliam of Elseth. I remember you.

She knew when she was.

But it was not the time for memory, whether fond or painful. She began to study the periphery of the wood itself, walking with great care, searching with the vision that was by now second nature: seer's sight.

She found what she sought. It was hidden from normal magic and normal sight, and it was subtle enough that she almost missed it at first. But interwoven with leaves, roots, and blades of wild grass was a net: a shadow-snare.

Shadow-magic was the province of the demon-kin and the priests of Darkness; they were at work here, now.

Lifting her arms, she waited for the path, certain that she had seen what she had been sent to see; as she stepped onto it, the forests faded from her view. She dared not linger, for fear of being spotted.

CHAPTER THREE

"Gilliam, stop fidgeting."

"I'm not."

Lady Elseth sighed before she stepped back to look at her oldest child. The robes that the Elseth Hunters were confirmed in looked odd and empty on the shoulders of their youngest heir. They hung low, and although pains had been taken to belt them, they looked awful.

But Gilliam, on the eve of his eighth birthday, did not, through no merit of his own. The blackened eye that had been the start of his friendship with Stephen had given way from yellow to pale pink. On the other hand, the large scrape on his cheek from their enterprise at the mill remained a thin mess of scabs and flaked skin. What, by the Mother's grace, had possessed them to try to climb the mill wheel, she didn't know—and at three days from his ceremony, not much could be done to aid him; the nearest of the healer-born was sixty miles away. Worse still, Stephen had quietly come forward, and in private no less, to take the blame for the escapade.

Elsabet was not a stupid woman; how could she be, and occupy the seat of judgment for her lands? She knew a lie when she heard it, but the heart beneath the lie was sound, and the reason for it unquestionable. Before he had even given his oath, Stephen had truly declared himself huntbrother. She wondered if he knew what those words and that false confession had meant, and did mean, to her. Of course, she had still had the duty of meting out just punishment for both the lie and the escapade, but the doing had not made her heart heavier.

She didn't understand completely how the friendship of her son—her two sons—had come about; the only time she had ever been caught at fist play herself still smarted as an episode of humiliation. She and Lady Eveston had never become friends, although age and experience had lent their rivalry a patina of civility.

Now was not the time to think of it. Her oldest child was about to enter the Hunter's rites and swear the Hunter's Oath. And he looked like an underfed urchin. Her own gangly son, with hints of his father's temperament already showing in all the little ways. Her son.

"Well?"

Boredan sniffed. "I think he will have to do. The Hunter Lords have already gathered, and they only wait on the final preparations of the Priest."

"Are you nervous, Gil?"

"Of course not!"

Ah, age. Lady Elseth smoothed the lines of teasing smile from her face, already regretting the loss of the small child her son had so recently been. Maybe, years from now, she would tease him again and he would smile. Maybe not.

Still, just as her mother had warned her when Gilliam was first born, the time would come to let go a little. She stood, smoothing out the simple linens of her own white robe. Her hair was one long, burnished braid that slid down her back, giving her dress its only color. Tonight, the only finery one could carry was in the heart. Not even the band of the wedding was seen upon her fingers; they were smooth and unadorned.

We are all the Hunter's people, she thought, and knew it for truth.

But only the huntbrothers and their Hunter Lords faced the Hunter's Death.

"Lady?"

"I'm all right, Boredan. It is . . . chilly this eve."

Ah, Elsabet, her mother had said, *it is hard when the first child is a son. When you let him go, you give him to the Hunter God, and the life and death of the Hunter's Oath. You gave him life, but it is not your province, or even his father's, to protect that life. It is in the hands of God.*

And the hands of the Hunter God were red indeed with the blood of his loyal servants.

She wanted to hold her son, one last time. Wanted to, but knew by the proud little thrust of his chest and chin that he would have been humiliated by it. Children could be so cruel in their race and struggle to grow. But they could be crueler still, by dying.

Elsa, you may love your sons for their youth, for their strength—but love them as the sacrifices they might become. Love your daughters more.

Yet she remembered her mother's wet, red eyes, and her trembling lips well.

They are all our children.

Yes. Her mother had answered, although her eyes had never left her son's bier.

For the first time, Elsabet understood why mothers of the Hunter-born looked so pale and quiet at the first of the ceremonies. And for the first time, she understood the folly of the Doomed King, who had attempted to halt the Sacred Hunt—and the deaths it always caused.

But the land had paid for it; the people had learned anew the lessons that had almost become fable and story. And the Hunter still claimed his blood in return for the life of the land. She looked quietly at her son, seeing only an eight-year-old child, like unto any of the Mother's children. How could he understand duty? How could he understand death?

The knock that came at the door was soft and insistent. It rescued her from the sadness of her musings. She knew who it would be.

"Elsabet?" Norn didn't enter. "Is he ready?"

"As much as we can make him," she answered. "Stephen?"

"I've been waiting hours. Gil's always late."

"It wasn't my fault!"

"Was too. *I* said we shouldn't go to the kennels."

"Would have been fine if you'd cleaned them."

"Maybe we could finish this argument later?" Norn's large hand fell to rest on Stephen's thin shoulder. Green cloth, bordered in gray, slid down Stephen's short arms and trailed upon the ground at his feet. Like Gilliam,

Stephen wore the robes of what must have been a much larger, or older, person. They were worn and simple, but the weight of a proud history was carried in each thread of woven cloth.

Elsabet smiled. *Do you know what you wear, Stephen?*

Perhaps he did. He carried himself with pride and a quiet awe as he touched his hem. Or maybe it was just her imagination; he had to lift the robes to walk.

"Well, Gil?"

Gilliam nodded smartly and stepped out into the hall. His eyes were wide and his breath was fast; flags of excitement colored his cheeks. He took his place beside Stephen, and stopped to whisper something to the boy who would become his huntbrother.

Norn placed an arm around his Lady's shoulders. He didn't ask her how she felt. He had lived with her for years, and knew well her mother's fears. But he knew what this night meant for both Stephen and Gilliam, and he almost pitied her, for she would never fully understand it.

Her smile faltered as she looked into his familiar face.

"Strength," he whispered.

"Pride." But instead of taking the arm he offered, she grasped his hand and held it tightly as she had once held her dead brother's. They followed in the wake of the two young boys, stepping cautiously into the unknown future.

Outside, the ground was wet and soft; new shoots of green leafed out over damp earth that threatened to turn muddy. The stars were out, and the moon as well; clouds had fled the sky. Torchlight glowed on the faces of those who waited, chief among them the Lord of Elseth.

He, too, wore only a simple robe. It seemed almost black in the scant light, but Lady Elseth knew it for the dark green that the Master Hunters were entitled to wear. At his left stood Lord Samarin, at his right, Lord Stenfal. They were older than he by at least ten years, but each had attained the rank of Master Hunter; Lord Samarin had even been named Huntsman of the Chamber two Hunts ago.

As witnesses, none could be found finer or stauncher

than these two. Lady Elseth felt a warm glow of pride, and smiled at her husband from across the green. He saw her and smiled back, the expression no less warm than the torch he carried aloft.

The villagers, holding torches and wearing their normal clothing, also stood on the green in an uneven circle. These, too, were witnesses that the ceremonies decreed. They were of the land; they were the Hunter's responsibility and support.

It was late, but even so, Elsabet was heartened to see small children standing at their parents' sides. The youngest were held in arms, although one or two of the most precocious were being chased down by very embarrassed villagers.

Perhaps the children knew best. Their understanding of life gave no pause to the solemnity of ceremony and oath—they laughed or cried as if all of life were encompassed moment by moment.

She had long since lost the ability to do so, but tonight she would not begrudge it to others, only envy it a little.

The circle opened to allow her to pass; she walked to its center, where the twin pillars stood flanking the simple altar of rough-hewn stone. It was weathered with time, and had stood here long before the borders of Elseth existed. She paused to bow low. Her hands came to her lips, held together in a solitary private prayer. When she rose, she looked to the east and west, at each of the stone pillars. Words were written there in row upon row; none could now read them, they were so old.

Will you take my only son?

Her lashes pressed against her cheeks, and she bowed again, unable to ask for mercy in the face of so much history. She was Elsabet of Elseth; she would be as the pillars—solid, strong, a testament to this moment.

She took her place in the foreground in front of her husband, and waited for Norn. Norn walked to the altars and drew a silver knife from his belt. This he laid before him, bowing as Lady Elseth had done.

He joined his Hunter, nodding quietly.

The priest came next. He knelt on the wet ground, unmindful of the robes that would bear the dirt's soft traces;

in the darkness they would not be seen. He lifted the
knife that had been left for him and pressed its cold
length to his lined lips. He was old, the Priest, and by his
colors, a Hunter also.

Greymarten, Elsabet thought. She was reminded again
of how well-respected her husband's family was. It was
no small matter to journey from the King's side to the
Elseth village, but even aged as he was, he had chosen to
make the trek.

The Priest rose, knife still in hand.

Only Gilliam and Stephen still stood outside of the circle.

"Breodani, we are gathered here to witness and to receive. We are the people of the Hunter. Who stands for
the Hunters?"

Lord Samarin stepped forward and bowed, his robes
flapping in the chill breeze. "I do."

The Priest nodded and gestured; Lord Samarin came to
stand at his side.

"Who stands for the people?"

An older woman, the village head, walked forward.
She bowed, and her bow was held long. Elsabet recognized Corinna with a quiet tilt of the head; more would
disturb the ceremony.

"I do." And she came to stand to the left of the Priest.

Greymarten nodded, satisfied. "Let them come
through."

A pathway appeared on the green; the circle broke into
a passage that Stephen and Gilliam could walk along. It
did not close behind them.

Gilliam came first, and knelt at the feet of the Priest.
Stephen started to follow, and one of the villagers gently
placed his hand upon Stephen's shoulder. It was not yet
time.

"You have chosen to walk the Hunter's path,"
Greymarten said to the young supplicant.

"I have."

"Do you understand what that path is, and where it
might lead?"

"I do."

"You are young yet to know it." The words were ritual, but Gilliam bristled anyway. "Tell me."

The young boy looked up into the old man's face; torches held aloft revealed only shadows and lines.

"In the time of hunger," Gilliam began, "we followed our God. But few children were born, and many died too young. There was no game, and we did not know the ways of the growers." He took a breath, and then his brow wrinkled.

Greymarten looked down benignly, waiting. After a few minutes, he whispered something.

Gilliam blushed and continued, knowing he should have studied his lines harder. "Near death, we called out for aid to any who would hear us. God in the Heavens answered our plea. He came to us and showed us all of the ways of the Hunter, and promised that we would know the full—uh, um—use of it. Them."

It came as no surprise to the Priest that the boy knew the lines so poorly. Very few Hunters had the patience for scholarly work, so it was not a bad sign.

"He showed us this gift and more, for the dogs at his side came to stand before us in silence. He fed us from the fruits of his labor." This line, Gilliam didn't understand at all. It sounded stupid. "Grateful, we accepted what he offered.

"For these gifts, we swore to become his people and follow all of his ways." And if he could just remember the rest, Gilliam would happily do that. "Ummm . . ."

"The Price?"

"But the Hunter demanded of us the one Price that those who accepted his gifts must face: the Hunter's Death. For to give us his skills, he must use them, hone them. Once a year, before the harvest, he asked that we call the Sacred Hunt in his name."

"Very good, Gilliam of Elseth." Greymarten placed a hand on either arm, and raised the boy to his feet. He had said enough, and besides, it was painful to hear all of the awkward pauses of ritual poorly understood, but it was warming as well. Year after year, such mangled words were offered as the young entered into the beginning of their full promise. "The people of Breodanir agreed, and the Hunters swore their oaths. And once a year, the Hunter Lords must gather, to be Hunted in turn by the God who has given us our lands. One of these Lords must face the Hunter's Death, or the lands will die around us, and the game will flee."

There was silence; all eyes were upon Greymarten. But only the oldest remembered the famines of the King's folly. Only the oldest knew that when the Sacred Hunt was finally called three years after its promised time, the Hunter God had been angry indeed. Fully two-thirds of the Hunters had died that grisly death. But the lands and the game had returned, paid for by noble blood.

"Then, Gilliam, do you swear by the Hunter's Oath?"

"I do."

"Will you promise to hunt in the people's stead, and to feed them your kills?"

"I will."

"Will you protect them from outsiders, defending them by force of hounds and weapons if necessary?"

"I will."

The Priest turned to Corinna. "Do you accept his word?"

Corinna remembered witnessing Lord Elseth's first majority—although she had been no headwoman then. Tonight was a window into her youth, so like to the father was the son. "I do."

"Will you succor him and his heirs in times of need?"

"I will."

"Gilliam?" The Priest held out one hand, and Gilliam placed his own into it. The knife very gently came down; it was cold and sharp, and left a well of red in its wake.

Greymarten nodded, satisfied, and then looked up, his eyes seeing both this darkness, and every other darkness that made this ritual endless. "Who comes from the people?"

Stephen was given a little shove forward now, and he walked quickly across the cool green. He knelt at the feet of the Priest, beside Gilliam.

"I do."

"And why do you come?"

"To pledge my oath, under the Hunters' eyes. The

Hunter God knew well the foibles of his people, for he knew all. He saw that those who labored under his gift might be driven too far from the people they had sworn to feed and protect. I have come, from the people, to take my place as huntbrother. To hunt, as my Lord will hunt, without use of his gift. To guard him and protect him and see all dangers by his side; to face the Hunter's law so that we may remain strong. To remind the Hunter, always, of the people he must defend."

"Rise, Stephen," Greymarten said, well pleased. The words, wrapped as they were by youth, had lost none of their power to move him.

Stephen did, holding out one hand just a little too soon. The Priest took it anyway, and gave it the kiss of the knife.

Stephen turned to face Gil, and the two clasped hands, right to left. Their grip was tight, and they ignored the blood that fell at the Priest's feet.

"I'll be your Hunter," Gil said. His grip grew tighter. "You'll be my brother and my friend." He looked at Stephen's shadowed face, and remembered the mill. "Everything I've got, I'll share with you. I'll defend you and listen to you—" he grimaced, "in all things."

"I'll be your huntbrother," Stephen said quietly. He saw the half-healed cut across Gil's cheek and smiled suddenly, lowering his voice to a whisper, "even if you're an idiot."

Greymarten coughed, and Stephen blushed.

"I'll be your huntbrother," he began again. "I'll stay at your side for all hunts, even the Final One." On impulse, he added, "I'd face the Hunter's Death for you." His grip grew tighter also. His hands felt warm and sticky, but they didn't hurt at all, and he wondered if it was his own blood he felt, or Gilliam's. Something began to change slowly.

He forgot about hunger, and forgot about the cold. He forgot all of the people who stood in a circle around him, watching and listening intently. There was only Stephen and Gilliam, and that was right.

"I call the Hunter God to witness." Greymarten's words echoed oddly in the stillness. They were full, low, loud—as if said by a throat that was no longer merely human. He reached out, placing a hand on either supplicant's shoulder.

"This is the last rite," he said formally. Neither boy looked at him. "From here, there is no turning back. Understand this."

As one, they nodded solemnly.

"Breodan, Hunter, accept this pledge." His hands grew suddenly warm as they rested against the robes of the two boys.

Stephen saw Gilliam's eyes widen in the same instant that his own did. He opened his lips to speak, and they froze as he felt a warmth, a heat that he had never felt before.

It burned like fire relieved of malice; it was hot, but it brought no pain. It was darkness, ringed with a light that grew brighter and stronger as he watched. His lids grew heavy, but he would not close his eyes.

From within, something rose to greet the warmth. Wings, invisible, unfeathered, spread out in awkward first flight. The warmth took him, and he soared to its heart, giddily at first, and then more surely.

Darkness was there; he heard the low rumble of a growl that even a dog could not produce. It was loud. It touched more than his ears. The horns he heard also—but they were dim and distant in their musical plea. This was the spirit of the Hunt, and he knew it fully.

Without fear. *This* was his home, his place.

Stephen?

Gil?

Gilliam laughed; the feel of it resonated with Stephen's sudden triumph.

This, he knew, would be his for life. Not even Marcus could change that, or take it away. The boy who had lived in the King's City, eking out a meager existence as a petty thief, had known little of friendship or trust, except in his stories or dreams.

But he'd remembered enough that he'd yearned for it. This was his answer. For just a moment, he could *see* as Gil saw, feel what Gil felt. The heart of the darkness was the unknown, and its shadows fled Stephen's approach.

He could see Gilliam's fears and hopes; could touch the web of his dreams. He knew that Gilliam was even now seeing the same of him, and he didn't care; the past meant nothing. The two of them would stand together, no matter what the future held.

Greymarten let his hands slide from the shoulders of the two who were no longer mere children. He lifted his arms, bringing his palms to touch either of the henges at his side.

The circle on the green closed at his gesture.

"It is done," he said softly. He reached forward and grasped the two young hands that remained locked.

Both boys turned to stare at him, a shadow of doubt in their eyes. He knew well why. Although his own huntbrother had long since perished, he had never forgotten his oaths and their special meaning: the bond that had been forged.

"It is real," he said quietly.

As always, he wanted to tell them of the risks; of the emptiness that waited in the hands of death. "Stephen," he said gently, as he touched the boy's hard fingers, "Gilliam, nothing but death will take from you what you have been granted. Do not fear to let go." The words were the truth, but the simple message, so slight and so soft, was almost a lie compared to the pain of the loss that Greymarten—and many a Hunter—had experienced in his life. More, he would not offer.

Gilliam relaxed his grip immediately; he had lived with the Hunter's Priests all his life, and knew the value of their word.

Stephen hesitated.

"Stephen, trust me. The oath has been accepted by God. No simple unfasting of hands can expunge it."

Clenching his jaw, he followed Gilliam's lead. Best to start now what would have to be continued. His hand slackened and he let it fall to his side, waiting for the loss to come, fearing it.

Minutes passed in his silence, and then tears came instead.

What his oath—his choice—had given, did not fall

away. It remained securely inside him, a warmth and a wholeness upon which a new life would be built.

He wanted to stop the tears, but they wouldn't be caught, not even by his will. Gilliam reached out and grabbed his shoulders gently. He understood Stephen now, and he knew what fears Stephen had faced in those minutes.

"Let him be, Gilliam of Elseth. It has been hard for him to trust his choice; it is not pain that moves him now."

If Stephen had been afraid of laughter, none came. In turn, each of the villagers that was old enough to know how came to offer their thanks and best wishes. They did all in silence, at the foot of the altar that signified the Hunter's Death.

Then the Master Hunters brought their previous day's kill. They placed it upon the altar with the help of the villagers, and Greymarten set about portioning it with the silver knife; the heart for the God, the hides for the Hunter, and the meat for everyone present. For this one special Hunt alone, the dogs were not allowed their portion of the felled beast; this stag was given in celebration of the coming-of-age of a new Hunter. A fire was already sparking to life in the pits to the south of the manor, and ale and wine were now brought in heavy, earthen mugs by manor servants.

Corinna was given an old harp, and she played it with both gusto and warmth. Several of the villagers, emboldened by wine, began to dance at her feet, and the blacksmith even approached the Lady Elseth, who was kind enough to join him in his jig. Truly, tonight, they were all the Hunter's people, and they lived in the moment of his blessing. The cost and the Price was a shadow made distant by merriment and celebration. Even Soredon, the most dour and grim of men, chose to catch a young girl in the circle of his arms and spin her about on the green. His son was Hunter-born, and by God accepted; this made a magic of the evening, and brought his past momentarily to light in the fires of his eyes and the warmth of a smile that was so seldom given it was truly special.

Stephen, too, was caught in the play of the rough coun-

try music, although not by any maiden; Norn grabbed him
from behind and placed him deftly upon broad shoulders.
Their robes blended together, becoming one moving tapestry of times past and times present. Of all the burdens
this huntbrother had carried, this slight, small boy was
among the most precious.

"Welcome," Norn roared above the laughter and out of
tune singing of the crowd, "to Elseth!"

The following week, Gilliam was inducted into the
Hunter ranks, albeit at the very lowest station: He was
made a Page of the Running Hounds to the kennels of
Lord Elseth. He was full of pride and happy pomposity
until he discovered that he would fail at the first of his
duties unless he paid more mind to the lessonsmaster.

Soredon was both amused and sympathetic to the
young boy's reaction, but, as he said, it was important to
take the roll of the dogs. Which meant, of course, writing
and spelling, as well as better reading.

There were two things that made this onerous chore
bearable. The first was that Hunter Maradanne of Corinth
would board at Elseth and begin the rudiments of weapon
lore, and the second was that Gilliam would have every
reason and excuse to be in the kennels with the dogs that
he loved.

Stephen was at his side for every moment of the lessons, although he took better to reading and writing than
Gilliam would ever do. They learned to spar together, and
although Gilliam was the stronger of the two, he was also
more quick of temper, and bore the bruises of it more often than his huntbrother did.

They walked the dogs, tended them, and learned to
write the letters of their names, but as promised at the
binding, only Gilliam could feel their presence and know
their minds. He shared this with Stephen, as he did all
that he was given.

But they rarely stopped their fighting. Indeed, it became as much of an annoyance to Lady Elseth as Norn
and Soredon often were.

* * *

Four months after Gilliam's birthday, he became a Page of the Scent Hounds, and he was given his first horn. It was not so fine or grand as his father's, being simple silver, but he wore it proudly, and even in sleep would not be parted from it.

Both he and Stephen learned the use of it; the different calls that comprised the Hunter's canon were intricate and necessary. Winding the horn was easier for Gilliam than for Stephen. The music came naturally to his lips, and he rarely forgot the use of a single note. He willingly prompted his huntbrother in the rote of the huntbrother's calls, which were different, but harmonious, with his own. Another source of conflict and companionship.

He learned the use and making of nets, as well as the coupling and uncoupling of the dogs. But he was still not yet old enough, at eleven, to be allowed out on the hunts. He did not bide his time with patience.

When they were twelve years old, just before they gained the rank of Varlet of the Running Hounds, they were called to the Valentin estates.

Lady Elseth was always quiet at this time of year, although there was enough to occupy her. It was the week that preceded the planting season, when the farmers were at their busiest and their requests had to be attended to immediately.

It was also the time of the Sacred Hunt.

Winter's chill was almost gone from the air; it lingered only in the face of the Lady and her most senior of staff. She counted the days in busy silence, watching the turnings and visiting the solitary altar on the green in the morning before her children rose. What had looked mysterious and almost forbidding on the night of the Hunter's Oath now looked like a thing of mourning and silence. And why should it not? It served to bind boys on the verge of manhood, and it served to lay them to their last rest.

It served the women differently.

This morning prayer was a custom of the women of Breodanir during the time of the Sacred Hunt. The Lords did not see it; how could they? They served their King and their country in the great forests that were reserved for the God's purpose. They found their prey, they loosed their dogs, they gave in to the wildness of the Hunter's trance.

A pained smile tugged at the corners of her lips as she waited at the stones for a response that never came. Next year Gilliam would begin his real training; he would come to know the Hunter's trance, and the greatest of all of the God's gifts. He was already growing into the role that the God decreed; the dogs, even though they were not his own, loved him and obeyed him; his use of weapons, if not words, had progressed immeasurably, if one were to listen to Norn. He talked of nothing but the Hunt, yearned for nothing but the ability to join his father.

To join his father. . . .

The smile dimmed and was lost for the day. Here, now, the price to be paid for the gift was writ large.

Where are you, Soredon? Is Norn still with you?

She no longer prayed for her father or her brother; the one had been lost through age, and the other the God had already claimed. But she knew the time was coming soon when two more names would be added to her small ritual. Why was it that all of the men she loved would always face this risk?

Duty. Responsibility.

She shook herself and rose, bending at the knee to lift the mat she'd brought with her. The sky told the time, and the sun's shadows beyond the henges bid her return to the manor.

"Mother?"

She froze at the sound of the familiar voice and lifted her head, her lips already straightening. Stephen stood, just outside of the green, as if aware that he should not disturb her here. His hands were behind his back, and his chin was close to his neck; it lent him that peculiar air of vulnerability that her blood-born son never showed. She was glad to see he'd worn his jacket; it was chilly without the full light of sun. She hoped one day that his common sense would rub off on Gilliam, but it was a small hope; Norn had never managed to have that effect on Soredon.

Norn. Soredon. "What are you doing out here so early?"

Stephen looked down at his feet. "I—I'm taking a walk."

"On the Hunter's green?" Elsabet left the altar. Stephen's shrug told her more than his words. "Are you going back to the house?"

He nodded.

"Walk with me, then. Is Gilliam awake?"

"No. And Maribelle's with Maria." He fell silent, matching the stride of her step. In a few years, it would not be he who needed to stretch.

They walked quietly until the altar was at a safe distance. Then Elsabet stopped and turned to Stephen, thinking him very like Norn at this moment. She couldn't explain her prayer, but felt that it wasn't necessary; she could see his worry, and a little of his understanding, at play around his eyes.

Stephen faced her squarely. "They're late this time, aren't they?" He held out a hand; it was still fine and slim. Growth wouldn't change this.

She wondered if he did so because he had seen Norn make a similar offer on many occasions. And she didn't care. Holding the heavy mat awkwardly in one hand, she accepted his solace with the other, gripping just a little too tightly.

"Not very late. The roads are poor."

Stephen nodded encouragingly, and she didn't speak again. They both knew that she was lying. But he held her hand as she walked. He understood fear and loss very well.

The Hunter God was kind, this season, to Lady Elseth.

Norn and Soredon returned in a ten-day, worn by the rigors of the Hunt and the journey by road. They came by horse toward the darkness of the turning, and the manor house flared to life at their approach.

Soredon dismounted and barely had time to place his feet upon the ground before he was nearly swept off them by his Lady's embrace. He returned it, hugging her tightly and burying the length of his face in her neck. Not even Maribelle sought to disturb their reunion—although it was more due to Boredan's heavy glare than her own consideration.

"Gil, the dogs," Soredon said, glancing up over his wife's shoulder. Gilliam nodded immediately and went to Corwel's leash; the care of the dogs after the Hunt was something not lightly entrusted to anyone. That the dogs were not his father's very first consideration worried him.

"You were late," Elsabet said, when she at last drew back.

He nodded heavily. "I'm sorry to worry you, Elsa. But we had the duty to perform." He watched her grow still.

"Who?"

"Bryan." He shook himself. "We're called to Valentin in haste. We must leave in the morning."

Norn joined them, looking just as weary as his Lord. This was only the second time in their long years of hunting that they had been called upon to guard the dead on the road with full honors.

"How is Lord William?"

"Shattered." Norn hadn't the strength to be diplomatic; nor, surrounded only by his Lady and her Lord, the need for it. He rested his head against the side of Soredon's horse before the servants came to stable it.

Soredon gripped his shoulder tightly. "Norn?"

"Fine."

"Have you eaten?"

"Some. Not much."

It was always this way—the joy of a safe return was marred by the shadow of another woman's loss. Lady Elseth nodded quietly to Boredan, who disappeared back into the house. "When the boys return from the kennels, I'll tell them."

All of the Hunter-sworn within a four-day's travel were honor-bound to make the trek to the Valentin estates. Lady Elseth, well aware of her own responsibilities at such a time, oversaw the wardrobe for all four of her men, although Norn was quite capable of dressing for ceremony on his own.

She, too, was well prepared for such an emergency, and

left Boredan in charge of the house and Maribelle, who was very much put out at being left behind.

One day, Elsabet thought, as she hugged her stiff, rebellious child, *you will be glad of the times you were spared this.* She bade her daughter be good, which didn't help, and then mounted to her seat in the carriage she would share with Stephen and Gilliam.

They knew well why they were going, and all of their arguments or enthusiasms were as subdued as their clothing. Bryan of Valentin had been huntbrother to Lord William, heir to the Valentin Duty. It was he, this year, who had faced the Hunter's Death, and paid the Hunter's Price. No Hunter, or aspiring Hunter, could do anything else but honor that sacrifice.

Still, the days were long, and after the first, Gilliam and Stephen grew undaunted by the shadows that haunted their elders. In the evenings, they shared a room, and during the day, a coach. Corwel and Maritt also traveled with them by wagon, and they spent each evening kenneling them properly, as was their duty. They argued, they spoke of their future as Hunters, and they played their learning games.

Until they arrived at the Valentin estates.

Black was the color of death in Breodanir, and it was everywhere in abundance. When they approached the manor road, the post that held the family crest was swathed in long ebony panels that bore only the crossed spear and sword of the Hunter God's dominion. The villager who met them at the fork in the road was also dressed in black. He directed the two carriages and accompanying wagon without so much as a word.

The guest houses were in readiness for the nobles who had come; the Elseth family was the last, waited for by three others.

Lord Valentin met Lord Elseth as they approached the manor house. He gave a low bow, his black cape skirting the ground.

"You honor my son." He was pale, his eyes darkened by rings that spoke of care and sleeplessness. His face, always long and thin, looked near-skeletal now.

"Your son has done all honor to us." Lord Elseth also

bowed, but when he rose, he reached out and gripped the older man's forearm. "Eadward."

"William would be here to greet you," Lord Valentin said, "but he has his duties upon the green. Please, feel free in the use of the House. Ah, Lady Elseth. Corwinna is also at the green, if you wish to greet her."

Lady Elseth curtsied, lifting her skirts with the ease of long practice. She looked long at Lord Valentin's strained face, seeing that the age in it had suddenly come to rest. She wondered if he would shake it later, or if, like a scar, its mark would always be seen. "Yes," she answered, taking his hand, "I would dearly love to speak with Corwinna. If it isn't too rude, I'll leave you now."

He nodded, working at a smile. Elsabet shook her head slightly, acknowledging much she knew must be left unsaid by him. She knew the path to the green, and took it, leaving her own two sons—her living, breathing sons—behind in her husband's care.

As promised, Corwinna was at the altars. So was her blood-son, and the Priest they had called for the last rites. No servant lingered there, and the three nobles who had gathered were conspicuous by their stillness.

Corwinna wore the black as well, a long old robe that had been passed from grandmother to grandaughter for years. Her hair was bound back in a knot of graying brown, and around her neck she wore the medallion of the Death. It caught the light and flashed in the high sun like the fall of a sword.

Elsabet approached her quietly, sparing a glance for the Priest. She paused before she reached Corwinna and looked at Lord William. He, too, wore the blacks, but they seemed to cover all of him in the heaviness of their shadows; his normally active, friendly face was sunken and pale. He heard her approach, she was sure of it, but did not stop to acknowledge it in any way. He had eyes only for the altar, which was empty.

"Corwinna?"

Lady Valentin turned at the sound of the voice "Elsabet."

Between the women, there was no formality at a time

of such loss. Grief took too much of a toll to be pushed aside for social niceties, and although the women were separated by twenty years of age and experience, in this there was understanding and common ground.

They moved away from the green in silent mutual consent, walking arm in arm. When they were far enough away that words would not carry on the wind, Corwinna looked back.

"He doesn't eat," she said softly. "He doesn't sleep. He doesn't cry." Her own eyes were pink and wet. "He won't even speak of it to Eadward." She looked down at her hands. "I don't know what I can do to help him."

Elsabet put an arm around her shoulders and drew her close, saying nothing.

"I'm sorry, Elsa. I've—I know you lost your brother. You must know what it's like. But I—the Hunter God has passed over my family until now." She struggled with words, lost them for a moment, and then lifted her chin. "I hate Him," she whispered, her eyes wide and red. "And I see all the people gathered here, all the villagers, my farmers—and I hate them, too."

Again, Elsabet said nothing. The words, she knew, were like water in a vessel that had fallen. They needed to run their course.

"Bryan died for them. And I don't know if William will recover." She shivered, and turned her gaze upon her companion. "He won't see the Priestess of the Mother, and I know he was injured. He doesn't want to live."

Quietly, Elsabet prayed that neither of her two would ever know a day such as this one. Prayed that she would not be there to see it, if they did.

"He was young. He was ... he had so much to offer us. And it's gone now. So that we can eat.

"He won't eat, Elsa."

She waited with Corwinna, offering her silence and the strength of her presence when both could never be enough.

In the morning, the rites were called. Three Hunter Lords and their Ladies joined the procession to the green. Elseth was there, as was Samarin and Cormarin. The sun cut between the henges to shine its light upon the altar that would not remain empty for long.

Everyone wore black, except for the Hunter Priest; he wore his colors and his crest grimly as he said the final words above the stone.

The circle of villagers, dark and still, had no children within it. There was no laughter, no anticipation, no joy— and not many eyes remained dry. They had come to witness, these people; to see the cost of their lands and lives in the blood that was paid to keep it. To honor, one last time, the sacrifice. It was hardest for the older people; each of them had also witnessed the ceremony that had joined Bryan and William to the mysteries of the Hunt.

Stephen and Gilliam were not the only young Hunters present, and like the others, they stood to the side of Lord Elseth, waiting and watching. They did not yet know what to expect; neither Soredon nor Norn would speak of it.

They had not yet reached their full height, so they did not see William until he was already within the confines of the circle. At first, they did not recognize him; he wore only black, and no horn or sword adorned his robes. His hood covered his fair hair, and his head was bent so that cloth hid his face. But two dogs followed behind him, and they knew him then.

Beside William walked another man; one old, judging by the length of his beard and the stoop of his shoulders. He also wore black, but not comfortably, and he did not bother to hide his face with a hood. Although it wasn't hot, he was sweating.

"Stephen, there." Gil pointed, even though it wasn't necessary; Stephen knew at once what held his Hunter's attention.

Five feet from the old man, suspended in midair at shoulder height, lay Bryan of Valentin. He was gray and stiff, wrapped round in a long, white cloth that was his only accoutrement in his final journey home. No hands touched him at all; the old man was one of the mage-born. How long he had held Bryan thus suspended no one knew, but all understood the strain he showed; Bryan had not been a small man.

The Priest, aware of this, moved immediately from his place by the altar, bowing low to Lord William. The mage-born stopped at center circle, and managed a bow of almost equal grace. From here on, Lord William, Cadfel, and Sorrel would walk by Bryan's side alone, as they had often done while he lived.

William stepped into place and held out his arms, bracing his legs against the ground. Bryan's body floated toward him, untouched by breeze, and was lowered slowly and carefully into the two arms that waited his burden. The Hunter staggered under the sudden weight as the mage released his care. The body went slack.

William drew strength from the Hunter's trance, and the trembling of his arms left as he cradled Bryan's head against his chest. His hood dipped, brushing what remained of Bryan's cheek. For a moment, he gripped the body tightly to his chest, and all watching wondered if he would have the strength to let go. No one moved.

"Hunter William," the Priest said softly, "it is time for his rest. Come."

Still William hesitated, and his grip grew even tighter. The Hunter Lords, almost as one, turned away; they did not need to see his face to know what was writ large upon it. Lady Valentin started forward, and her husband's huntbrother, Michaele, caught her shoulder firmly, shaking his head.

Then Cadfel, the leader of William's pack, darted forward with open jaws. His teeth snapped at air and the hem of the rustling black robe that William wore. William jerked his leg back, lifting his head. His face was pale and gaunt, too empty even for tears.

No one heard the words that he sent to Cadfel, but all knew, from the dog's sudden growling, that there was to be a testing here. Cadfel's hackles rose, and his throat rumbled in growling. Sorrel, the pack's bitch, suddenly lunged for William's other leg, catching the robe between her teeth. She began to back up, her growl higher than Cadfel's, but no less defiant, as she sought to drag William forward.

The villagers were surprised. They murmured indistinctly among themselves. The Hunter Lords were worried. In silence, they lent their strength to the dogs. The dogs who, in their animal way, understood a truth that only Hunters knew: William walked too close to Bryan, and his voice would be lost to them all if he could not be called back to life.

William's foot came up, connected with Sorrel's side, and then found the ground again as he staggered. His white cheeks took on flags of color; his eyebrows, fair though they were, could be seen to rise into the folds of cowl that framed his face.

Sorrel yelped, let go, and then started anew.

"Cadfel, Sorrel, go!"

Cadfel backed up a step, and then growled, hesitating. Sorrel grabbed wet robe in her jaws and started to tug again.

"Leave us alone!" William's face was suffused with red now—the most color that he had shown since the end of the Sacred Hunt. He kicked out, harder this time, and Cadfel caught the blow on the length of his face. He rolled, whining, to start at his master anew.

"What is this?" William shouted. His face had lost the peculiar tension of the Hunter's trance. "*I* am your Hunter. Do as I order!"

The dogs did not listen.

Stunned, William stared down at them as they worked at his feet. And then his eyes narrowed, and when he spoke his voice was low, deep-throated; his eyes were flashing. "And will you leave my command? Will you forsake your Hunter?" He bent all of his will outward, throwing it against the dogs' testing. "What was Bryan to you, but another commoner? You will not take him from me. *Let go!*"

This time, the dogs did as bid, growling all the while. They stopped when they touched the first of the gathered crowd. Stopped at Stephen's feet. He stepped back even as the growls changed, becoming the whining and wimpering that the pack offered only to its Hunter.

"And will you leave them?" The Priest asked softly, his voice breaking the silence. He did not move as William turned to face him. "They are yours as much as Bryan was. Must they pay the price of his loss too?"

William's eyes widened again. He stumbled and dropped to one knee, still clutching Bryan to his chest. Aware now.

"William, you have committed no crime. Your huntbrother made his oath at his own choice, or it would not have been accepted. Remember the King's folly. Remember what has always been the Hunter's Price."

"It should have been me," William said.

"The Hunter God did not choose, this year, to take your life—although you may well have your wish in another Sacred Hunt. You live. This is what your brother would have wanted. Bryan was no child. He knew the Price."

William closed his eyes and nodded, but bitterly, bitterly. He tried to rise and staggered again, but would not let Bryan touch the ground. No one moved to help him; they could not. Bryan was his huntbrother and his friend; to him fell the last task of rest. He was aware of it, even as he struggled; his pride, his duty, would not let him ask for any aid.

What aid, after all, had Bryan had, facing the Hunter's Death?

He rose and walked the last few feet to the altar. Then, very carefully, he laid his burden down. He started to stand once, but his arms would not release Bryan's body to the stone.

Now the Priest came. Now it was allowed. He gently but firmly caught William's shoulders and pulled him away.

William's eyes flared again, but he nodded and stepped back. He fell to one knee in front of the altar and bowed his head into his hands. Then he raised it, seeing the gray of sky and the sun. Silent, he called for the one thing that remained.

Cadfel and Sorrel bounded up to stand at his side. He reached out with a shaking hand to touch Cadfel's neck. Cadfel turned to lick his master's face. The bond between Hunter and dogs, tested so harshly, had not, and would not, be broken.

The ceremony started. The Priest spoke. And William, dogs at his side, paid his respects to his huntbrother, offering at last to share the emptiness and loss with the one who could never answer it, or comfort it, again.

Thus it was that Gilliam and Stephen first understood that the Hunter's Oath had two edges. They stopped by the body to pay their respects and looked long at the damage that the Hunter God had done; it had been no easy death, and not a painless one.

Stephen lingered longest, looking at the ruins of what had been a strong face. He touched the white cloth with one small, shaking hand. Death was no stranger to him— but this death . . . it was his. He felt certain of it.

Gilliam, who had almost left, came back to him. In silence, in awe of a loss he was old enough to fear, he put an arm around his huntbrother's shoulder and pulled him away. He knew what Stephen felt; he couldn't help but know.

"I won't let this happen to us," he whispered. "I'll protect you."

But Lord William could have meant to do no less, and even now he stood by the stone's side, the dead's side, a grim shadow of death and empty longing.

CHAPTER FOUR

Evayne a'Nolan was a young woman in search of truth in the libraries of House Terafin. Her hair was a perfect black sheen, her eyes were a pale, cool violet, and her clothing, if somewhat provincial, suited her perfectly.

She had been escorted into the grand array of domed rooms by The Terafin herself, and given leave to peruse any of the volumes that the librarian guarded so jealously.

"This is the first time you've met me," The Terafin said quietly. "But it isn't the first time I've met you. You saved my life, Evayne of no House."

Evayne was surprised, but she nodded gracefully and allowed herself to be led by the powerful, older woman. She could not imagine that a woman in her prime, with so much power and such a force of personality could need help.

"Did I tell you about myself?"

"Yes," the older woman replied. "But I would have guessed. It isn't often that a woman's age changes so drastically in the space of two days. Even I could hardly fail to notice it."

"She must have trusted you," Evayne replied.

"She?"

"I."

"Perhaps she did. Perhaps she still does. I confess that I do not understand how you walk your path. But come. The libraries are yours."

The doors opened, and Evayne saw, for the first time, the vaulted ceilings and multiple catwalks that were the pride of The Terafin. Books, many of them older than either of the women who stood before them, lined the walls in perfect rows.

"I hope you find what you seek."

Evayne bowed low.

And then she began her search into the rites of old Weston. Three days later—she was almost never in one time for three days—she found what she sought, and to the librarian's rage and sorrow, borrowed a volume bound in midnight blue with gold trefoil stamping for the next twenty years.

By the time she had finished reading it a third time, she met a man who could give her the truths of the knowledge that time had buried.

Had buried for everyone but Evayne.

On the tenth day of Fabril, the second month, Gilliam of Elseth entered his fourteenth year.

The Hunter's green became a place where festive poles and decorations, and pitched, painted tents in the Elseth pavilion, proclaimed the day a celebration. It was still cool, and the rains fell frequently, but the green showed the color of the new year well. Musicians of varying quality brought out harp and fiddle, and impromptu dances sprang up like wildflowers as the sun began to wend its way to its rightful place of rest.

Stephen's birthday was also celebrated on the tenth of Fabril because he told Lady Elseth that he didn't know when his real birthday was. He lied; he remembered well the frugal celebrations he had had with his mother when he was five and six on the fifth of Lattan, when there was no cursed snow.

Here, while the shadows lengthened across the faces of slowly tiring celebrants, he remembered his mother's long, gaunt face, her dark-ringed eyes, her shaking hands. She'd been two-thirds the age Lady Elseth was now when she died, but to his mind she seemed twice as old, her face sagging into tired lines. He wanted to remember loving her, but he felt nothing at all except unease and a little pity. She had been—they had been—very poor.

"Stephen?"

At fourteen, he was far too old to run into Elsabet's arms, but he was not so old that he couldn't, with dignity, allow her to put an arm around his shoulder.

Stephen? It wasn't so much his name, as the sense of his name. He looked into the crowd and caught Gilliam's eyes. His brother's concern and curiosity comforted him. He leaned back into Elsabet's arms, thinking only that he wanted no other brother, and no other mother, than these two.

She said nothing, but although no oath bound them, he felt her concern just as keenly as Gilliam's. They took a few moments of silence in the midst of the cacophony before duties took them, once again, to the middle of the Hunter's green.

It was the one time of year that the Hunter's altar was not forbidding or foreboding.

Soredon of Elseth was the only principal to escape the festivities almost before they'd begun. He was proud of his son, yes, and proud of his choice of huntbrothers; he was proud of his people and the festivities that had been planned, and executed, in his heir's name. He was proud of Norn, and Norn's ability to deal with inane chatter. He was even proud of Elsa, although he knew that, come evening, he would feel the sharp barbs of her words for his irresponsibility.

But his pride in people had never been worth very much to him, and on the eve of Gilliam's fourteenth year, it was worth less than usual. This year, Gilliam would finally be taught the Hunter's trance. If he could master it in the next season, he would finally answer the King's call. That would make him a Hunter proper; a Hunter Lord in his own right. He could choose and bind his own pack, and he could know, fully, the joy of the hunt.

The sun was indeed low; the foliage bore a faint, pink tint as the rising dew reflected it.

Corwel, sensing his master's mood, calmly placed his lower jaw into his Hunter's outstretched palm. Soredon smiled down at the leader of his pack. He would not be so for much longer.

The big black and white whined a little and placed a warm, wet nose against weathered skin.

I can't even hide that, can I? Not from you, old boy. He tried anyway, allowing the pride he felt in this, the best of

his hunting dogs ever to overwhelm the sorrow he felt at
his aging.

*I shouldn't hunt you this season. You've become slower
while I wasn't watching.* But he knew he would hunt
Corwel this year, as he had done the last. And he knew
that he would continue to hunt him until he couldn't
track, couldn't run, or couldn't catch the running beasts
beneath his jaws.

*You're the best hunter in Breodanir. You're Bredari-
born—you could have run with the first hunter in the first
pack at the dawn of the best age.* The stub of a tail
wagged happily. Soredon rested his left hand against
Corwel's neck.

This was the hardest part of being a Hunter Lord. Not
the risk of your own death, but the certainty of your
pack's. The first pack was special, always special, and
rare indeed was the Hunter Lord who didn't hunt that
pack until it was too old and a little sorry. Rarer still was
the Lord who didn't go into nearly open mourning at the
death of his first leader.

One learned better, of course, over the stretch of years.
One learned how to say good-bye; to look at the births
and deaths of so many friends, so many true companions,
as the Hunter's Way.

Soredon's hand tightened briefly as it rested against
Corwel. He thought of another time, a different fourteen-
year-old boy, a smaller dog. *Conner,* he thought, with a
pained smile. *I ran with you until you were what, nine?*
If there was any justice in the world, Conner was still
hunting in the deep, rich forests of the Hunter's Haven.

As Corwel would be.

Again his hand tightened. He could hunt for his people,
feed them, protect them, provide for them. But he could
do very little for his dogs in the end, and it was their loss
that pained him most. They understood him better than
any person ever could, with the exception of Norn, and
they were loyal to the point of certain death. Only the
loss of Norn would inflict a greater injury.

Out of the merriment of the celebration came a single
voice. "Soredon?"

"I'm all right." He didn't look up. He knew Norn's

voice better than he knew his own—he certainly heard more of it.

"It's Corwel." Norn's square hand came to rest on the black-and-white head.

"It's all of them." Norn could feel his Hunter's loss, but he couldn't understand why; no one could, who didn't make the bond with their pack. "I tire of watching my friends grow old and die while I do nothing. Go back to the celebration. Distract Elsa for me." He felt Norn's broad smile as it accompanied a gentle affirmative, and he returned to his brooding.

Tomorrow, Gilliam, Soredon thought, as he stared at the horizon, seeing not the sun but the roster of long dead hounds, *you'll begin to understand the Hunt's glory. And a few years from now, you'll know the Hunter's loss.*

Corwel nuzzled his master's hand.

"It never ends, Corwel," Lord Soredon said softly. "And it always does."

Stephen was lost in the earliest of the myths and legends of the empire of Essalieyan—Morrel's final ride against the Lord of the Hells. The Shining City was before him, and at his side, the Princes of the First-born; his sword was raised above him in the darkness of unnatural night, and the hooves of his horse strode above the broken, blasted plain.

He knew this story well, of course. It was the one that had first revealed the true purpose of reading: ancient glories. Morrel's ride would take him to the very foot of the Lord of the Darkness, and the blow he would strike there would end evil's reign and bring the Shining City down.

It would also kill him.

For in the time of such greatness as Morrel, the very gods walked the world, changing it and shaping it to their pleasure and their whims.

In the act of turning a page, his fair hair falling almost into his eyes, Stephen of Elseth looked up.

Seven books were spread out before him in disarray; the long table was covered by slate, quill, and parchment.

The shadows cast by the tall eastern window were long, hatched lines; it was early yet.

He sent his curiosity to his Hunter and waited.

The answer came back in a giddy rush that couldn't be contained by words. Gilliam of Elseth was more than happy, which was very rare.

Stephen stared up at the broad-beamed ceiling, and then slowly lowered his gaze to the shelves along the northern and southern walls. Lady Elseth's library was not the grandest, but it was by no means the least. Gilliam, at what distance Stephen didn't yet know, snorted in disgust. Of all the rooms in the manor proper, he hated this one most.

Stephen closed his eyes and saw in return a desk, an empty shelf, and an open window, which told him nothing. The vision shifted; he saw a fireplace with a closed grate, and above it the insignia of the Triple Hunt. Gilliam was in Lord Elseth's study.

After six years of practice they had learned this short form, a type of speech without words. The oath-bond wouldn't carry words between them, but pictures and emotions had a visceral quality that words alone could never convey.

Especially, Stephen thought, as he reluctantly set aside the last great ride of Morrel, when those words were uttered by a Hunter. He made haste to reach Lord Elseth's study. The Lord was not a patient man, and six years had done nothing to improve his disposition.

Gilliam met him at the halfway point between library and den of doom.

"Stephen! It's finally time! Get ready, and meet us at the kennels!"

Time? "Time for what?" Stephen shouted, at Gilliam's retreating back.

"Time," a much softer voice said in an icy, quiet tone, "To remember the rules of indoor behavior."

Stephen muttered a very quick "Yessir" to the keykeeper and retreated to his rooms, there to prepare to meet Gilliam at the kennels.

He found Norn before he found his Hunter.

The kennels formed a neat, almost tidy rectangle behind Norn's broad, green-clad back. It was cool, but both of the Elseth huntbrothers had dressed well for it, Norn in the green of the Hunter and Stephen in the gray-edged brown of the Varlet.

"Congratulations," Norn said, extending a hand. "As of today your hunter is elevated to rank of first; if you do well, at year's end you will be huntbrother to a Hunter proper."

"He's calling the trance?" Stephen said, lowering his voice to a whisper.

Norn continued to speak in a normal bass. "He's trying." Without further preamble they both began to stroll toward the enclosed runs near the west side of the kennels. Some of the puppies were at play in what could best be described as mud under the supervision of two of the village girls. Out of these dogs, or perhaps the next generation, Gilliam of Elseth—and Soredon, Lord Elseth—would choose their packs. They seemed diminutive, these pups; hardly the hounds and alaunts that would terrify the forest animals in their time. None of them showed the promise that Corwel fulfilled, but they were young yet; one might, again, resemble the Bredari of old.

"My part in the hunts won't change."

Norn laughed. "They will, and then they'll ease off again, all your lessons aside. Gilliam's able to call a trance—but that doesn't mean he's able to control it." There was a glee in Norn's eyes that Stephen was glad he wasn't the target of.

"Norn—"

"I remember when Soredon first called trance, the idiot. After all we'd been taught, all we'd been forced to memorize, he tried to run the full hunt on his first outing."

"But—"

Norn laughed again; it was a bark, not unlike a dog's. "He paid. Gilliam will, as well."

"Gilliam wouldn't be so stupid."

"Let us wager, Stephen. A huntbrother's bet."

Stephen grinned back. "I'd rather it were a Lady's bet; I want real money when I win."

"I don't think I can take advantage of you in good conscience. Watch, and be amazed at what your elders know."

Stephen started to reply, but the world spun in double vision and the words were forgotten. He stopped walking, blinked, and raised both hands to his eyes to rub them clear of whatever it was that was making them water.

"Stephen?"

Eyes closed, he could still see everything in a doubled, hazy way. *It's Gil,* he thought. *What in the hells is he doing?*

"Walk slowly, Stephen," Norn said, all gaiety gone from his voice. "They've started sooner than I thought. Remember your lessons."

"He's—he's called trance." Stephen opened one eye, testing his vision. It held, and he took a tentative step forward. Light flashed; color diminished. Images flickered by before he could properly identify them.

"Yes."

"But—" His vision altered and flipped again. "He's moving around all over the place; I can't even tell how many dogs he's trying to see with."

"It's too new to him. Remember what you were taught," Norn said again. "Or you'll pay the same price he does, and you won't be in any position to take care of him."

Remember? Oh, yes. Blocking. Stephen winced.

"You don't have to block everything," Norn said. "But block the vision well."

Very carefully, Stephen did as he was told. It was almost as if, in the darkness, he had to struggle to find each of a multiple set of open eyes and firmly pull the lids shut. But it eased the confusion and the tingling that he felt with each successive move.

"They can hunt like that?" he asked Norn, the lines of his brow bunched together.

"No." Norn shook his head. "But they've all tried it, and Gilliam won't be an exception." He shook his head as Stephen's expression changed. "You can try to talk him out of it if you want, but you'd have as much luck trying to talk Corwel out of eating his portion of the kill. Gil's *with* the dogs."

"I know," Stephen said, almost sadly. Although his visual link was gone, the emotional one remained. "He's—he's happy. It's like—"

Norn waited for five minutes and then looked at his pensive companion. "It's as if he's suddenly discovered that he's been alone all his life—and he never has to be alone again." The older man began to walk again. "They don't forget us, Stephen; they never will.

"But never try to compete with the dogs," Norn added. "The dogs are the hunt; they and your brother were born and bred to it, and they cannot be separated."

There were eight hounds in total; Corwel, Absynt, Terwel, Vellas, Sanfel, Tannes, Solsha and Browin. They had been wet down, dried, and brushed, and the sheen of their fur caught the sun and slanted it along ripples of gray and brown. Corwel alone was white with his black bandit's mask, but he would have stood out anyway; he was a full hand taller than the next largest dog and his carriage was almost regal.

Of the eight, Corwel was the oldest, and he relied on his experience and wit to keep his place in the pack. Corwel had found extreme favor in Lord Elseth's eyes, but not even Soredon would interfere with the instinctive natural laws his dogs obeyed. The hounds were the Hunter's method of pitting nature against nature, and there were some things that not even a Hunter Lord could judge as wisely, or as harshly, as was necessary.

These eight stood on the edge of the great, greening forests of early spring. Elseth Lords hunted here, for practice, pleasure, and duty. The ground was wet, almost too much so, and the trees were only beginning to show their leaves.

Both Gilliam and Soredon were quiet, which was usual. Norn and Stephen were also quiet, which was less so. Eight dogs were the minimum that were ever taken out for a proper hunt.

Gilliam's forehead was creased in a frown of concentration mingled with a little unease. In this, the first of his trance-run hunts, he was not the leader of his pack, not the Lord; he was Soredon's son, and a distant second to him. Only with Soredon's word and interior voice behind him did the dogs deign to obey Gilliam's commands, and they obeyed with obvious reluctance.

Get used to it, Gil, Stephen thought. *You'll hunt the full season with your father's dogs, and they'll always be your father's. Period.* He didn't say it out loud because he didn't want to embarrass Gilliam in front of his father and Norn, but also because he'd already said it at least ten times.

"Yes," Gilliam had said. "But at the end of this season, I'll be a Hunter Lord, and I'll have dogs loyal to me for the rest of my life." The implication that he would never give the key to *his* pack to anyone, son or no, was obvious.

Corwel suddenly moved, a restless lunge that ended with a distinct snapping of strong jaws.

"Gil," Soredon said, softly and sternly, "better control."

Gilliam nodded, lowering his chin slowly until his eyes were on a level with the pack's leader. "Will they do this to me?"

"Your own dogs?"

A fierce nod of dark, sweaty hair.

"Oh, aye. And more: If you don't exert your control from time to time, they'll test you—and they might win."

"And if they win?"

"They'll lead, Gilliam. You never want that to happen." He dropped a hand to Corwel's head. "If you're injured, they'll protect you; if you're fighting, they'll guard you. If you are upset, they will not leave your side unless you send them away. In all things, they will do as you say—but they *must* know that you are master." Soredon's sudden smile was a gleam of teeth; he looked not unlike Corwel. "And of *these* dogs, I am master. But you do well enough."

Stephen was surprised. In his life at Elseth, he hadn't heard Soredon say so many words at one interval. Gilliam, however, was not impressed or surprised. His eyes appeared to be all pupil, all blackness, as he swung his head to face the forest.

Absynt, a stately, fine gleam of gray, trotted forward. He met Gil's eyes, growled softly—and very, very quietly—and began to follow an invisible scent that a well-trained *lymer* could practically see.

Gilliam's lips moved, although he gave no voice to the command, and Absynt was swallowed by the Elseth forests. Gilliam of Elseth nodded curtly to his hunt-brother, and Stephen bent down to the doubled leads. He raised a brow in Gilliam's direction, but Gil didn't seem to notice.

"Should I uncouple them?" Stephen's hands hovered above the eyelets of chain that held Terwel and Vellas together.

"Wait for his command," Norn replied.

"What if he doesn't give it?"

Norn shrugged. "The Hunt is hard; it's best he learns it now, rather than at the King's call."

Gilliam did not forget. But the dogs were more disarrayed than Stephen had ever seen them when they finally moved in on the chosen stag's trail. Gilliam was already pale and breathing heavily from exertion when he disappeared from view.

Stephen was glad that he had placed no bets. He tightened his belt, securing water and dagger, and then nodded formally to both Norn and Soredon. It was time to join his brother in the hunt.

The first thing Stephen heard was the baying of the dogs. It was a bad sign; the Hunter's call should have been sounded first. He raised his own horn to his lips, knowing the Hunter's refrain. Both he and Gilliam had practiced calls with their silvered horns since they had reached the age of eleven.

"Late," Norn said, as the horn's triple notes—two long and one short—faded.

"And not," Soredon added grimly, "called by Gilliam."

Gilliam ran with his father's pack, almost as one of it; it was impossible for Soredon not to know who did what, and how, during the hunt's course. Norn felt something akin to sympathy for the cocky young man who was as much a son to him as he was to Soredon.

After fifteen minutes, Stephen thought he needn't be too concerned for Gil. It was obvious that Gilliam had called the second measure of the trance; Stephen could see, in the spring earth, the sudden widening of Gilliam's stride. He had been taught the art of tracking by Norn, and now understood why it was necessary. The dogs at full run, with Gilliam in trance, left him behind, and he didn't dare follow with a similar burst of speed. It would exhaust him before the hunt was properly finished.

He felt a sudden surge of panic—Gilliam's, not his own—followed by a sharp determination.

Oh, no. Gil, don't do anything stupid, please. But even if Gilliam could have heard it, he wouldn't have listened. Stephen's jog picked up incautious speed. A jog, even a quick one, could be maintained for hours if necessary; running just so, Stephen could find his stride—the perfect combination of footwork and breathing—and when he did, he was certain he could run forever.

But breathing was control and rhythm; Stephen lost track of both it and the even, steady pace of his feet when he felt Gilliam's sudden despair.

He found Gilliam and the dogs across a stream so swollen with the last of winter's runoff that it was almost a river. There were stones and fallen trees that made passage possible, but Stephen ignored them; they took time to navigate, and too much caution.

He plunged into the stream, wading up to the far bank and pulling himself out of water and mud with the aid of an exposed tree root.

The dogs were trembling, their sides heaving. Almost as one creature, their faces were turned toward the woods, and Stephen could see the evenly spaced hoofprints that were imprinted into the dirt. He didn't have to search for them. Gilliam's fallen body, his outstretched arm, lay in a perfect line with their retreat. An unhindered line. The hunted had escaped the hunter.

He ran the rest of the way, and then crouched down, unmindful of the dirt, to touch his brother's throat. The pulse was far too rapid, but it was there.

"Gil?"

Gilliam didn't stir.

"Gilliam!" He turned his hunter over and tried to lift him. Corwel suddenly came to life with a loud series of barks. "Shut up, Corwel!"

"No," another voice said.

Lord Elseth came up from the stream's bank. He gestured, and Solsha broke away from the pack, heading back over the trail he had made. "Gil's fine, Stephen."

"He's not even conscious."

"Well, no. And he's barely fine. But he stopped in time." He walked over to his son and held out his arms.

Stephen met his eyes squarely. *He's my hunter,* he wanted to say; his arms tightened around Gilliam's limp, dead weight.

"Yes, he is," Soredon replied, although Stephen had not spoken. "And you ran a good hunt until the end. You were slow." But he didn't really look at Stephen as he spoke; his eyes were on Gilliam's closed lids and flushed cheeks. "Norn will be coming; let's get Gilliam home."

Soredon waited, quiet, at his son's side. It had been hard to pry Stephen from it, which was as it should be, but irritating nonetheless. Sunlight tinged pink came in through the uncurtained window. Gilliam had still not stirred. Nor would he for at least the next eight hours. The Hunter's trance granted speed, endurance, rapidity of reflex—but it demanded its due when the Hunt was over. If the hunt were extraordinarily long, and the Hunter Lord weakened by some previous injury or illness, it could demand that due during the Hunt when the Lord's body couldn't answer it. Only a few had died this way, but they were lesson enough.

*I never thought you would make it this far. You will be
a Hunter Lord who will do Elseth proud.*

Smile turned to grimace; he knew that Gilliam would
be sick for the better part of a week. But that sickness
was natural, part of the history of the Hunter. Very, very
few had come as close as Gilliam had to owning that title
proper on his first hunt. Pride made Soredon gentle,
where very little else could.

You truly are my son.

The thought gave him a peace that not even the annoyance of the waiting pack could quell.

Gilliam was a good patient for the first three days of his
convalescence only because he slept through it. He managed to retain a grip on alertness for long enough to eat
before sliding back into sleep and dream. Stephen, Norn,
and Lady Elseth took turns watching over him. Soredon,
with duties to the Hunter title and its quotas, came in the
evenings but did not tarry long.

On the fourth day, Gilliam woke in a quiet mood, and
on the fifth, that mood turned sour. He hated being confined to bed, and his thoughts were not only with the
dogs, but within them as well. Lord Elseth made clear to
his sole heir how pleased he was with the hunt's progress,
but the taint of failure clung to the whole venture and as
Gilliam's memories of his first hunt were a patchwork of
motley scenes at best, he wanted to be up at once and
leading the pack again. This time, he swore, he would do
much better.

Lady Elseth kept him confined for a full week, and
Stephen was certain that had she been able to tolerate
more of her son's surly behavior, it would have been
longer. Stephen wished it so, but Stephen's temper was
easily the better of the two brothers', and in the end
Gilliam won out.

Suddenly, all of the duties of the huntbrother took on
their full, and often irksome, meaning. No longer was
Stephen allowed to spend time in his beloved libraries,
learning the intricacies of history and language that had
become his love. Instead, he was called to hold couples,
and the hounds, in the forested lands. Months stretched to

winter, and the busy Lady Elseth lost her evening reading
with Stephen to the demands of the mill and the farmers
of her demesne.

But the hunts, of course, never ended—and Stephen
was obliged to follow Norn, Soredon, and Gilliam wher-
ever it was that the season dragged them in search of food
and prey. In the winter, they would spend days or even
weeks away from Elseth Manor.

Stephen hated the cold. The dangers of winter had been
ingrained by childhood into his reactions, and even
though he was bundled in warm clothing with a hat,
scarves, mittens, boots, and layers of sweaters and furs,
none of these made up for the comfort of his own bed and
the security of a place that was home.

But he had made his oath, and some small part of
him—one that was firmly committed to silence—found
satisfaction in tending both the dogs and Gilliam when
they returned from their long hunts, exhausted and
weary. Sometimes they succeeded, and sometimes they
failed, but Stephen usually didn't move quickly enough
to catch the hunt's end—or Hunt's glory, as Lord Elseth
called it.

He was glad of it. He could barely stand the unmaking
of the poor beast that the hunt caught. He was certain he
would have no stomach to watch the beast's struggle as it
was brought down.

But at least after the second hunt, Gilliam didn't return
home ill. After the fourth, he didn't suffer from the head-
aches and nausea that always seemed to come with the
trance.

And after the eighth, both he and Stephen were brought
before the Hunter's Priest, and there they were given their
full rank of Assistant Huntsmen, while Norn, Soredon,
Lady Elseth and Maribelle looked on with pride.

From there it was only a matter of time before Stephen
and Gilliam completed the Hunter's triple: On their own,
and with the use of Soredon's dogs over the months to
follow, they brought back stag, bear, and boar.

The boar was the last, and the hardest, and Norn and
Soredon both waited at the periphery of the chosen forest
during their sons' four attempts. Two dogs, Vellas and

Browin, were felled there, and their bodies joined the boar's on the silent return home.

But it was the third, and come the spring of their fifteenth year, Gilliam and Stephen were ready to be called by the crown to take the rank of Hunter.

CHAPTER FIVE

High on the summer poles, wind curled round the flags of Cormaris, Lord of Wisdom, lifting them lightward. Rays of sun glinted off the gold in embroidered beams of the light that signified knowledge, sparkling as if on water. Multihued ribbons were entwined down the length of the poles, and later in the afternoon the young men and women of the King's City would choose their colors and begin their dances. Ironic, really, that this dance occurred under the watchful eyes of the Lord of Wisdom, for the young women and men in their light, summer colors were often anything but.

Wine, provided by the King's cellars, flowed perhaps a little too freely, and ale more freely still, but the Breodani had a knack for handling their drink, and they'd do nothing to embarrass themselves here, at the edge of the King's Forest.

It was the eighth of Lattan, the longest day of the year; it was always celebrated thus. Farther down the hill, toward the clear, cold waters of Lake Camrys, the Priestesses of the Mother were weaving willow wreaths; the unsuspecting were crowned with them to the amusement of their elders.

The Hunter's green was the only area that seemed almost unoccupied by comparison, but the Hunter's Priests and the Hunter Lords took no slight from it. It was the summer solstice, after all, and the time for death and mourning had passed with the chill of early spring and the land's renewal. Although the Lords did not join in many of the festivities, their Ladies did, adding color, grace, and a cunning wit to the proceedings.

First among these was the Queen of Breodanir; she

held her court at the center of the fair, and everyone, from the greatest of the Ladies to the least of the children, made their way there to bend knee and bow head at her feet. Yet for all that, it was not a somber or stately affair. There was a genuine joy in the air that no formality could stifle.

Into this day, she came.

She was tall, slender, pale; her hair, dark and straight, fell down her shoulders past the spill of her midnight-blue hood. Where the celebrants gathered to glory in light and summer, she was ice and night; obviously not one of the Breodani.

Evayne a'Nolan, in the cover of shade made stronger by a touch of violet mage-light, watched and listened to the gathering throngs. There were games being played that had lost all of the significance that once made them ritual; there were songs being sung that had lost all magic; there were prayers being whispered that had lost all power to invoke. Yet for all that, they were imbued with life, with an enjoyment of the moment, that they had not possessed at their beginning.

She knew what this celebration had once been, and what it no longer was: High Summer's Day, when the hidden paths of the First-born briefly touched the world of man. Twelve years of study had given her knowledge that had been lost to all but the most dedicated of the Order of Knowledge. Birth gave her the ability to use it.

And she knew, the moment that she appeared beneath the ancient trees, that that knowledge had been gleaned and gained for a reason. It was High Summer's Day, and she was to invoke the power of it. Why, she did not yet know.

When am I? She knew it was the eighth of Lattan, but did not know which year. Very slowly, with care to avoid the scattered rays of sunlight through the leaves, she reached into the hanging folds of her robes. The robes had been a gift from her father, and they sheltered many things, but none more precious than this: the soul-crystal; the seer's ball.

At faires and carnivals throughout the empire of Essalieyan, men and women who claimed mystical insights carried crystal balls. With light and smoke and mirrors, they huddled in darkened tents and wagons, mumbling cryptic nonsense and touching the edge of their customers' beliefs. The intellects among the Order knew that crystal balls were balderdash and children's nonsense.

But the wise knew that some children's rhymes held hidden and deeper meanings than the adult world could remember.

Evayne knew it well. She held in her hands the proof of that. *When am I?* She thought again and looked into the ball itself. It was smooth and hard as glass, but the light that struck it was absorbed, not reflected. *And where?*

Mists caught the sun's rays and turned silver as they rolled in on themselves. She looked into them, waiting for the visions to come. Resolving themselves out of formless clouds, they obeyed her silent supplication.

At first, all she saw was the faire itself, but it was closer and clearer than her cautious distance otherwise allowed. She studied the faces that drifted quickly by, searching for one woman, or one man, whom she might know. There were none—not directly.

But there were the Hunter Lords and their huntbrothers, and she recognized their green uniforms, although she did not know what the gold, gray, and brown embroidery signified. She knew she was in Breodanir, and as her vision scanned further, and she saw the Queen's pavilion, she knew that she was near the Sacred Wood, the King's Forest.

Her heart quickened; her teeth bit her lower lip. She scanned the crowd more intently, half-hoping. But no; minutes passed, and there was no sign of him. Stephen of Elseth was not here.

You aren't a girl anymore, she chided herself bitterly, *you're twenty-eight; you've work to do. Get to it.* But she looked a little longer. It had been years since she'd last seen Stephen, but she did not forget.

When?

But this time, at this place, she knew where to look. The mists rolled, resolving themselves into pale gray ghostly images. There. Stephen of Elseth was with Gil-

liam. They were hunting in the woods of the southern Elseth demesne. The corners of her lips turned up as she
watched them. The ball gave them no voices, but it was
clear that they were arguing.

She thought that they might be fourteen or fifteen; it
was hard to tell. Certainly, they were not the men that she
had met years ago, but there were traces of those men in
the lines of their jaws, the width of their shoulders, their
height. She lingered over the vision a little longer and
then let it fade. It was costly to maintain it, and she still
did not know what her purpose in this time was.

The mists shifted; she felt her hands tingle in a rush of
dangerous warmth. She was no longer in control of the
crystal. It caught her attention and held it fast, whether
she willed it or no. White light sparked like lightning
across the clouds; the silver mists folded and then folded
again, moving at an unfelt gale.

Then, suddenly, they flew apart like curtains pulled too
quickly. At the heart of the ball, creeping through the undergrowth, was a shadowy figure. Evayne watched in silence as the figure rose and became clearer. It was a
young woman with dark, wild hair. She was perhaps five
feet in height, with a round face and pointed chin. Her
lips were thinned over teeth that seemed a little canine,
and her eyes were so dark a brown they appeared black.
Her hair was a black, burr-infested tangle, and her skin
was darkened by sun and dirt. She wore no clothing.

She had seen this girl before, as wild and unkempt, but
almost never alone. There was something strange about
her, something that Evayne couldn't quite place—until
she realized that, in fact, she had seen *exactly* this girl;
there was no change between the then and the now.

It can't be time yet, she thought. *In the now, Gilliam of
Elseth is too young.* But the ball never lied, although it
was never completely clear, and she knew her task was
urgent by the color and immediacy of the vision itself.
She had to do something for or about the wild girl whose
name she had never thought to ask. But what? The mists
began to creep in; the girl was slowly obscured.

She almost set the ball aside, for there were dangers associated with its use, but some instinct held her back for

a few seconds longer. Because of this, she was prepared for the second vision—and the second vision explained the first too clearly.

In the shadows of the forest, cloaked in a seeming that shimmered when seen through the soul-crystal, was a tall, lean figure. It ran, catlike, on all fours, and then paused to stand and test the air with a flick of a sliver-thin tongue. Its eyes were obsidian, its teeth long and sharp where opened lips revealed them.

Demon-kin. Her fingers whitened as they clenched the crystal sphere. Not all of her journeys through the otherwhen were dangerous; this had just become so. Although she had studied enough to discipline her magery, her mastery of it was uneasy—it would be years before she had the power necessary not to feel so threatened.

The image began to slide away, and she concentrated on the fading details. *Tracker.* She had not yet encountered one, but knew them to be deadly—even the least of the kin posed a threat to the unwary, and the trackers were by no means the least.

Where?

The ball's light flickered; what had been warm against skin was now cool, calm blue. Her face went blank as she stared; her eyelids slowly closed. The answer to her question was not given in pictures or words, but rather in feel. She *knew* where she must go, although she couldn't have given a simple direction other than the word "follow," had there been others to speak with.

Before the last of the sense-light faded, the ball vanished into the folds of her sleeves. She murmured a word, and the sleeves retracted toward her body.

Evayne a'Nolan, seer, mage, and historian, began to run.

The leaves that grew closest to the sunlight were thick and plentiful enough to make the forest a place of shadows, which suited Ellekar perfectly. Hunting in shadow was his specialty, his existence. No matter that the scents were strong and oversweet in these mortal woods; the scent of his prey was unmistakable and singular. She was a light thing, with clumsy feet, but she was faster than most humans her size.

He had to be careful, cunning. Less than a mile away the humans who styled themselves the Breodani were playing the games of High Summer. Against High Summer, only the rites of Winter held sway. Shadows meant nothing, and shadow-magic was at a Nadir that made it virtually powerless.

None of the demon-kin would willingly allow themselves to be without power, but today Ellekar's power was weak indeed, and his ability to track was lessened. He had to rely on things physical not things magical, and he cursed High Summer as he hunted, for this was not a pleasure hunt, and the consequences of its failure would be extreme. He twisted around the trunk of a tree, head snapping at air as he ran.

The girl must not be allowed to leave the forest.

There are demons in Breodanir. Evayne tried to remember the canon of the kin, but she could not recall it without the aid of the seer's crystal, and she had no time to coax the information from the mists. *How did it get here? Who's the fool who plays at demonology?*

It was supposed to be a lost art, although there were mages—there would always be mages—who studied its lore and practiced it. In the debate in Averalaan's Order of Knowledge, there were always those who felt that the study of the lost arts—demonology, necromancy—should be allowed to come out into the open, if for no other reason than the fact that knowledge was a weapon against the dangers of misuse. The motion was always brought forward by the younger members of the Order, and always defeated by the elder.

Evayne, on the rare occasions when she was present for debate, always counseled the vote against. *You cannot control them all of the time, and it only takes one slip, one mistake, to begin the end of everything.*

"Evayne Doomsayer," she had been called. "Evayne Truthspeaker," was her reply.

She almost tripped over a tree root that had been exposed by the spring runoff. Cursing, she righted herself, leaving some of her skin on the bark. She had no time to lose.

The demon must not be allowed to reach the girl.

There is a wild keening that only animals can make. Part howl, it holds the essence of the forest nights, the sparse winters, the fires, and the storms that nature knows and accepts.

The seeress froze as that cry filled the wood. It was low yet loud, the tremor before the quake.

Evayne realized just how much noise and life there was in the forest when it suddenly ceased to be. There was a silence so encompassing that she thought, for a brief instant, it might go on forever. Into that silence, the howling started in earnest. Where there had been three in the forest, there were now four.

She raised a hand to her mouth and whispered a quiet prayer to the Hunter God. She had seen death, but the Death that he granted was one that she prayed never to witness again—certainly not to experience. Balling both hands into fists, she began to run once more.

Ellekar's hair would not come down; it rode the back of his neck and arms like iron spikes. He, too, felt the reverberations in the silence.

It cannot be. It is not the right time.

But correct time or no, when the second such cry came, Ellekar knew it for what it was: the Death of the human Hunters. Such a howling was almost akin to the Great Beast of Allasakar—and what made it could not be faced down. Not by a tracker.

He froze in place, becoming more rigid and still than the trees that surrounded him. Ears pricked, he listened as the silence returned, trying to gauge direction and distance. What he heard instead was the sound of snapping twigs and shaking leaves. The sound of human breath.

It was not his quarry, and it was not the Death. But it was human, and it was approaching him quickly. He'd listened to the sounds of their clumsy feet through the forests for decades, and he knew it well. He now had three problems; one, he could not face and survive; the other two he could not allow to survive.

He growled, but the sound was almost entirely contained by his throat.

The seer-born had instincts that they learned quickly not to question. Evayne a'Nolan suddenly leaped between two maple trees to her right, responding physically to the instinct before she realized it was there.

A claw shredded her hood, grazing the back of her neck.

She wheeled, crouching behind the broad back of a rotting log. A second later, she was rolling again—a controlled thrust of leg and turn of shoulder that ended with both of her feet firmly planted.

Ten feet away, staring at her with an expression of surprise that was already fading into determination, stood the demon-kin. He was tall, almost preternaturally slender; his head was roughly human in shape, except around the jaw. The skin there was extended around teeth that came out in a long wedge.

She moved again as he pitched forward, dropping his hands onto the earth. Trackers ran best on four legs, not two, and they never chose to be slow in the chase.

Only in the kill.

She rolled, dodged, ran in short bursts. He followed, slashing and snapping at empty air or the occasional fold of cloth that just barely slid out of his grasp.

Neither spoke a word, as if, by mutual agreement, they chose to make their combat as quiet as possible. The Hunter's Death was close, and even fighting for their lives, they had no wish to attract it.

But Evayne was tiring rapidly, and the tracker was not; the kin didn't feel physical exhaustion when on the mortal plane.

He's too fast, she thought, as she rolled again. *I'm not going to*— No. She bit her lip and took a second to catch his moving shadow. Jumped out of his way. Then, lifting one arm in a rigid line, she began the incantation.

As Evayne watched, a thin streak of lightning crossed the clearing in a blink of the eye. It wasn't going to work.

The demon-kin had a way of protecting themselves against the weaker magics, and her strongest elemental spell was considered unworthy of note by the Collegium and the Order.

Crackling blue light struck the demon's chest, transforming into a thin, erratic cage an inch from its skin. The creature screamed.

It was a cry of rage and of pain; there was no fear in it. Evayne didn't stop to marvel or wonder. She ran. And as she ran, she smiled crookedly, remembering what day it was. High Summer. She intended to make the most of it, although she knew it wouldn't last.

Come on, girl, she thought as she nearly flew between the trees, *where are you?* In the distance, the demon was once again silent. Evayne knew what it meant, and she cursed the Hells for it, for all the good it would do. She was tired, and she didn't have the energy necessary to contain the creature magically; she wasn't even certain that she had the skill.

Where are you?

Evayne paused behind the smooth, barkless wood of a stripped cedar. Breaths were shallow and slightly painful; she forced herself to inhale slowly and deeply. Standing thus, she found the girl.

Or rather, the girl found her. She came out of the woods in a sudden rush. The movement barely caught the corner of Evayne's eye before she was overrun.

Where the demon and Evayne had fenced in silence, the girl had no fear. She let out a strange, keening noise that was halfway between a child's whine and a dog's. Before Evayne could move, the girl bounded up to her, throwing her arms around the seer's waist.

Evayne pulled her arms free, and placed a hand on the girl's shoulders. "We don't have time for much," she said, her voice light with relief. "Hold on tightly and walk when I say walk."

The girl said nothing at all, but she watched Evayne with unblinking eyes as the seer reached into her robes and pulled out three things: a pale, speckled robin's egg for spring, a diamond—symbol of eternal beauty—for summer, and grains of the coming harvest for autumn.

She placed them on the ground and traced three concentric circles that enclosed them both, whispering quietly as she did. Then she placed the robin's egg in the outer circle, the diamond in the middle, and the grains at her toes. The sun was still high, the day was still strong. Fingers of light illuminated the forest floor.

The girl growled; Evayne looked up. A breeze blew strands of her hair into her eyes, but she saw nothing else. The growling intensified, and Evayne began the High Summer chant.

Reaching into her robes a second time, she pulled out her dagger. An amethyst caught the light and sent it scuttling down the perfectly balanced blade. It was an old piece, this dagger, and the getting of it had cost her much.

But it was not the time for memory. With a quick blade stroke, she drew her own blood, and then with another, the girl's. The girl stared down at her forearm as blood dripped earthward, but she made no new complaint; growling seemed to require all of her attention.

The breeze grew stronger and then died down. It felt nice to let the sweat evaporate in the summer heat. The wind reminded Evayne of Callenton in her youth. The wind . . . downwind . . . she looked down at the girl and realized why she was growling.

Evayne lifted her knife-hand skyward in supplication.

"I have drawn the circles, and I have paid the price. In darkness, and against darkness, have I fought and will I. *On this day, shadow shall have no dominion.*" She let her knife drop to the ground within the smallest of the circles. The outer circle began to shimmer.

The girl shifted restlessly. Evayne continued to chant. "Let the light be cast wide enough that I might see the paths hidden, the paths perilous. *For on this day, darkness shall have no dominion.*"

She raised her voice so that it carried over the sudden crashing in the undergrowth. She did not turn her face to see the tracker as he ran. The girl did; Evayne's one-handed grip grew pincer-like.

"As we see by the light, let the light see by us; on this day, let us be judged worthy to walk; we are suppliants, we will abide without fear. *On this day, evil shall have no dominion.*" The second circle began to shimmer.

Now, Evayne turned to see the demon-kin. She felt no fear and no exhaustion. She threw her shoulders back and felt the light of the High Summer circles warm her throat, her chin. The girl, she drew against her chest and held tight.

The demon's smooth skin glistened in the sunlight. She could see his muscles as his hind legs propelled him forward. Even as she watched, they locked; he froze as he reached the outer periphery of the High Summer Circle. His eyes were darkness and shadow, and these Evayne had already denied.

"You are," she said, raising her empty knife-hand, "too late. The path is open. I see what the darkness hides. Your name is clear." The demon began to back away. He gestured, but it was futile. He had no defense against the season, and none whatsoever against his name. "You are *Ellekar-sarniel* of the kin, and by the light of the High Summer Circle, I bid you begone!" And the last circle flared to life, glowing so brilliantly it hurt the eyes. Golden light bathed the clearing, the very essence of the sun at High Summer.

The creature screamed in rage and pain. He struggled against her knowledge and against her control. But the circles glowed brighter, glowed stronger, and he raised his hands to his eyes as he fell. His face sought the dirt as his skin began to burn.

"On this day, you shall have no dominion." Evayne felt the thread of his resistance snap. As quickly as that, he was gone; only the gouges in the ground were left to prove he had been there at all. She looked away as her charge stirred restively against her.

"Come," she said, in a voice full of strength and hope. "Can you see the path? We must walk it." She lifted one arm and held it wide; a fine, beaded mist seemed to trail from her sleeve toward the circles on the ground.

Evayne thought that this conjunction might resemble the path of the otherwhen, but in this she was mistaken. She watched as, for the first time in centuries, the hidden path was revealed.

The forest did not fade from sight. Instead, it became, by slow degree, older and grander. The trees became wide and wider still; they stretched skyward until their tops could not be seen. The forest floor became darker and softer, but where sunlight cut through the tree cover, it was distinct and golden.

"Come." She spoke quietly to her companion; the forest seemed to demand it. "We must be clear of the path by the end of High Summer's Day or we will not leave it for another year." Her hand, she placed upon the girl's bare shoulder. She felt a shock of kinship then, a recognition that words could not express.

The girl looked up at Evayne and uttered a soft, little bark. Evayne returned the girl's regard, and then shook her head softly. "You cannot speak?"

Silence was enough of an answer.

"It doesn't matter here. We will find another way to talk. Are you cold?"

The girl said nothing, and after a moment, Evayne reached out and gently took one of her hands. "Follow me, child. We will be off the road and in safe surroundings soon enough."

Her robe began to heal itself as she walked. It was a gift from her father, and it could not be easily destroyed. The same, she thought, in quiet reflection, could not be said of its wearer.

They came out of the forest so abruptly they were almost hit by a passing wagon on the crowded, city streets of Averalaan. What made matters worse, and a reasonable apology on either side difficult, was the fact that Evayne's companion had not, magically, become well-clothed, or even clothed at all, during their walk on the hidden path. Averalaan was the capital of the empire of Essalieyan, but although a more cosmopolitan atmosphere could not be found on the continent, or off it for that matter, nude, disheveled young women were not a common public sight.

It was one of the few times that Evayne did not wonder when she was before she wondered where—exactly—the path she traveled had taken her. She had friends in

Averalaan scattered across at least five decades, and one of them was certain to be able to help her. One of them could guard and protect a girl who was important enough that some mage had risked the forbidden arts to conjure one of the kin to hunt her.

Calm down, she told herself, taking a deep breath. *Where and when am I?* She looked around as people continued to shout or point, and the chaos of the crowds in front of buildings that overhung the street in a tight, disorderly fashion told her what she needed to know.

Of course, had the path not led them to the heart of the city's largest market square, life would have been less complicated. Or perhaps more so.

"You aren't going anywhere." Grabbing the girl's shoulder with her left hand, Evayne held her in place as she searched through the pockets of her robe, looking for coins. She carried gold solarii and silver lunarii, but coppers and half-coppers were not of interest to her; they weighed too much and proved, always, to be of too little value in her travels.

The dates of the coins were as early as 387 AA, and as recent as 433 AA. She took, as always, the oldest coin first and began to push her way through the crowds. Several people tried to stop her, whether to lecture her or show their concern, she didn't take the time to discover. She met their gazes with her now impenetrable violet glare, and they moved aside.

The girl was content to be pulled through the crowd, although she herself did not seem to feel any of the acute embarrassment that Evayne did. *I do not understand,* the seer thought, as she turned onto Crafting Street, holding fast to her charge. It was clear that her mind was not quite right, and Evayne worried about adding a fey child to the struggle—although she knew instinctively that this "child" was no helpless pawn, no easy victim.

We're all part of it, child, adult, weak or strong. One way or another we win or we die, and if we die, does it matter how the death's met?

It mattered, of course. But what was done was done; the girl had come to Essalieyan, and safety. Together, they entered the long, open stall of a clothing merchant.

* * *

The year was 402 AA, and evening was closing in on the eighth of Lattan. She would not be able to leave the city the same way she had arrived in it, but she was glad of it—the High Summer road, while quiet, was not peaceful, and it was said that there was always a price to pay for the traveling of it. Superstition, of course, but Evayne herself was proof that superstition was not always wrong.

The girl at her side did not seem to notice the strangeness of their transit. She did, however, seem to notice the oddity of her clothing, which was a simple, sturdy dress that could be pulled over the head and gathered at the waist. The color was a rusty brown with fringes of green and ivory, none of which suited the wearer—but it had been late enough in the day, and the buyer had been desperate enough, that aesthetics were not in question. Scratching and pulling at the dress, the girl kept an eye on Evayne as if to say, "You see, I'll wear it, but I don't have to like it."

The market square was a mile from the merchant's port, but in Averalaan the city streets near the dockside were orderly, clean, and most important, very well patrolled. Evayne led her charge along the open roadways until she reached the boardwalks. They were the pride of Terralyn ASallan, master builder. He said they could keep back the very tides of time, and if no one believed him, they were still impressed at the length and breadth of the builder's work.

"If we hurry," Evayne said, speaking more to herself than to her companion, "we'll be able to cross by the bridge. Otherwise it's the ferry for us." She caught the girl's hand and began to walk more quickly, listening to the thump of her feet against the planks.

They made the bridge, although they almost missed the hour; Evayne's pockets contained coins too large for the toll required, and the guards, after a long shift, were not in the mood to be lenient. Neither was Evayne, and after the ensuing debate, in which they implied that she wasn't fit to cross the bridge to the High City and she implied that they weren't fit to bear the emblem of the Twin Kings, she was at last granted passage across.

She let the wind across the open water play with stray strands of her hair. *Be calm,* she thought, *and as quiet as possible. He hates noise and bustle.*

Holding to that thought, she made her way through the High City streets toward the Order of Knowledge.

Before she entered the grand, four-story building, she took the time to pull her hood up and arrange it so its shadow covered all but the tip of her nose.

"Come," she said softly, taking the girl by the hand again. "But be as quiet as possible." The warning wasn't necessary; the girl hadn't seen fit to utter more than an outraged squeak since their arrival.

Together, they walked between the pillars of the entranceway and into the grand foyer. Here, the ceiling was one large arch that stretched from wall to wall. Sun, when the sun was high, streamed in through the slightly slanted windows above, giving the Order a sense of lightplay that otherwise dour mages would nèver sèe. There were guards lined up as they walked, one per pillar for a total of six, but they were less a matter of utility than show. As show, they wore the Order's colors quite well; their black shirts, white pants, silver-embroidered sashes, and gold shoulder plates were of a quality made only by the High City seamsters.

The girl seemed to find them quite interesting, and Evayne stopped to let her wander around both pillars and guards. When she returned, she wore a very quizzical expression.

"They're at attention," Evayne said. "They aren't allowed to move. Now, come."

The doors were opened by doormen who also wore the colors of the Order but without the dramatic weaponry that the guards bore. Evayne nodded politely, although she knew they couldn't see her face, and walked up to the gleaming, stately desk that barred would-be curiosity seekers from the Order proper.

A rather bookish man looked up from his paperwork. His face was as sour as the foyer was grand. Evayne wondered what mistake he'd made that had incurred the wrath of the Magi. Very few of the members ever manned this particular desk themselves. "What do you want?"

Obviously, there was a good reason for the lack. Evayne's hood hid her smile. "I've come to see Meralonne APhaniel."

"You've got an appointment, have you?"

"I don't usually require appointments to see him."

"You don't usually see him, then. He *always* demands appointments be made. It's a question of being orderly." The man returned to his notes with something just short of a sniff.

"Excuse me."

He looked up balefully. "Are you *still* here?"

"Yes. I've come to see Meralonne APhaniel, and I'm afraid I can't leave until I have."

"Well, we'll see about that," the man replied. "GUARDS!"

Meralonne APhaniel was one of the Magi, the council of twenty, and one that directed the business of the Order of Knowledge. He was not a young man, and Evayne often wondered if he had ever been one. He was tall, but somewhat gaunt, his skin lined and pale, his hair a platinum and gold spill that crept down the middle of his back when exposed. As one of the Magi, he was not only entitled to wear the colors of the Order, he was expected to.

But, as common wisdom held, the Magi were all a little insane—certainly, they were no ordinary men and women—and when Meralonne was forced from his room in the study tower by two of the Order's guards, he came down the stairs in his favorite bathrobe, and very little else.

The man at the desk—Jacova ADarphan—was consigned to desk duty for another three weeks, and there was every sign, from the mutinous expression on his face, that that stay would have cause to be extended. Evayne, however, was removed with extreme pointedness from that list of future causes by a rather irate Meralonne.

"You really shouldn't have been so hard on him," she said, as she climbed the tower stairs. "No, we want to go *up*." The girl gave her a look best described by the word dubious and then began her four-legged crawl up the carved, stone stairway.

"If I'm to be disturbed," he replied, his brows still drawn down in one white-gold line, "it had better be with good reason. ADarphan wouldn't recognize a good reason if it spitted him." He frowned. "And come to think of it, neither would you. What are you doing here, anyway?"

"I've come to ask a favor."

"What, another one? I've wasted years of precious research time with your education—for free, at that!—and you've come to ask me for *more?*" A head bobbed out from around the corner of the third-story landing. "This is a private conversation, ALandry—get back to your books!"

"Sir!" The head vanished.

Meralonne had a tendency to have private conversations that the entire High City had no choice but to hear. Evayne's forehead folded into delicate creases. "My Lord APhaniel, might I remind you that in return for your time, I've—"

" 'My Lord,' is it? Don't talk back to your master," he snapped. "I know perfectly well what we agreed to at the time, but if I weren't an honorable man, I'd demand more."

They reached the wide sitting area near the window of the fourth floor's gallery. Evening had almost fallen, and the curtains to the window had been drawn. Lamps, with a nimbus of light that seemed a little too strong be natural, gave the paintings and sculptures of the gallery of the Magi a preternatural glow; it was almost as if, at any moment, any one of the images, invoked, would come to life. Meralonne walked past them briskly, taking the time to reknot his bathrobe's belt as he did. Evayne glanced from side to side, wondering if anything the gallery contained was new to her. And the girl trotted—there really seemed no other way to describe her motion—from picture to sculpture to picture again, her eyes wide with wonder or curiosity.

But at last they passed the gallery completely, and entered into the chambers of Meralonne. As one of the governing council, he was permitted to keep a residence within the Order itself, and if it was small and suited only for living in and not for entertaining, no mage yet had been heard to complain.

"You realize," he said over his shoulder, "that I'm liable to be called upon to explain this public disruption?"

"Yes, Meralonne."

The door swung open into a chaotic jumble of papers, books, slates, and the occasional scrap of clothing.

"When you were a young girl," the mage said, "you knew how to be properly respectful. Of all the traits to grow out of, Evayne, that one is least pleasing. Well, don't just stand there gawking. I was in the middle of something important when you barged in."

"Yes, Meralonne." Evayne walked into the room, very carefully pulling the hem of her robes well above her feet in order to make sure she didn't step on anything vital. The girl followed with considerably less restraint, something that was not lost on the mage. He did not seem nearly as annoyed at the girl as he did at his student.

"Don't be condescending. It doesn't suit you." Meralonne found a chair beneath a small pile of clothing. He took it. "Now, what it is this time?"

"The girl," Evayne replied. But as her master sharpened the steel-gray focus of his eyes, she found herself watching him. It was hard, with Meralonne, to tell what age he was, he aged so well. His hair was perhaps a touch whiter, and his eyes slightly more creased than the last time she'd seen him; he was clean-shaven and ill-dressed as always.

And yet. And yet. At sixteen, she had found his curmudgeonly ways almost a comfort; at twenty-eight, she was not always certain how much was affectation, and how much genuine. There were times when she could catch a glimpse of something darker, something far more somber, in his words. Then, the lines of his body would alter subtly.

Only once had she seem him called to the private duties that were his, by right, to take on. He set aside his poor clothing for dress that could only be described as magical, pulled back his hair in a long braid, and girded himself as if for battle. She had asked him, then, where he was going, and the expression, distant and cool, frightened her more than his temper, his growling, or his pointed unkindnesses. He hadn't answered. She never asked again.

Meralonne was the teacher that the otherwhen had taken her to when she had started walking the path twelve years ago. For the first eight years, it had brought her to him every other day. He was the only living person that she had seen so regularly, so . . . normally. He aged as she did, and he remembered her almost as she remembered herself.

Not, Evayne mused, as every other person that she met did. They might be old yesterday, and a child tomorrow; they might remember meeting her ten years ago, when she would not meet them again for decades; they might be dead or dying, but live on in the otherwhen, compromised by the vividness of their end in her memory. They might have information for her that she could not use in any future she could see, but that she could not afford, ever, to forget. Evayne did not forget.

And they might gaze at her with awe and fear, and no understanding whatsoever.

"Evayne," Meralonne said, catching her attention with the flat of his hand against the crowded top of his desk. "I'm speaking to you!"

"I'm sorry. I was thinking."

Meralonne snorted. "And you do it rarely enough I shouldn't complain. But you can think on your own time. Give me explanations instead. What is this girl, and why did you bring her here?" He reached into his desk and pulled out a leather pouch so worn that it shone from years of accumulated oil and sweat. Evayne grimaced as he pulled a pipe dish from it. Of all his habits, this was the one that she found most odious. And, of course, the one he would take no criticism of.

She lifted her shoulders delicately and let them fall in a graceful shrug. "I don't know who she is. But as to why I brought her—let me show you." She let her hands tumble in the air in slow free fall, and as she did, she spoke.

The words had all of the rhythm of language, but none

of the sense; their cadence deliberate, evocative, and elusive. No man or woman, be they mage or merely mortal, could repeat what she said, even if they heard it all, and listened with a mind devoted to that purpose. She knew that if she were a better mage, she wouldn't need the words or the gestures to find her focus.

Meralonne knew it as well, but he nodded gruffly as the spell progressed, because it was a difficult spell—a subtle one, and not a spell for the warrior-mage.

Any idiot, he was prone to say, *can learn how to throw fire and lightning around. Look at nature—how much thought and purpose does nature show? But I'm not about to train just any sentient mammal. You'll learn* magery, *not some trumped-up sword-substitute.*

Yes, Meralonne.

And she learned as if her life, or more, depended upon it. Because, of course, it did.

As the last of the spell-words echoed against the sturdy stone walls of his chamber, Evayne lifted her hands as if to embrace the empty air. Light the color of her irises showered in sparks from her fingers, dancing across the air and leaving multiple trails. She looked directly ahead, her focus short, her violet eyes wide. Slowly, as she concentrated, an image began to form between her outstretched arms.

He uttered an oath under his breath, in a language that Evayne did not understand. "You're losing your focus, girl. *Concentrate.* Have you learned nothing?" But his heart wasn't in the complaint, and the words had no sting, no real energy.

He stood, lifting his pipe arm, and walked over to Evayne's illusion. Smoke wreathed his face, his hair. Carefully, he began to examine the details. "It ran like this?" He asked in a tone of voice that was almost subdued.

Evayne nodded.

"I see." He turned to look at the girl, who remained silent. "Well, little one, it seems you've attracted the wrong person's attention." He studied her more intently, steel-gray eyes meeting near-black ones. "Evayne, how did you see that creature and still escape with your life?" His voice was soft now, even quiet. There was no inflection to the words.

"High Summer rites," she said. It was hard to speak, think, and hold the image static.

"High Summer rites." The words were stilted.

"I—I walked the hidden roads."

"You did. And who taught you this skill?"

"You did! We studied them in the—"

"We studied their theory, Evayne. Trust the master to know when the pupil has been properly tested."

She swallowed. It was true.

"Still, if you managed to use the *theory* to escape such a creature, I will do my best to be grateful at a quickness of thought that you rarely reveal." He lifted his finger, and the room flared with an angry orange light. The image of the demon was torn into beads of spell-light that faded before Evayne could piece them together. "Very well. You've shown me what you had to show me. You will not image that in my presence again. Is that clear?"

"Yes, Master."

"Good." He passed his hand over his eyes. "You were the best student I ever had the hardship of teaching. You know what this will mean. Demonology is being practiced again; keep it quiet until we find the source, or we'll have widespread panic." His gaze narrowed. "Where were you?"

"Breodanir. In the King's hunting preserve."

"You think that the Breodani—"

"Absolutely not."

Meralonne raised a pale brow. "You aren't usually this defensive, Evayne. Are you reacting instinctively or because of experience?"

She said nothing, but blushed; both were as he expected.

"Still, Breodanir. There's something about it that seems vaguely familiar. There's certainly an Order there, if small. Let me see." He walked over to his desk, and began to search—sift, really—methodically through the papers and journals there. It was quite clear that the chaos represented some form of order to the mage, but what exactly it was, Evayne couldn't say. When she had studied more intensively under his tutelage, her desk had always been meticulously tidy and well-organized. "Ah, here it is."

Evayne held out one hand, and Meralonne gave her a piece of paper. It was a letter from Zoraban ATelvise. Something about the name was familiar; it nagged at her thoughts, holding knowledge just out of range of her immediate memory. "Who is he?"

"Zoraban? The head of the Order in Breodanir."

"The head of the—" she went pale. "I remember now."

"Remember what?" It was a sharp question, sharply worded. Meralonne's steel-gray eyes were narrowed to a dangerous edge; they glinted like blades. It was clear, from the color of Evayne's face and the momentary twist of her features, that the memories were not pleasant ones.

She fell silent; it was her only defense against the mistake she would otherwise make. The otherwhen held its secrets, and her life was hostage to them. She remembered, as she always did at times like this, the first step that she had taken on the path. She stood beside a figure whose features shifted so regularly and so completely she could not describe him at all. He spoke with a voice that was a multitude of voices, and gestured with an arm that was an infant's, an old man's, a brash youth's. *For the sake of the world,* he said, *I will let you walk my path at your father's behest. But it is my path, and I share it with only you, child. You will share it with no other. Remember this: that what is, is; what will be, will be. You are your own time, and you must live as if your time is all there is. You will never be able to change your actions, once taken. What you choose to do now, at forty you must abide by, as any other mortal; you cannot reverse it by use of the otherwhen, no matter how hard you try. And if you try . . .* He lifted a hand, and the path became molten, bubbling and hissing inches away from her toes. *There will be no path, and no future for you. After all, time will still exist, no matter who wins the war.*

And will I control this path?

He laughed. She could still hear it; a mixture of anger and sorrow. *Who claims control of his own destiny? Not*

I, not you. The path will take you where you need to go, little sister.

Meralonne hated her silence. It was these impenetrable spaces that had driven distance between them and kept it there over the years. He watched her still face, her opaque eyes, the way she bit her lower lip. He saw the struggle in her rigid stance.

Perhaps, had he not given his word at the outset of his tutelage, he would have forced the issue; he did not. But he returned silence with silence, and the distance between them grew a little larger still.

At last, she started, and turned to face him.

"What would you have of me, Evayne?"

"If you would, I would have you watch the girl. She is safer here than anywhere in Essalieyan, and until we understand what the demon-kin want with her—until we know which mage summoned it—I think she must be kept safe."

"Agreed." A thin stream of smoke trailed out of the corner of his mouth. For a moment, he resembled a dragon in the center of his messy hoard. "And you?"

"I don't know." She turned to face the blank wall of the mage's study; it was the only clear space in the room. "This has something to do with the Breodanir God. The Hunting God."

"Evayne, it hasn't been proved to the Order's satisfaction that such a god even exists."

"If he doesn't," she said, her voice sharp with sudden pain, "his avatar most certainly does." She bit her lip as the words left her in a rush. She wasn't thinking clearly, but she never did where Stephen of Elseth was concerned.

"I see." Meralonne raised both pipe and brow in unconscious unison. "Very well. I will see to the girl's safety. But you, student, you look peaked. I recommend something foreign to your nature: sleep."

She smiled bitterly and nodded. "I'll take my old room, if you don't mind."

"Evayne?" She turned back, framed by the door. Her eyes were shadowed with fatigue that was not feigned. "One day, I demand an explanation."

"One day," she said, as she always did, "I will give you everything you demand." It was as much an apology or explanation as either was willing to give.

"Tomorrow, then."

"Tomorrow."

CHAPTER SIX

The following morning, when Evayne returned to her master's study, she was forty years old.

It was not immediately obvious, for she wore the same robes that she always did, and the hood was pulled high and hung just over her forehead. But her stance had altered, and her gait had a surety that at twenty-eight she had not possessed. Her voice was a touch lower, her words, when she spoke at all, direct.

She did not speak now. The familiarity of the study returned to her slowly, as if from a great distance. Her hands shook as she touched the outer frame of the door through which she had passed, day after day, in her youth. The otherwhen had been kinder then, although she had not appreciated it.

She had seen—

Closing her eyes, she drew breath, finding the familiar question. *When am I?* But the answer was slow to come; the past that was, for her, hours old, held fast and would not easily be dislodged. Soul-crystal warmed her hands; familiar shadows, scattered with silver light, began to roll. Peace. Time.

Now?

402 AA. Espere.

She slipped the ball back into the safety of her robes. The otherwhen did not take her into horror without reason. Somehow, the wild girl, whose name she now knew was Espere, and yesterday's vision were linked, although any who lived at the time of the coliseum were less than dust.

The rings.

She had not been to Meralonne's study for well over

ten years. She remembered their final argument clearly;
the heat of their discussion still had the ability to burn old
scars. *But I should have known better,* she thought sadly.
*To come to a member of the Order and expect him to put
aside all curiosity without an adequate explanation was a
child's dream.* When she had stopped being a child, she
didn't know, didn't remember. But she wasn't one now.

She knew where she was in the otherwhen, and knew
that the argument had not yet taken place. But she also
knew, now, why he had started to increase his pressure
and his curiosity; knew what had spurred him and piqued
him too greatly.

She had.

She had never expected to be here; not like this. She
put her hands in her pockets and felt the curve of the
seer's ball as it pulsed against her palm. It was time. With
an outward calm that she didn't feel, Evayne a'Nolan
pressed her fingers against Meralonne's outer doors and
whispered three distinct words. They crept open.

It was not her way to try to sneak, and indeed she knew
that she would have no success—what had happened had
happened—but she tried anyway. She always tried.
Time—how could it be immutable, and she able to walk
between the here and now of so many different lives?

But it was. And as she crossed the threshold, she saw
the orange-white glimmer of Meralonne's spell as it
flared to life along the seams of stone blocks and oak
planks, seeking her identity, her mission, her reason for
intrusion.

"Evayne," she said, giving it what it sought. "I have
come for the girl that I left here last eve. We have far to
travel." She saw the spell shiver as her words hit it, and
she smiled in spite of herself. The years had given her
knowledge and experience. She had learned to hone her
sight so that it might be used without spell and focus.
Meralonne had always said he was a mage of no small
power.

At sixteen, she thought he was the most powerful wizard in Averalaan. At thirty, she believed him one of the
more mediocre. At forty, she knew better than to guess—

but she was aware that the spell of protection woven here had very few equals.

She took a chair—the old, orange leather that had seen the use of three previous members of the Order—and wedged her elbows and forearms along the winged rests. Her breath, she stilled. The otherwhen had never before taken her to him out of time; he was the one presence that had been steady—until their break.

He had nothing left to teach me, she thought bitterly, hating the path, hating Time, and hating her father. She waited, counting seconds. Stared at the room, eyes lingering longest over the scattered mess of books and papers nestled in with the dirty clothing. Meralonne, although he would never admit it, must have come from a family of means to treat so much of value with such casual familiarity. At least, so she had always thought.

Did you have to bring me here today? Wasn't yesterday punishment enough? But the path had no voice and no sentience that she could discern. It had never answered her, and she had raged, cried, and pleaded with it in her time. *Evayne. You are* not *a child. If you are here, it is for a reason; even a good one.* She reached into her robes and touched the seer's ball, pulled it, luminescent in th[e] shadow-darkness, from her sleeves. She gazed into th[e] silvered mists that she knew so well, and in but a fe[w] seconds, coaxed a distinct image.

The wild girl, indeed. She shook her head. Her life w[as] a series of loose ends, things half-finished because [the] otherwhen took her from them in mid-stride. The [wild] girl, in this place, was one such thing. It was clear [that] they were to walk the same road today—an echo o[f her] past. She shuddered, and took a breath to steady he[r.] *Think about yesterday tomorrow. Think about Mera[lonne] today.*

When the door to one side opened, she was read[y for] him. Or so she thought.

"Who are you?" It was his voice, and not his [—] She had heard him in many moods and in many t[ones] before, but this was new. She turned in surprise [to find] him quite alone; the girl was not at his side. She have spoken, but silence came in the wake of surprise as she looked upon the man who had been her teacher.

Standing just inside the door's frame, he was taller than he had ever been. He wore his bed robes loosely about his body, but she could see the very threads crackling with energy, with magery. Some of it was the orange threads of protection and cancellation, some of it was the white of discernment, and some of it was a deep, steady violet, so calm she might once have missed it. His hair was white and very wild, as hers was dark and wild, and his eyes were the color of a sword blade, but less friendly.

"Who are you?" He did not lift a hand or utter a word, but she could see the colors ebb and flow around him as a spell took shape.

"I am Evayne," she whispered, against her will. There was a command in his words that was almost bardic.

"So you've said," he replied. "And you are telling the truth, as you believe it." A little of the ice seemed to leave his eyes, but they were still hard, still keen. "But you are not the Evayne that I know, or that this room knows."

"No," she said, "I'm not." She rose, pulling her robes ightly to her body.

se are the same robes. That much, I can see." He other step into the room, and the door swung shut ack. It surprised Evayne. He was not usually a n to display, and the use of magic for the trivi-hutting a door was quite unlike the Meralonne new. "Very well, Evayne," and his voice was have you come?"

ome," she replied, as carefully neutral as she take the girl that I left in your keeping."

d where exactly would you take her?"

that is not a concern of the Order, and it is

id, his voice so soft she almost missed the r you to decide. You intrude here. You are

speak when she saw his power flare k; there was no hint of word-focus, no e the spell itself. Gray mage-light touched her cheeks, her chin, her eyes, as her hood was yanked back. She smiled grimly as the midnight-blue material struggled free of Meralonne's spell and settled around her face once again.

But he had seen enough.

"You are Evayne," he whispered. "What's happened to you?" He took a step toward her, and she a step back, although she could not have said why.

"We do not have time," she said. "Bring me the girl that I left in your care, and I will leave."

"We don't have—" His eyes narrowed. He walked the length of the room to his desk and pulled his chair free from the debris that inhabited it. Then he sank back, his fingers a steeple before his eyes. "Your age is not the effect of spell."

She said nothing.

He gestured; that single fact told her he used a greater magic. She needed to conserve her power. She let the rings of coruscating light spring up from the floor to the ceiling around her still body without raising a finger in her own defense. The circles flashed by so quickly it was impossible to discern their color, but she could guess what the spell conveyed to its caster. She knew that he wouldn't harm her.

When at last he finished, his eyes were slits, he was stiff, and his face, long and thin, had never looked so unusual. "You have great power," he said at last. "And more. You have walked hidden ways, Evayne."

"I walked," she pointed out, "the hidden path to bring the girl to you."

"You walked it," he countered, "but it did not change you. You invoked it on High Summer. No, you've walked in the Winter, along the dark road. I can see the scars."

She offered him no answer; he spoke the truth.

"What you've learned, I didn't teach you."

"Experience is a good teacher, Meralonne—but in magery, indeed, you were my only master."

" 'Were?' "

"Are."

He smiled, but the expression was neither friendly nor pleasant. Not for the first time, Evayne wondered who he was, and who he had been before he joined the Order. She did not ask.

"You have learned to cross time. It is not an art I would have thought possible."

"It is not an art," she agreed. "It's an accident or a curse. Meralonne, you must know that if I could share this with you, I would. But in no wise am I able; indeed, I am compelled to do otherwise. I ask your forgiveness and your indulgence in this, but even if you do not grant it. . . ." She let the words trail off into uncomfortable silence.

"Yes?" He would not let the silence lie.

"What do you think I was going to say? Why do you seek to force my words?"

"Why are you afraid to give them?"

She lowered her chin. *Why, indeed? We will argue, and we will part. Nothing I say or do can prevent it. It has happened.* "There is nothing you can do to take the information from me. If I have to, I will die to protect it."

"I . . . see."

"There are forces at work that even I do not understand. Meralonne—"

"You deny me this—this spell. And yet, you had not learned it, Evayne. Not . . . not yesterday." His eyes changed color and shape. "I would give much to be able to travel time; to correct old wrongs and old crimes." There was a hunger to the words. Evayne wondered if it had always been there, lurking behind the mercurial, peculiar man who had been her master, and would never be again.

I never came to you as an adult, she thought, *until now. I do not even know who you are.* "I would as well, Master APhaniel of the Magi. I would give more than you could possibly imagine. But I do not choose where I walk, and I can change *nothing* of what has been."

"I see." He spun round on the chair, showing her his slender back. "And what if I do not choose to release this girl to you?"

"Then you doom us, for she is part of what we need to face the demon-kin. The darkness is coming, Meralonne, and whether we are at hand to fight it or merely to be trampled underfoot is our choice."

"You ask me to make a choice without facts, without knowledge."

"I ask you to make the same choice that I have had to. Do you think I know what will happen, or why, or how?"

"You know more than I."

"Yes. But I have paid for that knowledge."

"There is always a price to be paid for knowledge!" He wheeled, sudden in his rage; his face was transformed. Then he lifted his hands to his face and fell silent, kneading his forehead with his pointed fingers.

"Yes," she said bitterly, although this blaze of anger was something that she had never seen from him. "There *is* always a price. But you would pay it, even knowing what that price was. I—" Bitter smile. She cast her gaze groundward, offering him silence.

"I am," he said at last, "nothing if not a judge of character. Whether I was willing to pay your price or no, you would not give me the answers I seek."

"No."

"What, then, do you know of the demon-kin?"

"Too much, Meralonne, and I have not the time to tell you all. Suffice it to say that they hunt the girl that you keep, as we surmised years—no, yesterday."

He did not blink as he met her eyes. "Evayne."

She looked away. "I don't know," she whispered. "I see glimpses, Meralonne, but never the whole picture. I see the facets, but not the gem; the trees, but not the forest." It was as much a plea as she was willing to make. She turned. "The girl?"

"She comes." He sank back into his seat, the fire gone from his gaze. "I know you well, Evayne a'Nolan. If you say it's important, it's important—that much I trust. But can you tell me where you go?"

"I'm not sure." As a pupil, she had always been a child; even in their final argument, their break, she had been a willful, headstrong girl to him. Not now.

He raised a brow, and then shook his head. From out of his bed robes he pulled his pipe. He lit it, and only when he did did Evayne realize that the room was covered in shadows. Smoke wreathed his face like a halo gone awry. "You . . . don't know." He smiled, but it was the veneer of an expression.

"Meralonne, I—" She drew her shoulders up and lifted her chin. "I am not a child any longer. We are equals, or we are nothing. My word that I will explain all will have to suffice."

"When will you tender this explanation?"

"When it does not threaten our future."

He chuckled and brought the pipe to his lips again. "I will accept your word."

But he wouldn't. She knew it, and knew that his inability would shame him. "Thank you, Master APhaniel. I've—I've always done my best to be true to your teachings."

His eyes shone with a genuine pride, and for a moment his expression was soft, almost gentle. "You are an odd student, but easily the best I have had."

The door to the study swung open. In the shadow of the door frame, lit by golden spell-light and not by day, stood the girl. She cocked her head to one side and gave Evayne a puzzled look.

"Come," Evayne said. "We have far to go today, if I have guessed correctly." She walked toward the girl, and then stopped to look back.

It hurt, suddenly, to leave his study as a stranger. She had never done it before. *Never look back,* she told herself bitterly, as she turned away for the last time. *Especially when there's nothing you can do but mourn.*

Meralonne APhaniel watched her leave, his lips tightening around the stem of his long, ancient pipe. When she was gone, he nodded and the door swung shut. On her. On their discussion.

But other doors had opened. A past that he rarely thought about, and never spoke of, had been recalled by the strangely aged Evayne's visit. Smoke wreathed the air again, eddying in the currents of his breath, his silent words. He brushed long, ivory strands out of his eyes as he stared into a past that he had thought lost forever.

He did not move. Were it not for the smoke that con-

tinued to curl in an upward spiral, he could have been
mistaken for one of the statues in the gallery.

Sunlight, filtered by exterior glass and interior shutters,
worked its way into the room. He had work to do; things
to see to. Perhaps it was time to investigate the findings
in Breodanir.

A rock skittered across cobbled stone as a sulky young
man let fly with a kick. His hands were jammed into his
pockets, and his hat was pulled down over his forehead;
stray, unkempt curls jutted out to either side. Were it not
for his expression, he would have looked quite pleasant.
He was slim, with a fine-boned face and large eyes. His
limbs were slender and his skin pale. It was obvious that
his day was not taken up with hard physical labor, or perhaps any labor at all. An elderly woman, walking by with
two attendants, gave him a distinct frown. He met it with
a scowl, but moved out of her way.

Kepton Crescent was lively enough for an off-market
street, and it would become more lively still as Korven's
Drinking Establishment opened for the day. The public
baths kept the morning traffic brisk, especially when the
day was bright, warm, and reasonably clear. Today was
just such a day, and the outdoor springs—although they
were no more than trumped-up fountains—meant that the
baths would be in great demand.

The young man found it hard to loiter without being
nudged off the road by any number of parties who were
making their treks toward the baths. Finally his patience
ran out and in a fit of pique and surly annoyance, he
stood his ground, glaring at a young woman and her attendant, a rather stiff, plainly attired matron.

The older woman in the mottled dress looked down the
bridge of her nose out of stern, violet eyes. "Excuse me,
young man, but you impede our passage." Before he
could reply, she turned to the young girl who walked behind her and took her hand, both protectively and forcefully.

The young man lifted the corner of his hat, and then
mumbled something under his breath. "Ma'am."

"Kallandras." Evayne a'Nolan, dressed in the matronly,

severe style of decades past, inclined her head slightly.
Her voice very soft, she said, "Are you almost ready?"

He shrugged, and then fell into step beside her as she
continued to walk down the street. His tone and his words
belied each other; the casual listener would have no reason to suspect anything other than wheedling ill humor.
"Where do we go?"

"I'm not sure. Not precisely."

He nodded as if he expected no more and then glanced
casually at the young girl who was fidgeting with her
skirts. "Who is she?"

Evayne was certain that although he had only just met
the wild girl, Kallandras was more likely than she to be
able to answer questions about her height, her weight, her
age. He would know, if he never looked at her again,
what she wore, what its colors were, where the style of
the dress originated. "She is a rather unusual young lady."

"Which means you won't say." He shrugged. "You're
old, this time. Does this mean trouble?"

"I'm *not* that old," she replied. "And, yes, it does."
Evayne at forty still did not understand the otherwhen,
but she could begin to see a pattern to the course the path
chose for her. She was a mage now of no little power; her
knowledge was up to the test of the best of the Order; her
ability to protect both herself and any she chose to cham-
pion had never been greater.

It was not a coincidence that, as she aged, the dangers
she found herself facing grew more potent and more
deadly. At least, it did not appear to Evayne to be so.

She glanced out of the corner of her eyes and saw that
Kallandras was watching her intently. He was young, this
time, but his youth was not the liability that it would have
been for any other.

"Which is why you summoned me."

"Yes," Evayne said softly. She looked up at Kallandras.
His eyes were, in youth, the same piercing blue that they
would always be; meeting them, she could almost forget
to notice the rest of his face. His attention always seemed
entirely focused, entirely absorbed. "You won't be
missed?"

"Evayne—Lady." He frowned a moment, and then

smoothed the expression from his face. "When you forced me to make the choice, I was already one of the best of my number. It's important to your mission that I not be missed; I will not be missed." He fell silent as they walked to the end of the street. "I've arranged," he said, waving his arm, "for transport—but it would've helped to know where we are going."

Evayne let herself relax a little bit as a single-horse cab pulled to the side of the road. As always, Kallandras had looked to the details of their meeting. He offered her companion an arm, and the girl looked at it dubiously before scampering up into the body of the carriage. He shrugged, offered Evayne his arm, and then joined them. "I've told the driver we wish to go to the northwestern quarter. Will that be out of our way?"

"No. You've done well." Evayne sat back in the padded chair and let the city begin to move by.

"Good." He gazed out of the windows as well, his face losing all signs of surliness or aimlessness. Then, after a moment, he turned to her and met her gaze. She knew what he would ask next, but it always unnerved her to hear it, especially on occasions when he was young. *But in youth,* she reminded herself, *we have less compassion and more of a will to absolutes, to brutality. When you are older, Kallan, even you will mellow.* But not much, if she was being honest; not much at all. The Kovaschaii took their members very young and trained them well.

"Who do you wish me to kill?" His expression was completely neutral; there was no judgment in it, and no curiosity whatsoever. He became, for the moment, just another weapon; one to be held with care and used with confidence.

She did not wish him to be such a thing. "Kallan," she began. "How has Senniel fared?"

"The college fares well, with me and without."

"And Sioban?"

"As far as I know, she's fine. She's still the headmaster of the college, if that's what you mean. I haven't seen her in a month, but I've been avoiding it. She means to give me my papers and my route and have me travel the empire between Attariel, Senniel, and Morniel."

They were three of the five bardic colleges in Essalieyan; Senniel was oldest and foremost. Evayne nodded
as if the conversation were a normal one. "And training
of the voice?"

"She says that she hasn't seen a talent as strong as
mine in all of her years at the college. She also says that
she can't train it further; it will grow with experience or
not at all." The reply was smooth and without inflection.
Kallandras took no pride or joy in being bard-born. It was
a fact, like the weather, only slightly more relevant. His
very detachment made it hard to envy him. It also made
it hard to like him much.

"Kallan, do you enjoy the music?"

He shrugged. "It's music, like any other skill." But she
thought his expression just a touch softer. "You haven't
answered my question."

She grimaced. "I don't want you to kill."

"You want me to kill, or you would not have summoned me." He turned his gaze back to the city streets.

She grimaced. "You leave me no illusion, do you?"

"You aren't a woman in need of illusion." He
shrugged, and she thought she caught a glimpse of anger
and impatience in the motion. It was hard to tell; all of
Kallandras' public displays were dramatic and not genuine. "You came to me because I was an assassin. You
showed me what you needed me to see. I gave up the
brotherhood for you, but I took my skills with me.

"Who, Evayne?"

Evayne looked at her hands, stiffly clasped in her lap.
How long had it been for Kallandras? She counted the
years at three. She did not often see him as a youth anymore, and she had forgotten how the choice she had
forced upon him could still sting.

For she had taken him from the brotherhood of the
Kovaschaii shortly after she herself had been forced to
give up her own life to walk the path of the otherwhen,
and she had not been gentle.

I was younger then, she thought. *And youth is always
cruel.*

"I play no game with you, Kallandras. I do not know
if we will be called upon to kill or to hold our hand. But

we travel in search of our history, and I do not know exactly how long it will take."

"What do you hope to find?"

"Nothing. But that's not what I think we *will* find."

"You've been walking again."

She nodded. Kallandras was so different from Meralonne. He knew that she traveled in time, but he never asked her what she had seen, or where she had seen it. The past was not his concern, nor was the future. The present was the time for action, and he concentrated his considerable power upon it.

"It was yesterday," she said softly. But she could not tell him what she had seen, although she greatly desired the freedom to do so. The dictate of the maker of the otherwhen was absolute. "But what I saw there is not what we will see today."

He nodded. "Today?"

So unlike Meralonne. "As I said, I'm not sure—but I think, if we see anything, we will see the kin."

"Servants of darkness," Kallandras whispered. "So soon. Do you think it will be over with this?"

She did not answer because she knew the answer was not the one he wanted—yearned—to hear. "Be ready," she said softly.

"What do you know of the history of Vexusa?" Evayne's robes had fallen back into their familiar shape. She did not regret the loss of the matron's dress, as perhaps she had regretted other gowns in the past.

She let the curtains fall back into place and turned from the window of the Imperial State's hotel room. Her eyes were light, yet somehow dark, as if they reflected both the aurora and the night sky.

Kallandras shrugged. He sat stiffly in one of three high-backed chairs. Both of his feet were planted against the floor, and his hands rested in his lap.

"You would have made a terrible mage," she said, and smiled.

"I never wanted to be anything but Kovaschaii," he replied. "And you cost me that."

It had been long since she had seen him in his youth,

and she had forgotten how much his words could cut. At twenty, he did not view her as the ambivalent friend he would know her to be when he became forty. She remembered, as well as she was able, what she had been like at twenty. Meeting Kallandras as an older man had been a shock, then. *We circle each other, Kallan. Will we never walk the same path?*

"I'm sorry," she said, and she meant it. "I would not have taken you from your life of death had I another choice."

"So you've said." He did not relent.

"Kallan—"

"Tell me what we seek, Evayne."

She turned back to the window, looking for a way out. To come straight from Meralonne to the intense chill of Kallandras ... "History, as I said."

"If you seek history, then you have far to go. Vexusa exists in legend and lore, but the annals of the wise have very little to offer in the way of truths. If you remember," he added coldly, "the city was destroyed by the combined wrath of the god-born; it was razed to the last stone."

"Vexusa existed in far more than the fancy of beautiful voices and children's tales." Her voice became remote. "You know the old Weston bardic lays?"

"Some."

"Do you know the *Fall of Light?*"

"Yes." Grudgingly, he added, "It was about the loss of the Wizard Wars, when the Dark League destroyed the last of the Dawn Rose."

"And do you know the *Hand of Myrddion?*"

He nodded again. "Shall I get my lute?" His voice was tinged with a trace of sarcasm, but his fingers began to flex where they rested against his thighs.

"If you wish it, yes."

He looked down at his hands and then back at her; he stayed his ground. He knew what compassion was although the learning of it had been difficult, but he would not lay it at her feet; not yet. "Myrddion was a mage of the Dawn Rose. He fought and failed against the Dark League when he was betrayed by Ancathyron, his apprentice. Carythas, who led the Dark League, stripped

Myrddion of his power, and put him on display in the coliseum in Vexusa, the capital of the mage-state. They cut off his right hand, and then they set him to fight.

"He died."

Evayne raised an eyebrow. It was hard to believe that Kallandras was so good a bard that he had already built a reputation for himself. She almost said as much, but she knew what his response would be, and she did not wish to hear it again. Instead, she said, "and the hand?"

"Myrddion's right hand had five rings. After his death, Carythas had the hand brought to him and attempted to claim the rings for his own use. He set them upon his hand, and they began to burn him.

"He died, as well."

"He did not understand their nature," Evayne said.

"No one did," Kallandras replied. "Or do you?"

She shook her head, and pulled the curtains, briefly, away from the window again; the sky above was darkening. With Kallandras, she walked a tightrope; the spirit of the law of the otherwhen had been violated on a dozen occasions, but never the letter—the letter, through no choice of her own, was kept and would always be kept. She discussed "known" history, of course. She did not discuss whether or not she had been present at its unfolding. And Kallandras, so unlike Meralonne, never cared to ask. "Not fully, no. They were a set, and they operated as a set, at a particular moment. Myrddion—he *knew* that he was going to be betrayed; I'm certain of it. He *knew* that those rings would be taken from his body by no less a mage than Carythas. It was a trap."

Her voice broke on the last word. "It must have been a trap." She closed her eyes, and prayed that it was so— because he had died such a hideous, demeaning death to lay it. In the end, although he had been a strong man, he had screamed and pleaded, and eventually, after the hours had whiled away and the crowds had their fill of their greatest enemy's torment, they granted him his death. And she had watched; all she had done was watch. Even prayer had been beyond her.

It was the third time that the otherwhen had taken her

to so distant a past. She prayed that there would be no fourth visit. "What happened to the rings?"

Kallandras shrugged. "After Carythas' death, three mages attempted to touch the rings. They also perished, although less hideously and less slowly than Carythas. Carythas fought Myrddion's trap to the end."

Evayne nodded. There was a grim satisfaction in both his death and the time it took him to surrender to it.

"The fourth mage attempted to lift them by spell, but they would not be coaxed by any magic he could cast. There was no fifth mage; no one was willing to touch them. The lays do not make clear what the eventual fate of the rings were, but it is believed, in legends associated with the lays and contemporary to them, that the rings remained a part of the coliseum—that they could not be moved, although they did not serve an active purpose after the death of Carythas." He stopped. "You think they're still in the coliseum in Vexusa."

"I don't know. But . . . yes, I do. If they could not be moved by the greatest of the mages of the League, the enchantment on them was one that defies description." She would not look at Kallandras until she could school her face. "Therefore, the coliseum in Vexusa is important— and it still exists, although Vexusa does not."

"Averalaan." His voice was almost hushed. "You think it *here* somewhere, or you would not be here."

"Yes," she said, and this time, pale but steady, she turned away from the support of the window ledge. "It stands near the heart of Averalaan." She was on safe ground again, for she could always speak of the here and the now.

He was silent a long time, absorbing her news. She thought him pale, and the arrogant ice of his expression was chilled for a moment by something other than his great anger toward her.

His lips moved over a single word as he bowed his fair head. "Where, Evayne?" he said at length. He knew the city better than any but another member of the brotherhood. "The coliseum for the King's Challenge was built after the founding. There is no other coliseum in Averalaan."

She slid her hands into the sleeves of her robes. Kallandras frowned with mild distaste as the orb of the seer appeared between her palms.

She did not notice the grimace. Her attention was absorbed by the silver mist as she stared into the world that only the seer-born could see. "It exists, Kallan. It exists in darkness, but it is part of the here and now." He did not ask her how she knew; he never did.

"You think our mission is to find these rings."

"I don't know."

"Assume it's so. What of her?" He pointed to the figure that slept, with her knees curled up to her chest, in the center of the crimson counterpane.

"It's important that she travel with us," Evayne's voice was a study in neutrality. "Our road is the same road for the time being—and I believe that only she can set us upon that road." The ball she held cast light against her face like a shimmering web.

Kallandras looked away. "Where is the coliseum?"

"I don't know. It's hidden." She smiled grimly. "Even the seer-born would have trouble piercing the darkness that surrounds it."

"And you?"

"I have trouble. If I did not know exactly what to look for, I would see nothing out of the ordinary." She lifted the soul-crystal high; the web across her face pulsed suddenly, a lightning mask. She walked over to the bed. "Child." She took a deeper breath. "Espere. Come. It is time to find the legacy that your father's people have long forgotten. Can you feel it? We are close."

The girl's eyes flickered open. She lifted her head and rested her chin upon the backs of her wrists as she gazed quizzically up at Evayne.

Evayne lowered one hand to touch the girl's upturned forehead. The girl flinched, and the seeress paled. The orb spun; the clouds within it grew murky and dark for a moment. "Let me lend you what you do not have, child. We cannot wait for your proper time. Tonight we must hunt in the city streets." Silver sparkled in a web of mist and light. It covered them both, melting like snow against skin.

The girl's eyes began to change color; the alteration gradual enough that an observer might miss the transformation completely. She frowned and then looked up at Evayne, meeting violet eyes with golden ones. She looked around at her surroundings: the bed, the curtained window, the empty desk, and the unused grate. Then she nodded almost gravely and rose, sliding her legs toward the carpets beneath her bare feet. Those feet were callused and padded; the stones and pebbles of the city streets made no impression upon them.

"We will follow as we are able," Evayne said, as the wild girl approached the door and reached for the handle.

Kallandras rose from the chair he occupied. He was tense, the line of his jaw hard and sharp. "Evayne—what did you do?"

"It's an old healing spell," she said quietly.

He met her weary gaze with narrowed eyes before nodding grimly. They both knew he knew she was lying.

Averalaan at night was the shadow-twin of its daylight self. The moon's light across the open bay was high and full, but it shone on an empty stage; the city's streets were almost deserted. In isolated wells of light and noise, people gathered for entertainment and company.

Evayne, Kallandras, and Espere avoided them. They each used the shadows in their own way. Evayne drew them up like a cloak, with a touch of magic to seal them; Kallandras used them as a wall to hide in and behind; Espere used them as a guide.

They did not speak. They felt no need of words, and indeed, words would have been more of a barrier than a bridge. Here, with night come and darkness a friend, silence was a shield and a weapon, and the better armed they were, the more confident they felt in their companions.

Espere moved with a purpose that was singular and new; her steps were lighter and her eyes quicker than they had yet been. She paid attention to the buildings that she passed in and around, staring at them in wonderment. Children gazed at the new and the unfamiliar in just such a way. She did not linger, though; her hunt drew her on.

Kallandras watched her dart back and forth. He saw her stop once or twice in the long stretches of cobbled road, turning her face to the breeze as if it bore a scent she could follow. He could make no sense out of what she was doing, and that annoyed him, but he knew better than to interrupt or break the silence with questions.

The hotel that Evayne had chosen was in the most sensible part of Averalaan; merchants patronized it, and many foreign to Essalieyan were also quartered there, with their followers or their companions. Among them, three people of any description were unlikely to stand out, and any business that had to be done could be done almost freely. Espere led them out of the quarter, which was unfortunate.

What was worse was where she led them. The roads narrowed; the buildings began to close in on the street. Here, the moon's light was blocked by the height of narrow, closely spaced buildings that housed whole families. Averalaan was as safe as any city could be—but it was a city, still, and even at its heart there were darknesses that wise men did not trespass upon.

He watched as the wild girl began to lead them to the most dangerous of the hundred holdings.

"What's wrong?" Evayne said softly, her voice coming out of silence and leaving no echo in its wake. Magery.

He had a like way of answering her, and wrapped his own reply in bardic tones, precise and cool. "She's leading us to the thirty-fifth."

"Thirty-fifth?"

"There are two holdings in the hundred that are dangerous. The thirty-fifth is the worst." If he thought it odd that she did not understand the shorter reference, he kept his own counsel.

"Why?" Again, the word carried in an unnatural stillness.

His shrug was answer enough. "It is known," he said again.

"Not to the Kings." She lifted her head as Espere caught the shadows and came sliding between them to stand before her.

Above them, the bowers of trees older than the city let

the moonlight through in a dappled, dark pattern. The freestanding circles were planted throughout the old city in a pattern that not even the wise understood. They were tended by the Mother's children, and hidden behind the bases of their broad, dark trunks, one could often find those who made of the night a private affair.

Beneath the height of their highest branches, the rooftops sheltered—and these roofs were three stories and more above the ground.

"If it were winter," the seeress said gravely to the young girl, "I would not have been able to pull you this far back."

The girl cocked her head a moment, as if listening to the wind. Then she lifted a slender arm and pointed. To the ground.

"Where, wild one?" Evayne said softly.

Again, the wild girl lifted her arm, but this time, in the shadows of buildings that blocked the full moon, it was clear that she pointed not to the door of the tall building in at best a questionable state of repair. No, she pointed instead to the trapdoor in the street beside it, where wood was placed by cutters' wagons, for the course of the cooler season. In Averalaan, winter was mild nine seasons out of ten.

Kallandras stepped forward. Dressed for the street and the night, he wore no lute—and the lute was the only thing that softened him in Evayne's eyes. His hair was pulled back so tightly it showed no evidence of the curl and bounce that was the envy of many a young court lady.

He raised a pale brow at Evayne, and she a dark one in return. If the stuff of dark legends stood here—in any age—it was in an age so long forgotten that nothing at all remembered it. Shrugging, he began to walk toward the closed trap.

Evayne watched as he unlocked and unlatched the banded, wooden door. It creaked on heavy hinges, but he lifted it as if it weighed nothing. Opening the slender, slight pouch strapped to his hip as part of his clothing, he pulled something out and held it for a moment in the flat of his palms. By it, the underside of his jaw was illuminated.

Curling his fingers around it, he let the darkness obscure him again. "I'll be back," he said softly.

He did not return.

CHAPTER SEVEN

An hour passed.

Evayne could feel it as clearly as she could see it; the moon moving across the sky, changing by slow degree the texture of the shadows the buildings cast against the dark road. The wait was difficult, and not only for her.

Espere looked up at the seer, and then away again. She had repeated this motion every few minutes since Kallandras had gone down into the darkness that the trapdoor covered.

"He's gone," Evayne said softly. The wild girl edged forward toward the trap itself, sniffing at the air before turning to face the seer.

It had gone on for too long already.

Sliding her hands into fabric that moved obligingly out of her way, she brought the round orb into the darkness, where she might better see its depths for the light it cast. The line of her hood fell forward, obscuring her eyes and her expression. Her palms cradled the sphere to either side, as gently as if they held another's upturned face. *Kallandras. I have searched for you before, and you are never easy to find, curse your training.*

To push the silver mists away was, after these many years, a trivial matter. To hide behind them, to see glimpses without revealing one's self to the vision of another seer who might be searching—that was a challenge, and one that a seer almost never faced. It took skill, but more than that, it took power. She spent that power; instinct alone made her cautious, and a seer never ignored her instincts.

Kallandras, trained and nurtured by those schooled in the arts of the hidden ways, was never an easy presence to find—not even with seer's vision. Unlike Stephen of Elseth, or Gilliam, or any of the other people whom Evayne had had cause to seek in the otherwhen, Kallandras was a shadow, someone who conformed to the mists instead of standing apart from them.

Her jaw tensed; it always did when she exerted herself in silent concentration. She did not tell the wild one to guard their backs because she knew it to be unnecessary.

Already, Espere tested the scent the breeze carried and watched the flicker of light and dark—an interplay of shadow and moonlight. The stars were there as pale companions to the moon's pensive face; the evening was clear, the breeze gentle. None of the Essalieyanese walked along these streets; nor did a walking patrol of the magisterial guards come by to disturb the silence, which was in itself unusual.

They stood, two lone women in the folds of magic-imbued shadow, in safety—the safety of the tightrope, or the razor's edge.

Time passed.

Espere looked up, but Evayne was still draped in silence and shadow; she had not moved. The girl hesitated, and then she reached out and grabbed the seer's arm.

Evayne cried out in shock as one palm fell away from the seer's ball. She fumbled and the crystal teetered precariously in the air before she caught it again and pulled it close. "What are you doing?" she said, eyes blazing silver. There was majesty to her anger, and power, and danger.

It faded as she met the gaze of the wild girl. The urgency and fear she read there made Evayne's anger seem as unreasonable as it was. She slid the crystal into the folds of her robes. "He is hidden," she told her companion.

"Yes. By us."

Evayne looked up, and up again as the moon cast a shadow across her face. Feet planted apart against the roof edge of the tenement, a tall, slender creature looked down upon them. His lips were turned in a smile, his arms were crossed. At his elbows and along the line of his shoulder blades, twin spikes jutted out to either side, and two long horns adorned his forehead. He wore no clothing and no armor—and he needed neither.

Evayne used a word that she hadn't spoken since a childhood she barely remembered had passed. She threw her hands up and light leaped from her fingertips, sparking and dancing in the shape of a translucent, orange dome.

The demon laughed and launched himself into the air, drawing his hands into fists above his head so that the elbow-spikes pointed down toward Evayne. His laughter died abruptly as they struck the barrier. Where they had broken through, they burned. Lightning ran up and down their length, snapping and arcing.

Snarling, the creature pulled himself away. Evayne staggered backward as her spell buckled. Underestimating one of the demon-kin usually had only one result.

Evayne was not the only person who could use the shadows to her advantage. Moonlight dimmed; starlight vanished completely. The demon sprang up, twisting in the air as if parts of it were solid to his touch. He was *fast.* Evayne had battled the kin before, but she didn't remember this speed.

At twenty-eight, she would have died.

At forty, she barely managed to resurrect her mageshield before the demon was upon her again. She was no fool. There was no comparison between them on a purely physical level, and she had no intention of allowing the creature to prove it. Her shield crackled as he forced it; he snarled, she grunted.

It was Evayne who was pushed back.

He saw her eyes widen and laughed. "This night, mage, you face a lord, and not a lackey. You will serve us well."

Demon lord. Evayne met his eyes without flinching. "I face one of the kin, no more, no less." But she paled, and he saw it clearly. From a demon, the darkness hid nothing.

"The Priests call me Lord Caraxas. You may call me master." Almost casually, he reached up and tore a branch from one of the freestanding trees. It was old, and the branch itself was the width of his arm. "I do hope you won't consider surrendering."

Lightning struck the branch. Wood cracked and shivered; splinters drove themselves into the demon's hands. He laughed and threw the branch away. "Ah, little human—you remind me of days long gone. The world was ours, and we had time to enjoy our distractions." He gestured suddenly, and the ground around Evayne's feet erupted into stony spikes.

Not one of them struck her. "Morrel rode," she replied.

"Morrel died." But he spat; the amusement gone to anger. "And Morrel had what you do not—strength and power. I am bored."

"And I." She threw her arms wide and spoke a single word. Pale fire roared up around him in a golden, glowing circle. Reflected off his teeth and his almost metallic skin, it grew stronger and brighter.

"I *am* impressed," the demon replied. "You are stronger than you appear. You will make our lord a fitting sacrifice."

She smiled, and for the first time, the hood of her robes fell away from her face, although she did not lift her hand to move them. "I think your lord would find me most unpalatable."

"You will have a chance to be proved wrong," the demon replied. "We've been searching for you." He smiled. It was the most threatening thing he had yet done.

Evayne looked at the fires, and at the demon. He was contained within her circle, and it burned brightly. "What—"

The wild one howled.

Evayne turned to see the young girl's dark, strained features. They were pale with fear, raised toward the open sky in near panic.

The moon was slowly fading from sight.

"I am contained," Caraxas said, and his smile darkened. "But I'm not alone."

She looked up. Espere was right, but wrong; the moon stayed where it was. *They* were the ones in transition. The shadows above grew darker and more solid; the moon became a ghost, and then an afterimage against her eyes.

She knew what the spell was, and as the sky above her grew completely solid and shadowed, she turned white. There were perhaps five mages in existence who could cast this spell—and only one of them could cast it on more than one person without paying the ultimate price.

She looked up. There was rock above her head— something dark and convex. There was no sky, no open air, no breeze. To either side of her, shadows slowly thinned as her eyes adjusted to darkness. She stood upon the steps of a building that took shape and form as she stared.

It was black and seemed to rise forever, gleaming in the light of her spell of containment. The steps went up to doors that were thrice her height. Towers stood astride the door, and a circular window above it. Only the building's face was visible in the poor light, but she recognized the style of architecture. It was a cathedral to rival that of Cormaris in the High City. And she knew it well. Having seen it once, she would never forget its dark face.

"Welcome," Caraxas said, his voice the purr of a demonic feline, "to Vexusa."

"Vexusa—Vexusa was destroyed in the cataclysm." Her voice was tense and strained; she could barely speak at all.

Caraxas laughed, the sound low and rich with pleasure. "So your histories have said—but the lords of the Hells know the truth of the matter. What was built here could not be destroyed by mere humanity." He threw his arms wide; light shone off skin. "No, when Vexusa fell to the Legion, the Dark League turned its hand to the city's heart—and they buried it, mage.

"Like a seed, it has bided its time, growing within the depths of the earth and waiting for its proper season. We tend it, we feed it.

"The City of Gold will rise again." The amusement warmed his voice. He raised a finger to his chin and shook his head, a very human gesture. "But you will not be here to see it." He lowered his hand and walked through the ring of fire without even flinching.

Evayne called light, and light came; a miniature sun burst into being in front of the demon lord's eyes. He cried out in shock and anger. "Espere—run!" she commanded.

"To where, little mage?" The voice was soft, feminine—and quite cold.

Of course, Evayne thought. *He would not be alone here.* Standing beneath the arched stone frame of the cathedral doors, a figure in perfect stillness commanded the seeress' attention. Her hair was pale as platinum, her skin alabaster, and her eyes very red. Her nails were long and iridescent, and her clothing was ... magical in nature. Beneath the walls and windows of halls hallowed by death, she looked every inch the High Priestess.

"To freedom," Evayne replied.

"There is only one freedom in Vexusa for you or your companion," the woman replied, stepping out from beneath the hard, curved arch. "And we call it Myrddion's escape." She raised her arms and a black, coruscating light shimmered up them.

Evayne swore. She did not need the sight to know that this demon was more powerful than any she had ever encountered. She could feel the presence of darkness, could see it as a fog, not a mist.

"You will be staying with us for a short while, mage. And after we have spoken, you will have the privilege of meeting a God."

"Thank you, but I fear I must decline. I have been in the half-world before and I don't find it very interesting."

The demon smiled softly. Evayne had never seen so attractive, so sensual an expression. "You don't have the option, I'm afraid."

"You can't force a person to the half-world."

"No."

Silence. The demon was patient enough to let Evayne figure it out for herself; it didn't take long. "By the Mother," she whispered softly. *It started here. Father—why?*

"Oh, yes. He's here, seeress. In this world. And the Shining City, when it rises and obliterates Averalaan above, will be his capital and the beginning of his dominion."

Evayne saw the black-light billow out in five distinct

tendrils. It closed round her like a fist. She had magic, yes—but against the trail of demon-magery that her enemy used, it would not last. She was not a fool; as bad as things were, they could get much, much worse before the end.

She knew it, having seen the coliseum of Vexusa in use once before.

"Very good. You will come with us now."

The hand of darkness lifted Evayne off the ground.

"And you, silent one. You, too, will have the privilege of suffering for the company you keep. Come."

Espere was surrounded by darkness, and by darkness lifted. Her arms were pinioned to her sides, but her head was free to move. She twisted it and stared at the seeress.

Evayne could think of no reply.

They began to move up the stairs of the cathedral as Caraxas joined his mistress. The doors swung open, creaking rather than gliding smoothly.

Evayne passed through them, head up, eyes focused.

As did Espere—but not in the manner the demons had intended. With a snarl that lengthened to a growl, she tore her arms free of the shadow that bound her. Her feet hit the ground, and she rolled along glistening black marble. The dark interior of the open cathedral swallowed her; she was gone.

Caraxas shouted in surprise. Fire leaped from his fingertips, leaving a molten trail in a thin, red stream in the wake of the fleeing girl.

"Sor na Shannen, you fool!" he cried, as Espere avoided flame and shards of rock. "Why didn't you warn me?"

"I had her!" The demoness snarled back. "There's no possible way she could escape that spell—she wasn't even a mage!" She scanned the darkness. "There!"

"She moves quickly," Caraxas said. "Leave her to me." He lifted his arm again. Fire flayed the darkness like a whip.

"No. If she could break that spell, she—" And then the demon called Sor na Shannen suddenly became quiet. "There is a way." She turned to Evayne and grabbed her chin, piercing her flesh with the tips of her delicate claws. "Mage, where was she from?"

Evayne said nothing. The claws touched bone in three places, but the process was slow, like a caress gone awry. "You *will* tell me. Caraxas, go to the orbs. Get Ellekar's report, and get it quickly."

"He's not due to report—"

"Send the message. We will use the power. *Now.*"

"But the girl—"

"I will deal with the girl, but I need that information."

Caraxas nodded and vanished. Sor na Shannen turned her attention back to her hands. Blood ran down her fingers and dripped onto her wide skirts. "You are quite clever," she said conversationally, "and skilled. It's a pity that you chose to interfere here.

"But you are not the only mage that has come across Vexusa in the past several centuries. Perhaps, if you offer us your cooperation, you might be allowed to join their ranks, rather than join my lord."

It was hard to speak with talons embedded in the lower jaw. Evayne spoke. "I'll cooperate. How?"

"First, tell me about your companion."

"I met her on the road." Evayne spoke quickly, as if aware that her time was very limited. "She—she's strange; looks very unusual under a magical scan. I convinced her to return with me to the Order, where I could study her properly, but she would only do so if I accompanied her here."

"What did she hope to find here?" The demon spoke softly and slowly, but the tone made a mockery of gentleness.

"I don't know—*I don't know!*" Blood fell faster. Evayne's face was white.

"It's a pity that I don't believe you. Come along. You will meet a better interrogator than I, and we will have answers."

Evayne slumped forward as Sor na Shannen released her jaw. "You are an attractive woman," the demon said. "I hate the waste, but I fear we do not have the time." Very gently, she planted a kiss on Evayne's bloodied lips.

"Do not move." The words were command embodied.

Sor na Shannen froze, her lips locked in a predatory smile. And then she cried out in pain, clawing at her back as she stumbled to the side. The shadows that held the seer began to unravel as their mistress lost focus and control.

"You should learn to lie," Kallandras said, as he stepped out of the shadows. "Or at least to negotiate with conviction." He watched, arms crossed casually against his chest, as Evayne's gesture burned the last of the darkness away.

Evayne cradled her jaw in her palm for a moment. "Where have you been?" Kallandras was bard-born, but he rarely demonstrated his power, relying instead on what the Kovaschaii had given him: assassin's skills. *I'd almost forgotten that you were this strong, so young. Thank the Mother. Sioban must be anxious indeed to have you travel the empire in Senniel's service.*

"I met—a demon. It brought me here." He shrugged.

She did not have to ask the demon's fate. "Come on."

Kallandras seldom showed surprise. Even now, he raised an eyebrow, no more. It was enough. "Evayne— where are you going?"

"To the coliseum—it's here; it's almost a courtyard, of sorts, to the cathedral proper." "The priests and the mages sat in the galleries or watched the entertainment from their rooms."

"Didn't you hear anything she said? We can't afford to—"

"We don't have a choice!" Her eyes were flashing violet; her cheeks were flushed. There was a pain in her eyes that had nothing to do with the injury Sor na Shannen had inflicted. She raised a hand to point. It was slick with blood. "Espere went there."

"Espere seems to be able to take care of herself."

But Evayne wasted no further time in argument. She ran down the grand hall of the empty cathedral. The vaulted ceilings echoed her hasty steps, but Kallandras made so little noise that the sound of one person, and one alone, filled the hall as they ran.

She wanted to tell him the truth. She wanted to tell him that it wasn't Espere she was afraid for; that it wasn't

Espere that drove her, half-crazed, into the heart of a cathedral that had once served the Lord of the Hells. She
wanted to tell him, simply, that yesterday—in her life, if
no one else's—she had seen Myrddion die the most hideous of deaths; that she had had to endure it, because to
leave would have been to draw attention to herself; that
she had had to pretend to enjoy the spectacle, for the
same reason; that she had counted each second of each
minute until, at last, he was granted peace. She could not
let that experience mean nothing. The path of the
otherwhen had taken her there for a reason.

And she needed to see the coliseum again. To see it,
empty and unused; dusty and cracked with the passage of
time, locked away underground in the darkness. It would
bring her a measure of peace.

Or so she prayed.

The halls were long and dark. She had sight enough to
pierce the shadows. She slowed down for a moment to
listen for signs of pursuit; there were none. Her robes retreated a little higher above the ground, giving her feet
room to take longer strides.

She pointed, Kallandras followed; words became sec-
ondary to breath, to breathing. The hall became a T, and
she turned to the right, catching the wall as an anchor and
pivoting lightly on one foot. She did not forget her way
to the cloisters, and through the cloisters, the edge of the
arena was visible.

She ran, her feet pounding stone, her throat growing
drier. Her right hand kept touching the wall at her side. It
provided her with sensation, with direction. Here and
there, her fingers ran over large cracks, places where the
walls had settled poorly after the cataclysm.

Evayne, she thought, *stop. You've got to be rational.
You can't—*

Thought stopped as the slaves' and combatants' entrance to the coliseum came fully into view.

Kallandras pulled up at her back; she sensed him stop.
He made little noise as he turned, scanning the darkness
at her back as she gazed at Darkness in front of her.

The floor of the arena was no longer dirt; it was marble, of the same texture and consistency as the stairs to

the cathedral had been. Gold and silver runes were writ large across the marble's face. The letters were almost as tall as she, and there was a pattern to them, and a magic, that defied her immediate understanding. Nor was this the only change.

In the center of the arena, there was an arch, a single, solitary structure. It was, at first sight, simple stone, but glints of iridescent light shot through it, concentrated at the arch's keystone. To either side, there was a pillar, each the width and height of three large men.

She froze in place, her hand gripping the edge of the wall.

"Evayne?"

She could not speak, her attention absorbed by the runes on the floor. They encircled the pillared arch in a permanent ring, radiating darkness; Winter power. She did not know the full arts of demonology, but she knew enough to be certain of two things. It was a summoning, and the kin were not its target.

In the center of the arch, suspended as if in air, was a growing darkness that curled in on itself in hunger. It was large; easily the size of two grown men.

"What—what is it?" Kallandras' question was hushed. For the first time in her life, Evayne heard a trace of fear and nervousness in his question. And her life encompassed many more ages of Kallandras than a mere youth of nineteen.

"It's—" But she could not speak the name. Because the name had power now. Because the saying of it could attract attention that they both desperately wished to avoid. She swallowed and very gingerly began to back out of the opening to the arena.

No. She stopped. *I am not done here, not yet. The path has not opened; the way is not clear.* Her jaw ached. She bunched up midnight-blue cloth and folded her sticky hands into fists around it. This she hadn't done since she was a youth not fully Kallandras' age.

She drew herself up to her full height, lifted her chin, and stared into the darkness. Her skin was white, her jaw clenched. Kallandras came in behind her, still watching their backs.

Very slowly, they made their way along the outer periphery of the arena. Evayne took care not to touch any of the symbols and wards that covered the marble floor. She swallowed. She never forgot anything important, but it was hard to remember in the face of the arched gate.

No. I was sitting ... there. Carythas sat on his throne ... there. The throne was gone; at another time she would have been grateful for it. *Myrddion died ... there.* It was the very spot over which the gate had been erected. A sudden anger displaced some part of her fear.

Kallandras sensed the shift in her mood. She could almost feel him relax. *Don't,* she thought, but did not say it aloud. She kept her concentration, forced herself to remember every detail of Myrddion's death—because she knew, if she remembered it well enough now, she would never have to think about it again.

Myrddion lost his hand there. And Carythas came to the pit itself and burned—there. There. She pulled down the hood of her robe—when it had risen to cover her face, to protect her expression, she couldn't say—and walked, with purpose, to the spot.

There, an orange, glowing ward pulsed in the shadows. It was not the same type or of the same magical texture as the runes surrounding the gate; it was older, and its power was not of darkness, but of a magery so strong she had only twice seen its like.

She could almost hear Meralonne's voice. *The knowledge here, the history, Evayne! Think of all that we could discover about the past!* She did not spit, but only because of the noise it might make.

Touching Kallandras very slowly on the shoulder, she pulled him to her right side. She lifted her finger to her lips and then lowered it toward the ground. He raised a brow, pointed to his feet, and then pointed a little distance off. She shook her head, no. He nodded.

She reached into her robes, found the cool, hard surface of the seer's ball, and then froze in place.

The lights went out.

"Welcome," A velvet voice said. "Welcome to the dominion of Allasakar."

* * *

There were ways to sense that did not involve the light. Hearing: the change of a voice's tenor and volume; its direction; and its strength. Touch: the movement of air as a door swings open and then shut. Smell: the nearness of bodies; of sweat. Of death.

Kallandras had trained in the arts of the night. Darkness was an efficient tool—not a weapon in and of itself, but an augmentation, an advantage. He was not a master of the night kill, but he was an able student.

With ease, he pivoted, crouching, toward the sound of the voice. He recognized it, of course. It belonged to the demoness. Somehow, he had failed in his mark. Shame warred with fear. Fear won. Caution moved him now. He recognized the name.

Allasakar.

Lord of the Hells. God of the Darkness. Reaver of the Chosen road.

"Yes, you were clever, boy. And foolish; you might have bought yourself time, had you run in any direction but this one."

He rolled at once. The ground erupted in a spray of shards and splinters. They bit into his neck, his back, and his arms, but not very deeply. He steadied himself as he rocked back to his feet.

"You missed. Have care." Another voice; male. Not Caraxas.

"I know what I do," Sor na Shannen replied, the velvet gone from her voice. "Do you think inconsequential magics like this could break the gate?" Kallandras rolled again, but this time the spell that struck ground was not dark; it was a sizzle of angry red lightning. Instead of shards, there was a spatter of molten rock.

"No—but the mage is the danger here; you waste time on the boy."

"Then, my lord," the sneer belied the title, "deal with the mage as you see fit."

She didn't understand why they chose not to use the darkness; Sor na Shannen's ability to weave it was greater than Evayne's ability to weave spellfire. But she did not suggest, and she did not complain.

In the stands, at the exact spot Carythas had once occupied, Sor na Shannen and a demon of more formidable stature stood side by side. Sor na Shannen was naked; all pretense of clothing and civility were gone. Her skin, like the light around the arch, was vaguely iridescent to Evayne's eyes; her body was distinctly nonhuman. The demon at her side was taller. At seven feet, he towered over his companion. His hair was almost white, and his eyes an unnatural black; he had no horns, no spikes, no fangs—indeed, he seemed to be a tall, very forbidding man.

Which was ill indeed.

There was an old Weston adage. *The more human evil's face, the more dangerous the threat.* It was, more often than not, true.

She was already prepared with a countersign when he leaped into the arena, a combatant assured of victory. It was a long drop, but he made no more noise than a cat would have when he landed.

"Greetings, mage."

She waited, ready for combat, but he did not try to approach her, and in a moment she understood the error of her assumption. He walked quickly, his arrogant demeanor melting into near subservience. He crossed the border of runes and wards, taking care to step between the golden lines, not across them. Then, in front of the pillared arch, he knelt.

"My lord," he said, his words the loudest that had yet been uttered in the arena. "We bring you two more." He bowed his head; Evayne could see, in the shimmering light of the keystone, the reflection of his face in black marble.

"Kallandras!" Evayne shouted. It was a command.

He heard the demon's words as he rolled, once again avoiding Sor na Shannen's strike. The hair on the nape of his neck stood on end as she readied herself for another.

It faded.

"Kallandras!"

He could not see Evayne, not clearly, but he could hear the command in her words. Taking care to avoid the arch,

he began to make his way back to her. His feet made no
sound; he held his breath as he moved, and stopped only
to renew it.

But there was no further attack.

She reached out for him as he approached; he heard the
familiar rustle of her sleeves. He hated to touch her. He
took her hand.

Together, they stood in silence.

The darkness confined by the pillars began to con-
vulse. The demon remained as he was, head bowed to
floor, shoulders curved to ground. Shadow shot over his
head, a living bloom of writhing tentacles—the twisted
version of a giant human hand.

Evayne had no time to draw breath. The tentacles
wrapped themselves around her body and lifted her above
the ground. Kallandras was likewise taken, but he was silent.

She screamed as the darkness pierced her flesh. It left
no mark, but it burrowed, searching her body for the
spirit it contained—for the shard of immortality that only
the gods themselves could touch. She wanted to fight, but
she couldn't; she couldn't concentrate. She was a mage,
but the center of her power had been distorted and shifted; it was unreachable.

Only the reaving was real.

Somebody uttered a piteous cry in the distance. It
wasn't Kallandras, but she didn't know the voice—she
had never heard herself scream so. She reached out with
one hand, then with both, trying to touch something that
was not darkness or torture.

Her right hand found Kallandras again. Their fingers
locked tight, their hands became rigid. Her left hand
brushed against cobwebs, or dust; something light, but
definitely real.

The cries that continued piteously in the background
were distant, the whisper that touched her left ear was
not.

Daughter of destiny, you have been long in coming. It
was a quiet, strong voice, the whisper of an older man
who had lived his life assured of his power. It was
Myrddion's voice; having heard it once before, she would

know it anywhere. *I have been waiting for you, and now that you are arrived, my travail is at an end.*

I was, as you, a seer-born. The future came in dream and vision, and I saw the end of the world—but so far ahead of my time that only by becoming fell or dark could I hope to survive to fight it. I could not chance it, for once the Winter road is walked, who can say what will become of the walker? Yet I could not turn away.

I went to Fabril, and to the houses of the Unknown lord called guardian of man. Guardian of Man. It was not a name that Evayne had heard before, but she would re-member it later. *And between us, we forged the five. Some part of our power is in them, and in this way, we give our legacy to those who must be mankind's warriors.*

I give into your keeping that which you seek. They are not yours, but they are your responsibility. You are their guardian, and I trust you to know when your guardian-ship is at an end. Do not attempt to remove them, or once they are removed, to retain them.

I give you earth, air, fire, and water; the elements that you know. But I give you a fifth ring as well. It is not meant for this world. It is haven on the darkest of roads, comfort in the most evil of places.

And now, I have kept my vow; I have fulfilled my re-sponsibility. May you one day know the peace that I will now know. For I do not think I could have traveled your road.

I have one last gift to offer: Be free!

Evayne lurched forward at the force of the words—and the magic inherent in them. She looked down at the darkspell around her and saw the shadow streaked with fissures of light. The screaming stopped as the fingers of Allasakar lost purchase. Suspended in air by the crum-bling remnants of the dark lord's spell, Evayne could see again.

The marble just below her feet was buckling and heav-ing. The solitary ward above it was a green, mottled glow. It twisted, resisting the movement beneath it.

"NO!" The voice was Sor na Shannen's and the demon lord's combined. "My Lord!"

But it was too late. A fissure cut across the glow, darkening and lengthening as the rock struggled to cast off the ward's magic. Another crack joined it, and another, and another.

Evayne watched. Everything moved slowly. Even the shadow that bloomed once again like a flower of darkness from the arch grew sluggishly as it crept toward her. She watched, and as the last of the pain receded, she saw a glint of silver light. The mists.

The path was opening beneath her feet.

She could not turn quickly enough to see Kallandras. She didn't have to; her hand still clutched his. *Mother,* she thought, *have mercy; we are all your children, no matter to whom we make our pledge.*

The marble shattered, but its shards turned to vapor before they touched her unprotected legs. A small, sharply-edged pit opened up beneath her, and it was filled with light.

Five stars rose, and behind each, a trail of magic seared itself into her vision; Myrddion's brand. Two were blue, one green, one red, and one a silver that stung the eyes. They came, across the shadow itself, to rest upon the fingers of her outstretched hand. Warmth tingled against her skin.

She did not look. Instead, she called upon her magic, upon the core of the power that she had used little of this eve. She could not take Kallandras with her; the path opened only for her, and no other living being, be they god or mortal. But she could see him to safety if he was not already consumed. That much power, she had.

Lowering her chin, she focused her will. Rings of gray light rippled down her right arm in a wave. They grew in number, in speed, in intensity, and as they touched Kallandras, they began to converge. Unlike all else, they moved quickly. Time's gift.

She whispered a benediction as the mage-rings connected and the spell's power fled her body in a cold rush. Shadow-magic collapsed in on itself and she heard the roar of an angry god as Kallandras vanished into Averalaan.

The otherwhen opened around her. Her feet touched the path and the silver mists shot up like impenetrable walls.

Her legs began to tremble. As did her arms, her back, her lips. She couldn't control them.

You pushed too hard, she told herself reprovingly. *Called too much.* Her knees and her palms struck the ground. Nausea hit as the shaking got stronger. She gave in to it—she hadn't the will left to do otherwise.

Slowly, and with great difficulty, Evayne began to crawl along the path. The road could only take her someplace if she journeyed along it. The distance didn't have to be great—it just had to be measurable. She threw up twice and gagged continuously, but concentrated on keeping her tongue flat against the roof of her mouth. The seizures were dangerous, otherwise. Her right hand moved. Her left. Her right leg. Her left.

The path delivered her slowly into the world. The mists cleared; day came, with a sun far too bright, and a season too cold. Her face was three inches above stone steps, and that distance grew less very suddenly.

CHAPTER EIGHT

Why did you have to bring me to this particular house?
Evayne asked of the otherwhen in a tone of mild disgust.
She received the usual answer: silence.

She was still in the year 402, although it was later as
the seasons went. She didn't understand why she was in
this particular time, but was certain that she would come
to. When she had the strength.

The roof in the house of healing was adorned by only
a single, fine crack in the plaster between the large,
darkly stained cross beams above Evayne's bed. She
knew it well. During the past week, between intermittent
seizures, she had done little but stare at it. The walls were
a shell-white, and the sill of the single window was the
same dark stain as the cross beams.

"Lady, can I get you anything to drink or anything to
eat?" The voice of the slender young woman contrasted
with the severity of her starched, stiff uniform. Her
smooth, uncallused hands and her pale skin identified her
as an apprentice healer, and not just an orderly.

"No. But thank you." She turned her head to the side
to see a look of disappointment cross the young attendant's features.

"Will—will you be staying much longer?"

"That," she replied dryly, "is probably a decision best
made by Healer Levec. You could ask him."

The girl's face told her just how useful that would be.
She dropped an almost courtly bow, and then wandered
out of the room, lingering a moment in the doorway as if
hoping to be recalled.

The orderlies and the attendants of the house were, for
the most part, young men and women with romantic no-

tions. The idea of a mysterious, wealthy woman, who was no doubt a mage given her unusual form of dress, spoke to their imaginations.

Evayne smiled, wondering what the truth would do. She propped herself up gingerly and tried to look out the window. The curtains were drawn; it was probably dark. Her elbows began to shake, and she sank back. Ruefully, she looked at her wrists. They were thin and fragile to the eye. She had come rather close.

Lamplight played off her fingers, glinting over gold.

It's no wonder they think I'm wealthy, she thought, as she turned her hand slowly in front of her face. On her forefinger was a thick, golden band. It wasn't plain, but rather delicately veined, as if a leaf had been pressed into the mold when the gold was being poured. At its heart was an emerald that flashed with the green of the first forest, cut in a rectangle with a flat, perfect face.

On her second finger was a band that seemed somehow orange in the light. Although it, too, was gold, it looked like liquid caught beneath crystal—molten precious metal. It held a ruby that was bright, not dark; the color of fire, not of blood.

Where fire stirred, water stirred also. The third ring, on her ring finger, was fashioned of white-gold. It almost looked as if the band were ice, for frost seemed to have covered the ring as if it were glass in a cold climate. The sapphire looked like the heart of the north wind, but no matter how long she stared at it, she could not see its depth. She stopped trying and turned her gaze to the last ring she had.

For some reason, it drew her attention away from the others, although it was a simple, rounded band, with no gems and no intricate design to mark it. She thought it made of white-gold, at first—but the weight was wrong. Later, she would have it properly identified. If she could find someone willing to do so when she couldn't take the ring off her finger.

This ring was the fifth that he had spoken of.

She was enough a member of the Order of Knowledge to feel a sharp curiosity. But she shook her head and let her hand fall back to rest against the simple, undyed woolen counterpane.

She had four rings, but she was not concerned; she knew where the fifth was. She had seen it many, many times throughout the years. She had even asked about it once, although Kallandras, at thirty-eight, hadn't provided her, at twenty, with much of an answer.

No, not true, she thought. A rare and genuine smile of pleasure touched her face in the privacy of her room. He had said, *It was the gift of a friend, and you will come to know her well in time.*

You would never have said that that eve. What changed you?

"Ah, I see rumors of your alertness aren't exaggerated this time." A dark-haired, dark-skinned man entered the room. It was obvious that he was the healer on duty, and equally obvious that he was the senior member of the house. He wore around his neck the open-palmed symbol of the healer-born. Upon his face, he wore an expression of distinct disapproval.

The healer-born could not affect someone suffering from mage-fever. Nothing—be it herb, spell, or potion—could. But there wasn't a healer alive who could accept that gracefully, or if there was, Evayne hadn't met her.

"You weren't terribly careful, this time."

"No, Levec," she replied meekly.

"You're never careful. Never."

"No, Levec."

"What's the excuse? Years ago, you could at least blame it on youth—but you aren't a child, or even a wayward, serious young woman, anymore—and it seems to me that you are often more severely injured or at risk than you ever were.

"If the young do not gain in wisdom as they age, what sort of example are they?" His fingers rapped the bedpost as he spoke, and his brows, which were lovely and thick, drew down into a single, fierce line. Levec was not a man who appeared, at first glimpse, to be of the healing persuasion. Nor, for that matter, at any glimpse.

The path had a cruel sense of humor at times; Evayne,

exhausted but recovering, could do nothing to stem the
flow of the healer's pointed tirade.

She knew that Espere survived, because she had seen
her, years ago, in the otherwhen—an older woman, if not
less dangerous. She didn't know how she had managed to
escape the cathedral in Vexusa; "how" was often the single question that she hadn't the luxury of asking.

*Well, forest sister, I hope you found what you hunted;
with your aid, I found what haunted me.* Light bubbled in
the ball she held between her palms. The room itself was
dark; the curtains drawn, the door closed. It was a pity
that it couldn't be locked, because she desired no interruption. The use of the ball often made her more vulnerable.

And if Healer Levec saw it, he would almost certainly
feel compelled to attempt to remove it from her keeping—a task which would see them both involved in . . .
too severe a disagreement.

*Don't push, Evayne. You've been here for a week
already—you can't afford more time.*

But ignoring her own advice was a habit of youth—one
that she had not entirely lost with wisdom and experience. She searched the mists again and again, but they
gave her no answers.

They did give her another glimpse of Stephen of
Elseth. He was fighting with his huntbrother—did they do
nothing but argue?—over the apportioning of a hunt's
kill. Youth robbed his features of their ability to sting. He
was fair-haired, slender of build, and graceful in
carriage—but he was not yet adult, even if he hovered on
the brink.

She watched him for a while before sleep took her
away from the vision.

And it was in sleep that her answer came.

The ball was a deliberate use of her birthright. She
summoned the mists and the strands of her soul's history,
her soul's light, and they came. They bore her examina-
tion, if not willingly. Not all seers were gifted with the
creation of such a ball. Evayne thought she might be
the only living seer to walk the Oracle's path, although in

the distant past, those seer-born had made the trek to the Oracle's hidden testing ground as a matter of course. If one could survive the Oracle's path, the Oracle would create the soul-crystal. If one died, it was no longer necessary. Many had died.

But before they walked the Oracle's path, they knew themselves seer-born because of their dreams and their visions. The dreams of the seer had a texture and a reality that a return to the waking world could not force one to surrender.

She had such a dream now.

It was brief, but unmistakable. In it, two men she did not recognize met in a well appointed room. One appeared to be a messenger; he handed the older gentleman a scroll. Their conversation had no bearing on the information it contained.

It wasn't important to hear their words; they were obvious. For one of these men wore a symbol of the Order of Knowledge—a bad sign, but not, unfortunately, a unique deviation. The other man wore, seared into his left ear, the mark of the chalice.

The mark of the Kovaschaii.

Their discussion was irrelevant; the name of the target was *never* spoken. But in the seer's vision, warped and guided by an unknown twist of fate, a face was superimposed, like a ghost, over the two men.

It was Stephen's face. He wore a green cape, Hunter's green, with gold, gray, and brown edges, and a cap that covered his hair and shadowed his face. The cap itself was embroidered with a crest: Against a field of green, a sword, crossed over a spear, beneath the horns of a stag in full season.

He was fourteen.

She woke with a start; the ball was already clasped between her palms. She didn't remember falling asleep, but sleep had provided her with the answer that had proved so elusive during her waking hours.

You never take me anywhere without a reason. Her hands were shaking. With determination, she began to search the mists of the now for sight of Kallandras. *Think, Evayne. What did the crest mean? When is it?*

* * *

The ring was made of gilded crystal. On his hand, it seemed to fade into nothing but a diamond's flash in the right movement of light. It was a marvel of craftsmanship, with a history that rivaled that of his—of the Kovaschaii. It was the only piece of jewelry that he had ever worn outside of the ceremonies of the brotherhood.

It would not come off of his finger. He had only tried to remove it once, and even then only for curiosity's sake. It was not small—indeed, it fit him as if crafted for his use—but it would not budge. It remained on the thumb of his right hand.

And that was of significance to the brotherhood's ceremonies. On that finger, he had worn, for the minutes of the calling, the ring of the Lady. By it bound, he made his oaths.

His right hand became a fist. He stared at his thumb, seeing, through the crystal, another ring, donned in a smoke-wreathed, darkened hall. His eyes grew opaque in the seeing. It was the one memory that any of the Kovaschaii could call at will—for it was the ceremony that made them one with the brotherhood, and no longer separate from it.

Light flashed; he stiffened and raised his left hand to shield his eyes. The diamond, large and well-mounted, had obviously caught a flicker of sunlight.

Eyes watering, he shook his head and relaxed both hands. Evayne waited for him in the house of healing in the northwestern quarter on Lowell Street near the boardwalk. He didn't know who she would be, this time. He had seen her very young and very old; she was never quite the same person as the woman who had forced him from the Kovaschaii almost four years ago.

He looked at the ring, swallowed, and started to whistle as he walked in a jaunty, purposeful way. The whole of his body was a mask right up to his calm, still eyes.

"I'm sorry, sir," Kallandras said, for perhaps the hundredth time.

"Her brother, are you?" Levec's raised brow bordered

on open disbelief, but he shook his head. "Well, I guess you'd have to be."

"Have to be?"

"If I weren't of the same family, *I'd* never claim her as blood-kin." He led the young man down the hall to the steps, and then began to climb them. "But I don't recall Evayne ever giving a family name."

Kallandras shrugged. "She's the boss." It was as close to truth as he'd yet come.

Levec raised a brow again. "Not," he said darkly, "in *this* house, she isn't. She's not well enough to travel—so if you've got any intention of taking her with you, I'd strongly advise you to think again."

"Yes, Healer Levec," Kallandras replied. He opened the door. "Evvie—you *are* here!"

"Evvie" raised a brow in a fashion that made her look quite similar, for a passing moment, to Healer Levec. "You took your time," she finally said dryly. "Are you going to stand there warming the door?"

"You've got an hour, because I'm feeling generous. Don't abuse it. Is that clear?"

"Yes, sir."

"Yes, Levec."

"Good." He was not a rude man, and left them to their discussion, drawing the door firmly shut behind him.

Kallandras half-expected to hear the door lock at their backs. He tensed, and then relaxed when Levec's heavy tread took him away from the door. "I don't think I've ever seen Healer Levec quite so . . ."

"He doesn't approve of my condition," Evayne replied. Then she sat up in bed, straightening her shoulders and raising her chin. *It's good to see you,* she wanted to say. But she didn't. Kallandras was still young and still very angry.

She watched as all show of friendliness slowly fell away from his face. It took a few seconds, but she always found it disconcerting. One instant he was alive with the gestures and habits of life, be it rural, urban, courtly—and the next, he was one of the Kovaschaii, cold and distant in his disdain for the lives that he could so effortlessly mimic—and take. "You summoned me."

"Yes."

"Why?"

"I have to ask you a few questions."

"Ask."

"Why don't you take that chair and pull it up."

He did as she asked; he often did. He could follow a command to the letter, yet still radiate an aura of hostility. Or contempt. "Ask," he repeated, as he sat, placing his hands casually in his lap.

"If you were Kovaschaii—"

He lifted a hand; his right hand. "I will not answer questions about the brotherhood. You know this, Evayne."

"It's not a specific question."

"It's a question. Of yours. I will not answer it."

"Very well. You know me—not as well now as you probably will in the future. Tell me what my chances against you would be if you were sent to kill."

"Kill who?"

"Anyone."

"Evayne—"

"Let me make it clearer. I would know, in advance, who the victim would be."

"Impossible," he said flatly. "You could not know."

"Just answer the question."

"If you knew, your chances would be better than if you didn't. But I wouldn't say they'd be high. Against what you fight, Evayne, we are not sent. You wouldn't be at your strength if you chose to fight me."

"No," she said quietly, and turned away.

"Is that all?" He rose.

"No," she said again. "I have a mission for you."

"And it is?"

"Go to Breodanir. Be there for the Sacred Hunt."

"The what?"

"The Sacred Hunt; it is the festival of the greatest import to the Breodani, and one of their number is always killed in it. It occurs, without fail, on First Day, although preparations leading up to it start weeks in advance. Go to the King's City, and there you will be able to find out all that you need."

"That is the whole of your order?"

"No. There will be a boy there. Stephen of Elseth. He must be protected against any threat. Tell him—tell him that I sent you." Her voice dropped, but she did not turn to face Kallandras. Instead, she waited.

"Evayne." She heard him rise. He pulled the chair slightly on purpose, because when he chose to be, he was completely silent.

"Yes?" She stared at her hands. The room was suddenly too small for both them and their memories.

"Your question. Why did you ask it?"

She didn't answer.

"Evayne."

She wouldn't answer.

It was answer enough for Kallandras. She heard the door open and close with force before she turned to look. Kallandras was Kovaschaii, and even young, he hated to show emotion.

Will you do it, Kallan? Will you do as I direct? She raised her palms to her cheeks and closed her eyes. When she opened them again, the silver-misted walls of the path rose to her right and left. She did not turn back, but a smile helped to erase some of the lines from her face.

Healer Levec was going to be most angry.

Kallandras the bard sat in the darkness of the empty theater, his harp in his lap. His lute was at his side; he always traveled with both. The wind from the sea was moist and cool in the open stands.

Two hours ago, the stands had been full. Every eye in the audience was turned toward him; reckless, he had used a touch of the voice to assure that. The stage lights, protected by large shells, cast a glow beneath him. At times like this, surrounded by light, he could almost forget his loss.

Music helped. The old lays, with their history and their grim tales of sacrifice to duty, were both a goad and a balm. But words, while they had their lovely cadences and intrinsic harmonies, were not necessary. The lute and the harp in isolation had their tales to tell, their sorrows to speak of.

Without words, he let his music weep for him. He offered the audience, in their ignorance, his fear, his self-loathing, and his final determination. He knew it disturbed them, but he had to release his burden—and no member of the brotherhood would now stand to witness or comfort the only member, in all of the Kovaschaii's long history, to betray them. Sioban might ask about his concert choices, but he doubted it. After the musical play, he had once again returned to the more traditional performance arts.

The audience offered him their left hands, palm out—a gesture of the highest approval. He accepted it gracefully and then melted into the stands to better hear the next performer. Two hours after the end of the set, both audience and performer were gone. He remained.

How could she ask this of him? His fingers strummed the strings of the harp rhythmically, seeking solace, not answers. He shifted the smooth, unornamented frame in his lap and stared into the darkness.

I have not seen my brothers for almost four years, Evayne. Am I to see them now as an enemy?

The air rippled with the dissonance of the chord that he struck. He was, to them, a traitor, but they were his family, his friends. Only for their sake, in the end, had the words of Evayne held sway. For in the end, even the brotherhood could not face a god.

It was a bitter fact: He would willingly have given his life to save the brotherhood—but giving up the brotherhood to save the brotherhood. . . . What was done, was done. But he could not say with certainty that, had he the choice again, he would choose as he had.

Silence surrounded him; the strings were absolutely still. His left hand held the harp, his right was curled into a fist so tight his nails cut the skin of his palm. *I won't do it. I can't do it. I will not confront a brother. I—*

Golden light flared in the darkness, half-blinding him. He recognized it as the flash of a diamond reflecting sunlight at an awkward angle.

Except there was no sunlight; not even the fires along the stage still burned. A mile down the boardwalk, near the docks proper, the lights were clearly haloed by the coming sea mist, but they hadn't the power to wake the gem.

He stared at his right thumb in bitter silence.

CHAPTER NINE

"Stephen?" Lady Elseth smoothed out the wrinkles her hands had put in the folds of her gray skirts.

"I kneel first, and if Gilliam doesn't remember, I knock his knees out from under him." Stephen's gaze was not upon Lady Elseth, but rather upon the head of the stairs.

"Yes, but do it surreptitiously."

Her tone of voice caught him, and he gave up watching for Gilliam. Gilliam wasn't late, after all. On this occasion it was Stephen who had finished packing and preparing early. He stepped over his single, modest trunk and made his way to Lady Elseth's side.

"Do you think Gilliam will remember—"

"I packed it," he said, placing an arm around her shoulders just as Norn would have done had he not been busy with Soredon. "With mine. If he forgets his trunk, we'll still have our uniforms, don't worry." He smiled, but it was only half real, and it vanished as she met his eyes.

"You'll know soon enough that I'll never stop worrying. Not now. This is the first year you won't be here when Soredon goes off to the Sacred Hunt. You'll be with him." Her hands had returned waywardly to the skirts, and were already kneading new creases into them before she caught herself.

Maribelle turned around a corner, catching their attention as she made her way down the stairs. At eleven she'd lost both curls and lisp, and she no longer tried to worm her way into the kennels at her older brother's heels. She could read better than Gilliam, which wasn't saying much, and she could write better, too, which said even less. Numbers were one of her stronger points, and already she had shown her willingness to take part in Elseth duties at her mother's side.

Still, her face hadn't lost all of its baby fat, and when it came right down to it, she was a full four years younger than Stephen, so he rolled his eyes at the tilt of her chin, a movement that she didn't fail to catch.

"Mari," her mother said, gently pulling away from Stephen's arm, "I was afraid you would miss the farewells." Her skirts rustled as she moved to her daughter and caught her in a hug.

Maribelle's arms returned her mother's embrace, and Stephen felt a twinge of envy.

But there's only so much comfort you can offer the Lady, Norn had said, *and it's very little when it comes time for the Sacred Hunt. You'll go with the men, now— and you'll have your chance to die like the rest of them. You can't do anything to make her feel good about it, Stephen, but if it helps you, you can try.*

He sighed as he watched his mother and his sister pull apart, wondering which was harder: To stay and to worry, or to go and be at risk. Loss or death? He shivered, feeling a morning chill that the fires couldn't protect him from. The nightmare image of Bryan's corpse warred with the empty hollowness of William's loss: his first funeral. Bryan was horribly dead, but William . . . even after five years, William was barely alive. He had his dogs, which helped—and he hunted without benefit of huntbrother—but even among Hunter Lords, William was withdrawn and silent. The glory had gone out of the hunt. The loss of Bryan would never be lessened with time; Stephen was certain of it.

"Stephen?"

He spun to face the open door, aware that he hadn't heard its hinges at all. Norn peered in. "We're almost ready. Is the young master down?"

Maribelle snorted. "Gilliam?" Her mother very quietly whispered something that neither Stephen nor Norn could hear, but the meaning of the words was made plain by the flush they engendered in the young girl's cheeks.

Soredon joined them before Gilliam did. He walked over to Elsabet's side and draped an arm across her shoulders. Her expression, as she leaned into his embrace, was one of resignation and fear. Stephen knew it well; for seven years he had waited quietly while Norn and Lord Elseth embarked upon their duty: the Sacred Hunt. This day marked the beginning of Stephen's adulthood in Breodanir, and he, too, would add to the burden of her worry from this moment on.

"Can someone help me with this?"

All eyes looked up to see Gilliam teetering at the railings. A large chest, one double the size of Stephen's modest choice, was precariously caught in a grip that was faltering even as they watched.

"Gilliam!" Elsa shouted, as Norn began to run up the stairs. She had been worried about whether or not he would show up in appropriate dress, but her eyes slid off the heavy gray jacket and the brown pants that were folded haphazardly into leather boots without comment. "Why didn't you send for the servants?"

He answered her by dropping the chest. It clattered down the stairs, narrowly missing Norn. Everyone scattered as the large, heavy box came to rest. That the lock held surprised them all.

Not an auspicious beginning.

"I don't suppose it will do any good to tell you all to keep an eye on each other?" Lady Elseth stood on her toes to give her son a kiss on the forehead. He was a boy for these few days more; not until the King called and accepted him would he be a Breodani Hunter.

"Mother."

"I'll take care of him," Stephen piped up. He held out his arms and caught Lady Elseth in a very tight hug. If Gilliam had become too self-consciously grown up for this sort of display, Stephen had not. He was going to have a few words with Gilliam on the subject once they were under way. "I'm sorry I won't be staying."

"So am I." Their foreheads touched. "You'll be back, though. I keep telling myself that."

"And you don't really believe it until you see it," Norn added. "Now enough of your time with the whelp—what about the real Hunters?" Breathing and being hugged by

Norn were mutually exclusive activities; Lady Elseth couldn't have talked had she wanted to. She caught his beard in her fingers and yanked almost playfully.

He set her down without comment. He had been through this routine for so many years, he knew there was nothing to be said. It would wait until they returned, because it had to.

Last, she turned to Soredon.

"This is his first Hunt," he said quietly, a hand on either of her shoulders. "Try to be as proud as he is, Elsa."

"I am." Her voice was soft. "The Hunters have their risk, and all of Breodanir depends on it. But we Ladies have our risk as well. I am proud for Elseth. I am worried for Elsabet."

He kissed her quietly, holding her face in the palms of his hands. Then he stepped back, still staring into her red-rimmed eyes. She wanted to cry; he knew it, and knew she would not.

"I love you." He turned. "Is everything ready?"

Norn nodded.

"The dogs?"

Gilliam nodded.

"Then we're off!"

The roads were very quiet for most of the journey. This year, because Stephen and Gilliam were to be presented to the Master of the Game, they had to arrive two weeks before the Sacred Hunt, rather than the usual four days.

Gilliam was in good spirits—this was the pinnacle of his youthful dreams. He would walk into the King's court with his huntbrother by his side, kneel, and be given the dress cloak and horn of the Hunter. He would be allowed to take part in the Sacred Hunt, and there he would further prove himself.

And on his return home, he would finally be able to form his own pack. Corwel's newest brood looked promising, and although Corwel was now too old to be the pride of Elseth, he was still capable of breeding true.

Soredon was happy as well, especially when he contemplated the arrival in the capital of his son and heir. Gilliam was everything that one Hunter-born could aspire

to. He was young, strong, fast—and his ability with the
trance had grown so quickly Soredon half-regretted that
they hadn't had time to choose a proper pack for
Gilliam's first appearance. Gilliam would hunt with a se-
lect number of Soredon's dogs.

Corwel would be at the head of the pack that Soredon
had chosen for himself. He wasn't pack leader anymore,
but he was second, and if Terwel was separated from him,
Soredon was certain that Corwel would still make a good
show of himself.

He knew it was foolish to take Corwel along; any of
the younger dogs would be better for show. He was becoming sentimental. Well, yes, but what of it? He would
hunt Corwel just this one last time, and they would face
the Hunter's risk together, as they had for so many years.

We're both getting older, he thought with wry affection.
He turned to look at Gil, who was positively impatient as
he sat astride his horse, and shook his head with a smile.
*It may well be time soon; the younger generation will
eclipse us both.*

But we're not doddering and useless yet.

"They aren't worried, are they?" Stephen wrapped another scarf around his throat, and fastened the highest
button of his jacket. It was chilly here; the wind across
the plain had few trees or rocks to break its passage.

"Them?" Norn looked over his shoulder. "No. probably not." He, too, wore an extra scarf for warmth, but the
color of his jacket was deep, warm green. Hunter's clothing. "I've rarely met a hunter who was. Not an oath-
bound Hunter, at any rate. Why?"

"Are you?"

"Worried?" Norn nodded. "Of course. I always am. I
have to be—I've got two people to worry about, since
one of us isn't worrying about himself. Why?"

"I'm worried." Stephen's voice was quiet. "I'm worried that Gilliam will make a fool of himself in front of
the King. I'm worried that we'll do something wrong before the Sacred Hunt. I'm worried that I'll forget all of
my horn calls—it isn't as if they're used anywhere but
the Sacred Hunt." He took a breath and shadowed his

eyes although the sun wasn't sharp, and the light was muted. "But mostly I'm worried about . . ." The words stopped, trailing into the quiet rush of wind against the ears. All of a sudden he didn't want to say them. For Stephen, words had always had a special magic, a feel of permanence, a ring of truth. To give voice to his fear was more than acknowledgment; it was empowerment.

"The Hunt is always a risk." Norn said quietly. He glanced at his companion, seeing an odd echo of the boy he had once been, traveling to the King's City and the duty of the Sacred Hunt for the first time.

If Soredon felt a pride and continuity in the legacy of his blood as he contemplated Gilliam, Norn felt something equally strong as he rode beside Stephen. They were not related, but in the end, they were bound by a choice and a purpose that made them unique in Breodanir. Hunters were chosen by birth and by blood, with all of the abilities that the Hunter God could grant. Hunt-brothers were the link between the Hunters and the rest of the populace, and they chose the same risk as their sworn oath brothers, without any of the God-granted advantages.

But they chose anyway, and they held true to their vows. If a brotherhood like this could extend forever outward, in all of the facets of Breodanir society, miracles could be achieved, he was certain of it. And proud of it as well.

"Why aren't they afraid?"

"You wouldn't want them to be," Norn answered. He shifted in his saddle, keeping an eye on the road. It was muddy, even with the chill, and the horses were not always as watchful as they could be. "Well, maybe you do now. But it isn't a pretty sight, and it feels wrong. Like a little breaking of the vow."

"But why aren't they afraid?"

"I don't know. Have you asked Gilliam?"

Stephen shook his head curtly. No.

Norn knew that Stephen would never ask. "Ah, well. I've never asked Soredon either. But I think it's because they live for the Hunt, those two and the others like them. You and I live for more because we can't feel what they feel—no matter what the Hunt or the conditions of it, we'll always be strictly human, strictly normal. The God-touch—the Hunter's trance—it's not for us. We'd never be able to attain it. So we want what other people want. Family, friends, a little knowledge outside of nets and couples and boar spears and dogs."

"You've never married outside."

"No." Norn closed his eyes for a moment. "And I won't either. Don't ask, Stephen; it's silly enough, and it isn't relevant. You may well marry as you please and find those who will be happy to accept your troth." His lips turned up in a smile, and his eyes softened.

"I don't know." Stephen shot a glance at Gilliam's straight, gray back. "I don't know how I could have a family and Gilliam at the same time."

Norn's laughter caught the attention of their brothers. He waved them on, still laughing into his beard. "Aye, there's truth in that. But he isn't your life, even though he may be your death in the end. You'll find a life that calls you yet, and you'll have to balance your vows with your aspirations." His laughter left a red glow at his cheeks. "It's the life of a huntbrother, Stephen. And it's true: when you're young enough to make the vow, it's always the easiest. Growing into it gets harder year by year." He shook his head. "Perhaps you will make the choice that we did, Soredon, Elsa, and I."

Norn's voice, full, deep, and tinged, every word, with affection, told no tale of regret at the choice he had made. Stephen gripped his own reins firmly and tried not to think of the Hunter's Death. He didn't want to die it, and he didn't want Gilliam to die it either. But he was certain that it was for him; so certain that he could not speak to Norn of it for fear that the speaking would make it real. Still . . .

"What does it look like?"

"What?"

"The Hunter's Death."

"No one really knows, Stephen. And it's better so—although, when we reach the King's court, you'll see at least five artistic depictions of it. The only thing these artisans agreed on is size: It's big. Everything else—fangs, claws, number of legs, number of heads, color, shape—

that changes depending on the artist. But the finest artists in the kingdom have turned their hands to the subject more than once—you'll even find a sculpture by Ovannen himself in the grand foyer."

It wasn't the answer he'd hoped for. He was silent, and after a moment, Norn continued.

"What does it look like? That's a question that every Hunter, and every huntbrother, asks. But the only way to get an answer is to die the Hunter's Death, and no one rushes eagerly into that. Well, no huntbrother. The Hunters ... I'm certain that each and every one of them dreams about facing the Hunter's Death and taking it in the full glory of a called Hunt.

"But say that it looks like this: Nightmare, fear, and a very dark desire. This is what the artists have done. When we arrive, I'll show you."

It gave Stephen a very odd feeling to pass through the gates of the King's City. Years had passed since last he'd walked these streets, and they were no longer snow-covered or cold. It was almost spring, almost First Day, the time of renewal when the new year began. Even this close to the city gates he could see the brown and greens of the Mother's followers as they set up their banners to line the main thoroughfare beside the banners of the Hunter Lords. He felt young again, in the worst possible way, as the arches of the gate trailed fingers of shadow down his back.

Since leaving the King's City with Lord Elseth and Norn, Stephen had never had cause to return. He wished that he had never been given cause, and then felt ashamed of the impulse. Gilliam glanced up, and steadied his horse into a waiting step as Stephen approached. He couldn't just bring the horse to a stop, no, not Gil.

"Something wrong?"

Stephen shrugged. He could say no, but there was really no point. If Gilliam hadn't known something was wrong, he wouldn't have stayed his horse. "Just nervous."

"Why?" It wasn't the Hunt, and Gilliam knew it. Stephen's fears about the Hunt were crystal clear and completely unique in feel. Gilliam ignored those because it had been made clear, by a succession of heated arguments, that Stephen wished them to be ignored.

"I keep expecting to see Marcus come pounding down the road looking for me." He said it sheepishly, and placed a hand firmly on the pommel of his sword. "Not that I wouldn't be able to defend myself now."

"But you couldn't then." Gilliam shrugged. "Maybe we should leave Father and Norn at the castle. We can go looking for this Marcus ourselves and teach him a lesson."

"Don't even think it, Gil." Norn's voice was crisp and clear. Not a hint of amusement gentled it.

Unfazed, although the interruption was unexpected, Gilliam whirled in his saddle. "But it's just—"

"Nothing." The older man replied, just as crisply. "You're here in your official capacity as Hunter-aspirant of Breodanir—you don't have time to settle some petty score from bygone years. You hunt for the land's blood, not for the blood of a den warden. Clear?"

"Yes, Norn."

"And you, Stephen. You aren't a child anymore, and you aren't a den rat. No den could claim you now, even if one were foolish enough to try. You're of Elseth, and you *will* leave your fears of childhood behind. Is that clear?"

"Yes, Norn." Of the two, only Stephen's quiet acknowledgment held any conviction. Norn hesitated a moment, and his hands bunched the reins in fists. Stephen could practically hear the older man's inner dialogue as he weighed Gilliam's impulsive determination with Stephen's ability to rein it in.

At last he nodded. He swung his horse around and sidestepped Gilliam's black gelding before looking back over his shoulder.

"Gilliam, you are here as an Elseth Hunter. If you embarrass your father or do anything to disavow the responsibility of that title, Lord Elseth will be furious. Rightly so."

Sullenly, Gilliam nodded. But he was too used to arguing with his own huntbrother to just let the matter drop into silence, even though the conversation had already drawn the ears of passersby. He glared rudely at an elderly matron who was obviously on her way to market. She blushed, pulled at her kerchief, and began to fiddle with the straps of her basket.

"Gil!" Stephen whispered, as he reached for Gilliam's shoulders. Gilliam ducked his hand.

"But we've got rights, Norn! We protect our own!"

Weary and annoyed, Norn shook his head. "You're your father's son!" He didn't even look back over the broad green of his shoulders to acknowledge Gilliam's shout.

Stephen didn't feel uneasy about Marcus anymore. Norn's words had penetrated deeply enough to drive that ghost away. Instead, he settled into the familiar worry about ceremony and custom.

Gilliam felt the change in his huntbrother's mood, and it only incensed him more. He knew what Stephen was worried about—but did *everyone* he was traveling with have to assume he was an idiot? With a very curt nod, he yanked at the reins of his horse and sent it cantering down the city streets.

Stephen sighed as an echo of Gilliam's anger flittered past. With more concern for his own mare—and her mouth—than Gilliam had shown, Stephen brought up the rear and followed the thoroughfare to where the King's castle lay in wait.

The castle did little to still Stephen's fears; it was a grand old building—and the work of the maker-born was in evidence everywhere, from the solid, sheer surface of the outer walls, to the high balustrades and buttresses of the twin towers. A stag seemed to leap in white, hard life, from the very heart of the gate; beneath it, the poles of the portcullis cast evenly spaced shadows.

The gate shadowed them, and it was not plain either, for above their heads in the archway was the bold relief of a Hunter and his lymer as they sought out prey in the quiet alabaster of the King's wood.

If he had just come to visit, Stephen would have been tingling with excitement and joy. Past the second portcullis, rearing on two legs, was a bear—but so ferocious a bear, and with such large teeth, that Stephen knew for a fact the artist had never truly seen one hunted. Yet even in ignorance, the sculptor had managed to portray nature's primal anger and defiance—thus did the hunted become, momentarily, the hunter.

"It's a fine work, isn't it?"

Stephen looked down at the voice, and realized that a man in royal livery was waiting patiently at the reins. He blushed and looked around; all three of his companions were unhorsed and waiting. Soredon looked annoyed—which meant, of course, that the dogs had been kenneled by someone other than a "real" Hunter. Gilliam was bored and impatient, and Norn was smiling quietly.

He slid off Dapple's back with a mumbled apology. The man in brown, green, and gold only smiled. He was older than Stephen, and his long thin forehead was obviously bereft of hair, although it was capped in gold-rimmed brown. "We don't mind it ourselves. It takes the eyes of a newcomer to lend a little life to the courtyard—and you've the right sort of eyes. Makes me remember how I felt when he," and he gestured at the stone bear, "was first dragged in here."

"Were you here then?"

"I've been here a long time. I'm good at what I do." The man bowed, his hands still firmly upon the reins. "I don't know if I'll be on shift to see you off, but if I'm not, we're pleased to have you. This your first?"

It was pleasantry, nothing more, for the warden knew that Stephen and Gilliam had arrived at the correct time for aspirant Hunters. Still, Stephen nodded quietly.

"We serve our King—and the whole of our country—in the ways that we can. But your way, huntbrother, is hardest; our thanks and our welcome to you." So saying, he turned and led the horse away from the flagstones.

Norn's voice cut across the quiet grandeur of the courtyard. "Don't worry about looking around for a bit. We've got a little wait ahead of us. The keeper of the outer estate is seeing to the Hausworth family, and we won't get our lodgings until he returns. Besides, the first time you cross these gates, they're significant. Do what you can to fix it in memory; it'll all become commonplace soon enough." Norn smiled, his eyes crinkled at the corners. "I did it myself when I first came." He turned, whispered something to Soredon, and left Gilliam in the care of his father. It wasn't necessarily a completely wise choice—two Hunters alone without the wisdom of a huntbrother to guide them—but they couldn't do much damage to their reputations, or each other, here.

"Did the maker-born do this?" Stephen asked, his voice hushed and muted.

"Aye. You can see their touch where their hands have been. Some little, perfect magic. Some quiet impressions. There—do you see the awnings with the ivy creepers? By the fountain."

Stephen nodded.

"They're stone. Solid as my wrist. But don't they seem to move with the breeze?" Norn shook his head in an echo of Stephen's wonder. "That's the maker-born though; if they can't have the raw materials they need, they'll force what they want out of the ones they do have."

"Have you met them?"

"Them?"

"The maker-born."

"Aye, some. Why?"

"What are they like?" Stephen reached out gently to touch the claws of the bear.

"Like anyone else with a mission or a talent. The Hunter-born live for the Hunt, the healer-born live for the healing—and the maker-born live for the making. Of course, they've got a little more leeway, and a little less similarity of personality, but that's to be expected. They choose what they learn to make, after all.

"The maker-born who worked upon this castle was a foreigner at one time. He came here to create a residence worthy of any king, and he stayed. You'll see his hand in the upper city as well. The maker-born who sculpted the bear—she's an artist. No buildings or carpentry for her; she works from different impulses. But the gift is the same in either." His arm caught Stephen's shoulders companionably. "You and I, we don't have talent to drive us.

Makes you wonder, doesn't it? Why do we do all of this? Why do we take our oaths?"

"I don't know about Stephen," Lord Elseth said, coming out of nowhere to stand at his huntbrother's elbow, "but in your case it was probably just another chance to talk."

"Aye," Norn's eyes sparkled, "and at that, a chance to do it without your interruptions. Are we ready to go?"

"*We* are." Soredon stood aside, the tilt of his brow bringing shadowed lines along his square forehead.

"Stephen?"

"Hey! Don't touch that! What are you doing? Get out of here! OUT!"

The raised voice was unmistakably Gilliam's. Stephen recognized it, muffled though it was by two doors and a wall.

Oh, no. The lid of his small chest fell with a bang, crunching dress breeches that were halfway out. He had no time to put his boots on. In the seconds that he considered it, he heard another shout.

He wasn't worried for Gilliam; Gilliam wasn't frightened, just angry. Well, not even really angry. But very, very annoyed. He wasn't quite out of his room when he heard Gilliam's door slam shut. As he peered out, he saw the flying brown, gold, and green of heavy skirts. Wisps of dark hair trailed beneath a golden cap and down a smocked back.

Lady Elseth was going to kill him.

Angry, he walked over to Gilliam's door and wrenched it open. "Gilliam, what in the Hells did you just do?"

Gilliam looked up from the mess of clothing and Hunter's wear on his bed. His face was red, and his brows dovetailed neatly; his hands were curled around his horn and hat. "What did *I* do?"

"That's what I asked." Stephen took a deep breath, crossed the threshold into the room itself, and closed the door behind him.

"I got back here from Father's room and found that—that girl snooping through my things!" He threw the hat down and pushed his dark hair out of his eyes. "So I asked her to leave."

"Asked? Gilliam, half the hall must have heard you!"

"So? Is it my fault if they were listening?"

"Gil . . ."

"Look, you aren't my mother, you're—"

"I'm your huntbrother. She was a *maid,* Gilliam, not a 'girl,' and she was doing her duties. You *don't* throw a maid in the royal service out of your room as if she were a common thief!"

As the full import of Stephen's words hit home, Gilliam had the grace to blush. "I was surprised."

"Great. And what are you going to do three days from now? Demand that the Queen get out of your way because she's looking at your sword?"

"I'm not an idiot."

"You're worse than an idiot."

"She shouldn't have been going through my things!"

"Did you leave them in that mess on the bed?"

"I had to find my horn." Gilliam let his hair fall as he picked up his hat again. "And this."

"So you left these rumpled things all over the bed, and it was her fault that she saw them and assumed they were to be put away?"

"She's got no business being in my room."

"Then don't leave things here like that—it's begging for her help." Stephen stomped over to the set of drawers against the wall beside the cherrywood headboard. He grabbed ornate brass handles and yanked so hard the drawer itself came off its rails and fell to the floor. Luckily the carpet muted most of the impact.

"Put them in here," he said, without bothering to pick it up. "Put the drawer back into the dresser when you're finished."

"This is my room, and I'll do what I like in it."

"Oh, really?" Lord Elseth leaned against the door frame with his left shoulder. Both boys gave a guilty start, and both cursed the fact that the door hinges were so well-oiled. Soredon's arms were folded neatly and tightly across his chest.

"Thanks, Stephen," Gilliam whispered as he straightened up and faced his father.

"It's your own fault, you idiot," Stephen replied, his voice as quiet as possible.

"I'm glad to see," Lord Elseth said, looking anything but, "that you've both decided to make yourselves at home here. But in case you weren't aware, this is the *King's* castle, and you are expected to behave like polite, happy young men while you're in it. I don't care if you want to squabble outside of his gates; it's expected from huntbrothers. But do not do it here. Understood?"

"Yes, sir."

"Yes, sir."

They cast very dark looks at each other, and Stephen, barefoot, stomped back to his room. Why, indeed, did anyone choose to take the Hunter's Oath?

"That was careless."

The woman knelt in the center of the golden mandala that had been worked into the large, dark carpet. Her hair, brown and straight, cascaded down her back and cheeks, obscuring her pale face. Her hands, palms out, lay before her; her knees were shaking slightly. The King's colors, caught in the common dress of a chambermaid, looked drab and unseemly in the room's light. She had removed the cap, but had not had time for any other changes.

"Yes, Lord."

The man so addressed nodded quietly. His eyes were hooded by frosted brows; his face lined by the long thin winter of a beard. His nose was his most pronounced feature, and he made the most of his height by looking down it. Silently, he let her fear take root before deigning to speak.

"Still," his fingers curled around a platinum medallion. Four symbols stood in shining relief along quartered lines beneath his hand; one each for earth, air, fire, and water. "The circumstances could have been worse. Are you certain it was only one of the children?"

She nodded without looking up. He had not given her leave to rise. "T–two."

"Two children? Ah, yes. I suppose one was the huntbrother." He let the medallion drop, and it nestled quietly against a black field with a white fur border; the robes of moneyed nobility. "Rise, then."

She lifted her head. Her pretty face, her widened eyes, met his.

"Did you find anything?"

"No, Lord."

"Are you certain?"

"Yes." She swallowed. "You said that I was to look for a very simple horn, with odd markings along the mouthpiece."

"Well, then. I think we can rest in peace for the moment." He smiled. "Our duty to God is done, and we may now consider our duty to less lofty principles."

She froze; her outstretched hands grew pale. Licking her lips, she turned only her eyes away. "I must—must return to my duties, Lord."

"Duties?" His voice deepened. "Ah, yes. But little Linden, that *is* what I spoke of."

"W–what do you mean?"

"Don't you know?" He gestured suddenly, and her whole body stiffened as the air crackled. The door that led to his sleeping chambers flew open and rocked on its hinges. "Your duty to the King of Breodanir means nothing. But your duty to Krysanthos, Priest of Allasakar may well save your life in the end. Or do you recant?" Even the mention of the Dark God's name was enough to ensure her loyalty. Still, it was a risk to speak it aloud.

Silence again, heavy on her tongue, and the ashen gray of her face. This was always the moment he loved best in these little charades: the sinking anchor of realization; the loss of hope.

He gestured again, with the slightest twist of his fingers, the merest syllable. Her hair fell away from her face, and the golden strings that kept tight the forest green bodice were suddenly undone.

With magic he held her still, although he knew she would not be foolish enough to run. Her breath, short and sharp, was nearly silent in its panic.

"Come, Linden. Surely others Priests have called upon your services before me."

He did not allow her to answer, but instead raised her to her feet. She walked past him stiffly and almost blankly into the waiting room, to the bed with sheets already turned back.

He would have to kill her sometime, but that was weeks away. Now, he indulged in the luxury of the moment. He would have to finish in hours and send her back to the castle. The Hunter Lords would be arriving within the week, and he still had need of her special access to their rooms.

But he was certain that he would not find the thing that the Dark God feared. After all, his coven had been watchful, and they had seen no reappearance of the cursed Horn that had somehow been stolen from their keeping. Neither had they seen the Spear, although it was less of a concern. It was harder—much—to hide, and had little use without the sounding of that Horn.

Anger lined his face and he turned away from it to view instead the ivory lines of a young maid's body. Soon, very soon now, the wait would be over—and the Hunter's Kingdom would be just another vassal for the Dark Lord's coming empire.

Allasakar would walk, whole, upon the face of the world, as no God had truly done in all of mortal memory. And Krysanthos, the mage-born Priest, would be there at His side, to reap the benefits of years of service.

CHAPTER TEN

Gilliam and Stephen waited nervously at the side entrance to the King's Hall. Although they were impeccable in their dark-brown velvet jackets, shadow-black pants, and gold-trimmed sashes, they were not nearly so ornate, so full of history, as even the door that lay closed before them. At a distance, that door seemed plain compared with the inlaid and wreathed great hall entrance that the nobles were using now to crowd the halls. But this close, one could see the fine quality of the darkwood beneath the cast-iron band; one could touch the cold stone frame, with its plain, gray surface free of any detailing or sculptor's fancy. This door stood as it had always done since the first day of its making—the passageway for those who would step between youth and adulthood.

"Stop it." Stephen's whisper came from the depths of a carefully placed smile which faltered only as he watched Gilliam fidget.

"When are we going in?"

"When they call us." Sighing, Stephen caught Gilliam's collars and straightened them, as much to soothe his own nerves as to clear away any wrinkles. "Do you know what we've got to do?"

"Walk down the side path to the—"

The door swung open, and a green-robed Priest of the Hunter nodded to them both. Like the door itself, there was a deceptive elegance and age to the man. His robes, although simple, were the purest green of the Hunter; they needed no ornamentation. "Who are you who seek to enter?"

"Gilliam of Elseth and his huntbrother Stephen."

Gilliam bowed low, and remembered to keep his arms stiffly at his side.

"And what is your business?"

"We have come to offer our service to the Master of the Game." It was the King's Hunter title, and as such, the only one of many titles that Gilliam found easy to remember. "We have hunted together and we've completed the Triple Hunt."

"And your proof?"

"Here." Stephen stepped forward and held out a small, plain chest. He flipped it open; the rounded and well-oiled lid rested briefly and coolly against his chest as the Priest examined the stag hoof, bear claw, and boar horn carefully displayed therein.

The Priest passed his steady, large hand over the open box. The air tingled around the three for a moment before the Priest nodded to Gilliam. Gilliam left the rigid stance of his bow behind.

"You have done as you have claimed. Come, then. You are judged worthy to seek His audience." The door swung fully open, and the dais which led to the King's throne, and to the Master of the Game, came into full view. The throne itself was inset too far back to be seen without actually entering the room. It bothered neither Stephen nor Gilliam, for they had no intention of turning away.

Gilliam went first, as was his right and duty. He walked calmly, if a little quickly, and he looked neither to the left, with its long, floor-to-ceiling tapestry depicting all of the greatness and glory of the Hunt, nor to the right, at the row of men clad in greens and browns, with their horns at their belts, and their weapons at their sides. They were not young men, not any of them—and they wore the scars caused by both prey and the passing years across their silent features. Stephen could not resist glancing at both the wall and the men, and it was Stephen who would remember it in detail. Quieted by the sight of so much finery and so much experience, he followed in Gilliam's wake, his hands still clutching the box that the Priest had viewed. The effort kept him steady.

He had thought that Gilliam would be the nervous one, because Gilliam hated both public occasions and the crowds that came with them. But Gilliam, in bearing and stride, was already one with the Hunters that he had come this far to join; he didn't falter or misstep.

Stephen did, but only once, when the dais opened up and the throne came into view, and he saw the King upon it. He had never seen the King before, although he had seen his likeness several times on most of the coinage of the realm, both in the lower city as a child and in Elseth as a youth. What he had expected, he did not know, or perhaps it just fled his mind, leaving only the reality behind.

The King was not a young man, but not as old as Soredon either. His hair was black shot through with a glimmering of gray that would one day overtake it all. His eyes, even from this distance, were a deep brown and seemed preternaturally large. He was not overly tall, but even seated he gave the impression of height, although the back of the throne dwarfed him, its simple wood edge bearing the horns of the very Stag itself above him. He wore a circlet of plain gold, yet without it he would still have been known as Master of the Game.

"Not yet," someone whispered with amusement, and Stephen spun around to meet the crinkled corners of gray Hunter's eyes. "You'll be kneeling soon enough—make sure that you do it at your brother's side."

Embarrassment drove awe back to its proper place. Stephen walked briskly up the aisle, closing the distance between Gilliam and himself. His hands stopped their shaking; his pace grew measured and seemingly more confident. But he did not look at the King again. Instead he fastened his gaze neatly at the point on Gilliam's back where shoulder blades bracketed spine.

He's only a man, he thought, but the words were a tickle at his ear. He could not believe them, not when the very air seemed to glow in the perfect, silent hush. During the long trip to the King's City, Stephen had been filled with many fears, most nameless—but among those had not been the fear of failure. He felt it keenly now. Although he knew his hunting craft as well as any huntbrother of his age, he felt raw and inexperienced. His hands began to tremble as doubt dwarfed the significance of the contents of the small Elseth chest.

Gilliam stopped walking and knelt three feet away from the King's throne. Stephen made haste to join him, dropping to one knee as he opened the box and placed it before them both in supplication. He bowed his head.

"Who are you and why have you come?" The Master of the Game spoke at last, his voice as deep and purposeful as any fancy could have made it.

"I am Gilliam of Elseth. In my father's name, I have hunted the Elseth preserves to feed her people and prove my worth." Gilliam's head, bowed, shadowed his legs in the flicker of torchlight and the sky seen through stained glass.

"And what have you hunted there?"

"The three."

"When have you hunted them?"

"In their proper time."

"And who will speak for you?"

"I will." Stephen started slightly at the words; they were distant enough that they offered scant comfort, although he recognized Lord Elseth's booming voice. "While Gilliam of Elseth has hunted in my name, I have hunted in yours."

"So be it. Look at me now, Gilliam of Elseth." The tone of the King's voice changed slightly, a hint of amusement warming its depth. "You have the look of your father about you—and his father before him, if the portrait gallery indeed holds truth." The voice cooled again. "But it is not in seeming that the Hunter judges. Who stands beside you?"

There was an eerie moment of silence before Stephen realized that his voice was meant to fill it. He remembered to keep his head bowed, and found fascinating creases in the dark folds of his tunic to hold his eyes. "Stephen," he said, and his voice grew steady. "Stephen of Elseth."

"And have you hunted at Lord Gilliam's side?"

"I have."

"What have you hunted?"

"The three."

"And when have you hunted them?"

"In their proper time and at the need of the people of Elseth." He almost looked up then, but he stopped himself; no permission and no order had been given. Still, the speaking of the words brought the comfort of an old truth, well understood by both speaker and listener.

"Who speaks for you, Stephen?"

Norn answered from a distance exactly as far as Lord Elseth's. "I do. Stephen of Elseth has hunted at his brother's side at the call of Elseth and her people."

"So be it. Rise, Stephen of Elseth. Rise, Gilliam of Elseth. Come stand before me."

Gilliam stood without effort and paused to offer Stephen a hand up. Stephen took it, leaving the chest behind. It had served its purpose and he did not think he could carry it.

"You have come to offer me your services, and I have seen that you are worthy to hunt with the Master of the Game. But I am also a worthy master. I will tell you of the risk and the Death that you face if you choose this path. There will be no other choice, and you cannot turn from it once you have begun—for all of Breodanir rests upon the choice once made." The King rose then, discarding the finery of his throne. Behind his head, the antlers drew level with the circlet of gold, and he looked like the heart of the living forest.

"You will hunt in my name from this day forward, and I—I hunt in the name of the Hunter. This is my pledge to Him, that once a year I will call the Sacred Hunt, that *he* might Hunt, in return, those who serve him. You will hunt in my name, and perhaps in that Hunt you will earn Breodanir's life by giving your own. But you might choose, in the King's Forest, your own prey, your own hunt; you might bring, on that one day, your own dogs into domains that are otherwise solely mine.

"I accept your service, Gilliam and Stephen of Elseth. Do you choose now to honor your offer?"

Stephen thought that Gilliam would answer immediately and be done with it. Instead, Gilliam turned to him, one eyebrow lifted in question. There was no doubt at all in Gilliam's mind, and no fear; this was the pinnacle of his years of training and hunting. He waited nonetheless on Stephen's word and Stephen's gesture—for no hunter came to the King without a huntbrother, and none left in his service without one by his side.

"We will serve the Master of the Game," Stephen said, his voice very small.

The King raised his hands, and from the recess behind his throne two Priests emerged, each carrying a heavy green cloak. In silence they came to stand, one in front of Gilliam, the other in front of Stephen.

"This is the color of your office. Wear it proudly, Lord Gilliam of Elseth, in my name."

Gilliam smiled and nodded as the gold leaf was fastened across his shoulders; the folds of deep, heavy green fell about his back like a perfect wave.

"And you, Stephen of Elseth, you share in your brother's office. Wear these colors, as befits your station, in the name of the people of Breodanir."

"And in your name, son of the Hunter."

Pleased, the king smiled, and his smile deepened his face, revealing the warmth that lay beneath severity. He nodded again to the attending Priests. Simple horns, with mouths of silver, appeared in their hands. These were offered in turn to Gilliam and Stephen.

Stephen's hands shook as he placed the horn in his sash. He could feel Gilliam's pride and excitement, but when he snuck a glance, no sign of it showed. Gilliam stood a little taller, and perhaps his chest was farther forward than normal posture allowed, but that was all.

"Turn," the King said quietly. "You wear the green of the Hunter now, and you have the blessing and approval of the Master of the Game. From this day forth, at this time, you will journey to the King's City at my behest, and you will hunt in my forest. If you fail to do so, you will be stripped of your title and the honors that you have accepted this day; you will be shunned by the Hunter Lords and cast out by the Priests. No Hunter will speak your name, and your deeds will be forgotten. Your children, should you have issue at that time, will inherit in your stead if you hold the preserves of your family. If you do not, your lands will return to the crown, to be given to

others who have proved themselves worthy." The words
were harsh, but the King's tone made it clear that they
were strictly a formality; he did not doubt those who had
become Hunters in his name. "You are among equals
now. Go into Breodanir in pride and with determination."

Stephen did not gasp as he turned, but only because he
lost his breath for a moment. The ranks of the Hunters
that had formed a human wall from the side entrance of
this chamber to the foot of the King's dais had somehow
changed shape and form. Leading directly to the double
doors the Hunter Lords had entered by was a dark, green
carpet with a border of gold filigree nestled around
brown. On either side of it stood Hunter Lords and their
huntbrothers in three evenly spaced ranks. They carried
spears by their sides, and they were now unhooded
as they all looked, as one man, to the two who had passed
the final test.

"Go now. I will call you again within the ten-day for
the Sacred Hunt."

Neither looked back; they had no choice, and no inclination, to do other than obey. Slowly, they began their silent procession, and as they did, banners unfurled above
their heads. The first, a leaping stag on a white field, held
by Hunter Lords, and older ones at that, on either side of
the carpet. The second was a golden bear on a green field,
held likewise. The third was a boar, black as pitch, again
on a green field. And beyond it there was darkness; a
field of ebony with a single, broken spear, a solitary broken horn.

Stephen paused before it; he had but to pass beneath it
and he would gain the door. But he understood well what
it was: the Hunter's Death. Gilliam didn't even seem to
notice the way it hung like a pall above the day's ceremony. He walked until its shadow covered his head before he realized that Stephen was no longer in step.

"Yes, Stephen of Elseth," someone said, but although
Stephen strained his eyes searching through the ranks
closest to him, he could not see the speaker, "you see
truly. But you will have no freedom now. You have accepted the path and must pass beneath this shadow, or it
will hold you back forever."

"Stephen," Gilliam hissed, before his huntbrother could come up with an answer to that strange voice, "it's just a bloody banner."

A breeze blew in through the open doors, and the spear and horn disappeared in the sheen of moving black cloth. Stephen shook his head and grimaced in sudden embarrassment. "Sorry," he whispered, as he walked quickly to join his brother.

"Doesn't matter," was the terse, but happy reply. "We did it. We're in." He crossed the threshold and waited patiently for Stephen to follow. "And do you know what it means?"

From the seriousness of the expression, anyone other than Stephen might have thought Gilliam had somehow managed to be affected by the ceremony. Bound by more than blood, Stephen couldn't make that mistake, although he might have been happier had he been able to.

"You get to choose your dogs."

"I get to choose my dogs!"

His father came out of the doors and into the nearly empty hall just in time to catch the echo of the words rebounding off beamed ceiling and walls. He arranged the hood to frame his head. "Gilliam!"

Gilliam turned and stopped. "Father?"

Soredon laughed. "Yes, there is the matter of your first pack. We'll have to discuss it now, you and I—after this Hunt, you won't be able to use my dogs anymore."

They started to walk, and Stephen hung back by the doors, waiting for Norn to come out. It was only a few minutes, but long enough to lose sight of the Elseth Hunters as they turned the bend in the hall.

"Stephen, you did well." Norn's hood was a fold of cloth against his shoulder blades. "Where's Soredon?"

"With Gilliam. Ahead. Talking about Gil's hunting pack."

"A bit premature, isn't it?"

Stephen nodded.

"But you didn't say anything?"

"No. He already knows. He doesn't see his death in any of this." His frustration was evident in more than the tone of his voice; his forehead was wrinkled, his brows gathered at the bridge of his nose.

Norn said, "I told you, they never do. Come on, let's get a drink. I'll take you to the Hunter's garden."

"The Hunter's presence was strong today," the King said softly, as the last of his Hunter Lords filed out of the hall. The banners that had formed a ceremonial rite of passage had been curled neatly against their poles. Servants would clear them away soon at the direction of Priests, and they would be held in keeping until next year's passage.

"Yes," was the quiet answer.

"And I gather from your tone, you've a feeling why." The King rose carefully and walked away from the throne, sparing a backward glance for the antlers that rose like white shadow above him. "I'm too old for this, Iverssen. Tell me what it was." He knelt, a solitary man on the dais used when he served as Master of the Game.

What a deadly game.

Iverssen's square jaw tightened as he pulled his brown hood away from his face. A single, white scar that sun and time would never remove ran from his upper right eyelid to the point of his chin. Only a miracle had preserved his sight.

"What it was?" came the testy answer. "Hunter's touch, I'd say." He walked over to where the King knelt and stood before him. The King bent his head a moment, both to hide his irritation and to murmur the Hunter's prayer—the one said only by the King.

Iverssen joined him with a counter-cadence. Their words mingled, at cross-purposes to begin, but in harmony at the end.

"They grow younger every year," the King said, as he slowly removed the gold-trimmed green greatcoat that the passage ceremony demanded. It was followed by the rest of his finery, of which there was little enough: cuff links; two rings; his crown.

"Yes." Iverssen took the coat and folded it, showing as much reverence as he ever did. He snorted as the rings hit his palm, and squinted as light circled the crown. "And not much smarter."

"Iverssen."

"Majesty."

The King rose, clad now in a fine tunic that simply bore his colors in a crest above deep brown; his leggings were even plainer, and of the same color. "I have almost never felt His touch so strongly."

Iverssen nodded gruffly. With a little twist, he made a bundle out of greatcoat and valuables that would set the seamstress screaming. "Almost never?" The question was grudgingly given.

"Maybe never," the King answered, his thoughts turning inward. "You are no younger than I; you know that memory is never a trustworthy truth keeper."

"I don't think I want to hear this." Iverssen said, but he stopped walking so his robes wouldn't rustle.

"It was when I was a boy," the King said quietly.

Iverssen's face became a set study of rigid lines. "Majesty, you—"

"I was four." The King's voice grew distant as he faced a memory that was never very far away. "It was the day I watched my father and my grandmother kill my grandfather for the sake of all Breodanir. I saw what my father was that day, and I never doubted that he would succeed. He looked older, more powerful, and more harsh than I ever saw him before or after. He came to the throne room. I followed him. And he stood," the king turned, "there. In front of the antlers. He was the very Hunter."

Iverssen knew the "he" the King spoke of. "Your father was of the blood, and it ran true. Your grandfather was a foolish and weak man."

"Was he?" The King's voice was soft. "He was a man of great heart."

"What great heart destroys the very people he is meant to rule and protect?" Iverssen's words were cutting; they spoke seldom of this, for this very reason. "Your father was Breodani."

"My father," the King replied, with only a trace of bitterness, "was still judged by the Mother for the crime of patricide. He ruled a scant ten years."

"Majesty," Iverssen said, conveying perhaps less respect than the word demanded, "we are all judged for the crimes we commit, and I believe the judgment was not the Mother's, but rather, Aered's."

"Yes." The King shook his head. "As heir to the Breodani, my father had little choice. I know it. I've been told no less for the entirety of my life—and I believe it's truth. But ... I remember my grandfather, although not well. He was a gentle man.

"It broke my grandmother and my father. Killing my grandfather was the worst thing that either of them ever did—and they did it for the Breodani.

"My grandfather hated sending the young to their deaths. He listened to the foreigners, and I believe—if no one else does—that he wanted to end the Hunt to save his people. Not more, and not less. If it would not weaken our people, I would make that truth known."

Iverssen's pursed lips and lined brow made his thoughts on that revelation quite clear.

"As I get older, Iverssen, I understand my grandfather's folly too well." The King shook his head, his voice very soft as he spoke what was almost heresy. Iverssen was disquieted, but he had seen the King in many moods. During the ceremonies of the Sacred Hunt—or those leading up to them—that mood was often the most bleak, the darkest. It was not easy to sentence your followers to death. Still, he was King, and the mood must be put aside. They would leave these chambers soon, and melancholy was not a public sentiment. "But the Hunter's power was strong today."

"Yes," Iverssen nodded.

"The Elseth brothers."

"Yes."

"You're being very agreeable," the King said wryly. "It's unlike you, and I'm not sure that I favor the change."

Iverssen snorted. "Agreeable, is that it?" But he started to walk again, absently swinging his precious bundle. "It was those two, yes. I don't know why. But did you see the huntbrother? I didn't think he'd make it to the throne."

"I saw him. And I saw what he did as he left."

"Aye, and I as well. The Death stopped him cold." Iverssen shook his head quietly. "Think he has a touch of the seer-born?"

"Not unheard of," was the equally quiet answer. "But I'm not sure that this is the case here. The Hunter God has some plan that requires one, or both, of them."

"You're certain?"

"As much as I can be. But time will tell, as always. Come; we have barely enough time to change and present ourselves for the festivities. Some young bard has journeyed all the way from Senniel College in Averalaan in order to woo the ladies of the court. I heard his song last eve, and it was . . . pleasant."

"From Averalaan?" Iverssen's frown made clear what he thought of that.

"He's not a dignitary, Iverssen—he's a bard, and a bard-born one at that. You know that the bards form no allegiances or alliances political. They travel with news and music, no more."

It was obvious that the Priest felt the presence of an outsider improper just days before the most important ritual of the Breodani. He started to say as much, when the King held out a hand.

"He makes the Queen laugh, Iverssen. And almost nothing does before the Hunt. I've accepted the young man in the court for that reason. Do you question it?"

"No, Majesty," Iverssen replied, bowing low. To that tone of voice, and that expression, there was no other answer.

"Good," the King said. He turned and continued to walk until he reached the closed door. Iverssen opened it for him, just as the lowest of servants might, and the King passed him by, stopping at the last moment to meet the eyes of his closest friend. The matter of the bard was forgotten, as was his momentary irritation. Only things Breodani remained. "I ask you to pray to the Hunter, Iverssen. I know what happened the last time I felt His presence so clearly. Let there not be so terrible a price associated with it, this time."

* * *

"No," Norn said, as he adjusted Stephen's jacket, "the King has no huntbrother. The closest he has is Priest Iverssen. Sometimes Priest Greymarten."

Stephen looked at himself in the long oval mirror; his face was pale, his hair brushed back and drawn up around it it. "Why not? He's a Hunter, isn't he?" It was a question that he had often wondered about, but had never pressed until now.

"Not just 'a' Hunter, no. You might have seen the difference today?" Stephen didn't answer the question; Norn shrugged. "The King is *the Hunter* personified, when the Sacred Hunt is called. In the beginning of time, it was the King of our people to whom the Hunter God appeared. And it was with the King that the covenant between the Breodani and their God was forged. The King is the living vessel of the God at the time of the Hunt proper, and that vessel need not be reminded of . . . commonality. Not in the way the nobility must. Because *the Hunter* is *not* common in any way.

"Hold still; I'm beginning to think you've caught Gilliam's jitters."

Stephen waited patiently until Norn drew out of the mirror's vision. "But the King hunts, doesn't he?"

"Yes—" Norn shook his head. "I forgot. You've never hunted with the King. Yes, he hunts. He has his pack, just as Soredon does, as Gilliam will. But he never hunts without the Priests. They tend to him, as you tend to Gilliam. There are also the Huntsmen of the Chamber; when they hunt, they hunt in the King's party. They offer him counsel and they offer him protection.

"Should you become such a one, you will learn an entirely new set of horn calls and obediences and services. The worst of which will be forcing Gilliam to conform to royal protocol.

"With all of that, a King doesn't need a huntbrother. A king has to be closer to God than he does to the commoners, I'd imagine." Norn shrugged. "Doesn't make a lot of sense to me. If the Betrayer had had a huntbrother, we'd never have had the famines and plagues."

"Why not? The Betrayer didn't listen to the Priests either. Why would he listen to a huntbrother?"

"How easy a time does Gil have when he's set on ignoring you?"

Stephen smiled.

"Well, and maybe there you have it. A huntbrother's bond is strong—maybe stronger than the sworn oath the King gives when he takes the crown. You and Gilliam will have Elseth as a responsibility, but you'll have the luxury of watching over each other as well. The King can't afford that partiality; he is sworn to all of Breodanir for his term."

"Do the Kings die in the Sacred Hunt?"

"Stephen, you think too much of death," Norn said quietly. He looked at Stephen's still face in the mirror, and then relented. "A king died once. Harald the Second, if I recall correctly," Norn answered as he walked to the window to see where the sun sat. "It was ... it was not a good time for the kingdom; his son was too young. The Hunt wasn't called the year after the King's death."

Stephen knew what that meant.

"And you'd know it, too, if you'd more time for our history. That'll come, now that Gil is a Hunter proper and both of you have less to prove. The King's vows are more complicated and subtle than ours were. One day, Stephen, you'll be witness to them, for they must be taken at a gathering of the Sacred Hunt, and the Hunter Lords."

"You've seen them?"

"Aye, but I was young and impressionable. Now come; these festivities are paid for by the crown—do you think to make me miss them?"

"It's a fine new generation of young Hunters, isn't it?" Lady Alswaine looked out at the crowd with a predatory sparkle in her eyes. She had two daughters of marriageable age, and had every intention of pressing their interests with a suitable family. She had been quite the beauty in her time, and even now, with the spark of youthful verve faded, she was still one to catch and command the attention. She lowered the powder-pink fan and turned her gaze upon her companion.

"Indeed," he replied softly. From long habit, his fingers

strayed to his beard as he smiled across at her. Few women were his equal in height; she was one.

"What is this, Krysanthos? Have the mage-born become dullards with words in some vain attempt to equal the Hunter Lords?" Her smile was warm and only a trifle edged as it glanced off the back of her husband. There, from the gallery, she could see him surrounded by his hunting companions. They were involved in an animated discussion which no one not born to the Hunt could possibly have any interest in.

"Ah, your pardon, Lady. I was merely looking at the young Hunters. It is, after all, their occasion." He leaned slightly over the edge of the gallery railings. "Who are those two?"

"Which ones? I'm afraid my sight is not as good as it used to be."

He knew that her sight was as poor as an eagle's, but smiled and indulged her; it cost him nothing. "The young, fair-haired one; he's smartly attired—or rather, he wears his clothing like a huntbrother. I believe his Hunter is the dark-haired boy with his hands in the canapes, standing beside Astrid of the maker-born guild."

"Ah, those two." Her voice took on a lilt of interest. "I don't know, but I believe they're from Elseth. Come, why don't we go down and congratulate them on their passage? It is why we're here, after all."

"Why not?" Krysanthos replied, offering Lady Alswaine a perfectly accoutred arm. She smiled as she slid her fingers around the black velvet of his sleeve. They took the stairs carefully and crossed the main floor with ease. The Hunter Lords didn't notice their passage, and the other guests usually made way for Krysanthos; he wore the emblem of the Order of Knowledge, after all, and all who saw it, save perhaps untutored children, knew him for one of the mage-born. Vivienne, Priestess to the Mother, nodded coolly at his passing before turning again to listen to the words of a shy young man.

All of the nobles and all of the noteworthy people of the kingdom came to this feast and this festival of celebration. There—heard more than seen—the bard-born trilled some ageless, deathless melody of a Hunter's bitter rite of passage. At the doors, priests of other orders could be seen making their entrance, chief among them Vardos, justice-born, with his gold-irised eyes, and his grim, severe face.

Lady Alswaine and her escort did not appear to notice their arrival; they were seeking other prey. "Hello," Lady Alswaine said, as she released Krysanthos' arm and walked up to one of the two young men.

Stephen looked up at her and smiled brightly. The hand that she offered, he took, holding it for exactly the right length of time. His hands were dry, and certainly not food encrusted. She would not have offered her hand to Gilliam.

"I'm Lady Alswaine. My husband is a Huntsman of the Chamber."

"I met him earlier. I've heard that he's a Hunter without match, except perhaps for the King himself."

Clearly pleased, Lady Alswaine bowed her head, tipping her fan in Stephen's direction. "You've been listening to him speak, then?"

A little "o" of shock came out before Stephen recovered himself. "He would never admit the truth of any of the tales, Lady." Especially not while she was present.

Lady Alswaine was a tall woman. This was made clear to Stephen when she bent down to whisper in his ear. "Gilliam of Elseth has found himself a fine huntbrother. You will do Lady Elseth proud—you already have tonight."

"Don't monopolize the young man, Lady."

Stephen turned at the words and stiffened. Years of etiquette lessons took over, and he held out his hand with a smooth smile as he performed the half-bow of equals. The bow was awkward. Stephen's gaze was drawn and held by the platinum medallion that clung round the stranger's throat. A slender crescent, a half moon, and the moon in full circle were raised in a triad that spoke of mystery and the light in darkness. Quartered in the moon at zenith were the symbols of the elements.

"Yes," the man said quietly, "I am of the Order of Knowledge. Let me welcome you to our city."

"Thank you, sir." The words were formal, as stiff as

Stephen himself. His fingers and legs tingled with the urge to be gone. The matters of the mage-born were not the concern of commen men, and Stephen knew well the folly of trying to bridge the gap. All children, no matter whether they lived as unparented thieves in the lower city streets, or as wealthy scions of the highest families in the land, had heard many of the tales that surrounded the mage-born.

"Let me introduce myself. I am Krysanthos of the second circle. You are?"

"Stephen of Elseth." He looked up and met the mage's eyes. They were brown, palely tinted with flecks of gold and green, and they were clear and unblinking. In stories he had often read about how hair stood on end at the nape of one's neck—and now he was certain it was no fanciful bardic wording.

"You've heard of Elseth, surely?" Lady Alswaine said, as she once again reached for the mage's arm.

"Lord Elseth is a Master Hunter, I believe—and Elseth is a well governed preserve." He did not raise his arm, or otherwise acknowledge Lady Alswaine's unspoken request. Instead he stared at Stephen.

Stephen couldn't look away. He froze as the eyes of the mage-born man came to life with a luminescent flare of blue. He could not even gasp as that light flashed forward toward his defenseless face.

"Stephen?"

Gilliam was there; suddenly Gilliam was at his side, instead of at the tables. His voice was quiet, concerned. He reached out quickly to place a hand on Stephen's paralyzed shoulder.

The white mage-light sprang forward and fell short, dripping into nothing like an awkward spray of shining water. Stephen felt warmth for a moment, a familiar heat that radiated outward from a center no mage-light could reach. He caught Gilliam's hand in his own and met the mage's gaze squarely.

The mage shrugged; there was no hostility at all in his expression. "It's been a pleasure to meet you, young man. May you fare well in the Sacred Hunt." He turned, moving neither too quickly nor too slowly, and left Stephen to wonder if his fear had grown fangs from his imagination.

"Who was he?" Gilliam asked, as he watched the velvet robes retreat.

"Krysanthos. Of the Order of Knowledge."

"Mage-born." Gilliam sounded as if he'd just swallowed something bitter. "I don't like him."

"Neither do I." Stephen shivered. "I—I don't know why."

"He's a mage."

Which was as good an answer as any. Stephen shook off the shadows, but he stayed as close to Gilliam as possible for the rest of the evening. Which meant, of course, that Gilliam was remarkably well behaved for a young Hunter Lord.

Krysanthos was concerned. Although he had tried several times throughout the course of the evening, he had not been able to come close to the young Elseth huntbrother. He had made a cursory scan of all the rest and found them to be common, uninteresting young men; certainly not eager to go to the Hunter's Death, but also caught up in their Lords' pride.

But this Stephen worried him slightly. No other boy had reacted so strongly to what was a completely invisible use of magic—it was almost as if the youth had seen the flare of power, which was impossible.

The mage-born recognized the mage-born; it had always been so. And Krysanthos had seen no kinship, no like spark, in Stephen of Elseth. But he was certain the boy knew that a spell had been cast on him.

Angry, he paced the length of his chambers, pausing when he reached the carpet's edge and turning on the ball of his heel. He hated Breodanir and longed to be quit of the place. Give him Essalieyan, and the most dangerous of missions there, and he would be content.

But no. He was here, with a mission that bordered on ludicrous for all its import, and a mystery that was not to his liking. For not only had the boy apparently been aware of his spell, he had also, somehow, negated it.

He pulled a tassled bell. He would call the maid back

and have her search, as thoroughly as she dared, the young man's chambers. Some sort of protection spell, perhaps a maker-born amulet, was obviously behind this.

Yes. Of course. And when he found it, he would conveniently replace it with one less ... potent. That done, he could catch the boy and mask out the memory of white-light and mage-spell. If that failed, he would have to resort to a common assassination—which might anger the Lord if any grew suspicious.

He walked over to the curtains and drew them aside. He had done it so often the finery of gold, brown, and green was beneath his notice. The sun was gone, the moon a crescent against the sky. Clouds ate away at the stars in blackness. It was time.

He let the curtains fall and left off tracing his impatient path into the carpet. The mirror in his bedchamber, perfectly dusted and gleaming in the light of his lamp, watched him like a sightless eye. That would change. He stood before it, saw the lines of concern around his lips and the corners of his eyes, and forced himself to smooth them into a cold, noncommittal expression. Pride made him pull his medallion from the folds of his shirt so it stood out as a proclamation of what and who he was.

The crackle of white mage-light came readily. It shot out and surrounded the mirror's surface, dancing against it as if the silvered glass were liquid. He felt the pull of power as it left him; the cost of communication from Breodanir to the heart of the city of Averalaan was high. He was glad that he performed this spell so seldom. Unfortunately, recent casting times had come relatively close together and it took him some weeks to recover.

The mirror grew murky as it lost his reflection. The light without dwindled, and the light within grew, taking shape and substance until once again the mirror's surface looked polished and reflective. It did not show his image.

"Sor na Shannen." His bow was indolent, at best half-respectful—but he bowed.

"Krysanthos."

He saw her back, and felt a flash of annoyance. She knew the time and the hour, and had had enough warning to comport herself with dignity. But no; the pale luminescence of her skin was completely uncovered. Her perfect shoulders rippled as she turned, slowly, to face him.

"You must be early." She was seated on a low divan. Her hair was a spill of finespun night that trailed around exposed breasts and perfect torso. Her lips were red and full, her teeth a pale glimmer.

Against his will he felt himself responding. Annoyed, he cast a distancing spell with his personal power; it robbed some of the glamour of its strength—but not all. Sor na Shannen was a powerful demon, and she held her demesne in the Hells with an absolute strength that many of the demon lords admired. No others of her kind had made the climb to such a height.

"You've been long away from the Hells," he said quietly. "Do you trust your lieutenant?"

Her smile fell away from sharp, white teeth. "I will return in good time." But she was cold now, and in coldness, quite safe. "You have a report to make; make it. I have waited until now to feed, and I am impatient to be out."

"It is as it has been for the last four years."

He knew what she would say, and she did not disappoint him. "Are you certain?"

"I am certain."

"The last four years and the last three months differ greatly in circumstance." Her voice grew sharper. "You saw no sign of the Horn?"

"I have seen no sign of it."

"The Spear?"

"The Spear is useless without the Horn," he said, through teeth that were already clenching. "But no. I have seen no sign of the Spear either."

She relaxed, and her eyes once again grew liquid and lazy. "I don't need to remind you of their import."

"No." He smiled, as cold as she had been. "Had they been in my keeping, I would not have been required to waste precious energy to speak about them."

She hissed, and his smile grew warmer. "Enough. The priests that were responsible have perished, and I, too, grow tired of this game."

"Then let me return."

"No. We know that the agent who stole the Horn and the Spear came from the King's Forest in Breodanir; Ellekar perished there. We know that the girl was not a Hunter, and we know that the Horn's power resides with the 'Hunter-born.' It *must* be there. We are less than ten years from the completion of our plans—the gate-spell goes well, and our Lord should soon have free access to the mortal lands. Find the Horn. Do *not* let it be winded."

Krysanthos cut the connection before his annoyance built beyond tolerable levels. As soon as he knew the succubus' personal name and sigil, he would send her back to the Hells—and into the demesne of her worst enemy. But for now he needed her, as she did him.

Another decade. Of this.

CHAPTER ELEVEN

"Stephen?" The word was muffled by carpets and curtains, but it was still conspicuous in the wide-open spaces and hollows of the King's library. The King's colors—the colors of Breodanir itself—had been deemed too loud for this particular wing of the palace, and were in evidence only in the banners that hung from the ceiling at the library's entrance. Wide, long tables and sturdy chairs were grouped in the center, surrounded by the library's many shelves; those shelves, lined with row upon row of books, rose up to the heights of the roof. Ladders and single-person walkways provided access for the many librarians who worked here. Norn could see one or two deftly pulling single volumes from their places.

"Stephen?" The single word was louder; an obvious affront to the quiet dignity the setting demanded.

"May I help you?" An elderly man appeared at Norn's elbow. The lines of his round face were heightened by a disapproving frown, the tone of his voice one that only respectable age could wield.

Norn gazed down his nose at the brown-robed man who stood with his arms folded. His clothing was rumpled, if clean, and he looked as if he lived within the bowels of the stacks.

"I'm looking for someone."

"I'd guessed. Who are you shouting for?"

It was hardly a shout, but the librarian's expression made it clear that any correction of facts would only be seen as an argument. Norn sighed. "Stephen of Elseth. Young man, about this tall. Fair hair, bluish eyes."

"You're with him?" Faint disbelief colored the words

before the librarian's face relaxed. "Well, at least one of you understands the concept of quiet study."

"Is he here?"

"Yes. You'll find him reviewing the Mythos of the Essalieyanese culture, or perhaps more properly, of the Weston culture the empire eventually supplanted. If you wish to converse, the sitting room beyond the east doors is appropriate." The librarian turned and started to walk away.

"Uh, excuse me?"

"What?"

"Where is that?"

"Beyond the east doors." The frown was back in place.

"I mean where would he be researching these myths?"

"Oh." The man shook his head. "Of course. I forget that it isn't obvious to everyone. If you'd care to follow me?" He was short, but for all that he seemed to shuffle, his pace was both brisk and silent.

Stephen sat with his legs curled beneath him, in the center of a chair with arms. It didn't fit under the desk, but it was clearly quite comfortable. A book was open in his lap, and he studied its pages intently. On the desk, a dozen books in various piles made an impromptu fortress.

"Stephen?"

Stephen looked up. "Norn? Is it dinner already?"

"Not yet."

The librarian cleared his throat. "The east room," he said, in a long-suffering tone. But he spared Stephen the ghost of a smile before he walked off.

Stephen nodded at the librarian's back and gently closed his book. He placed it on one of the piles with such care it became obvious to Norn that the stacks had their logical order. Standing, he stretched his legs, and then led Norn to the discussion chamber that lay to the east of the collection.

He stepped in, held the door for Norn, gestured at a chair, and closed the door—with great care to be quiet—behind him.

"What are you doing here?" Norn's voice was still hushed. "This is what, the third or fourth day in a row?

You've missed most of the festivities—and the food, mind—just to read religious texts?"

"I haven't missed them all," Stephen replied, with quiet dignity. "I dined yesterday eve with the Ladies Alswaine and Maubreche, and the day before, with Lady Devenson and the King's clerk for the Hunt. I had lunch with Lady Morganson and her two daughters, Lianor and Lylandra, and two days ago—"

"All right, all right—you've made your point. You've certainly kept up your end of the Elseth duties. But you've missed anything that might be fun in between."

"I've been doing research."

"I'd guessed. And I thought you didn't have time to study Breodanir history. I didn't realize that it was merely lack of inclination."

Stephen winced, and because it was the festival and the first Hunt, Norn relented. "What's so fascinating that you study it here?"

"God."

"The Hunter God?"

Stephen frowned as he nodded. "But there's so little here about Him. They have volumes about every other god, and more than just volumes about how the gods interact. But about the Hunter God . . . almost nothing. When the pantheon is discussed at all, there's never any mention of Him. Can He be that minor?"

"Not to us, no. But He *is* Breodanir's God; the only people outside of Breodanir who worship Him are envoys from our country. Why are you so curious?"

"The King," Stephen answered quietly. "And the ceremony afterward. I felt God. I know it." He shook his head, although Norn said nothing mocking. "But I don't understand why. The Hunters call themselves Hunterborn, but they aren't. Not really. Here—oh. It's outside. Well, I can tell you what it said. The god-born—they're obvious. First," he raised a finger, "they have golden eyes. Every one of them. Doesn't matter which god. Second, they have powers associated with their god. Third, if they study it, they can talk to their god. And fourth—most important—they're the *children* of a god."

"Yes?"

"So the Hunters *aren't* Hunter-born, not in the way that someone's Mother-born, justice-born or wisdom-born."

"And?" Clearly Norn was not enlightened by Stephen's discoveries.

Stephen was a little crestfallen, but he continued anyway, showing the determination of his age. "All right. No god is involved here, not that way. Which leaves the talent-born. Normal people without gods for parents, who somehow have power. The bard-born, the healer-born, the seer-born, the mage-born, the maker-born." His forehead wrinkled as he tried to remember the others. "Never mind."

"And you think the Hunter-born should fall in with the talent-born."

"No!" But he smiled, and his cheeks flushed. He was sharing the fruits of days of labor with someone who was willing to listen. "Because talent doesn't breed true."

"And the Hunter-born always have children who are Hunter-born."

"Yes."

"So?"

"Don't you see? The Hunter-born aren't god-born, but they aren't talent-born either."

"And what does that mean?"

Stephen's face fell, and his shoulders drooped forward a little. "I don't know. I've been trying to find out, and I'm not the only one. The Order of Knowledge first opened its Collegium in Breodanir when the mage-born came to study the Hunter-born. They call it a talent, but . . . well, they don't know why it works the way it does either. Andarion was first circle in the Order, and he spent a long time trying to figure it out. He didn't."

"Maybe," Norn said, rising, "it's just the power of God—it doesn't have an explanation to those who won't take the oath and be affected by it, the arrogance of the mage-born notwithstanding."

Stephen frowned. "We'd have all the answers, you know."

Norn nodded and reached out to grip Stephen's shoulder. "If not for the fire that destroyed the Hunter's temple over three hundred years ago."

Stephen's widening eyes made Norn smile. The arrogance of the mage-born was as nothing when compared to the arrogance of the young. "Yes," he said, trying to keep the amusement from his voice, "you aren't the only one to ask questions, Stephen, nor the only one to notice the Hunter's touch in the King's face at the ascension." He helped Stephen to his feet. "Let's put the books away for today."

"You knew about the fires?"

"In my day," Norn said, with the mock severity of a much older Lord, "we had to take *real* lessons; study history as well as weapon use and hunting. Of *course* I knew about the fires."

"That's Tallespan you're imitating!"

"Indeed. A man who knew much about everything— except perhaps enjoyment and relaxation. Now come; the library doesn't hold the answers that you're searching for. If you're really determined, you might petition the Collegium of the Order, and they might allow you to peruse the treatises that have been written on the Hunter-born."

Stephen nodded sheepishly, and remained in the library just long enough to make a neat stack of the books he'd been studying. Norn waited, and then made sure that Stephen was ushered to yet another dinner with the various Hunter Lords. The Hunt was gathering.

The temple walls were stone: solid; square; and obviously the work of competent masons—but no more. There were windows, long and open to catch as much of day's frugal light as possible, but the window seats were rough and lacked the greater dignity of most of the King's palace. A fireplace the width of the great hall lay blackened and silent; as silent as the temple itself. No one was there.

Stephen knew he was dreaming. He looked down upon leathered feet and saw the edge of real robes brushing the ground around them. The robes were simple and practical brown. He liked them, and after a moment realized that they reminded him of those worn by the Mother's Priesthood. There was no green here, no gold, no fanciful embroidery. He liked that, too.

But he was dreaming. He knew it. The world around him seemed imprecise, as if seen through morning eyes. He wiped at his to see if it helped. Felt his face and froze; it was strange, bristly, harder. He pulled his hands away and saw that they, too, had changed. They were lined, thicker, older—and covered in blood. Some of it was new; it was warm and liquid. Some was older, though; red flakes caked the crossed spears of his Order's ring.

He remembered then why the halls were silent, remembered what had filled them minutes—hours?—before. All of those voices were stilled now. There were no throats left for screaming or shouting or crying. A sudden pain flared up in his side and at his forehead. He was running, or he should have been running. He had stopped to listen for the little noises that spoke of pursuit. There were none.

He began to run.

It's a dream.

It hurt. He felt a trickle leave his lips and knew it for blood by the warmth along his tongue. He tried a window, for the third or fourth time, and found it sealed as the others had been; an invisible barrier protected the glass and soft lead that might have been his one escape. It was magic. The mage-born were here in force.

Yet it was not the mage-born that frightened him.

It's only a dream.

He began to run; he did not know where, but the feet did as they beat a steady, quick rhythm against the stone. The hall passed as did the great fireplace and the fading pinks of the coming evening. Torchlight caught his shadow, trapping it and making it seem more substantial in his wake. Worse, the winking torches began to go out.

They knew where he was, but if he moved quickly they would not be able to stop him before he reached his destination. He prayed, the silent vowels cracking his dry lips, although he knew it would do no good. They were at the year-end and the Sacred Hunt was mere days away.

Ah, the darkness; the darkness terrified him. The mages who bore it, who sheltered it and used it and fed it—they were the sword in the expert's hands. He heard the crackle of blue-light behind his back and leaped around the corner. The wall, inches away from where he had been, flared to life in a cloud of energy that shattered the torch holders.

The two ribs that were cracked pressed against his lungs as he drew breath and winced with the effort. It was a dream. A dream. A dream.

His hands were bleeding; the old blood had been completely superseded by the flow that trailed his arms from the height of his shoulders. His hands shook as he reached the doors and struggled to swing them open.

And then, for a moment, he was clear again. Into stone and silence; the steady quiet of temple life and its security. There, at the center of the room against the tiled inlay of gold and wood and marble, a small altar rose from the ground.

Against green cushions, the perfect edge of a well-oiled sword glinted silver in the light of the eternal flame that sat, like a miniature sun, in the flat, beamed ceiling above. The spearhead, silver also, topped a hardwood pole that had to be replaced every few generations, as it rested against the floor. The couples and leads were perfect, undisturbed, the very icons of the temple's inner life.

These were symbols of comfort and continuity; the regalia that went with the oath. But they were not what he sought. He ran to the altar. The wound had opened enough so his hand's quick passage above the cushions left a telltale mark.

Shaking, he brought away the last of the Hunter's hold in his hands; a simple, carved horn that defied time, temperature, and moisture to remain as perfect now as it was on the day of its making.

His fingers covered the only marking upon it as he brought it to his lips and called upon lungs that might not draw breath strong enough to wind it. Cold caught him in his midsection; cold and the heat of fire. He cried out in agony, and his hands closed rigidly.

He could not let go of the horn.

Wheeling, staggering, he turned to face the open doors that held his enemy. He reached out and gripped the altar's edge with one hand, needing to steady himself. He caught a glimpse of scorched brown cloth and the blistered flesh beneath it before he turned once again to the horn.

But the door held none of the mage-born, and none of the darkness. Instead, in the center of the frame, a slender figure robed in midnight blue stood. A hood was drawn over its face, and in silence it regarded him.

It's only a dream, he thought, and felt his shoulders sag in relief. The dream was turning. He saw his hands shift as age and blood reversed themselves and vanished into nothing.

"Yes," the figure said, in a voice that was soft and low. "It is a dream, but not only. The darkness waits without, but does not wait idly. Will you not sound the horn, oathtaker? Will you not fulfill your ancient pledge?"

Around the figure's feet, shadow pooled and began a slow crawl across the ground. Where it passed, stone began to smoke like kindling.

It's only a dream. But he could not escape it, and the darkness was drawing closer still. Shaking, he lifted the horn to his lips and his now beardless face. The horn had not changed at all.

It transformed the air in his mouth to a sound that he had never heard before. No horn, no simple hunting device, had ever made a sound so lovely and so full. It echoed in the air, filling the chamber and stretching ever outward. His body shivered and resounded with the single, low note.

The room blurred; he lifted his sleeve—now Hunter green and whole—and brushed his eyes free of tears. The figure in blue bowed low and stepped slowly out of the doorway.

Behind waited the Beast. It snarled, its voice as terrifying as the horn's note had been beautiful. The great, shaggy throat uttered no words—how could it?—yet Stephen understood its meaning clearly.

It had been summoned, and finally it had arrived. Its fangs, its claws, its very size defied his ability to absorb details.

"Yes," the figure in blue repeated, "it is just a dream, Stephen of Elseth. But it is the first dream."

He had no time for horror or fear at the words; all of his attention was upon the Hunter's Death.

Stephen woke in the morning with the webs of the dream still around him. He struggled out of bed, leaving a trail of sheets and counterpane in his wake. The curtains were heavy and stiff as he dragged them away from the window. Light, muted and diffuse, relieved the room of its dark edges. He peered up, saw the gray clouds above that moved at the wind's whim.

It was cool. The fire no longer burned in the grate. Hand shaking, he began to dress. He did not want to call servants to start the flames burning. He wanted to be free of his room.

He met Gilliam in the breakfast hall—a hall that was mostly empty. The Hunter Lords had reveled and discoursed for most of the previous evening and were still abed. Here, in the King's City, scant days before the calling of the Sacred Hunt, candles and oil were in plentiful supply. If any thought the expense frivolous, very few could be heard to comment on it.

"What's wrong?" Gilliam said, from halfway across the hall. He pushed himself away from the table and strode across the solid, cold floor. For a moment, as he crossed the path of the fireplace, he looked like a slender shadow surrounded by tongues of flame. "Stephen?"

"Why are you awake?"

"Same reason you are."

Stephen really wished that Gilliam would lower his voice. The few Lords and—much worse—their Ladies who had graced the hall so early were clearly listening. In a whisper, he said, "Did you have a nightmare?"

"No." Gilliam frowned. "But you did. Woke me up and kept me awake." His eyes narrowed. "You look awful. What's the matter?"

"Nothing." He tried to brush past, and Gilliam caught his elbow.

"It isn't nothing. You feel as if you've seen the Hunter's Death."

Stephen couldn't lie to Gilliam. It was always brought home this way. He would try, and Gilliam would refuse to let him be. The oath-bond between them was strong, even for huntbrothers.

"You aren't wearing your colors," Stephen said lamely.

"And you're wearing yours. Now what is wrong?" Gilliam caught Stephen's shoulders. "No. Don't say 'nothing.' Don't shrug your shoulders at me. We *promised,* and we're bound by it."

He might have added that he couldn't eat, couldn't sit still, and couldn't concentrate; might have pointed out that Stephen's fear was so strong that it overwhelmed everything else. But he was Gilliam; he didn't. It seemed too obvious a truth.

Stephen sighed and nodded; his throat caught and tightened. He gestured toward the nearest corner of the room, and they both turned in silence.

When they were as far from the hearing of others as possible, Stephen turned to Gilliam.

"I had a dream."

Gilliam nodded, waiting.

"I was in the temple. The temple that was here before the palace. I told you about it last night." He stopped a moment, and looked at Gilliam. Gilliam's brown eyes were unblinking, and unmocking, as they met his. "Everyone else was dead. All the Priests, the servants— everyone. It was three days before the calling of the Hunt.

"I was alive—I was a Priest."

At this, Gilliam snorted. "You'd make a rotten Priest."

Stephen nodded, as if he'd heard the words without understanding them. "I was the only one. There were mages. There was fire and darkness. I was afraid. But I—I *knew* it was a dream—I knew it. I just couldn't wake up." He brought his hands to his face and examined them closely. "I was injured. Bleeding."

"What happened?"

"I ran to safety. A room in the temple with an altar. There was a sword, a spear, couples, leads—but the most important thing was a horn. I picked it up. I sounded it." He closed his eyes, remembering the only peaceful thing that had happened. "And someone came, someone in blue."

"Who?"

"I don't know. The face was covered by a hood. But I couldn't ask—because the Hunter's Death came, too." Shaking, he lowered his hands.

"It was only a dream," Gilliam said quietly. But he waited; Stephen was not yet finished.

"I think I might have said that. And the person in blue—he said, 'It is the first dream.'"

"The first?" Gilliam shook his head and slowly sat down. It didn't bother him that there was no chair to catch him; he was quite comfortable on the floor.

Stephen nodded. He knew he should at least tell Gil to get a chair, but he didn't have the energy. Saying the words aloud had made them more real than the silence of fear did.

The first dream.

The Unnamed God dealt in dreams and visions, and if he visited these upon you thrice in three nights, you were his subject, you bore his wyrd.

"'One dream is a dream.'" It was a quote, and Gilliam offered it to Stephen knowing that it wouldn't be any help. Stephen didn't answer in words, but after a moment he, too, lowered himself to the floor. They sat facing each other as they might have done on a normal day in the kennels.

Gilliam reached out, caught his huntbrother's hand, and held it very tightly. "You believed him, didn't you?"

Stephen nodded.

"Wait. We'll know in two days."

He nodded again.

"And it doesn't matter. If we've got the wyrd of the Unnamed on us, we'll face it together—and we'll beat it. I promise."

The knot in Stephen's throat eased, but only a little.

Lunch went well, and dinner was another festive affair. The ladies and their eligible daughters were now out in force—a force to be reckoned with. Twice, Stephen had to rescue Gilliam before he said enough to earn his absent mother's wrath. Norn was even busier with Soredon, and it soon became clear to Stephen that all of the huntbrothers present watched over their Hunter Lords with an eye to social details.

The Elseth preserve was not a small one; indeed, compared to many it was quite sizable. But it was close to the eastern boundary of the kingdom, and farther from the capital, so in the early marriage-seeking forays, Gilliam was not besieged. He did speak with one or two of the young Ladies—and Stephen winced when Gilliam began his earnest, passionate discussions about how he was going to build his hunting pack to any who could hear.

The Ladies listened politely of course, as any hunt-brother would. Unfortunately, Gilliam could offer no like polite response when they attempted to steer the conversation to less specific topics. True to his class, he found it intensely uncomfortable to talk about the "weather," and it was impossible to draw more than a grunt or a nod from him about anything but the Hunt.

It was up to Stephen to fill the awkward silences, and again he did Lady Elseth proud. He talked, or rather listened intently, to matters of trade and governance; bowed with exactly the right amount of deference—forcing Gilliam to do the same by dint of a glare they both understood the meaning of—and complimented the women on their finery. That last was not hard to do. Any time a Lady, dressed in full evening wear, walked across the ballroom's threshold, he felt a hint of awe. The Hunter Lords had a grace that was born of agility and aggression, and honed on the Hunt; the Ladies had a grace born of the same, but honed on the dance floor, or in odd etiquette lessons—and Stephen found the mixture of delicacy and swift, sure steps the more entrancing of the two.

As well, although he didn't bother to say so to Gilliam, he found the colors that the Ladies wore much more pleasing to the eye; he'd had enough of Hunter green, brown, and gray to last a lifetime. Pale blues, azures, brilliant magentas, crimsons, golds—each dress as unique as the clothing of the Hunter Lords was uniform.

The only time he lost sight of Gilliam was when Lady Alswaine began her discourse on the problems with the seat of judgment in her preserve. For Stephen, to whom the law was still absolute and carved in stone, her ambivalence was both shocking and fascinating.

"There are mitigating circumstances for many crimes," she said, speaking more to the young women present than to Stephen. "For instance, Veralyn, what would you do if one of your villagers was caught stealing from the manor house?"

Lady Veralyn's cheeks clashed with her dress as she flushed. She opened her mouth to speak, and then closed it slowly, wondering at the game that Lady Alswaine, older and wiser, was playing, for Lady Alswaine asked no idle questions. Lady Veralyn was a year older than Stephen, and not yet pledged to any Lord or Lord's son. "I would—I would have to know more."

Lady Alswaine's smile held a glimmer of approval. "Indeed, and when you occupy your seat, you will have that opportunity. In this case, it was winter, and a harsh one." She tilted her head to the side and glanced at Stephen. "What of you, Stephen of Elseth?"

Stephen flushed, wondering whether or not Lady Alswaine knew of his origins. He was certain she must, and his response, defensive, was also a completely correct recitation of the laws of Breodani. "Fine, work edict, or finger. It would depend on what he'd stolen."

"Pigeons."

"Fine."

"He had no money." Lady Alswaine's lips turned up in a smile that was both friendly and annoying.

"Then work edict."

"Would you trust him in your manor?"

"Finger." It was the most severe of the sentences that could be meted out, and Stephen said it reluctantly, remembering his own fears, his own days in the lower city, surrounded by his hungry den mates.

"And what would his family do come spring and the common season? Death, I think, would be kinder—and death is not an option. Come, Stephen. I am the person who metes out justice, with the aid of the village head. In this case, the man committed a very real crime—but for foolish reasons, nay, stupid ones."

"But he committed a crime."

"Of course." She folded her arms very delicately. It made her look as fragile as a rock. "But the why of it was interesting. He was young, and had just taken a wife the previous summer. His wife was the pride of her parents, and the desire of many of the younger men—and he was still not comfortable in her choice of him. He considered the gift of her acceptance the whim of luck, and was afraid that if he failed her, she would revoke it. The house that they dwell in is simple, and was, of course, built with the aid of the village as a whole—but in order to impress her, he foolishly bartered and used supplies that were to have seen them through the winter."

Stephen shrugged uncomfortably, but did not look away from Lady Alswaine. She waited a moment before continuing, to judge both his expression and his temper. Satisfied, she nodded and went on.

"What would you have done, were you in his position?"

"Gone to the village head," Stephen replied promptly. "If the village head wasn't prepared to deal with the shortage and arrange for repayment, they could go to the manor proper and ask for the reserves."

"Yes. That is what's supposed to happen. But if he went to the village head, his young bride would be sure to know. So instead, he came to the manor at night." Lady Alswaine held out her cup as a signal to a passing servant. The young man bowed and carefully refilled it before moving on. "He was caught, of course, and his case was brought to me immediately. Now, Stephen, Veralyn—place yourself in my position, and more important, place yourself in his. He committed a crime against Alswaine, yes, but that was only a symptom.

"The real wrong was done to his wife."

For a moment, Stephen's brow furrowed; his face grew intent, and his eyes less focused. The lessonmaster would have known the expression immediately and approved of it. As the Lady Alswaine commanded, Stephen tried to place himself in the young man's position. He found, to his surprise, that it was easy. He was in the King's City, after all; the place of his birth and the first eight years of his life.

He remembered, although the memory was blurred and fuzzy now, how he had spent those eight years. Luck had smiled often on him, and he had escaped the notice of the king's guard—and therefore, of the Queen's judgment—but he remembered how the fear felt.

"Did he steal wood?" he asked quietly.

She chuckled. "The city isn't out of you entirely, is it? No, wood is not a problem in Alswaine. He took only food, and it was near the end of the season."

He nodded, and continued to furrow his brow. Lady Alswaine spoke of the thief's crime against his wife, but clearly there wasn't one. First, she had nothing to steal, and second, he probably only wanted to feed her. Of course, if he had wanted to feed her, and he'd had half a brain, he'd have just gone to the village head, admitted his need, and been done with it.

But then he'd have to tell her that he'd wasted all of their winter supplies, and she'd be angry and leave him.

Or would she? He stopped, and the lines in his forehead melted away. "He didn't trust her," he said quietly.

"No, he didn't. And if you see that, you might know what I demanded as restitution." Clearly pleased, she turned her full attention upon him, her gold-fringed skirts rustling as she moved.

"You made him tell her."

"Very good!" She almost clapped, but the goblet she held prevented it. "Yes, but more; I had her called to the manor. I'm afraid I was rather cruel to the young man, which certainly suited the nature of both of his crimes. I didn't tell him that I had summoned her, for I believed that I understood his motives. Instead, I had her wait behind a screen with the various servants who attend the judgments. When he told me, at length, of the reasons for the theft, she could hear every word.

"I must say that I had always thought her sweet and relatively even of temper." Here she smiled, but the smile was one that Stephen couldn't understand at all. "She knocked the screen over and stood with her fists by her side. I thought she was going to hit him in front of all of us." She was laughing; wine swirled over the rim of silver and slid in droplets down her fingers. It was some minutes before she could speak again. Stephen didn't understand what was funny about it at all.

"She didn't kill him—I mentioned that I thought it was rather too severe for his crime—but she made her displeasure quite clear." And here, her eyes softened. "And when he understood that she was angry, not because of the theft or the shortages, but because he hadn't trusted her . . . well, they left together, and in the end I think she was glad that she hadn't killed him." She set her glass aside when the servant next passed by. "So there you have it. Not everything is clear, especially to those of us who must judge. And before you think that you learn more with age, I've news for you both—you unlearn much. Things become more complicated and less clear."

Stephen nodded attentively before he chose to speak again. When he did, his voice was quiet. "But, Lady," and he bowed, "what would you have done if the thief's wife was exactly what he was afraid she was?"

"Your point, young Stephen." Her smile was sad. "But you've ruined my little story for the evening. Even the unclear becomes more unclear with time. What would I have done? As I did, I think, but I wouldn't remember it fondly, nor as a triumph. And I would have grieved for the foolish young man in the privacy of my rooms. It is difficult for the young when their dreams die.

"Now. Enough. Where is your Hunter? You've left him long enough that he's bound to embarrass your House; go, quickly."

Stephen showed her a hint of the man he might become. Although he did not understand her sudden change, and the loss of her little smile, he asked no further questions. Instead he bowed, low and formal in his respect.

"Wisdom," she said, as he rose from his bow, "is not knowledge. It is experience. You will find, as you grow older, that you are capable of many wrongs which you consider evil now; you will also understand much about people that you dismiss. You may even understand the fear that comes with love, and the love that transcends fear."

* * *

That night he returned to the temple. This time there was no silence and no isolation, and the air was full of smoke and ash—the rewards of fire. He was standing in the pews which were only half full when the wall uttered a roar and suddenly crumbled.

He saw four men in dark robes, and behind them saw soldiers with raised swords, and crossbows that were already loosing quarrels. Because he was spinning, he was spared. A wooden bolt grazed his forehead, leaving a red trail but no death in its wake.

He ran; he was closest to the doors that led to the inner temple. The sounds of slaughter had already started before he crossed the threshold, but he spared no backward glance. He knew that there was nothing he could do. This was a dream, after all.

But he couldn't shake it and couldn't defeat it. His feet carried him where his will could not prevent it; already the halls and the torches were familiar, as was the pursuit. He reached the inner sanctum, threw the doors wide, and ran for the altar. The passage of time did not slow; he could feel darkness and hear the approach of the mages. Gone was the moment where each item laid out for the Hunter could be studied and appreciated—only one artifact was of any import.

His hands curled around the horn. He lifted it, shaking. He sounded it and the call was clear.

And once again, the midnight-blue robes that concealed and presented at the same time appeared. He was bent now, as if from some great work, or great injury; he seemed older and more diminutive. Behind him, the darkness was held at bay—and beyond that, a glint of unnatural light on divine fur and fangs began to grow.

"But it's only a dream!" Stephen shouted.

"Yes," the figure said, and it sounded just as it appeared—older or weaker. "But this is the second dream."

Stephen had breakfast brought to his room the next day. Although he woke early, he could not bear to enter the dining hall. He tried to think on other things; caught the strand of Lady Alswaine's lesson, and held it firmly.

He even prayed to the Mother. It was foolish, but in the privacy of his room, there was no one to laugh or call him a child.

It was the last day of festivities; tomorrow, the hunters would leave the King's City—and the King's palace—to enter the royal preserve. There, when the Master of the Game called the Hunt, he and Gilliam would face the creature of nightmare: the Hunter's Death.

Before they could do that, there was the packing to attend to. In silence, Stephen rose and began to empty his drawers and closets of the things he would need: Sword, spear, horn. Norn had, for the moment, the couples and leads; he would hand them over with the part of the pack that Gilliam would lead in the Hunt.

The dress jacket and cloak, the breeches and shirt—all of these would be carefully set aside, to be worn during the great feast that followed the Sacred Hunt. He started to hang them properly, when the door creaked open.

It was Norn.

"I heard you had words with Lady Alswaine last eve," he said jauntily. Then he stopped, hand still on the door. "Stephen—what's wrong? Too much drink?"

"No," was Stephen's reply, but it held little indignation, little fire.

"You've not been swept off your feet by a young lady, have you?"

"No!"

"Well, good, then. The Hunter Lords are oblivious when it comes to the ladies, almost the entire lot of them—but the huntbrothers are sometimes a little foolish at their first Hunt. About the ladies, that is." He walked into the room and shut the door. "Gilliam didn't do anything really bad, did he?"

Stephen shook his head. "Spilled ale on Lady Marget's dress; I apologized."

"You're sure that's all?"

"Yes."

"What's wrong?"

"Nothing."

"Then if it's nothing, you'd better snap out of it." Norn's voice grew harder. He sat down on the bed, resting his elbows against his knees. "You're having your effect on your Hunter, Stephen—and he can't afford it now. Any other time of the year, yes—but not before the Sacred Hunt. He'll need his wits about him; he'll need to be sharp and focused, not distracted and exhausted."

Stephen said nothing.

"You're having an effect now," Norn said, pressing on. "Gilliam was up early this morning, looking for you in the hall. I caught him on his way back up here. He's out with the dogs—as his duty demands—but he's not paying attention. He wanted to find you, and only a direct command from Lord Elseth prevented him." He paused as the last of this sank in. Stephen's eyes widened; when Norn called Soredon "Lord," it was a fair indication of what Soredon's mood had been at the time: bad.

Norn's voice became quieter, but no less sharp. "Whatever it is that's bothering you, it's too strong. It interferes with Gilliam's concentration, his ability to call a good trance. Later—three, four years—he'll be able to do it without pause. But *not now.* You're here in the name of Elseth as well as in the name of the King. You've got to do well at this Hunt. It's your first—every eye in the kingdom will be upon you.

"Both Lord Elseth and I are willing to help you in any way possible, if you need help. But you have to admit to that need, Stephen, or we'll assume the worst. What is bothering you?"

"I—" Stephen swallowed and looked away. His feet were particularly interesting, clad as they were in slippers that clashed with the carpet. Maribelle's gift, as he recalled. "I had the second dream."

"Pardon?"

"The second dream." He looked up, almost met Norn's eyes, and looked away again.

For a moment the older huntbrother wore a mask of confusion. When it fell away, it was replaced by a mixture of shock and amusement. "Hunter's Oath, Stephen—do you mean to tell me that you're bothered by a dream?"

"It's the second dream," Stephen said, but his voice was less steady, less sure.

"I don't care if it's the tenth! Of all the things I ex-pected to hear—" He stood quickly and shook his head. Relief was evident in his smile. "Do you think that night-mares are uncommon for the Hunter folk? We have them all the time—especially before the Sacred Hunt."

"But," Stephen's word could barely be heard, "it's the second dream, on the second night. It was the same."

"Stephen, you sound like an impressionable child. A dream's a dream. The wyrd of fate, the Unnamed, was in-vented by old men who had nothing better to do with their time than terrify the gullible. Is that clear?"

Stephen nodded.

"I didn't hear you, lad."

"Yes, Norn."

"Good." Norn walked over to the door. "I see you've started packing—be done by lunch if you can. I'll come up then."

Stephen nodded again; his cheeks were bright red cir-cles. For want of anything else to do, he started for his dresser.

"Dreams, indeed." Norn snorted. He was a very practi-cal man, as all huntbrothers inevitably strove to be.

It was only a dream, a phantom of childhood and fear and gullibility. And like a phantom, it returned in the eve-ning, when Norn's jaunty condescension wasn't there to keep it at bay.

The temple was on fire now; the flames crackled loudly as they split wooden beams, doors, and joists. Whole sections of the twisted maze in the inner temple were no longer passable. A carpet of dead bodies, fallen stone, and blackened wood barred the way.

Stephen ran, but each step he took was painful. His robes were not dark enough to hide the spread of blood. He was certain his ribs were cracked or broken; each breath, hurriedly and deeply taken, was agony. But one hall, familiar now, was still standing. Nearly empty, it awaited his passage.

He turned and glanced over his shoulder. He knew it cost him speed and time, but fear forced him to it. The darkness moved like a sluggish wave, destroying the light and leaving fire in its wake. Yet as the darkness spread, he saw one of his many enemies. She stood quite tall, robed in shadows and very little else; her hair, a sheen of pale, white gossamer, flared round her shoulders like a ceremonial collar; her eyes—he could not see them well enough to know their color, and he was glad of it. At her throat, before all light was lost, he saw a large, gold medallion, with a tower against the midnight black of moonless sky. She smiled; he felt the tug of her lips over teeth as a command, and turned in desperation. He was almost upon the sanctum. He would not be stopped now.

The doors opened inward with no difficulty; the sanctum was not locked or barred. Who among the Breodani would seek to steal or destroy the sign of their God's favor?

And who would be foolish enough to use it? Hands damp with a mixture of blood and sweat, he reached out, running all the while. He caught the horn, felt it tingle in his hands, and drew it to his lips. It hurt to take the breath that was necessary; he coughed, tasted salt, and lost vision for a brief second.

Then, somehow, the pain was gone; his hands were clean, his arm steady. He sounded the horn. Its note was long and lasting.

And the blue-robed figure stepped over the threshold, while darkness surged beneath its feet. Stephen lowered the horn slowly as he looked at the hood, trying to see a face, a person, within its confines. Hands rose and reached for the edge of the fabric, rolling it gently back.

"Stephen of Elseth, forgive us."

He looked into the face of a woman; she was older than he, but younger than the Lady Elseth. Or so it seemed at first. Her skin was pale, her hair darker than her robe—darker than any black that he had seen, save for the shadows without. Her eyes seemed gray, then blue, then violet, and last an icy, pale gold—they flickered and changed so quickly he couldn't say which was the true one. But he knew that none of the colors were warm.

"Some of what you have seen these past nights is real. History has folded it into a secrecy that even the Hunter's

Priests cannot break. But some of what you have seen is yet to pass."

"Which?"

She shook her head, and seemed for a moment almost sad. "I do not know, fully—and if I did, my given oath would prevent me from explaining it." She lowered her hands and stood before him. "I am Evayne." She gestured suddenly, throwing her arms wide.

Warmth filled the room, different from the heat of the fires. A drowsy peace descended upon Stephen as Evayne brought her hands down, palms up, as if holding something precious.

"The world changes more than you know, Stephen. If I can be of aid to you, I shall—and you will need aid and more if the promise of all oaths is to be realized at last.

"This is the third dream."

CHAPTER TWELVE

On the morning after the third dream, Stephen woke before the dawn. He turned the counterpane neatly down and rose. It was chilly. The fire had burned down during the evening and the room smelled faintly of wood made ash. The curtains were pulled shut to keep the night out. He opened them quickly to give the sunlight that would soon come free passage.

He was afraid, but the fear had turned into something strange over the length of the dream, and he still felt a hint of the warmth that the woman, Evayne, had made manifest. Fear, he thought, remembering everything that Norn and Lord Elseth had struggled to teach him, was a type of wisdom. Terror was different; fear run rampant, with no control. He was no longer terrified.

He could not tell Norn of the third dream, of course. Norn's laughter still echoed in the bedchamber, reddening his cheeks. He began to dress. Breakfast today was important. It might be his last meal. When he was finished, he packed his small chest and left it beside the door for the porter.

Then he walked out of his room and down the hall to Gilliam's. He knocked quietly at first, listened for an answer, and then knocked more loudly. The sound that came through the door was Gilliam's attempt to make words. Stephen snorted and knocked, very loudly, before throwing the door open and marching in.

Gilliam's face was a bulge under the pillows. From the stretch of the bedsheets, Stephen could see that his back was to the door. He walked up, grabbed the pillow, and placed it gently on the chair beside the bed. As he expected, Gilliam's hands were over his ears.

"It's not even light yet—go away."

"Gil," Stephen said, as he reached for the rather rumpled clothing that Gilliam had stuffed, with nary a thought to proper folding, into the drawers of his dresser. "We were told that we had to be up before dawn proper. We've got to eat breakfast, and we have to join Norn and Lord Elseth in the courtyard. Or have you forgotten that we've got to find the right trail before we can hunt at the Master of the Game's call?"

Gilliam mumbled something that was inaudible. Stephen sighed, stepped over to the bedside, and grabbed the counterpane and the blankets beneath. With a quick, efficient tug—years of practice at work—he yanked them off. The cold would eventually force his lazy Hunter to find real clothing.

It worked; Gilliam yowled and scrambled up, taking the clothing that Stephen held out when he discovered the blankets were permanently out of reach.

"Are you packed?"

"Hmmmm."

"Good." Just to be sure, Stephen checked the contents of Gilliam's chest. He cringed at the rolled up jacket and the inelegantly folded pants. It was a good thing that couples and leads didn't require any forethought or care to stow away.

"Stephen?"

Stephen let the lid bang shut and looked up without rising.

"You didn't wake me."

He knew that Gilliam was speaking of the dreams. "No."

"Did you have it?"

"What?"

"Don't 'what' like that. You know damn well I mean the third dream."

"If I'd had it, you'd probably know, don't you think?"

The set of Gilliam's lips told Stephen very well what he thought. Prevarication was not Gilliam's strong point, but Stephen had learned the art from observation—and Gil knew that as well. Stephen hesitated anyway, although he could feel Gilliam getting more annoyed as the seconds passed.

He had wanted to wait until after the Sacred Hunt before seeking his Hunter's advice. He still did. It was something that he could keep to himself now. The terror was gone—and the Sacred Hunt, as Norn had pointed out, was indeed more important. But he knew, looking at Gilliam's face, that it wouldn't be right. He suddenly thought of the pathetic, stupid young thief of Lady Alswaine's odd story—and the lesson that had peered, half-formed, from the corner of his understanding, came fully to light.

I have to trust you. "Yes. I dreamed the third."

Gilliam exhaled, and his face lost the black expression that always brought an argument and often meant the fist play so despised by Lady Elseth. "But you aren't afraid of it now."

"Just a little. I—it was different, this time. The figure in blue removed the hood—and it was a she. She said her name was Evayne. She looked, I don't know, sad." He felt his stomach start to rumble and glanced at the door. "She said she'd help me if she could."

"Help you what?"

"I don't know." He shrugged. "And if we don't get downstairs for breakfast, we won't be around to find out. Norn's—"

"I *know* what Norn's been saying." Gilliam shoved his feet into his boots, and Stephen made sure that his breeches were neatly tucked in.

"We can talk after the Sacred Hunt—if we're both still alive." He smiled then, and it was genuine. "I mean, wouldn't it be funny if I died? The wyrd—and all the worrying I've done—would mean nothing."

Gilliam didn't think it was funny at all.

Krysanthos rose early as well. He often liked to rise and be fully awake by the coming of the dawn, but on this occasion it was more a matter of necessity than one of preference. The court would be ready to begin its long procession through the city streets, and he had to be among them.

He had had little opportunity, for the entirety of the two-week festival, to speak with the young Elseth huntbrother alone, and that worried him. It seemed too much of a coincidence that someone—or something—had consistently contrived to prevent his access. This single fact would have annoyed him, but it did not stand alone. The little maid had searched the boy's rooms at all hours, and found nothing that would give either magical vision or magical protection. The huntbrother had obviously managed to protect himself—which meant that he was dangerous.

Very well; he was a danger. Krysanthos smiled. Today, during the Sacred Hunt, the boy was, by law, placing his life at risk. There was always at least one death—but on occasion, there were more.

He managed to finish the onerous task of dressing well before the knock at the door sounded. It was precise, soft, and timely. Unlike many of the visiting dignitaries, Krysanthos traveled without a valet. He was forced to answer the door himself.

A slender young man in the blue and gray of messenger's garb bowed low. "Your pardon, sir, for this early interruption, but I bear a message that is most urgent."

"Please, come in," Krysanthos replied, holding out a hand.

The man rose and entered the room as Krysanthos stepped out of the way. The rolled sheet of vellum he placed in the mage-born's hand had no seal or distinguishing marks, although it was tied with black ribbon. Krysanthos gestured and the door swung shut.

The messenger nodded and stood, hands behind his back, waiting for a reply.

"You're almost early," Krysanthos' voice was casual as he looked at the message that slowly unfurled in his hands. One peppered brow rose, and he looked up. "This is more than your usual fee."

The messenger shrugged, neither affronted nor nervous. The long, thin lines of his face were like a mask; even the gray eyes were cold and still. "You've given little notice, and less chance to prepare."

Little notice, indeed. And he was exhausted with the

effort of that sending, too soon a̲
Sor na Shannen. "Ah, well. It wa̲
Krysanthos rolled the sheet into a
Kovaschaii were the best at their craft; wh̲
been spent in the training and perfection of then̲
won't mind if I ask to see your mark?"

Without a change of expression, the man compl̲d,
pulling white-blond hair away from the left side of his
face. There, shadowed by the arch of his ear, was the
small chalice that had once been burned into flesh.

Krysanthos gestured briefly, although by now it was a
formality. At once, his sight shifted into the odd haze of
magical vision. The room went gray and misty. In the
background, the mirror he used for communication shone
out, a stark, bright beacon. Beneath the bed, he could also
see the halo of a walking stick. These were not his concern. Instead, he examined the mark of the Kovaschaii.

It, too, glowed softly and elegantly with magic's fire.
Light silvered it and rounded it, giving it the appearance
of a tiny, perfect chalice, which contained the Kovaschaii
strength.

"Very well," he said, and the lights went out. He stood
in silence for a few moments, considering the fee. There
was no argument to be offered. He could accept it or re-
ject it. The Kovaschaii did not negotiate.

"Very well," he said again. "I accept the conditions.
Ten thousand Essalieyanese solarii. Success only."

"Who?"

This part of the operation was the one which Krysanthos hated most. Were it not for this, he was certain he
would utilize the services of the Kovaschaii more frequently. As it was, only situations of urgency could force
him to it. Gritting his teeth, he let one of his unseen magical shields drop.

The nameless man stepped forward and reached out for
Krysanthos' forehead. He placed the flat of his palm
against it and closed his eyes.

Krysanthos knew the routine well. He needed—and
would suffer—no instructions. Luckily, the Kovaschaii
were excellent at observation about human nature, and
the young man did not make this mistake. The mage-born

...rated until he forced a perfect mental picture of Stephen of Elseth to the fore of his thoughts. With it came all of the rest of the details; the first meeting, the several attempts, the growing frustration.

And the Kovaschaii drank it in, searching through the undercurrents of associated thought until he was satisfied with the answer he'd received.

The moment the pressure of his hand was gone, Krysantho slammed his shields into place.

"The other?"

"Other?" It was said too quickly; Krysanthos forced his hands to stroke the length of his beard to still their shaking. Nowhere in his long studies had he found any sensation so distressing as this: another man, rummaging through the privacy of his thoughts. Ten thousand solarii? He would have paid double to have been able to avoid the intrusion. It was never an option.

"The Hunter."

"Ah—him." With care born of experience, Krysanthos did not mention the name that leaped to mind.

"They will be together."

"Yes," the mage replied. "But the mission you've accepted is to make the death of the huntbrother seem an entirely natural occurrence. Surely the Hunter is your problem."

Kovaschaii shoulders moved up and down in a graceful motion that was almost feline. He asked no further questions; he had no need to. He now knew everything that Krysanthos knew about the intended victim. Krysanthos handed him the scroll that he had arrived bearing and saw him out the door.

Only the matter of the maid was left to be dealt with, and that was relatively simple—certainly less costly.

If Stephen had thought that two weeks of festivity showed the Breodani Lords and Ladies at their finest, he was quickly proved wrong. From the moment he set foot in the dining hall, until the moment he left it, he observed everything in the near-silence of awe.

The Hunter Lords were properly dressed in clothing that was well crafted but serviceable; this was expected.

What was not was the added finery of capes and greatcloaks and strangely plumed hats that somehow managed to be multicolored without ever looking ridiculous against the background of green, brown, and hints of gold that comprised the Hunter's uniform.

Of course, after a few minutes of standing in their midst, the glitter of their wear vanished beneath the tense excitement of the soon-to-be-called Hunt. Conversation revolved around dogs, goals, battle plans. There was camaraderie, yes, but also competition, which had remained, until this moment, unspoken. One or two, younger Hunters to be sure, even mentioned the Hunter's Death as a type of prey. The older Hunter Lords said nothing, but a shadow passed over their faces, stilling them a moment before anticipation returned—the remembered costs of each passing year.

It was the Ladies and the attendants who lost none of their aura. When they entered the hall, whether on the arm of their Hunter, or attended by other companions, it was clear where the power in Breodanir lay. The older women, especially, walked with a grace and confidence that spoke of experience and easily accessible knowledge. They were comfortable talking of the Sacred Hunt, but equally comfortable arranging the last few bits of trade and barter, giving the final words of judgment advice or supping frugally on what was placed before them.

Gilliam had to elbow Stephen twice, hard, in the ribs when his attention strayed to the less relevant members of the huge hunting party.

Norn had looked sharply at Stephen when they finally appeared in the hall, but Stephen's curt and controlled nod seemed to satisfy him. The edge of the anger the older huntbrother had shown the day before—had it only been one day?—was blunted and put aside.

Stephen was keenly aware of the fact that Elseth put on no fine display. Both Norn and Soredon—heads of the Elseth responsibility—wore good, solid, serviceable spring cloaks. They were also incredibly dull.

Well, he'd talk with Lady Elseth about it when they got back to the manor, and if it could be afforded, they'd look better next year. He consoled himself with the fact that all

of the finery would vanish the minute the King's horn
was sounded. Then the Hunters would be measured by
their true worth, not by their clothing. Still . . .

The drums sounded in the distance, and the hall quieted
as all eyes turned to the doors. No horn sounded to an-
nounce the coming of the King—no horn would be
winded this day until the start of the Hunt.

But the drums did their work, beating in time like an
unnatural heart. The doors rolled open, and the King entered the room, the Queen by his side. He was clothed in
the colors of Breodanir, all dark greens and browns, but
his cloak and jacket were emblazoned across chest and
back with gold thread. He wore no cap, and his hair hung
in a single braid, beneath a simple circlet. Behind him,
pages carried two spears, one long and slender, one thick
with protrusions near its iron point.

The Queen had left behind the greens and browns; nor
did she choose a simple dress for the outdoor occasion.
She walked, in full skirts, like sunlight made human.
Gold brocade danced just above her boots, and lit around
her shoulders and arms like spreading fire. Where the
King wore a circlet, she wore a crown, and the jeweled
work, even from the back of the hall, bore the mark of the
maker-born. It was perfect.

The King raised his Lady's hand and stood facing the
gathered nobles. "We welcome you to the King's City,"
he said softly. "On this day we are called upon to prove
our ranks, and their worth, to our people. Will you follow?"

The hushed susurrus of assent filled the room, as did
the King's grave smile. He paused only once, his eyes
scanning the crowd, until he found the one he was searching for. Stephen met his gaze and bowed; it obscured his
eyes.

They left the palace, perhaps not in as orderly a fashion
as one would wish; there was subtle jockeying for position between the various landed Hunters. But it was kept
to a minimum, and by the time the procession, with carriages and footmen, banners and flags, reached the palace
gates, the dignity of the occasion prevailed.

The streets were lined. It seemed that everyone,

whether gainfully employed or not, bore witness to the passing procession. Some merchants had even taken the time to set up stalls and displays, although they didn't attract the nobles. The smell of food and ale was in the air, and the musicians that led the royal procession carried tunes that even the children here could sing; cradle songs, school songs—tunes of youthful fear and hope.

The dogs were growling in the wagons that carried them. Small children, whose age gave them some excuse, and large youths, whose age did not, approached the wheels and peered cautiously in to see snapping, white teeth.

Through dint of will, the Hunter Lords kept their packs contained—but as they prepared for the Sacred Hunt, with all of its little competitions, so, too, did the dogs.

Gilliam didn't have to worry about it for this hunt. Later, he would understand why the Hunter Lords grew testy and snappish as they rode by in their carriages, past plain small buildings, stalls, and real storefronts. Stephen, fulfilling the function of the absent Lady Elseth, reached out of his window and waved, keeping both his hands and his smile stiff and formal. One or two people waved back, but these were mostly the young, or the parents of the young who wished to teach them a friendly example. The oldest among the watchers only inclined their heads gravely, standing as if in salute, which, indeed, they were.

It was a bright, clear day—crisp and cool, which was to be expected. Some of the lords and ladies rode in open carriages and smiled as if they little minded the chill bite of the cold breeze. They had furs, mind, and cloaks that were up to spring's test.

Stephen thought an open carriage would be splendid, but knew that it would have to wait until Maribelle was of age and she and Lady Elseth came to the court in person. Hunters just didn't have the necessary pomp and circumstance about them to merit it on their own.

But he thought better of it when he realized just how exposed the lack of a roof above his head would make him; one open side window was enough. He waved until his arm was sore, and then continued to wave, thinking that it couldn't be much farther. To his amazement, the line of gathered well-wishers continued right up to the city gates that led north—and beyond that, as farmers and those who did not dwell within the King's City also lined the road to pay their respects.

The villagers, for such they were, were old-fashioned and not so prone to the casual ways of the city dwellers. The older folk bowed, hatless, and held their bows until the last member of the procession rode by.

Of course, the younger children tailed after the last carriage with happy little yowls of delight, until caught by their grandparents, which didn't happen in the city either.

Outside of the preserve, gardeners had been at work since the snows had melted, clearing away dead branches, old leaves, and the occasional remains of winter food the forest's predators had left behind. There were no trees here. They had been cut down and uprooted centuries past, and none were allowed to encroach. Seedlings which were lucky enough to survive the northerly climate's snow and wind did not escape the gardeners and the wardens.

The ground was soft and damp, and tended toward mud in some places, but the King's servants were up to the task they excelled in. New grass had already been laid—at great expense—and the King's pavilion, with its flat planks and colorful tents, was visible the moment the road came to an end. Flowers, carefully tended to indoors in the off-season, had been planted and arranged so as to be in their glory for the arrival of the nobles. The pits were ready, and would not remain empty past the late afternoon. Stones lined them, and the spits that served to grill meat for the feast were already set up.

A dais that was neither simple nor new had been erected. Only one throne sat upon it, not the customary two, and it was clearly not meant for the King.

The King and Queen were the first to disembark, as they led the procession. The King dismounted first, setting both feet on the ground before turning to offer his Lady his hand.

The Queen came out like the sun, and if her smile was slightly sad, only the footmen saw it, and they never commented. They bowed, and held their bows as their monarchs walked by, her hand on his stiff forearm. The King led her up to the dais and to the throne. There, he withdrew his arm, and as she sat—with the help of two attendants who managed to stay in the background while they arranged her billowing skirts—he, too, bowed, falling to one knee. She reached out, and placed the tips of her fingers against his velvet hood, pushing it back and away from his hair.

For a few moments, in the silence of the cool dawn, she was all of the waiting Ladies, and he all of the Hunters at risk—both of whom had seen too many deaths to make any promises or any wishes known.

And then their somber silence was rudely broken by the thrum of harp strings struck badly for just that purpose. Without so much as a by-your-leave, a very young man holding a harp at his hip as if it were a comfortable sack, leaped up onto the dais, singing. His hair was soft, burnished gold, which fell in ringlets past his shoulders in such a perfect way that some of the younger Ladies watched with envy—and interest. He moved with grace, surety, and speed, and somehow managed to toss the edge of his pale gray cloak over his shoulder without interrupting the music.

Unfortunately, he was singing the song that most peasants knew as "The Drunken Hunter," a ribald and silly little ditty that one didn't sing around one's mother. His voice, perfect in pitch and sweet in tone, carried so that even those farthest from the King and Queen could hear it clearly. This was the talent of the bard-born, and by his brazen act, rather than by any symbol of any college, Kallandras the bard made himself known.

Shock kept the Lords silent, and the Ladies kept straight faces, although one or two of the younger girls shook silently behind spread fans, which made it impossible to tell whether they were crying or laughing.

But the Queen laughed gaily, and the sparkle in her eyes made it clear that the cheek of the young bard did no damage to her good opinion of him. The king raised an eyebrow, but made no comment as he gained his feet. Kallandras' voice was so buoyant and cheerful, it was a

delight to listen to, even wrapped as it was around such
a questionable series of stanzas.

For his finish, he coaxed from his harp a series of notes
that seemed impossible, and then bowed with a flourish,
drawing his small cap down and across his chest in the
manner of those from the East. A smattering of applause
followed, mostly from the Ladies and the servants.

"Kallandras, why have you come?" The Queen held
out one slender hand, her expression making clear her
welcome, as the question did not. He took it gracefully,
brought it to his lips, and smiled.

"Did you think I would miss such a festive occasion
without just cause? I've decided to accept your invitation,
Majesty. What other opportunity have I," he added, lowering his voice, "to spend so much time surrounded by
such elegant and powerful Ladies—without the interference of their husbands?"

"Have a care, young minstrel," the King said, mock-
sternly. "You give the studious and serious bards a poor
name."

"Indeed I do, Highness," was the reply. "But it's not
half so bad as the names they give—well, call—me."

Stephen, who had edged as close to the dais as he
dared, realized that the stories the servants told of the
bard-born were true: They would say anything at all, no
matter how improper or inappropriate, and give no of-
fense. Kallandras' voice was filled with a warmth and
friendliness that permeated every word he spoke in the
presence of the highest powers in the land. And they,
King and Queen, could not help but respond.

"And who is the young eavesdropper?" Kallandras said
quietly. The voice changed; it still held warmth, mixed
now with curiosity—but beneath that there was something as cool as steel.

Stephen started as the bard turned to look directly at
him. Then he cringed as the gazes of the King and Queen
followed.

"The young man? He's huntbrother to Lord Gilliam of
Elseth. Stephen?" The word, from the King's lips, had the
force of command.

Stephen walked to the side of the dais and quietly

mounted the steps. He took care with his cloak—the last thing he wanted, in front of personages such as these, was to trip or stumble.

"Stephen. Of Elseth." The bard came forward as Stephen hesitated, too aware that he had the attention of all of the Hunters and their Ladies. "I'm Kallandras of Senniel." He frowned when it was obvious that the name of the most illustrious of all bardic colleges meant nothing to the young huntbrother. That frown rippled and deepened; it became distant and cool once again.

This close to the bard, it was clear to Stephen that that coolness was not directed at him. He waited because he had nothing to say, and after a moment, Kallandras smiled wistfully. "I'm pleased to make your acquaintance, Lord Stephen." His voice was full, his bow, low. "I've heard about you."

Stephen's mouth formed a half "o" of surprise. He opened his mouth to speak, and the bard's ringlets shifted with the shake of his head. "Not now, huntbrother—you and I have other duties at the moment, or so the King's glare tells me."

The King was not glaring. "Duties? You?"

"Ah, yes. Didn't someone tell you?"

"Tell me?" The King turned his head to meet his wife's gaze. She smiled a little ruefully and nodded. "Tell me what?"

"It is almost the call of the Sacred Hunt. I join the drummers, Your Highness." Now, for the first time in the King's presence, Kallandras fell to one knee. "I will sing the Hunt's beginning with your permission, Master of the Game."

"And will your bard-born voice soothe the Hunter's Death and stave off the fulfillment of our promise?" It was said in jest, or at least it appeared so, but Stephen could see that the King's eyes did not smile with his lips.

"No. But perhaps I will give heart to your Hunters."

"And perhaps to our God." The King looked up to meet Iverssen's gaze. They locked stares for a moment, and then the Priest looked away. "Yes, if you will. Sing the Hunt's beginning." He reached up and unclasped his cloak. Before it left his shoulders, two attendants were behind him to smooth and preserve the folds of green velvet. "But, Kallandras?"

"Yes, Highness?"

"I charge you to do at the end what you claim you will do at the beginning. Lend heart to my Hunters."

To this, Kallandras had no reply. He nodded again, and bowed his head low until the King passed by him. When he heard the royal feet upon the stairs, he looked up to meet the solemn eyes of the Queen.

He mouthed a few words, and the Queen's eyes rose.

"No," she whispered. "*Not* 'The Drunken Hunter.' "

The drums began their sonorous roll at the edge of the clearing farthest from the preserve. The Hunter Lords had returned with their lymers—the best of the scent hounds in the kingdom. They had chosen their quarry well, if quickly, and all that remained was the Hunt. The huntbrothers coupled the dogs while their masters prepared as the drums beat on. It was an odd sound; steady and yet somehow almost musical. If the forest had a pulse, this was it: wild and primitive and endless.

The Ladies, those present, gave tokens to their Lords and wished them well—but it took mere minutes. The Lords were already in trance, and too far away from anything that was not either dog or huntbrother.

Stephen held the couples and every so often nudged a dog in the ribs with his boot. Terwel was the worst of the lot and could barely be kept from springing the leash and dragging his companion with him. He had sighted a competitor he dearly wished to test himself against—the big, red-brown hound that Lord Alswaine boasted as his pride.

Alair. That was his name.

Gilliam turned to stare wide-eyed at the leader of his borrowed pack. Terwel's growl grew stronger, but he settled back into the lead; the Hunt was close, he would soon be allowed to run and track and feed. Today was not the time to test the son of the master.

The strain in Stephen's upper arms and shoulders lessened. Freed from the intense worry and concentration the large gray alaunt demanded, he looked up to watch

Gilliam's face. What he saw was the Hunter in trance. It was time, now, to join him.

He closed his eyes, and as sight left him nothing but the faint red-black beneath his eyelids, sound grew stronger. The drumbeats grew louder and more insistent, although they remained steady and rhythmic. He felt his own pulse racing to catch time, and felt one other join it. He could almost hear the whisper of the dogs, almost taste the absolute necessity to be free of the couples, hunting the running, jumping, cloven-hoofed, frightened prey. He felt energy, excitement, overweening pride—and none of it was his. Shaking his head, he pulled back. His eyes flew open and he saw the clearing as it was: full of dogs and men, the former gray and brown, black and occasionally white—the latter, green, brown, and gold. He did not understand, in that moment, how Gilliam could live in the Hunter's trance; just the taste of it, seen through their oath-bond, alarmed him, and if he regretted not being born to the Hunter God's service, he also felt relief.

And then he heard it: The single, haunting note of the King's horn. It shattered the noise that Stephen had barely been aware of and, before silence could settle, continued with three shorter ones.

In answer, the Hunter Lords drew their horns, and lifted them as one man. Stephen was no musician, but he knew that the absolute perfection of timing, of inhale, start, and stop, should have been impossible. He waited until the drums commanded the air once again before fumbling at his belt. The horn the King had given him was cold to the touch against both fingers and lips. He drew breath around the mouthpiece and expelled it forcefully. One short note. One long. Two short notes. One long.

In the forest, the shadows stirred; the leaves rustled, unusually loud with the force of the wind and the morning. Stephen felt something *snap* into place as the notes died away. Almost reluctantly, he tied the horn to his belt once more.

The tenor of the drumming changed; single strikes became staggered and flew faster and faster against the

skins until, at the unseen hands of the Hunter Priests, the
clearing was filled with the roar of thunder. The sun and
the clarity of sky were anomalous; the Hunters of
Breodanir entered the storm.

And behind them, almost at one with them, flowed
dogs and huntbrothers alike.

CHAPTER THIRTEEN

Soredon walked the preserve with the ease of familiarity. At his side, unleashed and barely collared, walked Corwel. Even with his nose to the ground and his bandit's mask flecked with mud, his gait was regal.

The Lord of Elseth had chosen his quarry well enough; without the need to discuss the Hunt with any but Norn, it had been a gentle and quiet operation. He was certain that he would have a good, brisk walk ahead of him. Again, familiarity told him that the northern preserve was where he would find his stag.

Corwel was peaceful as well, if quick, but every so often he would stop and look up at his master, the glint of curiosity in his black eyes.

"This is your last hunt, old boy," Soredon whispered sadly. "Let's make it count." He used words, instead of trance-speaking. Corwel wouldn't understand them, but he needed the release of saying them anyway.

Norn's familiar footstep, not as quiet or as sure as his own, was gaining ground. He shook his head, scratched Corwel's ears affectionately, and then gave himself completely to the Hunt.

It was going to be hard to fulfill the Hunt's promise. The sound of the horns and the beat of the drums had pierced the forest's stillness, an absolute warning to any who heard it, whether they'd listened for it or no. The sounds lingered, caught in Stephen's chest and inner ears.

Gilliam moved quickly and, after the initial exhilarating run into the undergrowth, slowly. Absynt walked in front of him, nose to the ground, a single collar around his gray throat. He was older now, but the most important of the senses were still his to claim; he followed Gilliam's chosen trail without wavering once. Indeed, he pulled at the leash as if it vexed him, and after a few moments, Gilliam gave him his head. He made no sign to Stephen to uncouple the rest of the dogs; his concentration had to be reserved for Absynt alone.

The tracks, deep and evenly spaced in the soft ground, spoke of the size and unworried pace of the stag. They were fresh, which was more important. Absynt followed them without any difficulty at all.

Now that the other dogs were out of sight, and for the moment, out of hearing, Terwel had settled back into his couple. He wasn't graceful about it, and every so often he shouldered Stephen almost hard enough to knock him over—but not quite. He knew he could make his displeasure known to a point, but not beyond that, before he brought the anger of his young master, and although he was a dog, he remembered the one time that he had been forcibly denied the Hunt.

Stephen felt Gilliam tense and looked up. He felt a ripple of dismay and knew its cause at once: the tracks had widened suddenly; the stag had already bolted.

Hard? he thought, as he picked up his pace. It was going to be impossible. And today, of all days, they dared not fail. He nodded at Gilliam, caught Gilliam's return nod and the flash of his back as the Hunter and Absynt ran on ahead.

The Kovaschaii was also a hunter, and if his lessons had been in the labyrinths of Melesnea, and his training had been in the city streets and parlors of Averalaan, it would have been hard to tell. He wore Hunter's colors, less the gold, and he moved with his back to the shadows and an eye to the light. Birds saw him pass without comment or movement, treating him as just another predator who was not interested in their mates or their growing nests.

He had seen the huntbrother enter the sacred preserve on the heels of his Hunter, and he trailed them quietly. The dogs, coupled and held, were upwind; with care, they would not catch his unfamiliar scent and give warning.

He had to make sure that they were run in the Hunt proper before he approached his target—he made a practice of disarming his victims before a kill. The Kovaschaii were cautious.

The sun was barely above the horizon, but the trees here were thin and too new to provide good cover; his shadow was long and moved against the forest's patterns. He disliked it. But more, he disliked the sound of the other Hunters who had entered the forest at nearly the same point as his target. He had to avoid being seen by any. It was not the optimum situation.

Ah. There. He stopped when a flash of green, surrounded by four-legged browns and grays, came into view. His chest stopped moving; he stood as the trees did, but without their little rustles. Then the Elseth huntbrother was gone again, but he waited five minutes before picking up the trail. Timing was of the essence.

They jogged. The dogs weren't bothered by it, and Gilliam didn't notice at all. Stephen took deep and even breaths, forcing his feet into a steady rhythm. He held the dogs to his pace, knowing it dangerous to let them gain control here. They strained at the leads, testing his strength. Gilliam had vanished; the thin line of trees hid him from Stephen's vision. But the hounds knew where he was, and they followed unerringly.

Perhaps half an hour passed in the forced and silent jog before Gilliam appeared. He spoke no word, but by the signal made clear that all was well. Once again, the stag had slowed to a less frenetic pace. They could follow and hope to catch it at harbor.

Stephen breathed a sigh of relief—it was all the breath he could spare.

Ten minutes later, they came to the river.

From the cover of trees that were a little too thin for comfort, the Kovaschaii watched the Elseth huntbrother at the river's edge. Silt and mud were carried by the water's rush, and the banks were completely covered in the swell caused by melted snow.

It would be a good place to drown, if one slipped. The

single bridge across the river was nothing more than flat slats; there were no railings, no way to grab hold. And it was almost ideal. The young Hunter was far enough ahead that he could not be seen. Certainly, he would not be able to interfere.

But the boy still held the dogs.

The wind shifted, and the Kovaschaii shifted with it as if caught in the breeze. He lost his moment as the boy, dogs still in hands that appeared to be shaking, crawled his way across the bridge. Another passing minute brought the Hunter; he spoke, but the words could not be heard naturally, and the Kovaschaii wished to preserve his reserves of power. The meaning of the words became obvious soon enough. The young huntbrother uncoupled two of the dogs, and unleashed the only animal that did not share a lead. These three went immediately to the banks and began to nose around.

He crossed his arms, watching with interest. He could wait. The Hunt, or the running of it, had not yet started— and once it had, the huntbrother would bring up the rear in a very vulnerable position.

What?

Corwel's ears were twitching, and the hair on his neck seemed to stand on end. He raised his head, stopping astride the tracks that had led him this far. The scent was strong enough to linger in his nostrils, but it was . . . odd.

Soredon moved into Corwel, following the lines of his trance until their two senses were all scent-hound. The green and brown of forest, with its interplay of shadow and light, became gray shades. The ripple of muscles that gathered around neck and jaw hurt.

Yes. Something was strange. In the familiarity of this Hunt, a new element had appeared. Soredon tried to place a finger on it—he was certain that he had felt it before— but it eluded him.

"Soredon?"

He shook his head, calling for Norn's silence and receiving it at once. He tested the air, touched the tracks, and then slid out of Corwel's viewpoint.

"We hunt," he said softly, as his hand fell once again

to the wide, rounded head of his pack's leader. The words, a motto of the life he best loved, came out as if they were suddenly too large for his mouth. They were not for Norn, but Norn heard them anyway.

"Maybe we should leave this trail," he said, his voice quiet. "There were many that bore our interest."

But Soredon shook his head once, fierce in the motion, and urged Corwel forward. There was a light in his eyes, a ferocity in his step, that even Gilliam in the flush of first youth couldn't match. Budding leaves played against his face with their shadows, blocking the light; it made a phantom mask appear against his pale skin.

He looked not unlike Corwel as they continued along the track.

The stag was not young enough to be foolish, but not old enough to lose a seasoned hunting pack, and although it took time—and a backtrack across the river—Absynt found its trail again. His ears pricked up, his breath changed subtly, and he looked back at Gilliam with guileless pride. Gilliam wanted to leap with joy; he was wet from the river's edge, and cold as well, but at least it had not been without cause.

Stephen knew, of course. His sigh was louder than Absynt's, but just as unmistakable. "Gil?"

"What?"

"You'll be okay?"

Gilliam nodded. He had had to hold four dogs, jumping between them as they searched. It had been tiring, and would only get worse. The dogs had not yet been unleashed, and he would have to run at their head when he finally set them baying.

Stephen grimaced and hit himself in the side of the head for Gilliam's benefit. It had been a stupid question. If Gilliam were dropping from exhaustion, it wouldn't have made a difference; the Hunt had to be called, and it had to be run. This one day, no excuses would be tolerable—or tolerated.

The sun was well up by now, which warmed the ground and made it less pleasant to traverse. Stephen slipped once, but even that didn't slow them down. He jogged along, mud caked and drying along his back. His breath, short and sharp, came out in a mist that wreathed his face.

And then, in the distance, they saw it: a brown, fur-covered creature that had suddenly frozen in the wind, the white underside of its tail twitching. Its head turned in three-quarter relief, and large brown eyes met smaller ones unhindered by thin strands of trees.

Gilliam gave a wordless cry of excitement mingled with relief. His nervous fingers fumbled with his horn before it could be brought to his lips. The stag was gone in the blink of an eye. It left its tracks and the sound of its passing as evidence of its presence.

It was late to start the call, but the dogs lost all trace of exhaustion. They came to the Hunt as called, fresh and new—eager to prove themselves.

Stephen knelt, mud ignored, and uncoupled the dogs. His fingers trembled, not with cold—he'd barely removed mittens that practically made his hands sweat—but with anxiety. This was their first Hunt, their first act as real adults. They had to make it count.

Absynt was last to be freed, but he made way for Terwel, as did the other dogs that had gathered. Gilliam kept them in, but barely—they strained against his trance-voice as if it were merely the noise a groom made.

Stephen saw a flash of anger in his Hunter's eyes and bit his lip. *Not now, Terwel,* he thought, half-savagely. *We don't have the time.*

But the time had to be taken. Gilliam made them sit a full quarter-minute in order to show his control. He had no choice, this close to the quarry. Anything else ran the highest risk of an improperly finished Hunt. Not catching a beast was bad, but not portioning it properly was nearly as big a crime; it showed the Hunter's lack of control and will.

If we fail at this, Terwel, Stephen thought, as his hands formed fists in harmony with his thoughts, *I'll kill you myself.*

But the seconds passed, ending abruptly with Terwel's high, short whine. Gilliam's eyes shifted and changed; they grew strange even to his huntbrother.

The horn was winded. At last. Stephen had time to draw breath and brace himself before the pack was off and running, Gilliam at its head. He could barely hear, over the baying of the running dogs, the sound that left Gilliam's throat. It was a poor twin to their call, but he knew that Gilliam wouldn't notice.

He twined the leads carefully and shoved them into his jacket as he ran, trying to keep pace with dogs held back too long and a Hunter in trance. The gap widened between them, but Stephen had training to make up for the lack of blood-granted abilities—he lost ground perceptibly, but was not left behind.

Now.

The Kovaschaii felt the moment coming. He heard the horn call, and almost rolled out into sight before the notes had faded. Almost. Instinct whispered no, and he listened carefully, snapping his joints to a stop and drawing, finally, upon his many talents.

The terrain in the preserve was not always flat; indeed, small hills and short outcroppings that could almost be dignified by the name cliff abounded. The ground was slippery in places, more mud than dirt, and the undergrowth was new. A careless, anxious huntbrother, back from his Hunter and pack, might slip and fall in unfortunate foot play.

He came out upon the trail and began to jog in Stephen's wake. He kept pace with the boy, his eyes scanning the distance between his prey and the dogs. The gap was widening, but not as quickly as the Kovaschaii had hoped. Still, that couldn't last—the Hunter-born were known for their speed and endurance while hunting. Huntbrothers, such as the young Elseth one, were merely trained commoners.

The Kovaschaii had drawn no weapon, although by custom he carried three; he needed none for his chosen accident. He only need wait and strike quickly; it was that simple. But the boy was still too close to his Hunter.

The tenor of the dogs' raucous calls changed in pitch and frequency. He saw them disappear suddenly on their run, and realized that the time had come. They had

crested a hill of some sort, and the huntbrother was due
to follow.

A surge of energy, of otherworld calm, sizzled through
his body. He heard its tingle with his inner ear, and re-
joiced. It was time for silence, swiftness, accuracy; the
carefully hoarded reserve was drained as he put on his
last burst of speed and cloaked himself, momentarily,
from normal sight. It required no gesture, no mantra, no
foci—he was Kovaschaii, perfectly trained and aimed.

A foot from the boy's back, he raised his hand; it was
hard, flat—as much a weapon as a sword might have
been.

"HOLD!"

The arm stopped in midair, but not by the will of the
Kovaschaii. Pain shot up through elbow and shoulder at
the speed of his response. Anger, mixed with a foreign
emotion, danced in lines across his pale face. He tried to
force the hand down, to follow through on the imperative
of his given mission, and failed. The fair-haired youth
was already turning. His victim's motions were so pain-
fully slow—a gift of the Kovaschaii magics—they stoked
the fires of the assassin's anger. His plan had been perfect. There had been no interference, no followers, no
witnesses. It was ash now, burned as if touched by the anger that had momentarily shorted control. He watched as
the boy threw himself—again, slowly, slowly—off the
trail and out of reach of the fatal strike.

Defeat, then.

The Kovaschaii spun on his feet in the direction of the
single inimical word, casually relocating the joint in his
arm. Only the voice of one bard-born and bard-trained
had such raw and immediate power. He felt it still, although he could now deny its strength. He struggled to
cast anger aside, and this time succeeded. Implacable, his
face once again the cool, seamless mask, he met the eyes
of Kallandras the bard.

The fair-haired man in Hunter's garb was inches away.
His arm trembled awkwardly, like a branch in a stiff
wind, but Stephen barely noticed this; his gaze was
caught by a face of sharp, pale lines. It was calm, almost

still, but its eyes were a gleam of light over steel—
inhuman and dangerous. With a cry, Stephen threw himself to the side, forgetting the stag, the Hunter, and the
pack. He rolled through the mud and came to his feet a
little way off the track, his hands the color of dead bark
and dirt. He looked wildly over his shoulder, as he had
done many, many times as a thief in the lower city. Fear
brought back memory, and made of it a sharp, clear
weapon. There was no pursuit. He tensed further, brought
himself around, and saw why.

Kallandras the bard stood astride the trail, hands on his
hips, head tilted in the chill breeze. His hair, shoulder-
length curls of gold-flecked brown, rustled and blew
round his cheeks. Stephen thought it singularly stupid;
long hair, especially in a fight of any note, was an idiotic
risk.

But if there was any fear of risk in Kallandras, it was
buried well beneath a jaunty, arrogant smile.

"Well met, Estravim." His voice, rich, deep, and warm,
performed an invisible bow.

"It *is* you, Kallatin," the young man answered quietly.
The tone of voice made a curse of the words in its intensity.

"Oh, yes," Kallandras answered, still in the same
friendly tone. Stephen's eyes could only see the blur of
white sleeves—billowing, more fool the bard—and
Kallandras was suddenly armed. His weapon was a
sword, of sorts—it was long and seemed far too thin to be
dangerous. "I have your name." He whispered, but the
bardic voice carried the words easily.

The smooth lines of the pale man's face rippled uncertainly. Stephen thought he saw fear until he heard the
young man's words. "You *cannot* take a name now, traitor." He moved, and he, too, carried a sword that was, in
shape if not in guard, the twin of Kallandras'.

"I have your name." The answer was implacable. The
bard moved suddenly, covering yards of trail in long
strides that barely left time for feet to touch ground.

And this, too, Stephen understood. The other man was
moving easily as quickly—toward Stephen. The blade
that he carried suddenly seemed a significant weapon.

Stephen reversed himself, using the tree for interference as he ran. His cloak caught a branch, and he heard an awful tearing at his ankles. If he had the chance to explain it later, he'd consider himself lucky.

The Kovaschaii was furious. He followed the hunt-brother, quickly catching up with him. As the boy dodged behind a tree, he corrected his path. It took no time and no thought; pursuit was the earliest teaching.

He knew that if he reached the boy now and managed to kill him, he would still fail in his taking. It was bitter knowledge; he would dance the death spiral yet, and it would be his own. But he also knew that Kallatin—the blackest name in the history of the Kovaschaii—was here to protect his victim. If he were to fail in his taken name, Kallatin, also, would fail. That much he would see to. Kallatin the traitor had barely completed the first—and the lowest—tier of training before he had disgraced the brotherhood by refusing a kill—and by vanishing into complex shadows and magic that even the Masters could not follow.

Estravim the Kovaschaii was of the third tier, and proud of it; he was young to be so skilled. But pride was not foolishness. He knew that the voice of the bard-born, from the throat of one Kovaschaii trained, would soon be his death.

He called on the last of his reserves, called up a power that he was never meant to touch, and used it. The boy's progress slowed to near-halting; even strands of flailing hair ceased their struggle with the breeze. A second passed, maybe two, and the sword was raised above the back of the huntbrother's neck, just as the arm had been earlier.

It came down in stillness and silence.

The clang of metal against metal was unmistakable as it reverberated to fill his ears. Time started to turn again; the boy's back began to retreat. Estravim stared into the eyes of Kallatin the traitor. He spat.

Spittle, completely ignored, ran down the cheek of Kallandras the bard as he pulled back his blade and twisted it in the air.

Signal: now. Gesture, respect from one of lower tier to higher.

Estravim stepped into position with grace and deadly ease. He should not have granted the bard that respect, and he knew it—but it was automatic.

Kallandras held his blade in his right hand. His fingers shifted beneath the guard, his grip changed, and in a flick of motion, the tip of the sword cut his forehead, leaving a scant trail of blood in its wake. With his free hand, he gestured, a snap of motion from wrist to elbow that drove the cuff of his shirtsleeve momentarily up his forearm, revealing a slender bracer. Gold melded with silver glinted in the dull light; each termination of the ten-point star— the symbol of the Kovaschaii—glittered. The sword fell slowly, point to ground, and wavered in the wind—but Estravim knew that Kallandras drew the foci of the ten-point star in the air like a sigil. Challenge. And it was a challenge that Estravim could not avoid.

No Kovaschaii of the first tier would have been able to draw this sigil. A grimace tugged at the corners of his mouth, and he spoke, although this, too, was foolish. "How?"

"Second tier," Kallandras whispered, his eyes remote.

"No master would train you. . . ." Words failed him, and his anger, stiff to the point of breaking, shattered. He saw the star traced, could not help but see the beads of blood that struggled waywardly down a nose that had been broken at least once. With a motion twin to the bard's, he snapped his wrist. He also wore the golden manacle of the Kovaschaii—but he had the right to bear it. He wanted to decry the bard's use of the symbol, but again the words would not come. For he looked at the eyes of his enemy; they were very blue, very pale. Beneath their slate surface was a hint of sorrow, a touch of shame. Estravim grimly traced the ten-point star, taking it from memory and engraving it in the air. His response. "How could you choose treachery? We were brothers."

At the use of the familiar term, Kallandras winced. "I am wyrd-ridden. I was shown what the death of the woman would bring us to: the end of the Kovaschaii— and the end of the world."

"You were shown lies."

"I was shown truth. For nothing less would I have left you." His blade came up and he lunged.

"Even so—what of it? We are guaranteed to the Lady." Estravim dodged and blocked, the movement turning to a thrust at the halfway mark. He felt steel against his skin before it entered; it was a cool, clean pain. He smiled anyway. He could see the spread of crimson across the bard's cheek. They had each called blood; each touched in the step of this intricate, ancient dance.

Kallandras nodded grimly and began in earnest. Beads of sweat had time to line his brow and cheeks as he fought. Estravim was good—had always been good—and he attacked like one possessed. Because, of course, he was.

Here, in the open spaces of sparse woods and flat ground, Estravim gave in to his training; his sword grew wings, and the wind ran down the runnels along the crescent in a sibilant song that the Kovaschaii were trained to listen for. There was art in his movements, and in his attack; he chose the grace of line and action that was only displayed among equals. It didn't change the ferocity of his weapon-play, but rather, made an art of it.

Kallandras, in defense, could not come up with half of the beauty and artistry that Estravim displayed in attack.

But that grace couldn't last; the man who had once been called Kallatin knew it. Estravim had exhausted reserves of power that no Kovaschaii, not resigned to death, could call. That he could attack so perfectly spoke of his skill and his determination.

Estravim knew it, too—and his attack was a dance, almost a farewell. One second, he was dodging in midair, his feet clearing the ground by a good twenty inches, and the next, he was looking down the blade of the sword that ended—or started—in his chest.

"So soon?" His eyes shuttered and dimmed immediately; his face twisted in a pain that had nothing to do with the physical.

"I will remember. You had no equal here."

A smile broke through the pain before his eyes rolled up. Kallandras stared down at him as he started to fall.

* * *

The clash and clang of swordplay stopped abruptly; the silence that followed was chilling. Stephen watched, his face at knee level, his body obscured by the trunk of the largest tree he had found.

The assassin had just stopped in mid-step, as if asking for a deathblow. Kallandras' sword appeared out of nowhere to grant the man his request. The pale man sank to the ground, his knees bending and giving under his weight. Kallandras watched for a moment and then suddenly cursed. He yanked the sword free—sending a spray of red droplets across the ground—and threw the sword, hard.

It landed inches away from Stephen's hand.

He barely noticed. Rising slowly, he began to retrace his steps, twice tripping over small inclines. His eyes were upon the bard.

Kallandras, in an odd mimicry of the assassin's slow crumple, knelt to the ground and stretched out his arms to catch the body. Where the wound was open, blood splashed his breast. He ignored it as he gathered the body close, and cradled it against his chest. He heard Stephen coming and looked back. Only the trail of drying crimson across his forehead colored his face at all; even his eyes were flat and colorless.

"Go," he whispered. "This is not for you."

Stephen heard the anger in his voice and stopped moving. "I—thank you for—"

"Don't say it." Kallandras rose, still holding the body. "This is not for you, young huntbrother. *Go.*"

Stephen swallowed.

"It's been minutes," Kallandras said, as he lay the body down. "You won't have lost them if you run." He stiffened as Stephen hesitated. **"Go."**

This time, confused or no, Stephen had no choice; the meaning of the word was made manifest in a way that no other spoken word had ever been. His legs were moving, his feet following the trail broken by dogs and Gilliam both—without his guidance.

And he was weeping. Tears coursed down his cheeks, warming them before wind turned them to ice.

It was how he knew that Kallandras' smooth, pale face really was a mask over private pain; the bard hadn't been able to keep the grief out of his command.

He was ashamed. To use the voice on the boy was inexcusable; a poor display of self-control if ever there was one. But he had no time; the Kovaschaii spirit awaited its death dance, and there were none here but he to give it.

None here yet, he reminded himself. The Kovaschaii knew when one of their number had fallen. They would come as soon as possible unless the dance was done. Cradling the head gently, he stroked the hair out of the slack face. He sat thus a moment, contemplating. Then he shook himself. He had no right to dance the death, but he wanted to anyway.

The arms and legs he arranged properly, until they formed four points of a star, to the fifth point Estravim's still face made. Then he rose lithely, for all that he was out of practice, and hesitantly began to trace the five secret points—the five that completed the ten. His movements grew more sure as he progressed, his feet leaving shadows across Estravim's body without ever disturbing his rest. He opened his lips and began to sing.

Singing was common, and part of the death dance— and if Kallandras, who had been Kallatin, had never been particularly graceful at the challenge or the attack, none had sung a better death than he. Wordless sorrow, endless loss, a blackness the night fled from—all these rose in him, contained by the thrum of throat and the shape of lip.

Faster and faster he flew, his arms like wings, his face the Kovaschaii mask. But the mask was cracked, imperfect; tears fled it, leaving the face unchanged in their passage.

Come, Lady, come. He danced.

Set my brother free; grant him passage.

He danced, and the world shifted; the forest fell away into mist and gray softness that humans had no words for. He sang, and the mist took shape on the periphery of the ten-point star.

"Who calls?" a toneless voice whispered. "Who wishes to meet me in the half-world?"

He spun to a standstill, one foot on either side of Estravim's face. "I do."

"And you?"

He squinted but the mists fogged his eyes, becoming both solid and less substantial. "I am Kallatin. Lady, you hold my name."

And suddenly, the mist unraveled and fell away from his eyes like gauze too thin to trap sight. He saw *her,* and she him. Hair, so dark a black that ebony seem faded beside it, flowed around her thin, long face and past her shoulders. She was not tall, but height made no difference to her; she was majesty, a royalty that only the other gods could contest.

Upon her shoulder perched a raven, wings glossy black, beak pale orange. At her feet, where her flowing cape parted, a small, dark shape curled around her ankles and stared out through unlidded eyes.

"You are no longer Kallatin."

He bowed.

"But I know of your wyrd. I have not . . . forgiven you, little son. But I have not ordered your death either. I have heard your dance, and I accept it, although you have killed your brother, who served me truly." She stepped forward. "No, do not offer me your tears or your sorrow; they are not finished yet."

So saying, she lifted one hand, and her fingers curled up in calling. Estravim's pale eyes blinked open, the white sheen of lashes resting against dark, slack circles.

"I heard the music," Estravim said softly, and made to rise. His arms, weak and suddenly thin, would not move from the points of the star. Kallandras touched his forehead, which was still wet and sticky from the challenge. His fingers came away reddened, and he looked at them a moment before he knelt, taking care not to leave the points of the star that his feet formed. He placed his hands beneath Estravim's shoulders and concentrated.

Very slowly, Estravim rose out of his body. His face took on the color and the vibrancy of life that the corpse would never again have. But he did not look back to see who aided him.

"Have you come to give me back my name?" he said quietly to the Lady who waited.

"Yes," she answered. "You will find your strength soon; do not be concerned. When we walk, I shall guide you and protect your path. You are Estravim nee Soldaris Corasin. You have served me well."

He caught her hand, and with her help gained his footing. Before she could speak again, he was on one knee in front of her. Her smile was dark, but not cold, and her own hand rested gently upon his forehead as her pale, pale fingers stroked his hair. "Rise."

He did. And then he turned to see which of his brothers had danced his death, called the Lady, and lifted him from his prison.

"You." There was no anger in the word; only confusion lingered behind his otherworld eyes. "Why?" Before Kallandras could answer, he spun around to face his Lady. "Why did you come at his call?"

"Do you question me already?" She asked, but not harshly. "Very well. I hold his name still."

Estravim's smile was grim. "Then he will be trapped fully when he dies; none will call you to release him."

"It may be so," she answered quietly. "Come."

"Wait!"

They both turned to see Kallandras standing perfectly still. "What I saw—Lady, what I saw was truth."

"A truth." But she heard what lay beneath the words and the perfectly controlled tone. She nodded, ever the regal monarch.

"If I had killed her, we would have perished in time— each of my brothers, each of my teachers. Only for love of them could I make my choice; I have been as true to my Order as any. And I have lost all." He hated to plead.

"All?" One slim line of frosted black rose over a dark eye. What he left unsaid, she knew. Her expression grew remote as she stood, hand upon one of her chosen. "I have not forgiven you, bard. But you served me in your time, and I am not without compassion.

"Estravim of my Kovaschaii, this bard who was once

Kallatin spoke the truth that he believes—yet even so, his actions were a betrayal of his oath. You have done me nothing but honor; therefore I will leave your response at your discretion. Recognize him, or not, as you choose. I will make no judgment."

Estravim turned with eyes of death and looked long at the bard.

The bard stared back, unblinking, his face a mixture of apprehension, longing, and bitterness. He opened his mouth and lifted his hand, as if to start another explanation; silence fell as he bit it back. It was not his choice—it was Estravim's, brother, and lost.

"I could not have made your decision," Estravim said at last. "Truth or no. The loss would have been too great. I loved none but the Kovaschaii, and none but the Kovaschaii have mattered to me, save the Lady.

"You danced my death," he bowed. "None among us could dance a death so perfectly. We all know it, even though we do not speak your name. I thank you. You have honored me, Kallatin." Stiffly, as if movement were no longer natural, Estravim touched his forehead and fell to one knee.

"Thank you," the bard whispered; the name that was lost lingered in the air. "It is I who am honored." As the mists faded and the half-world went with the Lady, the tears rolled down Kalladras' cheeks. He reached out blindly and ran his fingers across Estravim's face; it was still warm.

Stephen did not know the exact moment when he regained control of his feet, but he thought it was when he heard the dogs baying. The tenor of their voices, the precision of their cacophony, drove away all images of the bard save one: the way he knelt, heedless of mud, to cradle the body of the strange, pale man.

Stephen was near the end of his running breath, his throat raw and dry. The bardic voice had left him little choice but to sprint full out up the trail.

Please, please, please, he thought, when his breath refused him even a whisper, *finish the Hunt, Gil.* The baying stopped suddenly. The sides of his throat clung together. He gagged, but kept moving.

This one moment was safest for worry, fear, and anger. Gilliam was with the dogs—so completely given over to the hunt that his huntbrother's voice was the slightest of tickles in his inner ear.

Don't let the dogs eat, Gil. Don't please please please don't join them. He'd seen that once, and it was an ugly, horrible sight. Soredon had thought it funny, and even Norn had worn a grim, tired smile as they had pulled Gilliam away from the carcass of the boar he'd been hunting. But not even the smell of roasting flesh and boiling broth at the end of the long, cool day could entice Stephen to eat any meat that night—or for weeks afterward.

The ground at his feet became a blur of gathered tracks and gouged mud; he was close.

Gilliam, please, please—

The call of a horn answered his frantic litany. Nine notes, nine perfect, fully winded notes, came back to him, carried downwind by a faint breeze. Hunt's end had been called. He pulled out his horn and leaned his back against the smooth bark of the nearest tree. His hand shook as he carried the horn to his mouth and blew back the proper response. It sounded like a strangling duck. On any other Hunt, he would have laughed at the pathetic noise the horn made.

He started to cry.

"Stephen?"

"What?" He wiped viciously at his eyes with the cuff of his jacket.

"I heard it." Gilliam looked exhausted but content; sweat ran down his forehead, matting thin dark curls to his face. "Come on, we're waiting for you."

"You didn't let the dogs—"

"No." Gil held out a hand, and after a moment, Stephen took it and crushed it as hard as he could. Gilliam grunted and returned the grip, and they stood that way a moment before Stephen suddenly surrendered and let his hand go limp.

"You fell behind," the young Hunter said as they started to walk.

"I'm sorry," Stephen answered. "Someone tried to kill me."

It took the better part of half an hour to convince Gilliam that the danger was past, and even convinced, the young Hunter wanted his enemy's blood. Stephen thought it the aftereffects of being so long at the Hunt, and did his best to put out the odd, reddish light in Gilliam's eyes. Only afterward did he realize that the tone of voice and the simplicity of repetitive words he had chosen to use with Gilliam were like those he would speak to the dogs.

They had made the initial cut the length of the stag's proud throat with a blade that Gilliam pulled from a long pouch at his back, one carried for only this purpose. The flaps of wet, supple skin were pulled back almost to the neck, and the dogs were given their reward for the baying of the hart—a few mouthfuls of flesh and blood that had not yet cooled.

Stephen coupled the hounds, treading with care around the muddy ground. The hounds' tails whapped against his thighs, and the occasional dog tried to knock him over with a none-too-subtle shoulder-check—but he was used to this.

While Stephen worked, Gilliam played out the nine again, slowly and surely calling a triumphant close to his first Sacred Hunt. The sun was not yet upon the horizon, and the day not yet too cold. He carried the last note with what little breath remained in his lungs. The dogs looked up at this and joined him in their own fashion.

Stephen knew that Gilliam would make—and break— the last trance-connection with each of his hunting dogs. He would praise them and feed their animal egos before he set the horn aside and began the onerous task of carrying the stag back to the Queen's pavilion.

Carrying? Stephen grunted as he tied the front and back legs of the carcass together. Dragging, more like. At any other Hunt, there would be aides to help with the task of returning the kill. But, no, on the one day when the

Hunter was most at risk, everything had to be done "independently." He grunted as he pulled.

Gilliam came to help him, and the dogs, tired from their run and satisfied with their master's praise, obeyed his terse commands. They followed at heel, and only occasionally got into the little territorial scrapes that so annoyed their master.

The Hunter Lord only called a stop once as they followed their trail backward, but the ground was clear and marked only by the many feet of the passing animals and their human masters. Stephen could not find the body of his would-be killer anywhere. He knew that he hadn't gone mad because the dogs found the scent—but even Absynt thought it weak and almost directionless, more like the scent of a place than like the trail of any living quarry.

"The thing I don't understand," Gilliam said between grunts, "is why anyone'd want to kill you."

"How should I—Terwel!—know?"

"Maybe he thought you were someone else." Gilliam stopped long enough to kick Terwel in the shoulder with the flat of his boot. Terwel whined and rolled over, and Gilliam started to lug again. "I mean, we're all dressed the same."

"I think he knew what he was doing."

"Oh. Maybe we should just ask Kallandras."

Kallandras had knelt by the body and gently cradled the corpse. There had been no anger in his eyes, in fact, no expression at all upon his face. But Stephen had had much experience with masking emotion, and he knew the sorrow the bard's stooped shoulders had spoken of. He felt that they were somehow cohorts in a very strange crime, and he didn't want to expose Kallandras to anyone else. Yet. "I will."

"We will."

"I will."

"Look, you're my huntbrother, and it's my responsibility to protect you. *We* talk to him."

"*I* talk to him."

"Oh right," Gilliam said, dropping the legs of the stag. "So you talk to him, and maybe someone else tries to kill you, and no one else is around to help. Forget it. I forbid it."

"If someone else tries to kill me, Kallandras'll probably handle him the same bloody way." Stephen's arms crossed his chest as his jaw tightened. "And what the hell do you mean, 'forbid it'?"

"*I'm* the Hunter Lord."

"You're an idiot!"

"An idiot. Right." Gilliam's shoulders tensed. "Idiot enough to finish the Hunt on my own."

Stephen drew breath sharp enough to cut his tongue; it meant he didn't have to bite it. *How dare you?* He thought, his face flushing. *You know damn well why I missed the last leg!* Red-faced, he spoke with anger's voice and anger's words. "What's the matter, Gil? Are you upset that Kallandras was a better protector than you'll ever be?"

Bull's-eye. Stephen had just enough time to recognize the hit before Gilliam answered anger with anger. Of course, Gilliam didn't answer with words, and the dogs watched in curious concern as their master and his closest ally began to roll around in the dirt, shouting, spitting, and punching each other with the happy abandon of sibling fury.

They were both so enraged that Stephen didn't stop to think about what Lady Elseth would say, which was just as well.

An hour later, they emerged from the King's preserve. The dogs, even Terwel, were quiet as they followed Gilliam's terse commands, walking to heel so perfectly that there was hardly any need for leads. Stephen's left eye was blackened, and his lip was swollen. Gilliam's lip was split and smeared with dried blood. Both of the young men were covered with dirt and the remnants of the previous year's fall; the careful crafted green velvet of Hunter's cloaks looked entirely brown at a distance. Blond hair and brown hair were a mass of knots and wild tangles, but at least the Elseth Hunters had come back successful.

Lord Maubreche, Lord Valentin and Lord William of

Valentin approached them in silence; the bare head of the eldest lord, framed in a ring of white tufts of hair, bent low. His huntbrother, Andrew, came to his aid, and together they lifted and dragged the carcass away to the center of the King's impromptu court—it would be unmade there, according to all of the proper rituals.

Lord Valentin bowed low; his peppered hair fell forward around his thin, lined cheeks. "Your Hunt," he said gravely. His huntbrother, rounder and shorter than he, also bowed. Michaele was not known for polite deference to either Hunters or huntbrothers, although he was still quite capable when it came to the politics of the Ladies.

Stephen was accutely conscious of the mess he presented. He glanced surreptitiously at Gilliam and cringed at what he saw.

But none of the Hunters or their huntbrothers seemed at all concerned—and not one of them was amused. No, their faces were grave, almost gray, in the afternoon light. He started to say something, and then his jaw stopped moving at all. All of the lords had removed their hats, and all of them wore the black sash of the Hunter's Death; it traveled across thin midriff and thick alike, clinging like a web.

Lord William of Valentin approached last; he fell to one knee and held out his hands. There, cradled carefully in the thin, scarred palms of the Hunter Lord were the three knives of unmaking; one to cut flesh and muscle, one to cut bone, and one to remove hide.

Each of these were much older than he—than any of the Hunter Lords who stood in silence before them—and they bore the crest of a stag over a field of stars in gold relief.

"The unmaking, Lord Elseth," William whispered with bowed head.

No one moved for a moment. William raised his head and caught Gilliam in the light of his gray eyes. They were red-rimmed and murky with held tears. "These are yours, Lord Elseth."

Stephen felt Gilliam's confusion turn. He knew a stab of fear so sharp, he wasn't certain whether it was his own, or his Hunter's. It twisted at him, doing more than a blade's damage. He bit his lip and looked at Gilliam's face. Gilliam didn't notice. He stared down at the three knives.

"Norn?" he said at last, and his voice was perfectly composed.

"Alive." William's response came quickly and easily—it was the only good news he carried.

The new Lord of Elseth swallowed and accepted Lord William's burden. His hands were sure and certain as he took the weight of the unmaking and the responsibility of his father's lands.

But Stephen of Elseth cried. Tears streamed down his cheeks, and his eyes were so full that the world blurred and moved incomprehensibly. He wanted to speak, but words couldn't escape the closed wall of his throat.

And he knew that it wasn't his pain alone that drove him to such an improper display. He was huntbrother, and linked to a Hunter Lord—and Gilliam had never been good at expressing pain; the only emotion that came easily was anger, and Stephen was certain he would see that later.

CHAPTER FOURTEEN

Soredon lay in death's repose atop an ornate altar ten feet from the Queen's dais. The King's Priest stood beside him in the silence of the Sacred Hunt, his brown robes flapping at his legs like crippled wings. He did not speak, not yet, but rather attended to the body with the ease of experience. The blood had been washed away, and the vital organs—what was left of them—were now bound to the body in a skein of pale green. Soredon's face was slack; whatever pain had been felt in the dying had left him with his life.

At the foot of the rough-hewn altar lay Corwel; his spine had been snapped, but he had not otherwise been savaged. The great white hound, with his bandit's black mask and a history of successful, even enviable, Hunts behind him, still attended his Lord.

No one watched the Priest at work. The Hunter Lords, drawn now and silent, went about the final responsibility of the Hunt. Beside the burning braziers that were meant as an offering to the Hunter God, they unmade their kills, working with sleeves pushed up past the elbows and cloaks discarded on the ground. It was cool, but warming as the season yearned toward summer. The meat had to be cut, cured, and hung if it was to serve as food for the people in the various demesnes of the kingdom.

Only the kills of the King and the Huntsmen of the Chamber were for the nobles who now waited, and even these were properly unmade with the quiet respect for the hunted that the Hunter knows.

Gilliam worked in silence, first anchoring the stag by his horns, then widening the cut along the throat until it traced the whole of the stag's underbelly. He removed the heart with care, and Stephen stepped quickly in to catch Gil's sleeves before they became blood-sodden. It was the only way he was allowed to help.

The heart was offered to the fire; there was no formal prayer, no formal thanks to accompany the sizzle of flesh that would soon char. But the beast's spirit would be free when the heart was ashes—he would go to the Hunter, and dwell in the afterlands in peace and plenty.

Maybe, Stephen reflected quietly, as he watched the heart burn, there were no formal words because the Hunter Lords, too new from their losses here, could not have been trusted to say them with the proper amount of pride and strength. Smoke, made heavy and dark with blood and flesh burning, wound its way up in a spiral of air, darkening the landscape and dimming the sun. He shivered as he watched, and then turned back to Gilliam.

A familiar figure barred his way. The pale, drawn face of the bard was a mirror to those of the Hunters, and any of the Lords who had thought his bawdy ballad a disgrace were mollified by the sorrow he now offered as his sole expression.

Only Stephen knew that the sorrow was not for Soredon's death, and he was surprised at the anger this brought him.

Kallandras saw the shift in Stephen's face and shook his head, smiling wryly. "It won't do, you know," he said softly. "You're too transparent by half, and it won't serve your House well in the company of the Hunter Ladies. They're all sharp and cold as hunting falcons—but only twice as deadly."

It was meant, Stephen knew, as a friendly comment; he smiled stiffly.

"Walk with me?"

"I can't. I have to attend to Gilliam—Lord Elseth."

Kallandras nodded and threw the folds of his newly donned cloak aside. Cradled like a child in the crook of his arm sat his small lute. "Salla," he said, naming her. "I wish to speak with your Lord, if he will allow it."

"About what?"

"I would—I would sing his father's death."

Stephen started to sidle away, and Kallandras caught his shoulder with his free hand.

"I offer it," he said quietly, "because it is the only thing I can offer. And not a bard in the kingdom, not even the foremost of the Masters of Senniel, could sing a better death than I."

"Why?"

"Why? Skill, perhaps. Too much practice."

"I meant, why did you save my life? How did you know?"

"Ah." Kallandras grew quiet. "If I answer your question—and I must say that you don't seem grateful for the saving of it—will you take my request to your Lord?"

Stephen nodded. Grudgingly, he added, "I'd ask him anyway."

"And honest, too." Kallandras shook his head, and ringlets glinted with firelight and dying sun. "Evayne sent me."

"Evayne?" The lady, robed in midnight blue and surrounded by shadows and dark hair, who had stalked his sleep for three nights.

"Yes. You are under the wyrd of her father."

"F—father?"

"She is god-born; that much I've been able to discover about her in the few years that we've ... known each other. She calls me when she needs me, and I do what I must to help her."

"Why?"

"Too many questions," Kallandras answered gently, but the distance had returned to his eyes. He stepped back, bowed, and then looked up again; Stephen's eyes had not left his face. "You are young," he said, relenting a little. "I help because I'm committed to it. She fights the darkness in ways I don't understand, but she fights it with everything at her disposal. I fight because I, too, am under Fate's wyrd." He lifted Salla and began to idly strum her strings. Without thought, he pulled melody and harmony from her; a pensive, wordless tune. "It always costs. Always."

Costs? Stephen's dream came back, an echo too sharp to be just memory. Suddenly, he didn't want to ask any more questions. "Let me go find Lord Elseth. I'm sure he'd be happy if you'd sing his father's death. But—but don't make any jests, please?"

"No jests," Kallandras said gravely. "In mourning, young huntbrother, we are closer than you will ever understand." But the last words were a whisper, and Stephen, already searching for Gilliam's back, missed them.

The ring of torches and glass lamps and fires strove to capture the dying daylight when at last the Hunter Lords were entirely finished and ready. Their Ladies joined them in their bitter silence, offering them comfort and support by merely taking, and leaning on, the arms held out to them. Each Lord was allowed the presence of four dogs for the ceremony, and the clearing was warm and crowded.

Seventy-seven Hunter Lords stood at attention as the Hunter's Priest walked to the altar, accompanied by the King, four of the King's hounds, and four of the Priesthood. He carried a burning brazier on a link of chain that hung from a dark pole. The smoke from it smelled sweet and pungent as it rippled through the crowd. Two feet from the altar, he took the pole and drove it, hard, into the soft ground.

That done, he knelt before the King.

The King wore black; gone were Hunter greens and browns, gone the bow and the spear. Only black remained; emptiness, an absence of color, warmth, and light. For one instant, Stephen could see great tined antlers rising from the King's forehead into the night sky above the deep, calm wilderness of his eyes.

"Master of the Game, is the Hunt over?" The words, firm and strong, were ritual. But they were also sincere; a question that began and ended without a surety of the answer.

The Master of the Game walked over to Soredon, Master Hunter, and formerly Lord of Elseth. He stared down at the slack, still face as if searching for signs of life; nor did he give off this quiet, desperate search until minutes had passed. Then, with infinite care and a respect that was tangible and not begrudged, the King reached down and gently closed his Hunter's eyes. "It is over."

He held out one hand, palm up, and curled his fingers tightly around the horn the Priest gave him. The drums started as the four who had accompanied the King and his Priest took their places on the green and began to play. Their faces were hooded by more than the night, but their pain came out in the throbbing of the skins. The horn sounded the end of the Hunt, and before the first note had died, every Hunter in the realm, Gilliam and Stephen included, had joined in.

The dogs, aware of their master's grief, began to howl in time of sorts—and together, men and beasts, they made enough noise to be heard even by a God.

The King stepped away at last, and silence was allowed to return. He gestured to the Priest, and the Priest took over while the King stood by his side. He began a quiet incantation over Soredon's body. The hems of his sleeves brushed pale white cheeks and shuttered eyes.

"Hunter," he intoned, and it was clear that he spoke to the God. "We are no oath-breakers; we have come, and we have hunted at your behest, in your lands.

"And you, too, have hunted; you have taken, with skill that we cannot imagine or match, one of the greatest of our number.

"Keep him in peace, and keep our lands whole and healthy for another year. Feed the very land as we feed our people, and we shall return again to renew our vows."

The silence that followed was also part of the yearly ritual—but it, too, was full and heavy with genuine emotion and a grief too deep for words.

Only one man moved in the gathering. He came from the shadows at the farthest edge of the clearing in silence, carrying no torch, no horn, no weapon. He caught the King's eye, and the Priest's, but instead of gently remonstrating with him, they bowed their heads and looked away as he approached the body, to give him what privacy they could in such a public circumstance.

Norn of Elseth knelt in the dirt, his back to the gathered mourners. His broad shoulders seemed so shrunken they barely supported his bulk; the red lights of his hair

were extinguished. His fingers moved blindly over
Corwel's cold fur before they reached for the edge of the
altar.

He rose. The drums stopped their beating, the breeze
stilled. In silence, the huntbrother joined the Hunter Lord.

Loss. Stephen understood it well. There had been many
deaths and disappearances in his past, in the years with
the den, and even those leading up to them. Lord Elseth
had changed all that—and now he lay as dead as any
commoner. The magic of his presence, the force of his
words—with their harsh anger and their prickly comfort—had been given to the Hunter and His Death. It hurt.

But not as much as it hurt Norn.

He knew that Norn shouldn't be alone. Gilliam caught
his shoulder as he started forward, and he shook him off,
quietly determined to go to Norn's side.

No doubt the death had been awful—it was hard to tell
from the body—but at least, dead, Soredon was spared
Lord William's fate. Norn was not. He had nothing now;
unlike his Hunter Lord, he couldn't hear the voices of the
dogs, and he couldn't anchor himself to their needs.

But when Stephen reached Norn, he found himself
without words to say or comfort to offer. He reached out
and placed one hand on Norn's stooped shoulder, but the
larger man shrugged it off.

"Norn of Elseth," the King said softly, "Lord Soredon
made his choice years before—as did you. All loss,
whether of life or of companionship, was accepted then.
We are Hunters and huntbrothers, and the Death takes one
of our number, always."

Norn said nothing, nor did the King expect a response.
The choice made as a child was bitter solace indeed for
such a moment as this. They waited—King, Priest and
huntbrother—but Norn did not touch the body at all. He
stared long into the frozen face and then turned away
with a whisper. "It should have been me."

Only Stephen heard it. He trailed alongside the older
man, afraid of disturbing him, but more afraid of leaving
him alone.

* * *

Kallandras was true to his word. When at last the King, a wounded Hunter Lord in his own right, retired to his place at the foot of the Queen's dais, when the Priest and the drummers quietly paid their final respects to their fallen and withdrew into the shadows, when the Hunter Lords were finally free to mourn as they chose, he rose, his small lute cradled gently and formally in his arms, and took his place before the altar. He bowed, a sweeping, serious motion, first to Corwel and then to Soredon.

The Hunter Lords looked askance at Gilliam, but as Gilliam did not demur, they kept their thoughts to themselves and waited.

He sang.

His voice was full with the emotion that the Hunter Lords kept carefully masked. They, who had always been strong, had no way to weep but through him—and his voice, accompanied by the sweeping range of lute strings that seemed too small, too inadequate to convey such sound, washed over them all.

There were tears on his cheeks; the fire from the brazier caught them and made pale rubies of their fall. His voice broke over words more than once, but that too became part of his song.

Stephen cried, and after a few minutes, Gilliam joined him. It was safe, after all; no one noticed. Their attention was fixed upon the bard.

Time passed, no one knew—or cared—how long, and Kallandras' song began to slowly change. Strains of grief and utter despair, of loss in the most primal sense, were joined by a thin strand of hope. The death of the Hunter Lord became a green, unfolding life for the land of Breodanir; the fields became fertile, the ground soft and rich. The children, untouched by sorrow and death, played in the peace of Lord Soredon's sacrifice, instead of dying in drought or famine.

All of this, they knew—but they had never *felt* it so clearly, and so cleanly, as at this moment. As Kallandras sang, the ghost of Lord Soredon moved slowly, and with purpose, before them. He smiled, if smile it was—it was hard to tell with Soredon—and reached for his weapons. He frowned down, and Corwel suddenly joined him;

Corwel remade, young and perfect and a little too eager. Together, they passed into shadow and were gone with the last strain of music.

In an hour, Kallandras had done what time would take months to do. A sweet, sad peace filled the clearing and spilled out into the forest. Hunter Lords and Ladies watched him quietly, seeing other deaths, other losses, from the perspective that peace allows.

They did not know that it was not the death of Lord Elseth alone that he spoke of; they didn't know that it was not the hope of the Breodani alone that filled the clearing. But they didn't have to; what they felt was Kallandras' emotion, and it was genuine, one with their own.

He bowed, first to Lord Elseth and Stephen, and then to the crowd at large. Their silence was their applause.

Only one man remained unmoved. He was like a lamp empty of flame. There was nothing at all left, not even for tears. Kallandras bowed to him as well, the third bow and the last of the evening. Norn nodded, but the nod, like the man, was empty.

Krysanthos, mage-born, was not proof against the magic of Kallandras' talent. He wept as freely as any of the Hunter Lords, although he felt only contempt for their loss. Only when the bard stopped singing did the spell fade, and Krysanthos was left with anger, and not a little fear. He wanted to approach the Hunter Lords proper, but did not dare. Observers—the gifted and exalted of the realm who were not blessed by the Hunter's gift—had a small area on the green that could not be abandoned until the full and proper end of the Sacred Hunt. As always, surrounded by Priests of various orders, and the official heads of many guilds, Krysanthos kept to custom. But magic augmented his vision as he watched.

The pale, muddied hair of the Elseth huntbrother, who stood shoulder to shoulder with his Lord in the gloom, was a taunt and a question that he had no answer for. The Kovaschaii had gone out in the morning, trailing the hunt in silence. He had not returned, which Krysanthos had expected—but the boy had. What had happened?

He felt certain that the boy could not have destroyed the assassin; or rather, he wanted to feel certain of it. But the boy's life was evidence against the assumption.

He didn't understand why more had not been made of the attempt, didn't understand why the boy had not mentioned the assassin at all. Unless the assassin had never even made the first attempt.

But, no, that was unthinkable. The Kovaschaii were almost a legend, and for very good reason. Krysanthos had called upon them twice before, and both times they had offered success and silence in return for their very high fee.

What a waste of an opportunity. He would have to hire again, or attend to the deed with his personal resources. He shivered; it was cool. The boy that had dealt with one of the Kovaschaii was not an opponent that Krysanthos was willing to challenge, however cunningly, without further study. None of the mage's plans took into account his own death.

Ah, the feast was starting. Perhaps food and a little wine would warm him. He began to walk over to the banquet tables set up for the perusal of hungry guests. Yes, he would eat, and then he would arrange for surveillance of the huntbrother to the new Lord Elseth.

Eadward Lord Valentin, his huntbrother Michaele, and Lord William of Valentin formed the honor guard. One of the mage-born—not Krysanthos, he was too highly placed—was called from the Collegium of the Order of Knowledge. He came with the dawn and attended to the body, with spells and potions made to preserve it on the long journey home.

Lord Maubreche and his huntbrother Andrew also honored the dead with their presence. They held the preserve closest to Valentin, and slowed their journey home to lend the strength and dignity of numbers to Soredon's last journey.

Norn rode, in black robes with a hood that showed little of his face, at Soredon's side. Michaele and Andrew tried twice to speak with him or offer their comfort, but he declined all human contact—and he shunned the dogs as well.

The young Lord Elseth proved himself to be the model of restraint; he held the dogs in check throughout the two-week journey, and never once let tears be shed in public. In all things, he was his father's son, but especially in this. Stephen knew how important the appearance of strength was to his Hunter, and he said nothing at all about it, pretending, as the other Lords did, that all tears had already been shed in the closing of the Sacred Hunt.

Lady Elseth saw the procession coming; she must have. When they arrived, she had food and rooms ready for the Lords who had served as guards. Dinner, for it was late afternoon, was hurriedly rearranged, and a Priest from the village was called for. He arrived within minutes, and he showed sorrow more openly than did any of the Elseth clan save Maribelle, who, while on the verge of adulthood, had not completely left the fields of childhood's open grief and sorrow.

Stephen heard Lady Elseth crying the evening before the funeral. He stopped outside of her drawing room doors. They were closed, and the rules of the house, made when he and Gilliam had been younger children, were quite strict: One did not disturb Lady Elseth if the doors were shut.

But he lingered in the hall, the lamplight flickering beneath his chin like ghostly fingers. He wanted to enter and offer her comfort, but didn't know how. If he hadn't been wandering the halls, he would never have heard her—and it was obvious that she didn't want to be heard, just as it was obvious that Gilliam did not.

In the end, he chose to knock.

The crying stopped; he heard the rustle of cloth behind the doors before they were opened. In the darkness, the redness of her eyes and the slight puffiness of lids and cheeks were not so obvious.

"Stephen," she said, and tried a smile.

He held the lamp higher, so that its light touched them

both. "Can I come in?"

"What are you doing awake at this hour? The funeral's tomorrow, and both you and Gilliam have to participate."

"I couldn't sleep."

"No." She stepped back and held the door open. He glided past the inlaid panels and into the room. She didn't wait for him to close the doors. Instead, she returned to her seat at the writing desk in the bay window. "I was—I was just working on accounts." She picked up a quill and set it to paper that was blotched and sodden with a liquid other than ink.

"The lamp is low," he offered.

She nodded. "I won't be up for much longer." But the quill trembled uselessly in her hands, and she set it aside. Gaining her feet, she turned to stare out of the windows. The curtains were pulled, and the moon, laced with clouds, glared down. Her feet, against the wood of the floor, must have been cold, but she didn't notice.

Stephen went through the drawing room and into her sleeping quarters, picked up the old knitted woolens and brought them out, offering them silently. She took them and bent down to place them on her feet, but her shoulders began to shake, and she left them in a messy pile on the floor.

"It isn't—it isn't for Soredon," she said, although it was hard to hear the words. "It's Norn. I can't reach him at all."

"He's lost his Hunter," Stephen replied.

"I don't care why," was her equally quiet answer. It showed him, again, how different their lives had been, because it told him clearly how poorly she, who had loved Soredon, understood the depths of his loss to Norn. "I can't reach him at all."

She opened the right-hand drawer of her desk and pulled out a crumpled handkerchief. She blew her nose, a most unladylike and inelegant gesture, and then rubbed her cheeks clean of tears with the sleeve of her night robe. "I'm so sick of the Hunter God," she whispered.

"I'm so sick of all of it. He won't even talk to me. He only said, 'Lady, I'm sorry.' That was all. I called for him; he came and he just sat here, saying nothing." The tears fell harder, and her voice became raw. "I've tried everything in the last day, Stephen. But he's lost."

"He'll come back," Stephen said awkwardly, "Lord William did."

Her laughter was harsh and heated, a curse, not an expression of mirth. "Watch," she said bitterly, "and learn. The Hunter has no mercy. It is not enough that I lose husband; I must lose huntbrother as well."

"What do you mean?"

"Norn—he's—" And then she dropped her face into her hands. "Go away, Stephen. I'm sorry, but I can't be what I should. Go *away*."

He left.

And in the morning, the Lords and their Ladies gathered to stand witness as the body of Soredon of Elseth was laid to rest in the cemetery of the Elseth estate. A headstone would follow soon enough, one as fine and unornamented and strong as Lord Soredon himself had been.

Norn accompanied the body into the Priest's circle, and Norn stood beside it as it came to rest upon the Elseth altar. He knelt in the mud and the dirt, and clung tightly to Soredon's lifeless hands as if afraid of being parted.

And six months later, at the height of the harvest season, Norn of Elseth joined his Lord. He never recovered from the loss, it was said. What was not said, and what Stephen learned only with the passage of time, was that huntbrothers left alive after the Sacred Hunt were left alive in body only, a shadow of what they had been, until even the body, like an echo, paled and faded into nothing.

Norn's funeral was quiet but well-attended, and Lady Elseth was the gracious hostess throughout. She had wept what tears she had had on the nights after they had brought her husband's body home.

Stephen cried as he stood beside Maribelle; she, too,

offered her tears. But Lord Elseth was as grim and silent
as his mother. It was the best display of strength he could
offer as his last sign of respect to the man who had been
a second father for all of his life.

CHAPTER FIFTEEN

In the glittering halls of Maubreche, beneath a flood of light made sharp and faceted by three huge chandeliers, Stephen of Elseth began to search for a quiet place to hide. It wasn't easy; the press of moving bodies and alert Ladies—many of whom wished his aid in cornering the Elseth title for either themselves or their offspring— created an eddy in the social currents that threatened to pull him under. To make matters more complicated— which was only barely possible—he could sense that Gilliam, lost to view somewhere in the ever-changing, ever-moving crowd, was angry with him. That was the last thing he needed at the moment. He felt as if he were eight again; the surety, poise, and skill of his twenty-two years were about to abandon him to a room full of strangers.

Luckily, recessed along the gold-foiled west wall of the ballroom, there were balconies, curtained heavily to close out the night and all hint of darkness. In the chill crisp air, he found his refuge. Lady Elseth would be disappointed, no doubt, and he would hear about it in the morning, but he needed the respite badly.

He shrugged himself out of his dancing jacket, taking care to hold tight to cream ruffles and lace as they tried to follow green velvet and satin. Better. The jacket he slung over the stone balcony before he turned to face the night. Music—the opening strains of Coravel's *Revelry* played with spice and skill by the small orchestra— reached above the din of conversation and tickled his ear. He knew, without checking his card, that he listened to the beginning of the fourth dance.

It was a three-step waltz, simple enough to maneuver

through without demanding much of the Hunter Lords who would always be too busy to learn the grace and skill a more difficult dance would require. And Lady Cynthia of Maubreche, the center of the evening's celebration, would no doubt be dancing with one or another of the louts who'd been told to court her. He ground his teeth in frustration.

Lady Cynthia had come late into her majority—she'd seen the turn of eighteen, when many young Ladies had already married into the fold of a Hunter Lord. She even had the grace to look—and act—her age; her long, slender body and her sharp, serious face had rarely been found in gatherings such as these. No, until now, Stephen had been likely to find her in the temple libraries—or the King's libraries, if the time of year was proper.

His fingers tried to dig holes in the balcony, and his mood was such that he wouldn't have been surprised had the stone not resisted. But even that satisfaction was denied him.

The music of the dance went on and on. He closed his eyes and saw more clearly the sweep of her emerald green gown as it flew above the floor; saw the twinkle in her eye, the smile on her lips, the pale, pleasing blush along her cheeks. Which Lordling held her made no difference to him; he had not even tried to reserve a dance for the evening.

"Stephen?" The curtains rustled and flew open, and Gilliam stepped out into the night. He was Lord Elseth now, which meant more to the Ladies than it did to the Lords, and he wore the title the same way he wore his clothes.

Had Stephen not been so moody, he would have stopped to yank the lace out of the stranglehold the collar of Gilliam's jacket had on it. He didn't even have the energy to comment on the crumbs that had been crushed into the pile of the pleats above Gilliam's left thigh. "Something bothering you?"

"No."

"Dogshit."

Gilliam was angry; had been angry for most of the last fortnight. His huntbrother hadn't been in the mood to deal with it, and frankly, he thought it would do Gilliam some good to deal with his tantrums on his own.

Stephen drew a breath and turned to face his Hunter. Air hissed out as his jaw stiffened. "Gil, now is not the time. All right?"

" 'Now is not the time.' " Gilliam shoved his jacket back and sat down, hard, on the stone. "It's been the same damned story for the last month."

"Gil . . ."

"You've come hunting, what, twice? If you can call what you were doing hunting."

"Fine." Stephen bent down, picked up his jacket, and shoved his arms into the sleeves. Even angry, he was careful with both linen and lace. "What did you want of me?"

Gilliam shrugged in turn, and his face, broader and harsher than Stephen's, set in exactly the same lines. "Nothing."

For a moment they glared at each other, and temper tightened their fists. But they were twenty-two now, no longer boys, or even adolescents, to be forgiven for fist play in public. Stephen, as always, turned away first. If Gilliam wanted to play out a stupid game, he could damned well do it on his own.

"It's her again, isn't it?"

Only the huntbrother's head turned. "Her?"

"Cynthia." No honorific, no title, and certainly no respect in the word. Stephen opened his mouth, but before he could answer in kind, Gilliam continued. "Why don't you do something about it, instead of fretting here like a bitch in heat?"

The color drained out of Stephen's face. His jacket slid to the stonework in a messy pile that also covered his boots.

"It's Cynthia, Cynthia, Cynthia! You think of nothing but Cynthia!"

"I—"

"Maybe you'd rather be her lover than my huntbrother—but you aren't doing both!" He slid to his feet and walked past Stephen, taking a moment to shove him to the side.

"Gil, I swear—"

"What?" Gilliam's voice was low as he stood, half in the light, half out. Already a quiet hush had built around the recess.

"You understand *nothing!* All *you* ever think about are your dogs and their kills! Maybe that's enough for you— who knows what—"

"Stephen." The voice was soft and feminine. The chill in the word had nothing to do with the air. "Gilliam. You do your House no honor by this . . . display." Her voice was not raised, and indeed her lips were turned up in the semblance of a perfect smile, which fooled no one. The Lady Elseth had grown in power over the years; if age had weakened her at all, none were there to witness it. She stood tall, although her cheekbones didn't clear her son's shoulders, and the regal fall of a perfect, night-blue dress made her face seem all the whiter.

"Lady," Stephen murmured. He dropped his shoulders and his head in a bow, and held it long enough for the flush to leave his cheeks.

"Good. Gilliam!"

Stephen looked up to see the back of Gilliam's head disappearing—none too politely—through the crowd. He was heading toward the doors.

"What was that about?" Lady Elseth asked softly.

"A private matter, Lady. Nothing important."

"Good. If you need a few minutes, take them, but you might consider making the social rounds soon." She nodded quietly to the alcove, and Stephen retreated as the curtains closed out the room once again. He picked up his jacket and brushed out the folds before they became wrinkles. All the while, his hands were shaking. In darkness, anger warred with pain; neither won.

For as Stephen stood alone again, under the eye of the moon, he felt a familiar tingle, an odd rush of warmth that surged through his skin and ran along his limbs. He cried out, but his throat passed a whisper, no more, and once again the jacket spilled to the stone like a liquid with no vessel to hold it. His hands found the balcony railing, for strength and stability's sake, as his vision floundered in the darkness like a wild, hunted thing.

He stood in the glow of the Hunter God's presence. And for just a moment, glimmering like fireflies near the perfectly kept lake, two golden, glowing eyes stared back at him. He blinked; they were gone. But the touch of God remained to sing its urgent, incomprehensible message.

He turned and the terrace became a spinning, unstable outcropping on the side of the larger building. His hair stood on edge, and his skin tingled so much it hurt. If the Sacred Hunt had ever threatened his life, he forgot it. Nothing had ever felt so full of danger as this moment.

Instinct, not any sure knowledge, guided his steps. He had to find Gilliam, and quickly.

Gilliam, Lord Elseth, was indeed an angry Hunter. His hair was a wild, dark mess, and his clothing, created at the behest of Lady Elseth, and chosen specifically for an occasion such as this, fit him both perfectly and poorly. Ashfel, the pride of his hunting pack, was safely kenneled at the Elseth Manor, as were the rest of his dogs; there was no release at all to be had in the streets of the King's City.

The fact that none of the other Hunter Lords had traveled with their dogs did nothing to still his temper. They, at least, had the attention and fealty of their huntbrothers, whereas he—

He swore, a steady stream of words that the Ladies would have heartily disapproved of—if they condescended to hear them at all. What was so bloody interesting about Lady Cynthia anyway? He kicked at a clod of dirt and overturned the edge of the flower bed that had been newly planted. A long green stem, topped by a stiff oblong bulb, keeled over into the cold air.

Oh, he supposed she was pretty enough, if you cared for that sort of thing; she was certainly quiet and not given to loud displays or political games; she dressed well and spent little time powdered and primped as so many of the younger Ladies did. So what? Any of her so-called good points were negatives; she wasn't like most of the other Ladies. And she still couldn't hold a candle to the glory and the stress of the Hunt.

He kicked something else that got in his way, a rock of

some sort that lined the garden path. Hurt his toe, too, although his boots were heavy. He didn't really notice.

If Stephen wanted to mope around after Lady Cynthia, he could bloody well do just that. But if he thought that Gilliam would stand around and plaintively watch, he was an idiot. Gilliam, Lord Elseth, had far better things to do with his time—and anyway, he hated coming-of-age balls with all their attendant frippery and stiff-lipped good manners.

Shoving his hands into pockets that were not designed for a bulge made of fists, he stalked off down the street under the watchful eye of the ever present moon-in-glory.

"Stephen?" Lady Elseth's fingers were gentle as they curled around the crook of his arm. "What is it?"

He shrugged her off as gently as possible, and once again donned the jacket that now seemed impractical and gaudy. "Did you see which way Gilliam went?"

"Out." Her voice made clear what she thought of his departure. It was enough to give Stephen pause, but not enough to stop him.

"I—I'm sorry, Lady Elseth. You'll have to give our regrets to Lady and Lord Maubreche."

She raised one graying brow, but her hands fell idle and disappeared into folds of blue velvet. "Why?"

"Gilliam's in danger." As the words rolled off his tongue, he felt them to be both true and false; later, perhaps, he'd have the time to wonder why. "I've got to find him."

She caught his face in her hands then, searching his eyes thoroughly—but quickly—before releasing him. His cheeks were warm with the imprints of her fingers as he bowed his head. "Oh, Stephen?"

"Lady?"

"We need to speak about Lady Cynthia when you return."

"Lady." But he felt no dread, and little embarassment; the urgency of his brush with God had put his life in perspective again. Gilliam, had he known, would have been pleased.

* * *

The guards at the door were not completely useless; they pointed to the damage that Gilliam had done to both the flower bed and the rock garden on his way out of the west gate. The keeper of the house was less helpful; he stopped Stephen once to comment quietly upon the state of the grounds, and twice to assure himself that Stephen needed no carriage. Stephen only barely managed to shake the man off before he made his way to the stables.

Gilliam was walking; Stephen would soon be mounted. Surely it wouldn't be that difficult to catch up to his Lord and bring him back to the estate. Whatever there was to be faced, they would face it together in the company of other Hunter Lords and their huntbrothers.

But the stables were shadowed and dark, and the stable boys too slow for Stephen's liking. He demanded a horse, and they brought out three that he deemed less than useless; they were fine-spirited, high-strung animals meant to be ridden by those with the time for odd tempers. They pranced about, evading bit and saddle and nickering their displeasure and their anxiety.

As if speaking in their tongue, he snorted to make his annoyance plain, and the fourth he chose himself: Greysprint, a horse used for riding that might as easily have pulled a great carriage without aid. He was steady, or so the stable boys vowed, but as Stephen mounted, he felt the beast shudder.

"Not now," he murmured, the words at odds with the soothing tone of his voice. He caught the reins, waved the hands off, and cantered out into the open air. The night, even with the moon to lessen it, was dark and shadowed. And unlike her sister sun, the moon gave off no warmth.

Gilliam had had enough of the social circus to last a long lifetime. He hated the odd dress and foreign mannerisms deemed necessary to interact with either the Ladies or the other Lords, who undoubtedly felt as dubious about the privilege as he. He hated the food, bits of ridiculous portions and equally ridiculous methods of preparation; hated the tinkling music and the constricting form of the few dances he knew; hated the milling servants with their stiff voices and perfunctory bows that so reminded him of his own manor's keeper, Boredan. He was angered by the strict adherence to the dogs-stay-at-kennel rule, angered by the idiotic velvet and silk that his mother insisted he wear, and annoyed by the fact that Maribelle, born of the same father and mother, fit so smugly into the whole charade.

But mostly, he was angry at Stephen.

The night was indeed cool now, and he'd left his jacket over the rails of the grand central staircase that pointed the way out of Maubreche Manor, so he walked briskly to keep the chill at bay. He had no idea where he was going; destination was not so important as escape.

Buildings, grand and recessed from the streets, loomed like hard shadow with hearts of orange flame where lamps were lit at entranceways. Guardhouses also contained a hint of light and movement all along the wide, cobbled streets. No one stopped him or attempted to challenge his passage; he strode the thoroughfare like a man with angry purpose.

But as he passed the last of the Lord's circle and left it at his back, the lights grew dim and intermittent. The buildings crowded in on the streets, as if no longer held back by gates or fences; they rubbed shoulders in a compacted, awkward way, and only garbage and refuse took up residence in the open air between them.

The scent—the awful, dank smell of the place—told him, more clearly than his limited vision, where he had come: the lower city. He slid his hand down to his sword belt, and smiled with just a hint of vindication. The Lords were allowed swords—not spears or axes or any other useful weapon—and daggers, but many of the older men chose to leave this formality in the comfort of their quarters. Or rather, many of the older men chose to let their Ladies direct them. Gilliam didn't have this problem, and as he refused to dance at all, the sword had been no hindrance.

He was glad to have it now. Out of habit, he checked his stride and glanced warily about. The wind rattled shutters and sent a hint of spoiled food from the mouth of an alley. He squinted, and the darkness settled in around his eyes.

He should go back. He knew it, but the moment he thought about returning, tail between his legs like any sorry dog, to the Maubreche estate—and to Stephen—the hairs on his neck stood on end. Stephen had no bloody time for anyone but Cynthia of Maubreche—and Gilliam had no time for Stephen.

He felt the raspy tickle at his throat before he realized that the sound he heard was himself. He was growling. He wanted a hunt. He began to breathe more deliberately. He knew of one way to make his vision clearer.

With moon full and at quarter height, Gilliam, Lord Elseth, called Hunter's trance in the lower city.

Stephen felt it.

He had spent fifteen minutes asking guards if they had seen his Lord's passage, and another five following their directions as he kept his horse on a tight rein. At least the streets had been empty; no steady stream of people, no farmers' wagons or merchants' train had slowed his passage with their right-of-way.

He was thankful. He forgot it. For the odd tingle, the strange and terrifying warmth that had been riding just above his shoulder, descended with a lurch. His fingers curled around the reins as if for support; Greysprint's mouth took the brunt of the shock.

The hand of God. But not God's alone; he felt something familiar, something raw and impatient and angry. Gilliam.

The Hunter's gift, he thought, as he urged Greysprint forward. *Gil, where are you?*

As if in answer, the feeling grew stronger as he rode. He concentrated on it, and on the horse, trying desperately to ignore the fact that they'd left both the Hunter's and the Priest's city circles. *I don't have my sword.* His shoulders stiffened. This one eve, Gilliam had probably been right to be stubborn and graceless.

The dagger would have to do—but the dagger seemed small and insignificant compared to the menace the lower city contained as Greysprint crossed its lip.

* * *

The world grew more distinct; the breeze slowed from a wispy brush to a gentle billow; the smell of the streets assailed his flared nostrils. Here and there, cedar burned in the fireplaces of those who had money to waste on that sort of warmth. These were few in the lower city.

There were shadows everywhere; deep and darker than the night. But they were still, and when Gilliam moved in near silence to confront them, he found them empty as well. The faces of houses and squat, tired buildings became so much scenery; he wanted to find something that moved.

The stories he'd been told of life in the lower city had made every dark alley a danger. Gilliam had half expected to see roving bands of thieves and cutpurses, each of whom carried glinting daggers as a substitute for fangs. He was to be bitterly disappointed as he stalked the city streets. Even the breeze seemed to die into stiff, unnatural silence.

The darkness brought back the dreams. Six years of quiet and relative peace had all but buried the wyrd. Although he walked in no faceless stone halls and heard no tortured screams or splintering of wood and stone, the three returned to him sharply. He shivered; Greysprint pulled at the reins in an attempt to turn around and head back.

"It's all right," he whispered, but his hands were shaking. Above his head, perched like vultures, the second stories of the street's buildings crowded out the sky. The road was narrow and poorly kept; weeds made new by spring were already claiming their territory.

These did not trouble him. But the shadows did. Even darker than he remembered, they seemed to have become a solid presence—one that absorbed both sound and light. And with every step that Greysprint took, each more grudging than the last, these living shadows grew substantial.

Stop it, he told himself firmly. *You're just being nervous about the past.* But Marcus' voice did not return to him, and the days that he'd lived in the den were far, far behind. The wyrd was not.

Greysprint came to a halt, and Stephen realized that he'd reined the horse in. Taking a deep breath, he forced the horse forward again. *Gilliam, where are you?*

He hated the answer.

He heard it before either his eyes or his nose could alert him. A loud, high-pitched keening threw off the silence of the city streets. Even the shadows seemed to shudder with the force of a wail that was either mournful or fearful. It was hard to tell; the voice was no human voice.

Gilliam froze, straining to hear as his eyes sought the shadows. Sound came before scent or sight did; the cry was either louder or closer. His hand dropped to his side; his fingers found the curved metal hilt of his sword. He drew it, and for a moment the ring of steel against the lip of the scabbard hid the sudden sound of running feet.

The Hunter's trance had set his heart to racing; he felt the pulse at his neck beat in time to steps that were many. Something was coming in his direction—and someone was following it. If he had heard the horns, he would have set his sword aside—the horn calls would have declared the hunt another Lord's preserve.

But blessed silence answered him; he had no reason not to interfere. His entire body tingled with the anticipation of action. All thoughts of Stephen vanished as a pale blur escaped the shadows. From an alley. Perhaps the stories had not all been lies.

It was a woman, or maybe a girl—it was hard to tell in the poor light, even in trance. She was wrapped in shadow, and her hair, from this distance, seemed knotted and dirty. Her face was long and thin, her jaw slender but angular, her forehead short. Whether or not she was pale or dark was impossible to tell; her skin was made blotchy by dirt and sweat. She saw him, but instead of halting, swayed her course. It should have surprised him. It didn't.

In silence, he waited to see what would follow her; she was headed directly for him. But she was at least a minute ahead of her pursuers, and in trance a minute is a long time. He watched her lips as they stretched thin over her teeth, and saw the lids of her eyes flutter down over irises so black they seemed to be all pupil. He waited to hear what she had to say.

And the long, thin sound left her lips. There was no mistaking it: it rose in the air like a howl in a throat not built to utter one. But there was no mourning or fear in it any longer—in fact, her expression was one of recognition. His eyes met hers and pressed against them across the distance as he struggled to remember who she was and how he knew her. He felt a tingle, an odd lurch, and a dizzy, spinning warmth. The moon changed position.

Suddenly, he saw himself, standing with his sword at the ready, his feet planted slightly apart, his knees gently bent. He wore no jacket, and he could see the sweat of the Hunter's trance along the linen of his shirt. His face was set and grim, but that expression slowly changed into one of astonishment.

With a cry part curse and part fear, he pulled himself out from behind her eyes.

Not since his very first Hunt, with his father to supervise and guide his steps, had he felt so disoriented and out of control. He staggered as she knocked against him, butting him in the center of his chest. Righting himself, he reached down to place a hand on her shoulder; he missed—it was unnaturally high. Her lips parted; this close he could smell her stale breath and hear the low growl in her throat. She wore clothing, but it was poorly made, an ill fit, more remarkable for the fact that it covered her at all, it was so torn and frayed. He couldn't say what the color of the shift had originally been, but hoped it wasn't white. She looked at him, as if asking for guidance. No, not as if. She was.

Stand left side. Be ready. The thought was automatic, but he shook slightly as she snapped to attention, just as Ashfel would have done, and turned her face to the shadows. Her lips drew up over her teeth; her eyes narrowed.

The shadows burst out of the alley's mouth.

Greysprint's mouth was flecked with foam; his eyes were wide and whitened. He stepped stiffly, his hooves so heavy against the ground, Stephen thought they might take root in the cobbled stone and dirt. Still, he coaxed and gentled the horse as he tried to move forward. He knew, now, that the fear of the beast this eve was a natural and understandable fear, and he almost regretted his haste in cursing both the stable hands and Lady Maubreche's choice of riding beasts. For if Stephen, both rider and a huntbrother used to facing death, was terrified of the darkness in the lower city, could more be expected of a mount?

Greysprint didn't throw him and didn't flee in panic, but his breathing grew more labored and his sides began to heave. Stephen knew that more time would be lost trying to ride forward—he'd be faster if he dismounted and walked. But then he'd have feet in the shadows and no sense of motion and life beneath him.

What choice did he have? He felt Gilliam's trance, like a delicate pulse, unseen but still a light in the shadows. Gripping the saddle, he relinquished the bridle and slid down the left side of the horse. The buildings, with their second and third stories overhanging the street, closed in like a poorly-made roof; he felt them keenly although he was now closer to the ground.

Greysprint nickered softly, and Stephen gripped the reins once more. He led the horse in a half-circle, and then gave him a forceful slap on the rear. "Home," he said softly, although the word wasn't necessary.

The moon, where it breached the top of densely packed buildings, cut a path in the darkness. Alone in the twilight world of sleeping dens and hidden bars, Stephen of Elseth began his search. He moved slowly at first, but whatever power rode him became less kind and more demanding. Without realizing it, he began to stretch his stride into a near-silent run.

Three men came out of the shadows. They were in clothing that was dark—near-black—in color, but light of weight. No dress jackets or odd robes impeded their progress. They wore masks that darkened their faces and left only their eyes visible. They carried long, slim knives, but no swords, no obvious scabbards. And they ran, in step, like a single man.

The wind blew at their backs, a soft huff of night's breath. It carried a scent back to Gilliam and his companion—one unlike any he had ever encountered. It was faint, pungent, and repulsive. He was reminded, although he couldn't say why, of the perfumes and heavy oils that were applied to a corpse to hide the stench of death. They were never completely successful.

He felt the heat of her anger flare up and mingle with anxiety. He felt, rather than saw, her gaze turn to his profile. *Not now.*

The three stopped in a web of shadows as they saw Gilliam Lord Elseth, and the woman who stood a foot behind and to his left. In silence, they gazed at one another, but the mouths beneath their taut cloth masks didn't move.

Kovaschaii. Who else could speak without speaking; which others could move so precisely and so perfectly? He knew a moment of fear, then; against even one of the Kovaschaii, he would have had difficulty. But the breeze blew their scent to his nose, stronger and less cloying, in denial of his fear. These were not Kovaschaii.

The Kovaschaii were human.

Fear—what fear a Hunter Lord allowed himself to know—gave the shadows form and substance; they roiled up, thicker than mist in the season before the snows came, and lapped at the knees of Gilliam's newfound enemies. He blinked his eyes and saw that the darkness had moved, did move. Four enemies then, and he wasn't sure which was most dangerous.

Until the man in the middle lunged forward, knife held flat and to the side in his left hand. Gilliam brought his sword up to deflect the long knife's passage. He missed, or rather, the knife stayed on its unaimed course. But the man's right hand, black as the shirt he wore, shot out, fingers forming a v. The edge of Gilliam's blade met the fold of skin between the second and third fingers—and the sound of metal against metal rang out. The man twisted his hand, and Gilliam's grip faltered. The sword spun out into shadow, and all sight of it was lost, although Gilliam could hear it skitter to stillness against the uneven stone. The man had worn no mailed glove—in fact, no glove at all; his skin was ebony.

Gilliam didn't pause to wonder or gape; instead he spun low, into a roll that carried him away from both knife and attacker. He felt the whistle of air as something cut into the ground a fraction of an inch from his back. They were fast, these creatures.

By the time he gained his feet, he had his dagger in hand. He could see two of the enemy and their shadow; the third was beyond him. Without thinking, he slid behind the girl's eyes, and saw what she saw; an arm, disappearing into shadow near the ground, biceps and shoulder blades taut. She was close; too close for the details of the cloth-covered face to be made clear. He felt, through their connection, the rough, hard skin between her teeth—and heard, with his own ears, the low, pained grunt that his attacker made. If there was blood, he tasted none. Which was probably for the better; he needed his wits about him, and even that would have been a distraction.

The moon suddenly disappeared; he leaped to the side, and something brushed against his ribs. Sharp, cold pain cut along the nap of his shirt, exposing the side of a rib. He pushed the trance, prayed for speed, dodged again; this time, only the shirt was abraded. He faced two, and he had no idea how the girl fared.

Stephen knew the shadows now. Even though there was no burning temple and no dying Priests surrounding him, he knew what they presaged. The dreams had returned, and they were his only reality. Blackness and death came under the cover it chose. What chance had he? The lower city held no sacred chamber, no hidden retreat—and none of the regalia of the Hunter God. But it held Gilliam; perhaps that would be enough.

He rounded the corner, and found that it was the final one. In the moonlit street, with shadows as carpets and flooring, he found Gilliam, Lord Elseth, as his Hunter struggled for his life.

He didn't recognize the two who attacked him. They were enemies; that was enough. His dagger slid out of his

sheath, and he crouched into the nearest wall, trying to
keep even with the shadow, and at the same time trying
to stay out of its reach. His breath came heavily; his
throat felt raw.

One of the men dressed in black turned suddenly. In
the moonlight, his dark fingers were gloved by a red, liquid sheen. He moved so quickly, Stephen thought of the
Hunter in trance, and involuntarily, his gaze found
Gilliam. Lord Elseth was injured; the night couldn't dis-
guise it.

He had never wondered, in all the years since the
wyrding, why he ran in those dreams; he didn't wonder
now. The assassin—what else could he call it?—leaped
through the air, both hands extended. He carried no
weapon, and took no time to dance the intricacy of mage-
spell through the air. Just the same, his presence was
death. Stephen used the wall to push himself into the
ground. The hands of his attacker splintered wood above
his head as they drove themselves into the exterior of a
building.

They were stuck there for seconds; long enough for
Stephen to raise the dagger and slash out at the man's
neck. Steel grated as if being sharpened; the dagger hilt
shook in his hand as he drew the edge against stone, or
perhaps something harder. The only damage his single,
free strike had done was to cut away the lower edge of
the mask.

Black cloth rolled up, revealing another layer of
darkness—ebony and a glint of white that overhung obsidian lips.

Gilliam didn't know the exact instant that he became
aware of Stephen; certainly his huntbrother shouted no
greeting or warning. But he felt a sudden surge of fear
that was neither his own or his strange, new companion's.
And where two had attacked him, one stood alone.

The knot in his chest tightened. He fumbled for his
dagger, but without any hope; the hand that had twisted
his sword from his grasp was not likely to be affected by
the smaller, thinner blade. The attacker lunged low;
Gilliam jumped high, and dragged the blade across his

back. He heard again the scraping of metal against stone, and felt it rumble up his arm. The black cotton shirt was split from collar to waist. There was no skin beneath it.

Yet there had to be some way of injuring these assassins; the girl had done it. The taste of cold, hard arm, alien to him, lingered in his mouth. His mouth. She'd *bitten* down.

It meant something, he was certain—but he had no time to think what; he was moving, at the farthest reach of his trance, while the creature kept up its attack. He felt pain along his back, and his skin split as easily as the black shirt had done along his enemy's.

They were not going to survive this. From the moment wood splinters had cleared his head, he knew it for fact. He didn't have Gilliam's speed or skill; there was no Hunter's trance to draw on for protection. The dagger, dragged across an exposed throat, had done no damage. Were it not for the fact that the assassin's hands were caught in the wood for a few seconds longer, Stephen wouldn't have been able to avoid its next strike. He just moved too damned slowly.

He had to run; he knew it.

But he couldn't leave Gilliam behind.

Frantic, he began to race across the street, out into view of the silent moon and the cold, pale stars. The shadows roiled at his feet, growing more substantial as they tried to impede his progress. His heart wouldn't still; it filled his ears with its beating, although he needed to listen for any sign of his pursuer.

The cold, full laughter that suddenly broke the silence told him more than he wanted to know. Like a rabbit, he froze and looked over his shoulder. The assassin had not bothered to follow in his steps; he had waited, timing the perfect, deadly leap that would carry him to his quarry.

Stephen's knees unlocked. He tried to throw himself to the side, but too late, and far too slowly. The assassin fell like a perfectly aimed sword strike.

And the lightning that suddenly flared in the street answered his attack, an equally perfect shield.

Laughter was dwarfed by sudden screams, the sickly

smell of death replaced by the scent of charred and charring flesh. The impact of the strike sent the creature flying in a direction, and with a speed, that mirrored its attack. The shadows reached up, caught it, and appeared to consume it; the screams halted suddenly.

The remaining two assassins stopped and drew back; the one that had attacked Gilliam without cease now threw up its arms and spat out syllables that no one could understand. Together they sprinted out of sight, back the way they'd come. The shadows seemed to pull in around them.

"No!" Gilliam shouted, and a small, dirty girl skidded to a stop. Her lips were black, as were her teeth, and the growl in her throat was feral, inhuman. "Stephen?"

Stephen rolled to his feet. His forearm was bruised, but he'd managed to keep hold of his weapon; it glinted with a light that had proved too pale to pierce the darkness. "Gil." His voice was shaky. "Who?"

"I don't know. I found her. Maybe she found me." He drew closer to his huntbrother; close enough to give Stephen a full view of the various bleeding gashes he'd suffered. Stephen reached out automatically, but instead of pulling back, placed one hand on his Hunter's shoulder. They took two seconds to gain their breath as the smoke slowly cleared in the breeze.

"Hunter's power?" Gilliam asked quietly, as much awe in his voice as there had ever been.

"I don't know."

"No."

Two heads turned at the voice; only the girl seemed intent on her enemies to the exclusion of any interruption. Another shadow stood in the darkness.

And Stephen of Elseth recognized her voice.

"Well met, Lord Elseth. Well met, Stephen. You must follow me now. We have no time for explanations. The demon-kin will be back in minutes—and I do not have the power to strike again. Not from here. I am late, and the spell was . . . costly."

"Where?"

"Back," was the soft answer. Stephen squinted into the night, but the figure stayed out of moon's reach. He saw the hood pulled low, and the sleeves, long and flowing, that entirely covered her hands. "To Maubreche."

A cold, shrill cry rode on wind.

"Not yet!" Her words, soft and urgent, were not spoken to Gilliam or Stephen. "They return too soon." She gestured, and white hands broke free, for a moment, of concealing cloth. A light flared in her palms; it was a pale orange, beaded like fine mist as it trailed to the ground. "Follow the path the light reveals. Do not stray from it, or the lower city will not let you escape."

Gilliam turned to the girl, met her eyes, and gestured. Without further question, he stepped upon the path this stranger had created.

Stephen hesitated at the last moment, caught perhaps by strands of dream, or perhaps by the great weariness in a voice that still held power and decisiveness. "What of you?"

"I will join you if I am able. Now go!" So saying, she turned to face the darkness, shoulders slightly stooped, hands shaking but infinitely strong, as those she had named demon-kin burst once more from the night, wielding shadow that was edged in bright lines of shining blue.

Stephen ran. He followed Gilliam's lead, aware of the fact that Gil slowed his pace in order not to leave him behind.

CHAPTER SIXTEEN

Blood mingled with mist as it made a wet, slick trail down Gilliam's exposed flesh, but acknowledgment of the injuries would wait; the path, faintly luminescent as it cut a trail beneath their feet, wavered and flickered like a lamp run low of oil. It was safety. It would not remain so. All around it—and it was not wide—shadows reared up like small garden hedges. Even the buildings that had seemed so tightly packed to Stephen's eyes now seemed a river away; they no longer blocked the moon's vision, but they offered no sense of comfort or familiarity.

The streets were still empty—or almost.

Stephen thought he saw people at the shadow's edge, but before he could give warning, they screamed with their young, terrified voices and melted away. It stopped him by stopping his breath; he turned as if to reach out, and faltered.

Gilliam caught him firmly; Gilliam, unperturbed by the shouts and the awful silence that followed. Like any Hunter Lord, his concern was first for his huntbrother and his pack, second for the people in his demesne and preserve. For street urchins and thieves, as these must have been, he might have spared either pity or contempt had he time—but he did not. Tonight, he, Stephen, and the odd, dirty girl were being hunted. No matter that the methods of the hunt were foreign and heretofore unknown—it was still a hunt, and he had no intention of falling prey to demon-kin.

Demon-kin.

He pulled Stephen more squarely onto the path. The lower city circle was almost breaking; he could see the perimeter of the merchant's circle—and beyond that, Maubreche lay nestled in the highest circle in the land.

Stephen's shoulder trembled. He was still fit and trim, used to the rigors of accompanying Gilliam while the Hunter's trance was deep, so the shiver had nothing to do with exhaustion.

"You're injured," he said.

Gilliam nodded. There wasn't much else to do. "We're almost there."

"Great. What are we supposed to do when we get there? We can't lead those—those—into the ball; they'll kill everything in sight!"

As if talking to a testy child, Gilliam replied. "Lord Maubreche has his pack on the grounds."

"His pack?" Stephen laughed hysterically. "Gil, our daggers couldn't touch the God-cursed things at all— what the Hells good will a bunch of hounds do?"

Their situation was too urgent to allow Gilliam the luxury of bridling; he did anyway. "Maybe teeth have more of an effect—she bit them!"

It was difficult enough to argue and run, but they'd made a practice of it, and become near-experts. Throwing a third person into the process put Stephen off his stride, and for the second time that evening, he looked at the dirty girl. He also chided himself, very briefly, for being so unkind in his appellation. Except that she *was* dirty; filthy. She smelled rank and stale, even though the breeze and the pace pushed her scent away from, not toward, him. She looked at him with only a faint trace of interest in her eyes, and those eyes were all of a single color; either black or a very dark brown.

If they ever reached safety and light again, he would have to look more closely.

"Who in the Hells is she?"

Gilliam shrugged, and Stephen felt him turn and shy away from the question. It wasn't like Gilliam; he was usually direct to the point of rudeness.

Not the time for arguments; not yet. Stephen swallowed, and asked a different question. "Why is she with us?"

"They," Gilliam said, motioning with his head toward the darkness behind, "were hunting her. She found me."

Again, Stephen felt an odd shifting.

"I had to help—you would have."

I would have, yes.

A scream broke the night again, shattering the conversation. Cold, long, with a hint of sibilance to underpin its ringing clarity, it gave the shadows more force as they crowded the path.

It certainly made it easy to remain with the light.

Maubreche Manor was still brightly lit, and even as the path brought them racing across the threshold of the grounds, the strains of orchestral music joined the rustle of leaves. There were guards at the front gate; Stephen saw them as he ran past, at Gilliam's heel.

Perhaps they were enchanted, or perhaps they were sleeping—although, with Lady Maubreche as their commander, he very much doubted that was the case—but for reasons that he did not understand, they did not stop or challenge the newcomers. Indeed, they stared straight ahead, like the Queen's guards at attention, rather than stooping to notice the noise and the scramble that passed yards away from their torchlit vision.

"Something's wrong," Gilliam said, breathing hard.

"You mean, beside the fact that demons from the Hells are hunting us?"

Gilliam didn't answer, and Stephen gave up—but he had a feeling that what he had said in sarcastic jest was, in fact, true. Any hunt, no matter who the intended victim and who the hunter, was "natural" to a Hunter; it probably felt somehow natural to Gil. Mouthing a quiet, heartfelt curse at Hunter Lords in general, Stephen dropped his eyes down to the misty path and continued to run along it.

To his great relief—or perhaps just to his relief—the path veered away from the grand manor, with its lovely lights and the carriages that stood as stately emissaries in the long, cobbled drive. He had no idea at all where they were running, but as long as the path still arched on ahead, he didn't worry.

Until he heard the screaming again, keen and icy. Until he heard the human voices that followed, and quickly died into stillness. The guards. Gilliam slowed; Stephen felt the sudden lurch of tension that revealed itself only in the squaring of Gilliam's jaw. The thieves had been prowling the lower city on their own, and their death was inconsequential to him. But he had led the demon-kin to Maubreche, where the two guards would never have met them otherwise.

It was Stephen who pushed him on this time; they had exchanged roles, as they sometimes did under duress. For if the demon-kin were so close on their trail, it meant that Evayne—if the ghostly, hooded apparition had indeed been the woman of his dreams—would no longer be there to offer them her protection.

And solid steel had availed them nothing.

The path never forked and never faltered; it remained wide enough to follow easily by foot, and straight enough to follow with eye. And although the moon was at her peak, with no buildings to hide her open face, she cast no shadows to bleed the light from the mystical road.

Stephen wasn't sure exactly when it all changed; he was too concerned with running, and too certain that their flight would soon be halted by the demon-kin. He had seen how quickly they moved, and was certain that they were mere inches away, waiting and preparing. They didn't come, but the hedges did, springing up like dark life on either side, with a scent of dirt and water, of leaves and bark—of green. In the night, they had no color, but they had shape and height, and they were so perfectly kept, so solid in appearance, they seemed to be walls.

Looking down at his feet, Stephen saw the only shadows there were the ones the moon cast. He took a deep breath, tried to hold it, and winced as his lungs expelled air, seeking more.

"Stephen?"

He shook his head and kept running.

They came at last, through a maze of dark hedges and perfect new grass, to light's end. The hedges stood at a respectful distance in an almost uninterrupted circumference. There was only one way in—and one way out—from this center. The light crawled the last leg of the journey, and ended abruptly at the base of a tall, solemn statue. Even in the poor light, it was obvious that this was carved in the likeness of a man—one tall and proud, perhaps a little severe. He stood, completely straight, and a simple robe fell gently to his feet. His face was long, his chin rounded gradually to a point; his hair, long as well, fell away from his face and forehead, trapped only by a circlet across his brow. It was hard to read his expression, and Stephen would not have been surprised to find that that expression was both changeable and changing. One hand was raised, palm out; the other held a spear or like weapon that ran from his feet past the height of his shoulder. Stephen had no doubt that one maker-born had fashioned the likeness, and he wondered who the original model had been; something about the man was familiar.

"This is it," Gilliam said, softly and irrelevantly.

Stephen barely heard him. He walked quietly, his steps gentle and almost hesitant, his right hand outstretched. "Is it a King, do you think? Maybe the founder?"

"It's no King," was the quiet reply.

And hearing the voice, Stephen lost his own. He spun in the darkness, his heart ice. Hidden, until this moment, by the folds of the robe and the base of the statue's pedestal, was Lady Cynthia of Maubreche.

She was pale, white even in shadows and moonlight. Her dress was of a simple and pleasing cut—but its make was no such thing; it had cost a fortune. Stephen had, many times, bought the bolts of cloth and the reams of lace that Lady Elseth and Maribelle required, and he knew how dear they could be.

"Stephen?" She stepped out and away from the statue; her finger trailed along its hem before pulling away. "What are you doing here? I wouldn't have thought you could navigate the maze on your own—not in this light."

He swallowed; the sides of his throat formed a neat trap for words—none came. Her smile faltered; her eyes widened, and even though he couldn't see their color, he knew how brown, and how deep, they were. Then they narrowed; her shoulders straightened, her jaw came up. Even her voice changed subtly. "Is that Lord Elseth, then? And who is your companion?"

"It's—"

The shrieking of demon-kin rescued Gilliam from a rather large social crime. A plume of fire flared up into the sky, dampening the light of the moon with its brilliance and its harshness. It burned itself into Stephen's vision, lingering until the very slight breeze, carrying the smell of burning leaves and wood, arrived.

"What was that?" Cynthia said softly. Her voice was steady and very cold.

"What are you doing here?" Stephen's words overlapped hers, but where she had chosen ice, he held fire. She was no Hunter Lord, trained to death or dying—she was a Lady, skilled in lore, history, politics, and the management of the Maubreche preserve, which would one day be her own. He felt certain she would die here, because she had been rude enough to leave a gathering held in her honor alone. A few short hours ago, he would have been overjoyed.

Another person would have taken a step back from the force in his voice. Her nostrils flared, and perhaps her cheeks grew a little more red. "I could ask the same of you, Lord Stephen. This is a private area of the Maubreche Estates, and is *never* open to the ... public."

"Ask later!" Gilliam snarled. He had no sword, but his dagger was readied—and useless. He hated it.

Silence reigned a moment. The moment stretched.

"Why are they waiting?" Gilliam muttered at last. "They're fast enough to have followed."

Fire answered, stronger and closer. The smoke that the hedges surrendered drifted up in a thick, pale cloud. During the day, it would have been darker; now it wended its way on the thin breeze, the ghost of flame.

Cynthia's eyes widened. "They're—they're burning the *maze!*"

"Maybe they can't follow," Stephen offered quietly. "There's no shadow here, Gil. Look at the ground." It was a faint hope, but better than none.

Gilliam nodded; the shallow dip of chin told Stephen that his Hunter wasn't really listening. He was testing the wind, seeking the unfamiliar scent, readying himself for quick action and quicker response.

Slim fingers, strong and firm for all their lack of size, closed tightly around Stephen's forearm. "Stephen, who are they?"

He swallowed, fear for himself and fear for her becoming so tightly entwined they were inseparable. "Demons."

"Demons?" She laughed in astonished disbelief; her eyes seemed to sparkle.

"Damn it, Cynthia—demons! Look at Gil—I know he's barbaric, but he usually doesn't run around in bloodied rags!" She didn't have the chance to follow his command; Stephen caught her shoulders.

Angry, she wrenched herself free. He reached out again, but his hands met the invisible wall of her icy wrath. They fell, shaking. "Maybe," she said, and for a moment she reminded him of Gilliam—her jaw was clenched, and the tone of her voice walked the thin, tight line between anger and all-out fury, "they're of the mage-born."

Another scream, chill and loud. Yet another bolt of flame. Smoke and the smell of fire had become so common they barely noticed it.

"Oh?" He turned away, feeling a helpless anger of his own. "And what gives you that idea?"

"This is the Hunter's Hallow." Her lips curled up in what might have been a smile; it was an unpleasant expression. "The mage-born have no easy entrance here."

"It doesn't have to be easy," Stephen snapped back. "If they get here, we're lost. We met them in the lower city. We tried to fight. Steel doesn't affect them at all. Does that sound like the mage-born to you?"

"Not immediately, but mages are cunning and capable creatures." Her voice lost a bit of its edge. "Why did you call them demon-kin?"

"It's what she called them."

"She?" The edge returned, redoubled.

"Will the two of you shut the Hells up?"

Both Stephen and Cynthia spun, their mouths open in

angry unison. The odd, dirty girl sprang suddenly to life, half-leaping and half-running to stand between Gilliam and his huntbrother. Her throat seemed to grow larger and thicker; the sound she made was unmistakable and loud. She was growling.

Cynthia took a step back; she couldn't help it. The black tongue, darkened teeth, and wild, wide eyes made the girl look mad, and dangerously so.

"No!" Gilliam shouted. "Get out of the way!"

Stephen's bond with Gilliam was strong enough that his shouted warning was unnecessary; he was already flying through the air with the force of his leap.

But Lady Cynthia did what a normal person would do in the face of just such a command. She spun around to see where the danger lay, her hand already falling to a well-adorned hip, and a lovely, functional dagger.

The hedge-wall erupted.

She would never laugh at Stephen again. It was absolutely clear, from the moment the strangers burst into the maze-heart, that they weren't mage-born. They weren't even human. Shreds and scraps of dark clothing barely clung to their arms and legs; their faces, in all their dark glory, were obsidian, ugly masks. But the teeth that rimmed their lips like serpent fangs were white and gleaming.

The demon-kin were children's games and children's fears. Cynthia was suddenly a child again. But not a foolish one. Her knees bent into a roll; her shoulders and upper thighs provided the necessary momentum. The long, plush skirts she wore were heavy and impeding, but she didn't take the time to fuss with them.

"CYNTHIA!"

Gilliam, Lord Elseth, had his dagger to hand in the shadows. His breath was harsh and heavy; he had pushed the Hunter's trance almost to its upper limits, and once his endurance flagged, not even the benefit of consciousness would be left.

He knew it; he even considered it on an instinctive level. But he showed no sign of doubt or hesitation as he leaped forward, dagger extended like a claw. He had pushed himself to survive to reach the center of the maze; he pushed harder, finding new strength. He was terrified, yes—terrified that it would not be enough.

The first of the demons touched earth, slamming its hands into the ground; catching folds of velvet and embedding them in the dirt. Lady Cynthia jerked, hard, to a stop; the demon's obsidian hands came up.

Cynthia raised her pale hands to her face; they were white in the moonlight and shadows. A ring glinted as her fingers trembled. She opened her mouth; her lips parted as if in a scream. But the scream held a word, and the word held command.

"Sanctuary!"

The demon's hand sliced down in the darkness; Gilliam cried out, a rush of air against a raw throat. But before the lethal blow could cut across Lady Cynthia's face, another shadow met the first, snarling in dark fury.

Stephen had his dagger as well; he gripped it tightly, his fingers almost molding themselves to the bound twine of its hilt. He had no words at all, and very little breath; his knees were weak with momentary relief as the dirty, wild girl—somehow at the heart of this conflict—hurled herself at the demon who stood, like a death, over Cynthia's fallen body.

He was four feet from her spilled, torn skirts, but the distance seemed immense, uncoverable. Whatever anger or pain he had felt at the beginning of the evening was gone, a victim of the fear of her death. He ran, his free hand outstretched.

He was not gentle as he pulled her to her feet; even less so as he shoved her, hard, toward the statue in the maze's center. If he'd had voice or time, he might have broken all etiquette and commanded her to hide—but he had none. Gilliam's sudden terror, bright and clear, hit his throat through the Hunter's bond. He jumped, wheeling, and felt a sharp sting at his back.

Without thought, he struck out, his dagger only an extension of his hand.

Against hope, the demon growled. Stephen drew back.

In the dim light the moon cast—if it was dim; it seemed now, to his eyes, bright and luminescent—he could see the trail of dark liquid that ran the runnels of his knife.

What he knew, Gilliam knew; in danger, their bond had always been strongest. He did not need to shout or gesture or otherwise catch his Hunter's attention. Instead, he began his dance across the grass and the flower beds, his pale eyes narrowed, his attention upon the demon.

But if the demon was somehow vulnerable now, it had not lost its great speed; lunging in, in off-step to Gilliam's attack, all concentration bent upon his opponent, Stephen almost lost his arm.

He screamed as something wide and sharp scraped bone.

Even had she been so inclined, Cynthia could not hide; the cry that Stephen uttered, his voice barely recognizable, pulled her forward. She saw him fall; saw it clearly, as she saw all things in the Hunter's Hallow. She saw Gilliam's desperate lunge; heard his low-throated, guttural snarl, and saw his dagger deflected.

Demon-kin. She took a breath, trembling. Let her eyes flicker off the second demon. He was shadow, tall and narrow, to the red-tinged back of the wild child who attacked him. She, too, growled—like a Hunter boy, too new to his pack, gone feral. There was none of Gilliam's control or concentration about her—yet somehow, she still stood.

Somehow.

Slowly, the shock began to drain out of Cynthia. She took a deep breath, and leaned back, gripping the pedestal of the Hallow's single statue in tight white fingers.

She was the heir to the Maubreche demesne, with its country preserves and its near-legendary labyrinth in the very heart of the King's City. And although she had never been given to the care of a weaponsmaster, never run or linked with a pack of Hunter dogs, never faced the truth of the Hunter's Death and all its implications—she had nonetheless learned to fight.

But her voice was thin and young and vulnerable as she began to speak.

"I am of Maubreche," she whispered, her voice slowly gathering strength, "and I am of your line. We have kept this garden and this maze and this mystery that is the Hunter's Hallow."

Stephen cried out again, and sudden tears welled up in her eyes, filming their surface without falling. Her throat grew tight. She struggled with the words, won, and continued to speak. But she closed her eyes, flinching and turning from his cries; she could no longer watch.

"We have kept our pledge and our word, and now I turn to you, Keeper and Lord of the Covenant. Grant me your Sanctuary!"

Stephen heard her pale, trembling words; heard it above the din of his own pain and his own cries. He looked up weakly, his eyes seeking hers in the shadows, as her words rippled through him with the force of an oath made, an oath kept. What she had said sunk roots and became planted in memory. He would not forget it.

Only twice before had he felt so.

But never so strongly and so completely. Dawn came to the clearing, springing like life into the heart of the labyrinth. A nimbus of light touched leaf and branch and bent, sticky blades of grass, spreading outward. He felt it along his upturned face, and his lips turned in a smile of sudden, inexplicable jubilation.

And the demon-kin screamed, both at once, their fight momentarily forgotten. Stephen rolled, almost drunkenly, to his feet, clutching his wounded arm, his shredded jacket. He glanced up, and up again, to the very height of the skies; they were dark and clear.

The dawn that prevailed in the Hunter's Hallow had nothing to do with the turning. His eyes followed the light as it grew stronger and clearer, and at last his eyes found its source: The statue at the center of the maze.

No light this bright should be easily viewed, and Stephen raised his hands automatically to shield his eyes, before he realized that he felt no pain, saw no searing intensity. As the demons screamed, and the dark smoke of burning flesh reached his nose, Stephen gazed into the stone face of an angry God.

Angry? No. Or rather, not angry alone.

Stephen stumbled forward, staring now and trying to understand what his eyes saw. Before him, upon a perfect pedestal, surrounded by the greenery of the maze and the broken silence of night, stone robes seemed to flow in the wind. A man—no, the very God—stood, one hand held fast to a Hunter's spear, and the other, palm slightly extended, as if in welcome. And then stone *moved*. The lips of the God formed near-silent words.

Help us.

He felt each one as a blow, and his knees collapsed, first the right and then the left, beneath him. He reached out with one hand, palm up, as if he could somehow bridge the distance between them. But even Stephen could not say, at that moment, whether his gesture was one of supplication or comfort.

Lady Cynthia of Maubreche squared her shoulders. The stone at her palms felt warm, almost living; the light at her back shone like a beacon and haloed her stiff form, growing stronger. She wanted to turn, then, and study the face of the God; but some instinct stopped her motion, and instead, she watched the demons as if from a great distance.

They burned. Just as the hedges had burned, shriveling and dying as the breeze blew their scent across the whole of the maze. It was hard to imagine, as they writhed and shrank in on themselves, that they had ever been a danger.

The wild girl, her lips black and wet, stood snarling as her enemy burned; she seemed leashed somehow. Cynthia heard the growl that came from this stranger's lips and shivered. Had she been in any other place, she might have felt fear—but under the watchful eye of the God, she had none to offer.

And then Cynthia saw Stephen, and even the deaths of her enemies were forgotten. She left the comfort of warm stone and crossed the grass quickly toward him, wondering why he knelt, frozen in position, upon the grass.

The look on his face was more than she could bear, and without a second thought, she lifted her overskirt, pulling both her dagger and a swath of thick cotton from her petticoats. These, she cut into long, wide strips.

Gilliam appeared at her side; it was clear that he, too, had suffered—but none of his wounds were as dangerous as the one Stephen had taken.

"How is it?" Lord Elseth asked bluntly.

"Take these," she murmured, handing him her newly made bandages. "Wash them in the fountain basin and bring them back. Quickly."

He followed her orders; she had known he would. Kneeling, she touched Stephen's face, one palm to either cheek, as she had never dared do before. He was cold; ice had settled beneath his skin. She closed her eyes, suddenly unable to look at the expression on his face.

"Stephen," she whispered, and then, pulling him out of his kneel and toward her shoulder, *"Stephen."*

He came, as if suddenly released, a heavy weight. His arms, both the injured one and the whole, found her shoulders and held them, convulsively; his face, he buried in the side of her pale, white neck.

He was shaking. She rocked him gently, wondering how the minutes could stretch so unbearably. At last she heard movement across the grass and pulled her head up, turning it in the direction of the noise. Stephen would not let go.

Instead of Gilliam, she saw the girl. This close, the blackness at her lips resolved itself into more than just liquid. Even Cynthia, raised on the unmaking of the Hunter's kill, flinched. The girl did not seem to notice. Instead, she shuffled in, her head forward, her nostrils flared.

Like a dog.

"Not now," Cynthia said, her voice quavering slightly. Stephen raised his head.

"Stephen?" Cynthia turned, forgetting the girl. But Stephen's eyes, wide and round, caught and distorted that feral child's expression. The girl darted forward suddenly, butting Stephen's shoulder with her head. He bit his lip on a cry and winced; the arm she had struck was the injured one.

"Go away!" Cynthia shouted.

The girl came forward again and began to nuzzle Stephen; there really wasn't another word for it. Cynthia, caught by Stephen's arms, nonetheless tried to physically shove the girl backward.

"What's wrong?" Gilliam said, and then, as he saw the three of them huddled upon the ground, "No." It was to the girl that he spoke. She looked up at him, guileless, and then began to whimper.

That whimper stretched out into a full whine.

Gilliam did not look away from the open darkness of her eyes. "Cynthia," he said, holding out the dampened strips of cloth.

She took them and eased herself out of Stephen's grip. "Who is she?" Her voice was soft; she did not look up at Gilliam.

"I don't know," he answered, each word measured.

"What is she?"

"I don't know."

But she heard, as she began to bind Stephen's wound as tightly as possible, the quiver in Gilliam's voice. Had she been in the seat of judgment, she would have called him forward and asked for the truth. She did not.

Instead, she worked in silence, aware that Gilliam had not turned or wavered at all. The girl's whine grew higher and sharper, but at least the girl was somehow contained, for she did not approach Stephen again.

"It's all right," Stephen said softly.

"Shhhh." She touched his fingers with her lips. "Lord Elseth, will you aid me? I do not think Stephen will be able to walk."

"I can walk," he said, ever so faintly. He started to prop himself up on one elbow. "I can walk; I will walk for you, Lord." His eyes were wide, almost glassy; Cynthia knew, as she stared at his face, that they did not see her. She paled.

Gilliam was at her side at once.

"What is it?" she asked him, grabbing his arm and holding it tight, as if to somehow shake the answer out of Gilliam. "What is he feeling?"

Gilliam pulled himself out of Cynthia's grip and bent down, placing a hand under each of Stephen's shoulders.

"Gilliam!"

He looked at her, over the pale thatch of Stephen's hair. "I can't answer that," he replied evenly. "He'll tell you himself, if he wants to."

Lady Cynthia, heir to the Maubreche responsibilities, was a very tired young woman. Her hair, carefully coiffed and secured at the evening's start, had come loose from combs and pins, and curled in darkness around her dirt-stained face. Her gowns were askew, and the very lip of her undergarments, cut so jaggedly with her personal dagger, hung loosely at her feet. Her body ached; her head felt so heavy, it hung with the weight of exhaustion.

And none of this mattered as she met Gilliam's suddenly shuttered face. She spoke, although she knew it was unwise.

"Lord Elseth," she said, her voice very cold, "we are not enemies, or even rivals, in this."

Gilliam's jaw set as he hoisted Stephen to his feet and draped one strong arm under Stephen's shoulders. "I never said we were." If possible, his voice was colder than Cynthia's.

Cynthia snorted. "You didn't have to say it. For the past two months you've been barely civil—and this evening you were a positive disgrace to Elseth!"

"Cynthia," Stephen said weakly. "Gil."

They ignored him. "That isn't for you to decide," he said, grinding his teeth. "Lady Elseth will make her opinion known, and I answer to her alone."

"Gil—"

"He isn't yours," Gilliam continued, brushing aside Stephen's weak plea. "He'll never be yours. You've got no right to interfere with the huntbrother's bond."

As Gilliam bristled, so did the wild girl.

Cynthia heard the snarl, turned, and snapped. "Be quiet!" The girl took a step back, but her growl grew tighter and lower.

"I'm not trying to interfere with what you and Stephen share," Cynthia said evenly, her cheeks suddenly crimson. "I know full well that I'll never have it—or anything else of his, besides. I was—concerned for him. That's all."

Gilliam made no reply. They stood, in the darkness of moonlit sky, their faces shadowed by more than night.

"Gilliam," Stephen whispered. "You idiot."

Gilliam bridled; he always did. But he did not let his brother fall. "Come on," he said, to no one in particular. "Let's get inside. We'll have to call healers."

Cynthia nodded stiffly and turned to lead the Hunter and his brother out of the damaged maze. As she did, the girl darted forward. Gilliam shouted wordlessly, and the girl whined—but she continued forward until she could butt her head against Stephen's bloodstained chest.

Stephen staggered; Gilliam caught him in both arms.

The girl shoved her hands into her dirty, torn shift, still keening softly.

Gilliam shook his head, but the girl ignored him. Hands trembling, face quite still, she watched Stephen. After a second, she shoved her head into his midsection again, demanding some attention, some gesture.

Stephen put his hands out to gently push her aside. Before he could so much as brush against her shoulders, she pushed something into his shaking palms and jumped back, skittish. His fingers closed reflexively against something smooth and cool.

Gilliam, Lord Elseth, felt his huntbrother's sudden lurch of terror. "Stephen?"

Stephen shook his head. Even in darkness more complete than this, he would have known what it was that the wild, strange girl had given into his keeping. He could not look. He did not have to.

The wyrd of Fate and mystery, so long suspended, settled heavily upon his frail shoulders, contained as it was by the deceptively simple form of the Hunter's Horn.

CHAPTER SEVENTEEN

"Gilliam," Lady Elseth said softly. "What happened?"

Gilliam knew that his mother's soft-spoken question was nothing short of a demand for information. Unfortunately, he also knew that Stephen did not wish that question answered. As he hadn't Stephen's faculty for words, he shrugged instead. A poor substitute.

The Mother-born Priestess, Vivienne of the King's City, had come as quickly as the night roads and travel allowed. She had said nothing at all as she entered the room that was to be Stephen's sick chamber. But she quickly cleared it of idle spectators—even, and including, Gilliam of Elseth. As always, he bridled.

"A shrug," his mother said quietly, "is not an answer that I find acceptable."

Lady Cynthia, newly changed, and now much more simply attired, stepped forward and placed a gentle hand on Lady Elseth's shoulder. "May I? Gilliam is also exhausted; the doctors prescribed rest for him."

Elsabet's eyes narrowed as she glanced at her son. Her son wisely refused to meet her eyes, but made a display of a yawn that was only part act.

"Lord Elseth, why don't you tend to your other guest?"

"Other guest?" Lady Elseth's voice was even softer.

"What a good idea," Gilliam said lamely. He knew it would spark his mother's curiosity further—but that was unavoidable now. Grudgingly, he nodded his thanks to Lady Cynthia of Maubreche and slunk out of the room, figurative tail between his legs.

"Lady Elseth, please forgive us for allowing this tragedy to occur on Maubreche lands. We've prepared rooms for you, should you wish to stay in the manor."

Elsebet nodded almost absently. "Yes, I'd appreciate that."

"Then let me show you to your rooms."

Lady Elseth was a shrewd and perceptive woman. For that reason, Cynthia had always both admired and feared her. As she walked now by her side, fear was the stronger emotion. She felt Lady Elseth's keen gaze upon her face. In silence, and without turning once to meet her elder's eyes, Cynthia led the way to the manor's west wing.

There, she paused in front of the door.

"Why don't you join me, Cynthia?"

It was not a request, no matter how politely worded. Swallowing, Cynthia nodded assent, and together they entered Lady Elseth's rooms. A fire was already burning in the grate, and a cozy tea had been newly set in the sitting room. Lady Elseth took the chair closest to the fire and motioned for Cynthia to join her.

But if Cynthia had thought to be questioned about the events of the evening, she was mistaken.

"Tell me," Elsabet said softly, "about Stephen."

Cynthia swallowed again. "You know him better than I ever will," she replied. "Tea?"

"Yes, please. And as for the other, I'm not so certain."

Cynthia poured slowly and let the liquid, still steaming, reach the gold rim of the cup before she passed it on. She poured for herself as well and then sat, cup between her hands, staring at her reflection upon the clear, brown surface of the liquid. Silence stretched widely between them before she ventured to speak. "Why do you want me to talk about Stephen?"

"Because," Elsabet said quietly, "you talk to no one else of him—and perhaps you need to speak."

"Am I so obvious?"

The smile that touched Lady Elseth's face was a wry one. "Perhaps only to me. Certainly not to Stephen."

Cynthia lowered her gaze to stare moodily at the table-top. "It won't make any difference. We both know that."

"Yes."

The word hurt; it still hurt.

"But it already has, Cynthia. You are eighteen now, and

not even at the start of your year. You have met and been courted by many of the younger Hunters, although that should more properly have waited until you came out."

"I know," Cynthia said, her voice surprisingly bitter. "And I know that I'll marry the younger son of some Hunter Lord, and both he and his huntbrother will forsake their family name for Maubreche. Because, of course, the line must continue."

Lady Elseth said nothing at all.

"But that's not what I want." There. It was said.

"No," Elsabet replied. "And you have less choice than most of us had when we searched for our husbands. We had plans to tend to their estates; you are hampered by the fact that your estate will be—can only be— Maubreche. If you were not the only child, Cynthia, I would have happily recommended you to either of my sons. But Gilliam *is* Elseth; he cannot take Maubreche responsibilities as his own. And Stephen is no Hunter Lord, to offer Maubreche's services in the Sacred Hunt."

Cynthia set her tea down on the table; her hands were trembling. "Do you think I don't already know this?" she asked, her voice too low. "Do you think that I've thought about anything else for the last two years?" She rose, upsetting her chair; her cheeks were flushed and dark.

Lady Elseth did not move.

"Why are you asking me this? Why do you want me to speak openly about the impossible?"

"Because only by admitting it openly will you ever truly dismiss it. You parents are concerned; this you know well. Let me tell you that I, too, am concerned. For the sake of Stephen. Between you and I there is no pretense. What we do, we have little choice in, if we are not to abandon our responsibilities and our birthrights." This voice, these formal words, were those that Lady Elseth used when she sat in judgment. "If we are lucky, then we will have love; if we are not, then we will have duty. Love is for children, Cynthia."

Cynthia drew a sharp breath, but before she could frame a reply, Lady Elseth continued, sitting very, very still as she did.

"I was a child, too. I listened to the musings of the

bard-born, and I dreamed. The man I chose was no
Hunter Lord. He was a student, an academic in the King's
City seeking admission to the Order of Knowledge. We
met by accident at the Sacred Hunt in the year I came
out."

Cynthia was silent now, watching the pale, neutral cast
of Elsabet's calm face.

"After the Sacred Hunt, when death and loss were in
the air, I went to him. I don't know why." She smiled,
briefly, and shook her head. "I do know. I wanted no taint
of loss or death; I wanted someone whose life was living.
Or so I tell myself now.

"I contrived to stay in the King's City for three weeks,
Cynthia. I met with Ladies and their sons, and began to
search in earnest for the Lord of my future—during the
days. But in the evenings, I went to him, stayed with
him."

"You didn't—"

"No; I asked for the intercession of the Mother-born to
aid me in my cycle."

Lady Elseth set her tea aside and closed her eyes, remembering. The fire crackled; not even breath was loud
enough to be heard.

"Was it—was it worth it?"

"I thought so for those three weeks. For the next two
years, I regretted it."

"And now?"

"Now? I regret nothing."

Cynthia met Lady Elsabet's gaze; their eyes locked; the
room vanished around them. "But what if I want more
than three weeks? What if I want forever?"

Elsabet knew what the question would be before it was
spoken. There was no softness in her when she answered.
"What if you have a choice between nothing and three
weeks?"

Silence again; the evening had been measured by the
quality of their silences, rather than the force of the words
spoken. Cynthia's eyes were watery and red, but she allowed no tears to fall. "What if three weeks aren't enough
for Stephen?"

Lady Elseth looked down at her skirts; she brushed

them out carefully and methodically, almost automatically arranging them into the most pleasing drape. "I cannot speak for Stephen. Perhaps you should let him decide." She stood, then; the work on her skirts was undone. "I am fatigued by the evening, Lady Cynthia; I must retire. Perhaps we shall speak more of this tomorrow."

Stephen feigned sleep under Vivienne's gentle ministrations. It was only a partial act. Although the pain had receded, and the bleeding had stopped, he was exhausted. To be nursed and tended by the Mother-born was a balm, but it had its price. For to heal the body, the healer had to understand it, and to understand it well, she had to become, however briefly, a part of it. She brought warmth with her, sure knowledge, a deep understanding of all pain, all sorrow, all fear.

And when the healing was done, she left. His body, whole, let him feel the ache of the Mother's passing, as he had done only one other time in his life. It hurt.

She knew, of course. She could feel his pulse, unnaturally quick, at her fingers. But she, too, was weary. She had asked no questions about the injuries when she had first arrived, as Stephen had not been in any condition to answer them. Now that he was, she felt too weak to ask.

"Stephen," she said quietly, as she rose from his bedside. "If you feel the need to ask any questions, I will still be in the Maubreche estate on the morrow. Summon me, if you will."

He did not open his eyes; did not move or nod, or in any way acknowledge her offer. Trembling, he saw the shadow of her passing against his eyelids. She paused once; he heard the rustle of her robes. The lamps in the room were doused, and Stephen lay back against his pillows in the darkness.

He had not allowed them to take away the horn. He reached for it now, as it sat completely vulnerable upon the table beside his bed. As his eyes adjusted to the moonlight filtering in through the uncurtained window, he stared at his new burden.

He could still see the eyes of the girl in the moment that the horn had passed into his hands. And he did not understand what he saw there; a flicker of desperation, fear—something else. It had not lasted; her dark eyes had darted away, horn forgotten, to seek Gilliam.

The horn was smooth and curiously unadorned. It was simple bone or antler, but from what beast, upon close inspection, he couldn't say. Around the horn's lip, burned there as if by a brand, were two interlocked circles; they were perfectly round, unbroken.

Three times he had lifted this very horn, and three times—in dreams—he had sounded it. He pressed its mouth to his lips; both were cold. He could not draw breath to wind it.

Evayne, he thought. But this was no dream; she did not appear in the doorway to answer his questions or offer her unfathomable pity.

In the morning, he woke to a knock at the door. The sun was high; higher than it should have been. He began to scramble out from under the covers when the room spun back into focus. Maubreche. Not Elseth.

"Hello?" He expected breakfast, or lunch, judging the hour; neither came. Cynthia opened the door quietly and entered the room.

Speechless, he pulled the covers up to the tip of his chin.

"I see that your arm is better." She smiled, hesitant, her hands behind her back. Gone was the unfamiliar young Lady who had danced in fine silks and velvets; gone was the proud and beautiful solitary heir to the Maubreche estates. She wore a simple brown dress, and her hair, no longer combed and jeweled, rested at her back in single braid.

"It's—it's much better." He swallowed and sank farther back. "I—if you—"

"I brought you a book," she said, too quickly. She started to step forward, stopped, and pulled the volume from behind her back. Advancing upon him, she held it as if it were a shield.

He held out his hand; she placed the book in it. Neither of them so much as glanced at the title. Their fingers touched, and Cynthia pulled back. The book tumbled to the floor.

She blushed, bent, picked it up, and shoved it firmly into his hands. "I'll speak with you later," she said, and turning, fled.

On the third day of his recovery at the Maubreche estate, Stephen accepted Lady Cynthia's rather formally worded invitation to a tour of the grounds. He did so because he was curious; he wanted to see, in daylight, what night had shadowed. But he also wanted to see Cynthia, unwise though he thought it might be.

She met him in his rooms after breakfast had been served, and waited at the doors while one of the Maubreche valets helped him dress. Then, in near silence, she led him along the corridors and down the stairs of the wing. Only when doors opened into sunlight did she seem to relax.

Wind swept the strands of hair not caught in braids up along the sides of her cheeks; it ruffled the pale brown of her stiff, heavy skirts. She closed her eyes a moment, took a deep breath, and then accepted the arm that Stephen offered almost hesitantly.

"Is there anything that you'd like to see?" she asked. Her voice was soft, almost a whisper.

Several answers came to mind, but when he finally spoke, all he could say was: "The labyrinth."

She seemed to be expecting that, or perhaps that was what she had intended to show him. She nodded and began to lead him toward it.

Even from the house, the neatly kept sweep of tall, green wall dominated the perfect landscape of the Maubreche gardens. In their foreground, there was a tall stone slab, cut deeply across the middle, as if by a sword. Water trickled from the edge of the gash.

"What is it?" Stephen questioned quietly.

She didn't answer; instead, she approached the fountain to let the monument speak for itself. It seemed to be marble, shot through with hints of smoky gray and green. Etched into the grained pattern of the marble were names; Stephen recognized very few of them. But he knew them for Maubreche ancestors. Cynthia bowed very quietly to both the monument and the names it housed; after a moment, Stephen did likewise.

"Corason built the maze," she said, pointing to the very first name on the list. "Let me show you his work."

Stephen looked at the hedges as they approached. On first sight, they were not so different from any other shrubbery that he had seen—they were carefully tended, carefully pruned.

"The outside face," Cynthia said, as if she could hear his thoughts. She led him slowly around the circle of greenery. They came, at length, to a gap between the circumference. It was too narrow for them to walk through abreast, and Cynthia relinquished her hold on Stephen's arm to precede him.

"Where is the damage?"

"Damage? Ah. Around the other side." The momentary darkening of her features told him, clearly, what the hedge meant to her. "It was . . . not so bad as we first feared. Later, if you'd like, we can inspect it, but I want you to see what the labyrinth looks like when it's whole."

Stephen barely heard her answer. For as he stepped clear of the labyrinth's one entrance, he saw what the outside face hid. The walls of the maze were alive. Captured in green, as if the shrubs were stone, all manner of creatures stood. There, to his left, an elderly woman sitting upon a rock; to his right, an elderly man bent over some task that the leaves swallowed.

"These are the pride of the master gardener. He tends them every day he can. Every year the maze changes, very slowly and very subtly. I used to come out with him and try to guess what was different, when I was younger. I asked him once why he didn't sculpt—real stone, I mean. He laughed and walked off. It was two days before he decided to answer the question."

There, in the wall just ahead, one figure caught Stephen's attention. He almost missed it, it was so slight, but perhaps the light caught the figure at just the right moment, or perhaps Cynthia guided him toward it. He saw the face and hands of a young child, peering out of the greenery. Green eyes, branched limbs, wavering in the wind the way a child shivers in surprise or fear.

"These walls—that child . . ." He felt acutely aware of his lack of words, although words had never been his weakness.

"I know." She walked toward the leafy child. "He was so much younger the first time I thought I saw him. So much more hesitant. Just his nose, and his chin, and a couple of fingers. He only came up to here—" She motioned toward her waist. "He's coming out a bit, sort of escaping whatever life he has on the other side of that wall."

"I wonder what he's looking at."

"So do I."

"Cynthia?"

She nodded, reaching out at the same time to touch the small hand of the boy.

"You said the master gardener answered your question."

"Eventually." Her lips were curved in the same delicate smile as those of the green child.

"What did he say?"

"He said 'Look in my garden, child. Come back and tell me what you see.'" Her smile didn't change, but her eyes did, although Stephen could never afterward describe the difference. "I went out and spent the day wandering in the maze. I spent some time sleeping under the arms of the God, and some time talking to the rabbits— they were like the boy, but they're gone now—and when I came back, I'd almost forgotten the question. But he hadn't. He asked me what I'd seen there, and I told him."

"And?"

"He told me that it would change. He said stone is lifeless, cold, hard—you have to fight it and once you've finished, it's still stone. But life—he said life was the best material because it changed, and grew, and surprised one."

They were silent a moment, thinking on it. "I'd like to meet this gardener of yours someday," Stephen said finally.

"Perhaps we will see him today." By the forced lightness of her tone, he knew that she didn't mean it; he did not know why. "Come; let's go to the heart of the labyrinth." She released her tentative hold upon the green child. As she did, Stephen felt a sudden, sharp loss. He let it pass silently as she moved away; in a few seconds, he joined her.

As he did, Stephen's full attention returned to the hedges; he barely stopped to offer Cynthia his arm. If she begrudged him this rare breach of etiquette, none of her disapproval showed on her face; indeed, she was slow to place her hand upon his arm.

These bushes, they were like any other. There was no way they should have been so much of a presence. But try as he did to tell himself that, he still felt that they were more than alive—they were life, in expression, in intent, and in the odd quirkiness of their design. Every so often he would point out something that caught his eyes—the carved representation of birds nesting, of a sly fox darting for cover, of a group of men gathered around it with a clumsy sort of grace. There were people sitting under carved boughs; they were green but he could feel flesh, breath, and a slow, stately movement about them that more than wind through their tiny, delicate leaves could explain.

"This master gardener," Stephen said softly—for no loud words, he was sure, could be uttered in this maze, "he's maker-born, isn't he?"

She did not answer. "Here," she murmured softly. "You must look at this one. It will be gone very soon, unlike the others."

Stephen followed her obediently, and as he turned a corner, he came face-to-face with a stag leaping out of the hedge. Only half its body could be seen, and that half well above the ground, its front legs straining for height and speed. Its head was held high and crowned with strong, branching antlers. Its face was determined, noble, and touched by a sadness that almost overpowered his silent watchers.

Not until he was forced to exhale did Stephen realize that he'd been holding his breath. He pulled back, without a word, and they continued on, allowing the proud animal to continue undisturbed and untouched.

But to Stephen the stag crystallized what he felt in the hedges, and why. They were like forest, like hunting grounds in an inexplicable way; teeming with hidden and silent life, undisturbed by common human interaction. They were more than that, though. He knew, with a profound sense of loss, that were the animals in the hedges real, were he to encounter them at the side of his Hunter, he could no more allow them to be hunted than he could hunt in a ballroom. For the first time in his life, hunting felt almost profane. It disquieted him deeply.

Cynthia, not born and bred to the actual, physical hunt, could not know all of what he felt, but she sensed his silent mortification. "Here, Stephen," she said, as if to distract him. "Now we come upon the only thing that interests most of our visitors. The tapestries."

He shook his head; the stag slowly receded. The walls to either side were teaming with scenes from life, in different reliefs; they had none of the quirky reality that the other hedges had—they indeed seemed to be, as Cynthia had named them, tapestries. In green.

Acts of war were carved there, war and the heroism it often evoked; acts of sacrifice, love, pain. Figures melded in and out of each other, giving the whole a feel of continuity. Of Maubreche's lineage.

"These are the exploits of the Maubreche line," she said, although it wasn't necessary. "That—" she pointed almost reverently, "is Harald of Maubreche." She shivered, and Stephen came to stand at her side, wondering what in the young man's countenance could cause her reaction. The figure could not have been older than Cynthia. He stood on the edge of a cliff, looking outward insensibly upon his audience. His face was an open expression of grief, shock, and loss, but beneath that was a determination seldom seen in any his age. Stephen did not know the history of the family, but he knew that somehow, somewhere, this young boy had given up more than his life to protect something he loved. It radiated outward from him.

Cynthia bowed low and pressed her fingers against her

lips. Then she stood and moved on. The scenes changed.
Some of them featured women, some men, and some children. In one or two, the pride of the Maubreche hunting
packs long past came to bristling life. But none of those
had the resonance, and the sense of bitter, inevitable loss,
that Harald did. Stephen was afraid to ask the story.

They walked together in silence until at last the tapestries ended. To Stephen's surprise, the hedge that preceded them into the heart of the maze seemed wild and
untended. He turned to glance at Cynthia, and she smiled,
as if she expected his reaction.

"These wait for the future deeds of the Maubreche
family. We know that one of our line will be greater than
any who have come before—and this whole wall will be
his. Or hers. I hope I live to see that day." She swallowed,
and, for a moment, her eyes were stripped of pride and
assurance. She hoped for that day, but Stephen saw fear
there, also.

And he wondered, as she did, whether that greatness
would exact more of a price than Harald had paid—
whatever that price had been.

"Come," Cynthia said, shaking herself. The moment—
and the vulnerability—passed. She was again the adult
heir to the Maubreche demesne. "We're almost upon the
center. I want you to see the God in daylight."

Stephen stopped walking, and Cynthia noted this because her hand was upon his arm. "Stephen?"

He did not want to see the God in daylight. He realized, suddenly, that he did not want to see the God at all,
even if it was a statue, a representation, no more. He
opened his mouth, but he found that he could not tell her
why; the horn at his side, hidden in the folds of his jacket,
weighed heavily upon him.

But heavy or no, he walked with it, at Cynthia's side.
The last of the wild hedge fell away, and in the center, as
Cynthia had promised, the God stood in daylight.

But in daylight, the God was different; without darkness, some of its frightening mystery had been stripped
away, concealed by the sun. There was a fountain that
bubbled at his back, and although this maze was a testa-

ment to life, the fountain and the statue were both of stone.

There are some things, Stephen thought, *that do not change with time.* He stared up, following the lines of the statue's stone robes, until he could clearly make out the details of the God's face. There, his eyes stopped. For what he saw in this unchanging representation, he had also seen in the Maubreche living tapestries. In Harald's face. Sorrow, deep and profound, as well as determination and a measure of peace, were evident in the solemn line of jaw and forehead.

Without thinking, he dropped to one knee and bowed his head—just as he would have done in the presence of the Master of the Game.

"He doesn't look so horrible, does he?" Cynthia asked softly. "It's hard to imagine that he hurts us so badly each and every year." She walked past Stephen's bowed form, and came to rest both hands upon the pale stone, as if seeking warmth.

"Why did you ask for sanctuary here?"

She looked back, met Stephen's raised eyes. "Because here, there is no Hunt." She looked away. "And because here, in this hollow, we have promised to keep the Hunter's word in return for his peace."

"His peace?"

"It's an old custom, Stephen. A family custom. I don't understand it well, myself; I won't until my father dies."

It didn't make any sense. "But if your father's dead, how he can tell you anything?"

She did not choose to answer, and although he was curious, he lost the desire to push her. Instead, he stared at the pale profile of her face. Her eyes were closed.

"Cynthia?"

"Yes?" She did not open her eyes.

He hesitated, and then rose, treading carefully across the grass to stand before her. "Why are we here?"

"Ever?" she returned softly, "Or now?"

"Now."

She swallowed, and to Stephen's surprise, her cheeks reddened. She opened her eyes, searching his; they stood very close. Words started, half-audible; words stopped.

They were both afraid, and the fear was an old one, a common one.

"You know I'm going to have to marry soon," she said at last, uncomfortable and uncertain.

It was Stephen's turn to look away. "Yes. Do you—do you know who?"

She shrugged, an elegant rustle of cloth against skin. "One of three. It doesn't matter."

He wanted to tell her that it mattered to him, but he couldn't bring himself to say it. Awkward in silence, he matched her shrug.

"I would—I would have married you, if we had held different positions."

He had always thought it was what he wanted to hear, until he heard it in truth. But hearing the pain behind the words, hearing the farewell, he took no pleasure in them. "Cynthia—"

"Stephen," she cut off his question, her voice low. "Must I say everything?"

"What do you want from me?"

"Everything." Her face was pale and stark. "But I cannot have it; you cannot give it. Ask me a different question."

"What can I give you?" He reached out; traced the line of her cheek with his fingers.

"It's a better question," she said, not withdrawing. "Only you can answer it. I've asked it of myself, and I know my own answer. I brought you here."

He kissed her then, gently and hesitantly. She stiffened, and he pulled back, bumping her nose and the line of her forehead. She laughed shakily and reached up to encircle his neck with her arms.

They kissed again, less awkwardly, their nervousness blending with something else. And then, when Stephen pulled back, he caught her face in his hands and met her eyes. She did not look away, did not avoid him, or make any move to leave.

He buried his face in the nape of her neck and pulled her close, hugging her as tightly as he dared. In awe, almost, at what she had asked, what she had decided. He knew that nothing that happened today, in this labyrinth,

was permanent; knew, no matter how much he thought
and planned and plotted, that Cynthia of Maubreche
would go on to marry—and bear children to—a lesser
Hunter Lord. None of it mattered. He held her close,
closer; he lifted his head and found her mouth, still
clutching her tightly.

Something sharp pressed into his hip.

He pulled back, as did she, and then looked down to
see the plain, carved horn. And he remembered, clearly
and suddenly, the last time he had been in the maze with
Cynthia. He saw the eyes of the wild girl, as she had
shoved the horn into his hands, and felt once again the
presence of God.

He knew that he could not stay or accept what Cynthia
offered; the time was poor for it, and dangerous.

But he bit his lip until he drew blood.

She knew. He did not have to speak. Her eyes filmed
and then snapped shut; water glistened at her lids and
along her lashes, but did not grace her cheeks. "I—I understand. I'm sorry to have troubled you."

He caught her by the shoulders, then. "You don't understand, Cynthia. I'm—I'm under wyrd; I would stay
with you if I could. But that girl—that wild creature that
Gilliam brought with him four evenings past—she gave
me this." He lifted the horn at his hip.

"What of it?"

"It's the God's."

She did not believe him, or else she thought him mad.
She turned her face to the statue and once again gripped
the edges of its pedestal. "Then give it back to God." Her
voice was shaky, angry.

"Cynthia," he said, but she would not turn. "Let me see
to the horn and the girl; let me solve the problem they
present. I'll return then."

"And what if you return too late?" Her voice was
proud, almost haughty.

He swallowed. She was right; he was a fool to lose this
one day, this one chance. He took a step toward her, and
then another, but as he reached out, he felt *power*. The
clearing glowed with it. Cynthia, unmoved, still kept her
back to him.

The face of the God moved. His lips formed a single word or perhaps a snarl; it wasn't clear. Its meaning was. *Go.* Cynthia had not seen it, and Stephen doubted that she would.

"If I return late?" he asked, determined to at least answer her. "Then I'll curse myself for a fool until I die."

She turned in an awkward rush. "Stephen—"

He pressed his fingers against her lips. "I'll return, Cynthia. I'll come back to you. We'll meet here again." But even as he said it, he felt the shadows growing. The wyrd was upon him, and in each of the three dreams, he had called his own death.

She had always been aware of him, or of part of him; she saw the shift in his face and the shift in his promise immediately. "Swear it," she said, her voice suddenly hard. "Swear it, Stephen."

"I so swear."

"No—not like that." She bent down and lifted her skirts in trembling hands. He watched as she removed the small knife that all Hunter Ladies carried. Before he could stop her, she dragged it across her hand, as Gilliam had once done, years ago.

"Cynthia . . ."

"You did it for him, when you were a child. Do it for me now." She was crying, her eyes almost as red as her palm. He took the knife.

"Tell me that you'll return to me, Stephen."

"I'll return to you. I swear it." His hand shook as he placed the knife against his palm.

"No matter what happens."

"No matter what." His blood flowed then. Before he could offer her his hand, she had taken it. He pulled her close, and she let him, although it was awkward; she did not release his hand.

"Lord," she whispered softly, her lips and eyes swollen. It was not until she continued to speak that Stephen realized she did not speak to him. "We've kept our oath and your lands. Bear witness to this vow; give it your blessing and your curse."

They were no Priest's words, but in their choked rhythm, Stephen felt a stirring. He could not identify it, could not name it; it was almost as if a different God's approbation drifted past on the quiet breeze.

But Cynthia stopped crying almost at once, and he held her in his arms for as long as he dared, thinking that not once had they spoken of love.

CHAPTER EIGHTEEN

The first person that Stephen met, when he returned to Elseth Manor, was Lady Elseth herself. She had had word of his coming, and perhaps contrived to meet him upon his return. Gilliam was nowhere in sight, and Boredan was also about his duties.

He was not tired from the journey; indeed, he had chosen a leisurely pace along the road. He had wanted time and privacy in which to think—and these would best be obtained in the company of complete strangers at the inns or along the roads.

"Stephen," Elsabet said, coming down the long hall, her skirts rustling, as always, in her wake. Fashions had changed since he was eight, and with those fashions had gone the plain, long skirts. Now, there were thin hoops, and panniers that reminded him, oddly, of saddlebags, around Lady Elseth's legs and petticoats. He thought them ugly, and hoped that fashion would be kind and turn again.

"Elsa," he said, grabbing her hands firmly in his own, and leaning down to kiss her cheek. "What news?"

"I was about to ask you that," she said, smiling. She pulled back, although she did not let go of his hands, and her eyes were distinctly appraising. "You didn't stay long."

"No."

"I'd sent word that you wouldn't be needed."

"You lied."

She met his eyes and the lines around hers deepened. Then she smiled, almost shyly; a hint of the young girl she might once have been. "I didn't," she said dryly, "realize that it was a lie at the time." She leaned forward into his chest, and he let go of her hands to place arms around her shoulders. "But I'm worried."

"About Gilliam?"

"Who else?" She laughed, but the laugh was too high, and a little too brittle. Then, as if remembering herself, she said, "You look well, Stephen."

He felt her shiver, and he smiled broadly. "Vivienne could raise the dead. But, yes, I'm well. I apologize if I frightened you."

She played at batting the side of his head. "Frightened me? The very thought of being left alone with Gilliam— say that you terrified me instead, and all will be forgiven."

They hooked arms together, but instead of entering into the house, Lady Elseth led Stephen out the front doors. She ambled along the kept area of their grounds, and to any watching servants, there was little out of the ordinary. Except that Stephen had not yet bathed, or even seen to the accoutrements of his travels.

"Stephen, what is happening?" Elsa said, when they were far enough away from the manor so she could be certain no servant's ears would hear her. All playful banter was gone from her voice, and the very set of her eyes and lips were exactly those she wore when she sat in judgment.

"Happening?"

"You did not see fit to explain your injuries; neither did Gilliam or Cynthia. I can understand, perhaps, your reluctance." It was, of course, a lie. "But the girl that Gilliam brought home with him—she's not normal."

"No," Stephen replied gravely. "But . . . how has she been?"

"I don't know." The words were clipped and cold. "She hasn't spoken a single word. Not just to me, Stephen. To anyone. Gilliam is constantly with her—or rather, she is constantly with Gilliam. She does not eat at our table, and . . . she cannot be made to dress in an appropriate fashion."

"Do you fear madness?" he asked, hoping that she did.

"No," Lady Elseth replied. The women of Breodanir were far too perceptive. "Not madness. She's possessed

of a certain cunning, and a certain intelligence. I have
seen it before, often.

"In the dogs."

"But surely only a madwoman—"

"Stephen, enough! I am the Lady of Elseth, and all
who dwell on Elseth lands answer to me. This is a matter
of safety for our people and our responsibilities, and I
will have the truth. Now, if you please."

"Elsa—"

"Now."

He told her, of course. And she knew that he would.
Gilliam could turn her aside with a word or a dismissive
gesture, but his huntbrother understood too well her cares
and concerns.

He hesitated before he told her of the wyrd, but with
her gentle prompting, he found it impossible to be afraid
of her derision. He told her of the dreams first, and when
she nodded gravely, he found himself speaking next of
Krysanthos, the mage-born, and Kallandras, the bard-
born. When he told her about the man who had tried
to kill him in his first Sacred Hunt, she stopped him
briefly.

"Why didn't you tell us?"

"I—it didn't seem important after Soredon's death." It
was half-truth, but Soredon's death, even at years distance, could still stop her in her steps, and she didn't
question further.

Last, he told her of the creatures who had hunted them
in the lower circle of the King's City. "She called them
demon-kin," he said softly.

"She?"

"Evayne. The mage who saved our lives."

"The woman of your wyrd."

He nodded.

"And this girl?"

"I don't know. But—" But very gently, he reached for,
and opened, his belt pouch. Hands shaking, he pulled the
simple horn out, into the light of day. When she reached
to touch it, his hands curled up reflexively. She drew
back. "She gave it to me."

Sun touched the horn, casting little shadows in the palms of Stephen's hand. For a moment, it looked too simple, and too real, to be the cause of such concern. He expected Lady Elseth to laugh—if only a little—or to demur. She offered him neither comfort.

But her face was very pale, almost gray. "Stephen?"

He had to lean down to catch the word; the wind, weak and playful, pulled it from her lips.

"Walk me to the Hunter's altar."

He offered an arm, and without hesitation, she took it. Together, in silence, they made their way to the Hunter's green. There, at its edge, she let go of his arm. "Leave me," she said softly. "I need time to think."

"Elsa—"

"Leave me." There was no anger or rancor in her words; there was hardly any emotion at all. But her chin was set a little too high, and her lips were a little too thin.

"Elsa—" he tried again.

But she would not hear him. Instead, she drifted over the invisible circle, a quiet vision of deep blues and bright reds across the open green. She did not look back; she walked like a ruler who needed, and wanted, no aid. Stephen did not know what to offer, although Norn might once have, had he lived. Instead, he watched until she approached the altar itself. Then, abruptly, he turned, knowing what he would see, and unwilling to watch it.

Elsabet, Lady Elseth, knelt in the grass, unmindful of dirt or insects; she had brought no rolled carpet with her to protect her skirts. She pressed her forehead to the cool stone of the altar's edge, forced it, just to feel and to know that it would not give at all.

What must I do? she thought, afraid to even whisper the words; afraid to give them solidity, grant them reality.

She did not lie to herself, did not try—especially not here, in the sight of God. What she had heard, she felt as truth. *It is never over, is it?* She lifted her face, then, to look up at the henges, with their ancient, impassive runes.

The women of the Breodanir were never trained in the

Hunt; they were trained, rather, to face its wake. They were not trained, or rarely so, to fight with the weapons that the Hunters bore—although they each had some knowledge of dagger play—yet they granted death, on rare occasions, from the seat of judgment in their demesnes. They did not face the Hunter's Death—but not a single one of them, upon becoming mothers, would have hesitated to face it if their children might be spared.

And if they were not fighters in the Hunter's scheme, they were warriors in their own. Elsabet, Lady Elseth, was tired—but she still held her title, and all of the responsibilities that went with it. She longed to find Gilliam a wife; she longed to leave, just for a moment, the duties that had shaped and scarred her.

But she would never hurt her line and her people by stepping aside to let them pass untended. She did not cry; she had long since learned that tears were a language that the Gods did not understand. Instead, she raised her face, looking almost serene in the dying light.

"What will you have of my sons?"

Grass rippled in the breeze; nothing else stirred.

"Very well, Lord. But I will not let them go lightly. What I can offer them, even in your game, I will."

She rose, and her pride settled upon her shoulders like an honorable, ancient mantle.

Stephen saw to his horse; he wanted the time to think about all that he had revealed to the woman who was his mother and his ruler. The stable hands, used by now to the moods of quiet and business that Stephen sometimes displayed, stayed out of his way; they did not even offer him brush or blankets.

When he had finished in the stables, he turned to the house. He greeted the keykeeper with studious politeness—he was still, at his age and station, measured and too often found wanting in Boredan's eyes—and then retreated to his rooms to wash and change.

But he did not sleep, and he did not eat. When he had finished, he left to search for Gilliam. It was not hard to guess where he would be found.

The sun was low, and the sky had given way to pinks and tufted clouds; the air was cooling rapidly. Stephen did not bother with a heavier jacket; the kennels, he knew, would have a fire burning in two places. He paused only to light the lamp he carried before he opened the small door at the kennel's side.

There, haloed by the light that he carried too tightly to his chest, he stopped in silence.

He understood, in an instant, the concern that Lady Elseth had failed to make completely clear. The dogs lay in their beds, resting before their final evening meal. Although he could not make them out clearly, he could read the names graven in plaques at the foot of each bed; he knew which ones woke to sniff the air before they settled their heads back down against paws and straw. Although Gilliam was Lord now, and master of the Elseth kennels, there were no younger brothers or cousins to tend the dogs, and the responsibility remained Gilliam's.

Ashfel, at three years of age the leader and pride of Gilliam's alaunts, growled softly and gently; a warning to Stephen, but not a threat. Stephen met the dog's eyes, reddened in the lamp's glow, and nodded, as if to quiet the dog. He did not have the kitchen scraps that he most often brought as a bribe—and had he carried them, he would have forgotten them in an instant.

For in a bed that should have been disused, the wild girl lay upon her stomach, her cheek to a pillow that looked incongruous upon the bed of straw. She wore a pale shift—one that was dirty and torn—of indeterminate color, and her hair was a tangle of darkness and shadow.

And beside her, in the tunic and vest that Gilliam wore when he tended the dogs in their kennels, Gilliam himself lay sleeping.

Stephen blinked rapidly, as if to clear away the fog from his vision. He even closed his eyes and bit his lip, something he had done only rarely since his Ascension, but when he opened his eyes again, Gilliam still lay in repose at the girl's side.

Mother's breath, he thought, as he leaned back against the wall. *I'm not seeing this. This isn't real.*

The girl suddenly raised her head, squinting against the light. She opened her mouth, and something midway between a bark and croon left her lips.

Stephen felt Gilliam stir, and wake, as he watched. He didn't know what he would say; didn't know what he wanted to say. Gilliam saved him the trouble.

"What in the hells are you doing here?"

Elsabet heard the kennels as they erupted into cacophony. A tight smile fixed itself to her lips; she did not so much as pause as she made her way to the house. The dogs were howling, and no doubt the litter that Gilliam's best bitch had recently whelped had joined their elders. She shook her head, glad that Stephen had at last arrived home, if not to set things right, than at least to argue sense with Gilliam in the way that Hunters knew best.

She was not surprised to see them come into the house. Bits of straw and dirt clung to their jackets, and it was clear that Gilliam's shirt had lost buttons. She could see, even down the stretch of the hall that held her sitting room, that they were both still very red-faced and angry—and that one, if not both, of them would have bruises around their eyes. She held her peace, but an echo of the children they had once been touched her heart, and she almost smiled.

Until she saw that Stephen's arm was bleeding, and he held it close to his chest. With an ease that spoke both of custom and unquestioned authority, she pulled the rope that would summon the keykeeper, and then set off down the hall at a quick stride.

They both looked up, as if seeing her for the first time. "It's all right," Stephen said quickly. Gilliam said nothing, but he would not meet his mother's eyes.

"What on earth—Gilliam, did the dogs do this?"

"No!" They both said it in unison.

"Did you?" Lady Elseth said, her voice high.

"No."

She knew, then, what she thought might have happened, and she paled. But on this one point, she was too weary to press Gilliam. Stephen was his huntbrother, and on Stephen's shoulders, she would let it all rest.

"Elsa—we haven't finished talking yet," Stephen said, smiling rather dryly. "We'll be in the side room if you need us."

She nodded, but very, very stiffly. "Your arm?"

"It's not as bad as it looks," he said, but he winced.

"When you've finished this, you will see Boredan." It wasn't a question. Stephen grimaced and nodded. Then his face tightened as he looked at his brother.

"Come on," he said.

"Gil," Stephen said, the moment the door had closed, "what in the Hells is going on?"

"I told you, it's none of your damned business."

Stephen stiffened. "Why is the girl sleeping in the kennels? She isn't one of your damn hounds!" But looking down at his arm, he wasn't so sure. He tried not to remember the night of the demon-kin, and failed.

"She doesn't like sleeping in the house," was Gilliam's stiff reply.

"You said that already."

Gilliam turned. His jaw was set, and his face was nearly purple—and not just from their fist play.

"Don't start it again, Gil. What the *Hells* were you doing sleeping there?"

"I don't answer to you, Stephen!"

"You goddamned well do! You might have forgotten this, you flaming idiot, but you aren't a dog!"

Gilliam, never as good with words as his huntbrother, took two steps forward.

"There's no excuse for this—this sort of behavior. You're not fourteen anymore, and you aren't with your first pack. Remember who you are, Gilliam—you're the Lord of Elseth, for the Mother's sake!"

" 'This sort of behavior?' " Gilliam's eyes narrowed, and Stephen felt a sudden pull along the bond that they had shared since they were eight. Then Gilliam's eyes widened, before narrowing again, this time dangerously. "You think I've—you think that she and I—you think that *of me?*"

There was not, and there never could be, any lie between a Hunter and his huntbrother. Stephen said, "What the Hells am I supposed to think? You want to!"

And those last three words were the truth, too. But if there was honesty, there was also incredible anger—and that was never easily hidden either.

"You son of a bitch!" Gilliam roared.

Stephen didn't bother with words; the time for them had passed. He had time to dodge the full force of Gilliam's furious charge before they connected again. This time, free from the dogs and the need to control or confine them, they tried, as brothers sometimes will, to beat each other senseless.

"Look at the two of you," Lady Elseth said, as she picked up her napkin. Breakfast had been set and served, and the sun that filtered in through the windows of the breakfast room was bright and unforgiving.

Stephen did not reply, but looked across the table at his Hunter. Gilliam did not look up from his plate. Neither of them had gotten much sleep during the previous evening.

"You do realize," Lady Elseth continued, her frosty voice belying the warmth of the early day, "that the servants haven't had this much cause for gossip in years?"

"Mother." Gilliam's single word was a warning. His face was set and etched in lines of sullen anger.

Lady Elseth was not to be put off, but she did not ask, as she had every previous breakfast, where Gilliam's guest could be found. "I think, Gilliam, that both Maribelle and I have been tolerant enough."

Maribelle, following her mother's lead, had seen to her napkin and her serving, but her eyes, openly curious, followed her brother's face. Gilliam was bruised; there was a cut just under his eye, probably caused by Stephen's signet ring.

Stephen looked no better, although it was a wonder, given his smaller stature, that he didn't look worse. His arm was bandaged and hung in a sling across his chest. The servants that had just been mentioned had been called to help him dress, and although on one other occasion he had likewise been tended to, that had had the excuse of a hunting accident behind it.

He ate stiffly and awkwardly, and although he made polite conversation with both of the Ladies, he never once looked at his Hunter.

Lady Elseth did not have a good morning. For that matter, lunch was no better, and by the end of the day's second meal, only Maribelle dutifully tried to keep conversation light and pleasant. The only boon to Elsabet's day was the fact that Gilliam, whom she subtly kept watch over, did not once go down to the kennels after seeing to the dogs' morning run and feeding.

When dinner commenced, weighted down by the same heavy silence, she finally put both her fork and knife to the side—setting them down so heavily, the wine in her glass sloshed over the brim.

"I have had enough of this," she said, the anger behind the words so forceful that for a moment the similarities between mother and son were obvious. "Stephen, Gilliam—both of you have things to discuss."

Stephen, ever obliging, rose. He knew a dismissal when he heard one, and he wasn't particularly hungry.

Gilliam looked at his mother. "There isn't much else to discuss," he said. His voice was not quite the match for hers.

"Then discuss nothing," she replied evenly. "But do it like civil adults. And do it now."

He looked as if he might speak, but enough of his anger had played itself out the past evening that he had the sense to be cautious. He rose, scraping his chair against the floor and dumping his napkin, in an unceremonious white pile, on the floor.

They approached the closed door at the same moment, and stopped, neither willing to open it first and allow the other to precede him.

For a moment, Lady Elseth wished she had never had sons. She rose, her cheeks reddened by a sudden wash of color, and walked evenly to the door. Her dark eyes were wide as she cut both of the Elseth men with her glare.

Stephen had the grace to blush and look away; Gilliam did not even meet his mother's eyes.

She opened the door. "Out," she said. That one word contained as much anger as she ever showed.

But in the face of it, neither Stephen or Gilliam dared to offer a word of resistance. They went—Gilliam first, and Stephen in his wake.

"I hope you're happy," Stephen said softly, as he leaned against the fence that kept the Elseth horses at pasture. His arm hurt, although Boredan had done what he could to insure it would not become infected, and he took care to favor it.

Gilliam said nothing. Instead of leaning forward, he let the rough-hewn wood of the fence cut into his back. He stared ahead, in the growing darkness, to the walls and runs of the kennels.

They were uncomfortable; it was rare that anger between them lasted this long. But Stephen tested the bond, and he felt the anger, mixed and folded into every other emotion, that lay between them. He would have been proud if he could have said that the anger was solely Gilliam's. It was not.

"You took your time getting back," Gilliam said at last.

"Yes," Stephen said, equally quietly.

"Did you spend the time with her?"

Stephen's hands tightened into fists at the tone in his Hunter's voice. "Hunter's Oath, Gil—let it lie!" He could see clearly the glint of Gilliam's bitter smile; there was triumph in it. "You might recall," he said, his voice cold and sharp, "that I nearly died. Unlike the Hunters, I'm merely human. I was abed four days."

"You didn't want to come back." It wasn't a question.

"No."

Gilliam started to speak, and bit back the words in disgust. He was silent a moment; the air felt heavy, was made heavy, by what he said next. "Go back to her, then. We don't need you here."

It was meant as a slap. Stephen shut his eyes and clenched his fists. He exhaled slowly. "What of the girl?"

Gilliam did not reply.

"What about the girl, Gilliam?"

"What about her?" His voice was low; deep. Stephen had heard him speak just so before, although it took him a moment to remember when. He paled.

"Gilliam, she isn't yours. You can't keep her here. She's not right. She needs help."

The low rumble at the back of the Elseth Lord's throat was a growl. He turned toward Stephen, and then away, slamming his fist into the fence post.

Stephen reached out through their bond, pulling at Gilliam; urging him to understand. He felt an echo of the strangeness that drove Gilliam—and then he felt a terrible lurch as Gilliam leaped forward into the night. Anger was forgotten; pain and the bitter taste of betrayal vanished like morning mist. All that was left was panic and a desperate drive to action.

Stephen knew why an instant before it would have become obvious to any other observer.

The kennels burst into sudden flame, a symphony of night fire.

There were men on the grounds.

In the sudden flare of light—a light that burned and crackled with the faintest aurora of blue haze—Stephen could make out their shapes as they ran across the grass. He had not marked the setting of the sun, but although the edges of the sky were still bright, darkness had settled, and these intruders sought to take advantage, or cover, in it. They moved lightly on their feet, but he saw the glint of weapons; they wore no armor, or very little of it.

Gilliam, no! He did not shout; he did not want the attackers aware of his position or his place. Indeed, they moved so quickly, and with such a determination, he wasn't certain that either he or his Hunter had even been seen.

Gilliam's panic ebbed. He took a breath, and then another, deeper one. His heart was beating too quickly. He was frightened—terrified—for the dogs. It was never fear of his own mortality that drove him; it was fear, always, of the loss of things loved.

The dogs.

And the girl.

Stephen felt the shift as Gilliam called Hunter's trance. And he felt Gilliam recoil as the dogs began to whine.

Steady, Gil, he thought. He had no time for more. Passing his hunter, he made a direct line to the kennel doors that faced the pasture. For good measure, he drew his sword, and felt its weight settle comfortably into his hand. He tried to ignore the throb of his arm as he threw off the sling that Boredan had been so insistent upon.

Gilliam joined him in seconds, weapon likewise drawn and ready.

"Hold the dogs," Stephen said tersely, as he struggled, in a light blackened with tendrils of smoke, to free the latch and open the door.

Gilliam nodded, his eyes almost glazed. "She felt it," he whispered.

"Felt what?" Stephen did not pause until the latch had been lifted.

Gilliam shook his head, frustrated; Stephen knew, from his expression, that the thing felt could not be put into words that a human could understand. But he had a very bad feeling that he knew what that word would be, if Gilliam could find it.

Then he heard, through the door, the change in the tenor of the dogs' voices.

Gilliam cursed, and the anger that had been replaced by concern flared up, just as the fire had. "They're in through the other side!"

"Mother!"

Lady Elseth rose at once as Maribelle's high voice broke the silence of her sitting room. She left her papers, and the month's numbers, in an even neat pile, and although she rose with both haste and force, not even the inkstand was upset.

The hall was empty, although Maribelle's single, imperative word had certainly come from outside of her doors.

Lady Elseth looked around, concern growing. She began to walk down the hall when one of the younger boys threw open a door and came careening into the hall, his arms full.

"Talbet!"

He skidded to a stop, stumbling into the closest wall. "Lady?" His breath barely forced the word out.

She stepped forward to see what he carried, and her face paled. "Where did you get these?"

"Maribelle sent me, ma'am. The kennels're on fire and there are intruders on the ground." His pale hair was matted to his forehead with sweat, and his eyes, normally bright and crinkled, were a deep, wide green.

Without another word, Lady Elseth helped to lighten the boy's burden: She took from him one of the several crossbows he carried and began to wind its spring as she walked. "Run," she said softly. "I'll catch up with you."

Almost before the door was fully opened, Gilliam wedged his body through the darkened gap. His face gleamed with sweat, and the dirty smoke had added grime and circles to his eyes. The fire was eating the wood of the building; Stephen had expected that.

What he had not expected was the destruction of the stone walls. He bit his lip, narrowing his eyes as something—not human—shrieked in pain. Gilliam's back, and the clouds of smoke, were all he could see— and in seconds he lost sight of his Hunter as well.

But he heard the sudden clash of steel against steel; heard a grunt and a scream.

Send the dogs out, Gil, he thought, as he dropped to his knees and began to crawl, sword still at hand, into the heart of the kennel.

"There," Maribelle whispered softly, pointing into the night sky.

Her mother nodded quietly as she followed Maribelle's finger. Three men stood, near the cover of the great trees that alone had not been cleared when their ancestral manor had been built. They carried a light, but only a small one. Even during the day, the distance would have prevented any recognition on Elsabet's part.

She had sent out an urgent request for the aid of the villagers, but the rising flames that encompassed the kennels were probably beacon enough. Soon, the wagons, with sand and what little water there was available for such an enterprise, would begin to wend their way up the roads.

She had two questions. The first she could not give voice to; the second she concentrated on. But Maribelle did not have her mother's sensibilities.

"Where are Gil and Stephen?" Maribelle scanned the horizon even as she asked.

Swallowing, uncertain of her voice, Elsabet lifted a perfectly steady hand and pointed. To the kennels. She heard Maribelle's sharp intake of breath—but Maribelle offered no argument to her mother's silent answer. It was obvious, after all. Where else would Gilliam have gone?

As if in taunt, the fires suddenly blazed again, becoming a solid, near-white wall.

Young Talbet jumped back; this far away, the surge of heat could still be felt. Elsabet remained steady. Maribelle, at eighteen the youthful pride of her mother's training, did likewise—although if she betrayed herself by starting, no one noticed.

But she looked to Lady Elseth for commands.

Lady Elseth closed her eyes, weighing and deciding all actions. "Are these three the only intruders?" she asked at last.

"The only ones we've seen," Talbet volunteered.

But Maribelle shook her head. "I think there are others," she said softly. "The kennels."

You have, Elsa thought, *your father's vision.*

The fires there were so bright and so high that the kennels were out of the question. Lady Elseth narrowed her eyes and shaded them as she turned, rigidly, to examine those very flames. The stone itself was on fire. Which was impossible, unless . . .

Stephen's words came back to her. Grimly, she looked back to the great trees. Those trees would not serve as shelter to enemies of Elseth for one moment longer. She took a breath, deeply, to steady herself. "This is my judgment," she said, and for a moment she might have been sitting in the ancient, Elseth seat. "Kill them."

"But the kennels—the Lord!" Talbet's eyes widened.

"We cannot go to them through those fires; they will not be banked by sand or water." Lady Elseth's voice was ice. "But we may find another method of putting the flames out." *Stephen. Gilliam.*

Maribelle nodded grimly. "Your judgment," she said, lifting her bow, "is accepted in the eyes of God, Lady of Elseth." Turning, she nodded to Talbet.

But Elsabet was not to be left behind. Not if one—or all—of these isolated three were, as she suspected, mage-born.

She had thought, one day, to lose either of her sons to the God. She had been born to it; she accepted it with the sorrow that was the burden of every noble mother. But if her sons were lost to her this eve, through unnatural fire and human malice . . . she struggled, holding her anger, tightly confining it. Control, especially in crisis, was everything.

"Approach them by the pastures," she said. That was all. She did not need to mention speed or silence.

Five feet into the kennels, the smoke vanished. It had not dispersed; indeed, Stephen could feel the heat and see the blackness that the flames shed. But some wall, some sort of barrier, had been erected here; he could mark the circle of it very clearly.

He knew what it was, and in silence he named it. Magic. He stayed low to the ground as his eyes adjusted to the muted, unnatural light.

There were four men in the kennel's confines. Four men, all of the dogs, the girl—and Gilliam. The intruders wore black—why was it always black?—masks and clothing; they had shoes of soft leather, and each carried a sword and small buckler. The smoke, and the magical absence of it, did not deter or bother them at all.

But the hounds did.

For once, Stephen was glad that he had no bond with

the dogs. Through his link with Gilliam, he could feel an echo of their pain and their confusion, their anger and their determination—and that echo sent him reeling, his back to the smoke and charred embers of wood. Eyes stinging, he looked away and down; upon the rushes strewn along the floor he could see three of Gilliam's pack. Two at least would never rise, or hunt, again; in the darkness and smoke, he could not tell who.

He shook himself, and started to rise; he wanted to be at the side of his Hunter in this most dangerous of fights. Then he stopped, and let himself sink back into the ground, unnoticed. This was no Hunt, and these no animals; the danger that they presented could not be met by force of spear or hounds alone.

Swallowing, Stephen began to trace the perimeter of the smokeless circle in the hope of getting behind those who attacked.

Gilliam had never been so close to insanity in his life. Each and every voice, from the youngest to the most experienced of his hounds and lymers, clamored for attention. Only Piper and Vorel were silent, and their silence filled him with a bitter rage.

The kennels were dark, and the space in them far too confined, to be used to advantage. As well, the intruders were very good at what they did. He had almost misjudged their skill—and his arm, cloth and skin split by the same swift stroke, bore witness to that stupidity.

He had never before fought men with his hounds. He could not count on their fear, as he did with stag, or bear, or boar; nor could he predict their rages. He needed the dogs now more than he had ever done, but he did not—quite—know how to use them to their full advantage.

The girl fought at his side. Her, he had ordered back, and of all times, she had chosen this one to test him. She remained at his side, spitting fury, although his mental shout should have given her little choice but to flee. He did not dare to see from her eyes, for fear of being lost behind them.

But it was she that they wanted. Although they might

cut at his hounds—at he himself—they had eyes for her, and her death.

Snarling, Gilliam rushed forward in a barely controlled frenzy of flickering swordplay.

If smoke could not fill the inner circle, the snap of crackling fire could. Stephen tried to ignore the splintering sound of wooden beams and tried not to think about the rushes on the floor and the way they would soon catch fire. They were damp now, damp and warm—but they would not remain so.

Stop it. He took a breath of the air closest to the floor; it was acrid, but it did not hurt his lungs. He listened again to the noises that came with fire. Against them, his movements were hidden and silent.

Straw scraped his cheeks and chin and clung to his jacket and pants as he moved. He felt little, sharp ends against his shins as his boots caught and held them. But he moved, struggling with Gilliam's anger and fear; afraid to let it in, but terrified to let go of it.

And then he saw the backs of the intruders, black-clad and wraithlike through the smoke.

Don't look, he whispered, his eyes turned up in supplication as he tightened his grip on his weapon. *Don't look back.*

Trembling with tension, he rose in the poor light, a multicolored, rush-strewn shade. Hands shaking, movements precise, he brought the edge of his blade down in a tight, forceful arc that ended with the back of the closest man's knees.

Maribelle moved, just a shade more quickly than her mother, through the tall grass. Elsabet could see her by the movements of the tops of the grass, but that was all. She counted three and then saw the grass move again, a little more forcefully, at Talbet's passing. They did well, although they had not been trained to this.

For that matter, neither had she. And if she had, she would certainly not have chosen the long, formal skirts of the evening meal for such an enterprise. Every crinoline rustled as she crept along. She swore, then, that she would forsake fashion entirely after this night's work. But she did not stop.

When she came at last to the old, slanted fence post that marked the farthest reach of the horses' pastures, she dared to glance up, dared to attract the attention of the three who waited.

And she saw, although she only looked up for an instant, that they were three men, all oddly garbed, with a light at the center of their triangle. They wore robes that were darker than the sky, with hoods drawn up and around their faces. The light that hit their cheeks made them appear skeletal, threatening.

She crawled beneath the fence, gently disentangling her skirts. Maribelle's head bobbed up; she bit her lip, and then exhaled slowly into the passing breeze. These men stood downwind—but they had no dogs to guide or warn them. Good.

And then, at last, they came to the edge of the tree's farthest roots. She saw her daughter's face in the moonlight, and she nodded quietly. They exchanged no words; none were needed. Maribelle's posture told Lady Elseth everything that she needed—or wanted—to know.

You have never killed a man, she thought, as she saw the silhouette of her almost adult daughter shiver, *but you will be called upon to do it. We are those who sit in judgment, Mari—and when we judge a crime worthy of death, that weight is upon our shoulders. It is time to learn.*

Still, she hesitated. She herself had never learned this bitter truth so completely bare of pretense or tradition. Perhaps this was something to spare her daughter— Maribelle would, in the end, prove true to her lessons.

Or perhaps not. She realized, as she slowly brought her bow to bear, that she did not know which of these three, if not all of them, were mage-born. Taking a deep breath, she made the only quick decision she could: to trust her daughter's speed.

She crept as far away from the base of the tree as she dared before she rose to add her silhouette to the night.

"Hold!" Her voice was strong and clear in the darkness. As one, the three turned to face her. But only the man in the middle, bereft of all of the insignia of the Or-

der of Knowledge, moved. His hands cut upward in a
sharp steeple, his movements graceful, precise, controlled.

But before he could speak one word, utter even the beginning of a syllable, Maribelle of Elseth fired. The small
lamp, carried by the man farthest from her, guttered suddenly.

As did the fires that surrounded the kennels like an
impenetrable wall.

Lady Elseth fired into the night; heard a sharp cry followed by the sound of stumbling, running feet. She herself did not dare the darkness to pursue. Instead, she
began to rewind her bow.

"Damn," Maribelle whispered softly, coming to stand
at her mother's side. "I didn't kill him."

"Your aim was off," her mother agreed.

Stephen's entry into the fight proper changed the balance of the game—and Gilliam was quick enough, instinctive enough, to take advantage of it. The dogs found
their openings, and moved from a defensive crouch and
snap into full leaps beneath the swords of their attackers.
Gilliam's strike was less lucky, or less deadly; the moment he stepped forward, his dark-robed assailant suddenly snapped back into the present, and the very real
threat to his own survival.

They had scant minutes before the smoke, dark and
thick, suddenly began to cross what had been an invisible
boundary. The smoke changed everything again, for with
it, came fear. Gilliam could almost smell it rising.

It was then that he knew he would win. One of the
standing men suddenly broke and ran—an obvious, stupid
mistake. Ashfel took off in pursuit, the embers and little
flames disregarded. *This* hunt was Ashfel's territory and
strength. Gilliam cursed, but let him go; he renewed his
attack with ferocity and the last of his Hunter's strength.

Fear did not make his enemy a more tenacious fighter,
and in the end, he fell. As did the man that his dogs now
savaged. He waited a few seconds before calling them,
sharply, back. It was bad to let the dogs eat flesh outside
of the confines of the Hunt's end.

Only when he was certain that they would not test him further did he lead them out of the kennels, calling them quickly and giving them their positions. Ashfel also waited, angered.

"Gilliam," someone said, and Gilliam squinted into the darkness to see his mother's stiff form.

At her feet, unmoving, lay the one man who had seen fit to run. "Your work?" he asked softly.

She nodded. "Stephen?"

"I'm here, Elsa," Stephen said, emerging from what remained of the kennels. He was shaking and pale.

"What of the girl?"

Stephen twisted his head sharply to the side in denial. "She's—she's safe." But his color, if possible, became worse. He tried to close himself off, tried to keep the disgust and fear from Gilliam. This time, the Hunter Lord didn't need to test their bond. He turned sharply.

Stephen caught his arm. "Gil—"

But Gilliam shook him off without a word and returned to the kennels to call the girl out.

"Gilliam, you don't want to see her."

"Go away, Stephen. I'll—"

The light in the kennels was poor; moonlight came through the walls with barely perceptible rays of light. It was enough. On the rushes of the kennel's floors, the girl sat crouched over the twitching body of one of her assailants. Her eyes were narrowed, and her lips, where they could be seen, were flecked with blood.

Her teeth were planted firmly in the throat of the man; her jaw muscles were tense, and the high rasp of a growl filled the silent air.

Stephen closed his eyes, reaching for his dagger. He expected Gilliam to interfere—to say something, do something. But Gilliam was frozen, his mouth open in surprise.

As Stephen approached, the girl's wary eyes followed his movements. Her hands tensed, flexing as if they were the claws of some wild, dangerous beast. He hoped that Gilliam could hold her. He didn't care if he couldn't. With a soft, decisive strike, he planted his dagger firmly into the would-be killer's heart.

He left it there, his hands suddenly too weak to hold the hilt. The body stilled.

Sickened, Stephen walked away, past Gilliam and the sounds the girl made at his back.

CHAPTER NINETEEN

In the morning, Lady Elseth rose early, refusing to feel her age. She called for the village head and saw to the burying of the bodies that remained. Sourly, she noted that the mage-born man, and one of his associates, was not among them.

She had seen the dead before; had, indeed, seen deaths much worse than these. She didn't flinch when it came time to inspect the bodies. Letters would have to be written, and some dispensation from the Queen's Justice would have to be granted. She also made a note to begin her own investigations into the Order of Knowledge within the King's City. She did not, however, expect to find the mage harbored there any longer.

"Lady!"

She looked up from her musings and saw one of the caretakers of the dead approaching her. He carried something that glinted in the sunlight, cupped carefully in hands held away from his body, as if he bore a serpent. "Kelset?"

Kelset was obviously tired; there was much to be done, and quickly; the air was warm, and there were many dead. He wore a hat to protect himself from the sun's light, and had she desired to do so, she could have pretended the shadows in the hollows of his face were cast by the hat's wide brim. "Look. On one of the dead."

She held out her hand, and after a minute's hesitation, the older man gave over what he held. It was a pendant on a long, thick chain, by its coloring platinum. She knew this because she knew that silver warmed with age and wear; this metal was still a cold, shining gray. The pendant itself was simple; a deep obsidian held by a platinum circle. No design, no engraving or carving, marred its black surface.

"Do you recognize it?" she asked, glancing up to see Kelset's intense gaze.

"No, Lady," he said hesitantly. He reached up to massage the growing knots of tense muscle along the top of his neck.

"But?"

"What good can come of it? It's black; blackness. And the man was wearing robes of some sort."

"Was he god-born?"

"No. Wrong eyes for it."

"Good news, then," she replied lightly. "It wouldn't do to anger any one of the Gods." But she held the pendant more carefully.

Stephen knew that he'd overslept when he heard the knock at his door. He had closed the curtains, just before he'd come to bed, as a precaution against the night. Unfortunately, it had served as a shield against the dawn as well. He swung quickly out of bed, sliding his feet into the slippers that stuck out beneath the wrinkled counterpane and reaching for his robe.

The knock came again.

Before he could walk the length of the room to answer the door, it opened. The servant that he had expected was nowhere in sight, but Gilliam of Elseth filled the door's frame for a moment as he lingered between the hall and the room.

There was no anger at all left in him, but Stephen didn't need their connection to know it. The night, with its fire and death, had killed the rage in them both.

Hesitant, perhaps a little too quick to offer, Stephen said, "Come in, Gil."

Gilliam nodded stiffly. He entered the room, closed the door at his back, and then used it as a support. His face was lined—creased almost as deeply as Stephen's sheets—and his eyes were circled and dark. It was obvious that he had had no help dressing; the buttons of his shirt were askew.

"Mother's seen the bodies," Gilliam said at last, when it became clear that Stephen would not speak first.

"Does she have any information?"

Gilliam shrugged. "She's waiting to speak to both of us. After lunch."

They stared at the carpets and walls in uncomfortable silence. It was Gilliam who, at length, broke the silence again. "I slept in the house last night."

Stephen started to speak, but with Gilliam's words came the image of the girl as he had last seen her. He paled. But he did not keep his queasiness away from his Hunter.

"I know," Gilliam said. His voice was low and unsteady. Had he been a dog, he would have been halfway between whine and growl, were it possible. "Stephen?"

Stephen nodded.

"The girl—she's part of my pack." There was no anger and no possessiveness in his words; his voice was even, but his hands shook where his words did not.

"Part of your pack?"

"I can see behind her eyes," Gilliam replied. "I can call her; I can command her. I know when she's near." He turned away. "It happened the night we were first attacked."

At once, Stephen understood everything. It happened like that, sometimes—information gathered in bits and pieces suddenly coalesced to form a whole that could never again be forgotten. His shoulders sagged slightly, and he thrust his hands into his pockets; they were fists. "How?"

"I don't know. I—I didn't think about it."

He hadn't wanted to think about it. Stephen didn't point it out; they both knew it, so there was no need.

"And I don't know how to find out." Gilliam turned again, his hands, palms up, before him. It was as close as he would come to asking for aid.

Stephen could not demand more. "I think we can help her," he said quietly, mind racing. He swallowed. "Does she—does she feel different than the hounds do?"

His Hunter nodded, hesitant. "She—she's more than an animal. But less than—than you and I. And I hear her all the time. Even now." His voice dropped. "She's unhappy. She knows I'm upset. Knows it's because of her, but doesn't understand why."

"Gil—has she ever spoken to you?"

"Never. I thought that she didn't know how. At first."

"I'd still say she doesn't know how," Stephen said mildly.

Gilliam shook his head. "It's there. Somewhere. If I get close enough to her, I can almost hear the *words*. She's more than a dog. She's stronger, too."

"Then maybe you can—"

"I can't. Don't ask me, Stephen. I can't."

This, too, Stephen suddenly understood. He looked across the room to his Hunter, and then bowed his head. He was proud of Gilliam, but he would never say so in words that would only embarrass them both. Instead, he let the feeling thrum down their Hunter's bond.

"Is Elsa waiting?"

Gilliam smiled. "Impatiently."

"Then I'd better finish dressing."

"Well?" Lady Elseth looked up across the length of the table as her luncheon dishes were finally cleared away. She had eaten little—but that was in keeping with her three companions at the meal.

Stephen met her gaze first. "They were after the girl," he said quietly.

She raised one slightly frosted brow. "The girl?"

"We think so."

"Do you know why?"

"No." Stephen shrugged.

"I've taken the liberty of sending for a member of the Order of Knowledge. No, not that one." Her own lips turned up in an imitation of a smile. "I don't believe that Krysanthos will be found within the Order's walls after last night's work."

"I'm not sure that we want one of the mage-born here."

"I'm certain that you don't," Lady Elseth said, a little too pointedly, "but in this case, I think it wise. A mage wanted the girl dead, Stephen; it only makes sense that a mage would be able to explain her . . . condition."

In matters of difficulty, it was Gilliam's custom to let Stephen speak for them both. He did not even venture a syllable now.

"Elsa, is that wise?"

"Perhaps." It was her turn to shrug. "Perhaps not. But truthfully, Stephen, it is not just because of the girl that I summoned a member of the Order. I want answers—and some restitution—for the attack last evening. And answers, I *will* have."

Stephen nodded; when the Lady of Elseth used that particular tone of voice, the matter was already settled. He tried to change the direction of the conversation. "Did you find anything of interest this morning?"

"On the corpses?"

Maribelle's eyes widened slightly at her mother's bluntness. Stephen didn't even blink. "Yes."

Lady Elseth closed her eyes and raised a hand to her forehead. "I'm sorry, Stephen. That was uncalled for. But I like these affairs no more than you, and I'm not in the best of moods for delicacy." She smiled wanly. "Yes. I did find something that may be of significance." She rose. "If you wait, you can look at it and tell me if it has more significance for you than it does for me."

They waited, still uncomfortable, while Lady Elseth left the room. Stephen did not even try to keep up light or pleasant chatter, and Gilliam certainly wasn't about to start what he had avoided for most of his life. Maribelle's silence was unnatural—but Maribelle looked very much like Gilliam; sleepless, dark-eyed, haunted.

Lady Elseth's return was a relief.

Until she stopped at Stephen's side and very gently unfurled one hand. Like liquid, the pendant she carried fell free, stopping to swing as the chain pulled tight against her thumb and finger. "This," she said, studying Stephen's face.

Stephen stared at the pendant in fascinated horror.

"Stephen?"

He shook his head, reached out to touch the obsidian surface of the flat oval, and then pulled back sharply before his fingers made contact.

"You recognize it." She put her free hand around his

shoulder, as the pendulum continued its gentle swing. "Is it your—from your dreams?"

He nodded quietly. "But I also recognize it from my studies. In the King's library."

"Yes?" Her voice was gentle, but the question demanded an answer nonetheless; Lady Elseth had that kind of voice.

"It's the emblem of the Priests of Allasakar." Stephen glanced up and met the eyes of his Lady. "The Lord and ruler of the Hells."

Lady Elseth was silent a moment, absorbing the news. "Well," she said at last. "I think this merits a visit to the King's City. And perhaps even a visit to the Queen herself." She caught the pendant firmly in a tight, solid grip. "If I guess correctly, that religion has been forbidden practice in Breodanir."

"And in every other civilized land since the birth of the Twin Kings," Stephen replied. "But so has thievery, and thieves have never died out in the history of *any* people."

"True," Lady Elseth said, her gaze remote. "But it is not the habit of the seat of judgment to ignore those infractions that are brought to its attention. Especially not when that seat is the High Seat. I have work to tend to here, and accommodations to arrange in the city itself.

"We will wait upon the arrival of the member of the Order of Knowledge before you set out."

"How do we know they'll send one?" Maribelle asked.

"They'll send one," her mother replied grimly. "And quickly."

She was right, of course. She was the Lady of Elseth.

The Hunter Ladies had an informal messenger service and route that they used in circumstances of great urgency only. Elsabet had deemed this to be such an occasion, and had ordered her courier out on the roads with a horse and the writ of summons that bore her blood-red seal. She knew that once the messenger reached Valentin, he would turn his horse in to the Valentin stables in return for a fresh one; this operation would continue along the straightest path to the King's City. Therefore, a messenger that might normally travel for weeks would take perhaps five days to arrive. She expected one of the mage-born to arrive at the month's end.

He arrived two days after the earliest possible moment of the message's receipt.

His arrival was not an auspicious one to start; he walked, unhorsed, up the long and half-tended path to Elseth Manor. He was met by villagers who carried the long, wooden planks that were necessary to frame the second story of the half-completed kennels, and given the stories of attempted murder that had been whispered at the hearthside of each and every cottage and shanty in the Elseth village, his arrival was greeted with suspicion and worry.

Were it not for the fact that he arrived at midday, looking tired, travel-worn, and not a little exhausted, they might have been tempted to take matters into their own hands. Instead, the village head ordered him contained— much to his obvious chagrin—and marched, in the center of the village's most able young men, to Elseth Manor proper.

Elsabet discovered this oversight in her people's hospitality when a very harassed-looking keykeeper all but barged into her study. He knocked, yes, but entered without giving her the grace of time to give him leave to do so.

"Lady," he said, his face pale and lined, "an emergency that requires your attention has arisen. If you would be so kind?"

"Is it Gilliam?" she asked, rising immediately.

"No. I believe it is a visitor that you've been expecting."

"That hardly seems an emergency, Boredan." But she followed him quickly down the long hall and out to the manor's wide doors. Stephen met her in the hall.

"What's upset Bōredan?" he whispered.

She shook her head, and he let the matter drop, but did pause to offer his arm. She took it.

When they at last went through the doors that the keykeeper held open for them, they found most of the village gathered at their steps.

"Lady!" Corinna said, her voice a rather hoarse shout.

She was dressed in the daywear of a busy, village headwoman, and her sun-lined, darkened skin was covered in a fine mist of wood dust and dirt.

Lady Elseth surveyed the crowd quietly. "What has happened, Corinna?" she asked at last.

"We've brought another robed intruder. He came with no papers and no letters, and we thought it best you dealt with him."

"I . . . see." Lady Elseth had turned a very becoming shade of white. Unconsciously, she put an unadorned hand to her throat as she searched the crowd more thoroughly. Then the color returned to her cheeks in a blush. "You've done well," she said, her voice so faint it could barely be heard. "But I believe all is as it should be. Have the men release him."

Corinna raised a peppered brow. "You're sure?"

"Yes," Elsabet said, her voice, if possible, weaker. "I had a summons that has been answered rather earlier than I thought possible." She was furious with herself for the oversight. "You haven't—he hasn't been hurt, has he?"

The tightly knotted crowd pulled back, and the intruder in question, a slender reed of a man in rather wrinkled traveling clothing, was given leave to speak for himself.

"No," he said wryly. "He hasn't."

Stephen felt Elsabet sag against his arm in relief. He, too, felt some relief—but that was understandable. One did not anger the mage-born often and survive it. Or so legend said.

This particular mage did not even look annoyed, although his smile was perhaps a bit thin at the edges. "I give my apologies for arriving without the proper seals and writs, Lady." He bowed, low, to her, and then to the amazement of all, also bowed courteously to the headwoman. She frowned at this and turned her back.

"Well?" she asked the waiting crowd. "What are you all hanging about doing nothing for? You heard the Lady—she's safe enough. Get back to work!" For good measure, and as an emphasis to the command, she whacked the nearest strong-arm on the side of his bronzed face.

Nobody argued with her, just as nobody argued with

Lady Elseth—but it was always a wonder to Stephen how two such powerful women could carry themselves so completely differently. The villagers trickled away until only the mage was left standing at the foot of the Elseth steps.

"Where is Gilliam?" Lady Elseth whispered to Stephen.

Stephen rolled his eyes. "Out running the dogs."

"The girl?"

"With him." He started to speak, and then shook his head. He did not want to discuss his Hunter, and his Hunter's situation, in front of a stranger.

"I see." She turned back to the member of the Order of Knowledge. "Please accept my apologies—"

"Zareth. Call me Zareth if you don't consider that to be too informal." He bowed again, brushing his dark hair from his face as he straightened. In the light, the medallion that swung against his brown tunic glinted perfectly clearly; the quartered circle was obvious, although the elements each quarter contained could only be imagined.

"Very well. Please accept my apologies, Zareth. My people are not normally this . . . cautious."

"Given the circumstances—and the fact that I remain uninjured—I'm inclined to forgive and forget." He came up the steps, his stride both weary and long.

"Come in, then. You might appreciate the chance to rest. You arrived here at better speed than I would have thought possible."

If the mage heard the question in her voice, he ignored it politely. "Yes, I would appreciate it. I'll be ready to speak more properly in perhaps a few hours."

The few hours stretched out to encompass most of the next day. Stephen was well aware of the servants' gossip, as each and every one of them who had time to be interested in such affairs made guesses—most wrong—about the status of the stranger who had arrived with such indelicate fanfare. He busied himself with the dogs and his Hunter, trying his best to keep away from the stranger's rooms.

The kennels were not yet complete, and although

Stephen was no carpenter, he spent time as an unofficial
overseer while the villagers worked their shifts. The sun
was free from clouds, and the peak of the day hot and
dusty, but he heard no word of complaint pass any man's
lips. These villagers, perhaps better than any, knew how
important their task was; the Lord of Elseth was, in some
ways, in their care. Gilliam kept his dogs away from the
rising frame of their new home—but he kept that building
in sight as well, almost as nervous as a new mother.
Stephen thought it funny; no other building, no other
structure, could command this amount of Gil's attention—not even the magnificent arches of the King's castle
had moved him. He watched his Hunter, chuckled, and
became aware that he was not the only person to notice
Gilliam's anxiety. He was just the only one to think it
amusing.

Still, in watching, he noticed that Gilliam's relationship
with the wild girl—the still unnamed visitor—had mark-
edly changed. Although the girl accompanied them in the
runs, Gilliam took care to keep his distance. But he was
stiff and a little awkward with the new effort. Stephen almost felt sorry for him. He did pity the girl, though; she
whined and fretted in her inarticulate way, and her eyes
rarely left her master. No—not her master; not that.
Gilliam.

Stephen had to admit that it was hard, watching her,
not to think of her as one of the hunting pack. It was clear
that the rest of the dogs did. They nudged her, butted her,
and even snapped at her, depending upon their own pack
standing—and she returned their attention in kind.

It was after dinner—a dinner still awkward with tension and worry—that the mage-born visitor finally made
his second appearance.

Lady Elseth, clothed in the near-finest of her apparel,
rose at once to greet him; Maribelle and Stephen quickly
followed her lead. Only Gilliam remained seated in bliss-
ful ignorance of custom and required manners. Had it not
been a public first meeting, Stephen would have spoken
with him.

Stephen noticed that Lady Elseth had forsaken the odd,
ugly panniers for a skirt that was more easily maneu-

vered, and therefore more practical. It was odd; he wondered if perhaps Elsabet did not trust the mage. Still, in the formal, dark greens of her station, with a sash of burgundy and golden velvet to give brightness, she was a commanding figure.

The man who had named himself Zareth was not nearly so striking a presence. He wore clothing that was a cut above common, or so it seemed; the robes of the Order of Knowledge allowed only a glimpse of what lay beneath. Those robes didn't suit his coloring; they were smoky-gray, and fell heavily, like ill-hung drapery, over his gaunt frame.

For all that he cut such an odd figure, he was above ridicule. Perhaps the pendant, much clearer now in the light of the hall, was enough of a significator of power that clothing mattered little. Or perhaps it was his eyes; they burned with a striking intensity, even though they were dark and ringed.

"Zareth," Lady Elseth said, approaching him. "Have you eaten?"

"I don't require food," he said, and his smile was wan. But he bowed and held that bow longer than strict etiquette demanded. "What I do require—what we both require—is an exchange of information." He glanced around the room, noted Stephen, Gilliam, and Maribelle, and raised one eyebrow in question.

"Yes," Elsabet said quietly. "Anything that you have to say can be said freely here."

"Would you not rather retire to someplace where we might be less likely to face interruptions?"

She thought a moment. The servants would be clearing the table soon. "Yes. Follow."

Stephen watched the mage as he walked down the hall. It was clear that exhaustion still marred his step, and he placed a hand upon the wall to serve as a crutch. Whatever magics he had used to travel so quickly had obviously cost him dearly. The thought comforted Stephen.

They retired to the parlor, and Zareth chose the seat closest to the fire. Only after watching the mage press his hands tightly together did Stephen realize that he felt

chill. Rather than call the servants, Stephen began to
build up the small fire himself.

"Thank you," said Zareth, a trifle dryly. "I'm sorry to
be so obvious in my infirmity."

"I'd rather see an infirm mage than an active one,"
Stephen replied, equally dryly.

Zareth laughed softly. "I imagine you would. You're
Stephen?"

"Does it show?"

Zareth spoke much more softly. "Yes. I was told there
would be a Hunter and his huntbrother—and I've rarely
heard of a sullen and suspicious huntbrother."

Stephen smiled and turned back to the fire. He had surprised himself—he hadn't thought to like the mage that
the Order would send.

Lady Elseth, however, had not apparently warmed to
the visitor at all. While she was polite, even solicitous,
and certainly a graceful hostess, her face was very set,
and her eyes were free from the lines that bespoke a genuine smile. She waited until Stephen took a seat before
she began to speak, and it quickly became clear that she
intended to do all of the talking for the Elseth contingent.

"Let us come immediately to the matter at hand." She
rested her elbows upon the arm of her chair, and rested
her chin upon the tips of her pale fingers. "Ten days past,
my estates were invaded by unknown men—led by a
member of the Order of Knowledge."

Zareth nodded intently. "So you said in your letter."

"That member's name is Krysanthos."

"Are you certain of that?"

She nodded, not even glancing to the side to look at
Stephen's face. "He is not, I assume, still in the capital?"

Zareth glanced down at the ground between his feet.
"No, Lady. A summons was sent for him, but I do not believe it will be answered."

"How convenient."

This time, Zareth flinched. "I have come with an offer
of restitution for any damages caused; the Order will
cover your costs."

"That is acceptable," Elsabet replied. It was her turn to
wait.

"You haven't brought this to the attention of the Queen's court?" Zareth asked softly. His hands, resting also against the arms of his chair, now gripped the rests almost convulsively.

"Is there any reason why I should not have done so?"

"No, of course not."

She watched him, her face set in the lines of judgment. After a moment, unblinking, she added, "But, no, I have not yet notified that court."

His relief was obvious, although his stance changed very little. "We appreciate your forbearance in this, Lady. As you well know, the mage-born are feared by the populace at large. We wish to avoid panic or any hasty reactions."

At this, the lines of Elsabet's mouth curved into a sardonic smile. "Such as the reception my villagers gave you?"

"Such," he said, returning her smile cautiously, "as exactly that."

"Perhaps if the mage-born were more open about the limits to, and extents of, their powers, they would be less feared. The Hunter Lords are not feared."

Zareth raised one dark brow. "Are they not?"

"Not in general," she said, conceding a small point. "But, yes, I have no wish to upset the Breodani for no reason. There *is* no reason?"

Zareth moved his head restively.

"Master Kahn?"

His eyes widened in surprise. Then he shook his head, and this time, he did laugh out loud. "I'm not of Breodanir," he said apologetically. "I constantly underestimate the Hunter Ladies. Yes, Lady Elseth, I am Zareth Kahn. Do you know the names of the rest of our Order?"

"Only its foreign members."

"Which are almost all. Very well. There is no reason to worry. Let me be blunt."

"Will you be?"

"As blunt as is prudent. Krysanthos is of Essalieyan, and a mage of the second circle. He has power. In Breodanir there is only one mage to match him, although they are generally considered to be equals in magecraft.

The Order of Knowledge cannot explain his attack upon your manor; there is no reason—nothing at all to be gained—by such an obvious assault.

"The very fact that there were no casualties is suspicious. We did not understand why, given the fact that he had chosen to mount such an attack, he did not proceed with more force."

"More force?"

"He is capable of far, far worse than he showed. If the man you saw was indeed the same mage. We assume that he was."

"Explain."

Zareth glanced away, to the fires that burned in the wide, open hearth of the room. His eyes were lambent orange; a reflection of heat. "I cannot," he replied at last. "Forgive me."

Stephen was surprised when Elsabet returned a shrug for the mage's refusal. "Very well. Continue."

"There is little else to say. I have come, at your summons, to ascertain what it was that would attract a member of the mage-born to this household. This information will be reported to the head of the Order. You have our word," the mage added, "that we will pursue our investigations to the full extent of our combined power."

She listened. Her expression had only changed once in the course of the interview—and that small change could hardly be considered encouraging. Slowly, she folded her hands and let them settle into her lap. The fire crackled; breaths were drawn. No one moved.

At last, she nodded. "Gilliam. Stephen. Bring in our visitor."

Aside from an argument that threatened to delay them long past Lady Elseth's tolerance, Gilliam and Stephen obeyed her command. The subject of the argument made it clear that she would be presented, as she was, to the mage. Gilliam, of course, could see nothing wrong with it—but Stephen, taking in the torn, dirty fabric of her shift, and the matted tangle of straw and darkness that passed as her hair, shuddered.

He would have pressed his point had the mage not

been at a disadvantage with Elsabet. As it was, he gave in
to Gilliam's insistence, and together they returned to the
manor, the girl trailing Gilliam in the wide, happy circles
that the dogs usually did.

". . . and here she is," Lady Elseth said, as they made
their way into the parlor.

Zareth looked up immediately. His eyes, shadowed
now as the sun crept down the horizon, were wide and
unblinking. "This one?"

Gilliam bristled at the incredulity in the voice, but held
his tongue. Which was, considering his mother's mood,
the only wise option possible. The girl, catching Gilliam's
anger, bristled as well. Her growl, lower than a pup's, but
certainly high compared to a full-grown hound, filled the
room as she raised her lips over bared teeth.

"I see," the mage said. "May I?" Without waiting upon
an answer, he rose.

Gilliam placed a hand firmly on the girl's shoulder. She
didn't seem to mind, although it was perfectly clear that
the hand was meant to restrain. "Hold," he said softly.

"You're certain that the girl was the object of the attack?"

"Stephen?" Lady Elseth said, looking quietly across
the room.

"Yes, sir."

"Why?"

Stephen shrugged. "I don't know why he attacked her."

"Why," the mage said again, his voice less soft, "are
you so certain it was the girl he sought?"

Stephen did not answer. The mage looked up, his eyes
leaving the girl for the first time since she had entered the
parlor. "Stephen of Elseth, the question is not idly asked.
I would have you answer it."

"I understand," Stephen answered. "But I can't."

The mage drew himself to his full height and lifted a
hand. For a moment, the hand played against the air.
Stephen felt the faintest tingle of something odd, something wrong. It had been many, many years since he had
last encountered this strangeness, but he knew it at
once—it was not something he would ever forget, no
matter how he might desire to. His hand was on his

weapon at once; he fell back two steps, his midsection folding into a defensive crouch.

Zareth Kahn's eyes widened in surprise. In haste, he dropped his hand. "Your pardon," he said softly and bowed his head.

"You may have his pardon," Lady Elseth said, and her voice was undisguised ice. "It is not the pardon of Elseth. What has happened here?"

The mage looked warily at the Lady, suddenly reminded of where he was and why he had come. He met her eyes, unflinching beneath her cold regard, and then bowed his head again. When he raised it, his face was free of all conviviality; his eyes were dark and unblinking.

"I attempted to use my magics," he said softly. "To compel Stephen to speak more freely."

Even Elsabet was surprised at the bold frankness of this confession. Words left her; she once again raised her hands to her chin.

"You arrogant son of a—"

"Gilliam." Lady Elseth raised one hand, calling for silence. Not even her son dared gainsay her gesture, and although he bristled, he waited her word. As did Zareth Kahn. "I don't like the mage-born," she said at last, as if coming to a decision. "And I do not like foreign dignitaries. Twice in our history they have almost been our ruin."

Zareth Kahn nodded, offering no argument. His face, bland and expressionless, showed nothing.

"I particularly dislike the way both of these groups assume that because we are not of their number, we are ignorant or savage."

At this, the mage opened his mouth; she waved him to silence.

"But I imagine that our own opinions are worn just as gracefully by either of these two parties: mage-born or foreigner. Stephen, if it pleases you, you may speak freely without regard to the Elseth fortunes. The Order of Knowledge will likewise speak freely—through its representative—without regard to its reputation. If the one is hurt, I give you my word that the other will suffer."

The mage bowed. "You are gracious, Lady."

"No. I am pragmatic."

At this, the mage laughed again. "When you retire from the running of your demesne, you might consider foreign service—you would do well abroad."

She did not warm to his compliment, but did incline her head. "I have considered this. Stephen?"

Stephen, straight and once again composed, nodded and bowed to his Lady, with all the formality due her office, and not their relationship. "Zareth Kahn. We know that it is the girl who came under attack, because less than a month ago, on the eve of the majority of Cynthia of Maubreche, we found and saved her. She was beset by three creatures that we know for a fact were not human."

Zareth raised a pale hand; it was shaking slightly. "Hold. What do you mean, you know they were not human?"

"They could not be cut by our swords. They had blades for fingers. They had skin of stone. Is that enough?"

"There were three of these?"

"Three."

What Zareth Kahn said next could not have been repeated in the company of Ladies—should not have been even whispered in the parlor. "I will take my seat again," he said quietly, and proceeded to almost stumble back until the chair caught and held him. "How did you survive this?"

"Through the intervention of a mage," Stephen said shortly.

At this, Zareth Kahn's dark eyes narrowed. "Who? And how did you know for certain that this person was a mage?"

"Because the non-mage-born don't usually call lightning and have it answer."

"Stephen," Elsabet said, her voice quiet. He took the warning from it.

"She said her name was Evayne. She saved our lives, and lit a path for us to follow. They pursued the girl to the gardens of the Maubreche Estate. There, we finally managed to defeat them. I was injured and spent some time recuperating in the King's City.

"When I returned home, this same girl was attacked again, or, rather, her . . . rooms were." Even given leave and command by Elsabet, Stephen could not say everything to this stranger. "And this time, we found one other item of interest. You might know it, but let me describe it."

"Please do."

"It's a platinum chain with a simple oval obsidian stone at its end. The stone is ringed by platinum as well."

"I see," the mage said, very, very quietly. "Come, then. Let me examine the girl. I will use magic," he added, the words tentative.

"You will not!"

"Gilliam!"

"Gil . . ."

The girl began a low growl; it was almost as if she spoke the words that Gilliam had been forbidden.

"I will cause her no harm, Lord Elseth," the mage said, swiveling his head to meet Gilliam's angry glare. "If you wish, you can stand behind me with your sword. I seek answers only."

Gilliam nodded curtly, and strode across the room, his hand on his sword hilt. Stephen cringed.

"Gilliam. *I* have seen fit to trust this visitor, who has come at *my* summons."

"Lady," the visitor in question broke in. "I made the offer in all seriousness. It appears clear that the girl . . . responds to her master's unease. If this will make him feel more easy, I'm willing to submit to it without calling your hospitality into question."

She frowned, but grudgingly nodded her acquiescence. Gilliam did indeed come to stand behind the mage's chair, sword drawn. He was a dark shadow—the only one that didn't flicker with the fire and the lamplight. Steady in his defense, poised for some unforeseen battle, he looked more at ease—although the mage could not see this—than he had in the last three weeks.

A hush formed in the air, part magic, part shadow, part absence of sun. Zareth Kahn, instead of reaching out, settled back into his chair, striking a pose not dissimilar to the Lady Elseth's. Lines settled into the circles beneath his eyes; his forehead creased. Only the fire snapped and crackled as it burned away at the wood.

And then, growing so slowly it was hardly visible, came the faintest hint of blue light, as if lightning had indeed been harnessed and forced to stay its quick strike. Strands of the mage's dark, long hair began to rise.

Stephen drew breath and held it. He was uncomfortable, and as the blue light grew, his sense of unease increased. The gaunt contours of the mage's face drank in shadow until he looked skeletal; the horrors of a young boy's nightmares. For just an instant, Stephen was glad that Gilliam could not see the mage's face.

The mage gestured; the light leaped suddenly from his fingers. His fingers danced heavily, but certainly, through the air, like a drugged athlete. When they were again still, perfect blue rings surrounded the girl's body.

Stephen did not understand why she did not move, or snarl, or fight them. His hair, much like the mage's, stood on end at the back of his neck, and he was only an observer, not a participant.

The rings began to move, but Stephen saw that they cast odd shadows; they did not touch her skin, or even what remained of her ruined clothing, at all. He exhaled slowly, caught by the strangeness of the spectacle. For a moment, he could see an eerie beauty played out in her features, the perfect smoothness of her skin, her suddenly closed eyes. And then it was gone.

The lights vanished, and the mage sagged forward, visibly exhausted.

"Zareth Kahn?" someone said.

He looked up to meet Elsabet's concern. "It cost much to arrive here in such haste," he said softly. "But I think I have an answer for you." His forehead creased; his lips tightened. "Although I admit that I don't understand it."

"What answer?"

"The girl is god-born."

"God-born?" Stephen's brows vanished beneath his hair. "But that's impossible! Look at her eyes!"

"I know," the mage replied, and his sourness grew. "I

don't claim to understand it either. But she *is* god-born. I
have tested that to the limits of this spell—information is
my speciality." He sat back heavily against the chair.
"And the study of historical magics was one of
Krysanthos'." He raised a hand to his brow. "Apparently,
Mother watch us, summoning was one of those magics."

CHAPTER TWENTY

The room was awash in the heat of flame; the fire had been piled high, and quiet servants tended it at the mark of each hour. But Zareth Kahn still felt the chill. Blankets, pulled from winter storage, were piled high around him; he shivered against them, pulling them closer and higher.

This was the mage-fever, the result of pushing too hard with too much power and too little energy. He contained what he could of it in the presence of the Elseth family. But the act of examining the god-born girl had been madness, a symptom of the disease of insatiable curiosity.

He would pay for it; was paying for it now.

Yet even as his body was racked by shudders in the moon-touched room, his mind was elsewhere. On the girl. On Krysanthos. On Stephen of Elseth. It was not possible that Stephen was mage-born; a talent as strong as his sensitivity to magic indicated would have destroyed him, untrained as he was, before he left puberty behind. And he was certainly not god-born.

Or was he? The girl, to everyone's surprise, had proved to be just that. But the girl was mad, not nearly so human as Stephen showed himself to be. It was a puzzle. Zareth Kahn hated puzzles, and lived to defeat them. The puzzle of the Hunter God had brought him to Breodanir—and years later, the God's mystery remained unsolved. The mage was certain that Stephen and the girl were somehow involved in it.

Answers come from strange places. He told himself this, as the cold attacked again. It was bad tonight. But not nearly so bad as it had been when he first crossed the Elseth threshold.

Krysanthos was also a dire portent—of what, Zareth Kahn could not say. But although he had not concentrated on it during the course of the eve—had barely acknowledged the Elseth huntbrother's words—he recognized the medallion that Stephen had described.

Allasakar, the Lord of the Hells, was the only God to claim such an insignia.

Krysanthos, you fool, what have you done?

And why are you interested in the girl? Is she hellsborn?

The question was rhetorical; the magical scan that Zareth Kahn had slowly and deliberately completed ruled out that possibility. Ah. The cold subsided further; perhaps sleep had a chance to claim him, should it move quickly.

But even as his lids flickered down over his eyes, he felt annoyed. Not at Krysanthos' involvement—although that had consequences for the Order that he did not have the strength, or desire, to fully contemplate now—but rather at the fact that the mage of the second circle somehow had answers that he, Zareth Kahn, did not himself possess.

He would change that. He would bring the girl to the King's City.

"Elsa," Stephen said lightly. "Aren't you here early in the season? The time for the Sacred Hunt has passed us."

Lady Elseth looked up from her prayers. She was simply dressed this morning, favoring the practical over the fanciful. Her dress was a crisp brown, with long, plain sleeves that were wide enough to give her elbow play, but narrow enough not to be a nuisance. The skirts were wide and split at the hems; it was obvious that she planned some sort of physical labor this day. Perhaps the overseeing of the kennel's construction.

"Stephen. Is it that time so soon?"

He nodded and approached her, crossing the soft green to do so. "Will you come to see us off?"

She offered him a hand, and he took it, helping her to her feet. She rolled up her mat and handed it to him; he caught it carefully and placed in under the crook of his free arm. "Gilliam's excited about this, isn't he?"

Stephen drew a slow breath. "Yes. But worried, as well. And the mage tells us little, for all that he asks."

"You tell him less, Stephen. You failed to mention the horn the girl brought—and I think we both know that it is important. Perhaps important enough to launch such an obvious assault on our grounds for."

He nodded. "Later, if he proves trustworthy."

Lady Elseth inclined her head. "I will not gainsay you; if you do not see fit to trust a mage—especially one who has attempted magics in my presence—I will trust your judgment." She fell silent. Her lips were set, and her chin was tilted; she looked severe, or tired, or both.

"Elsa," Stephen said, placing an arm around her shoulders. "This isn't the Hunt. We'll be fine."

"You tell me that?" she said, turning sharply. "When you don't even believe it yourself?" Her voice was taut, like a rope pulled so tight and fine it might snap if touched.

"We don't have to go," Stephen said, leaving his convivial—and hollow—smile behind. He caught her cheek in his hand. It was cool to the touch.

She met his eyes; hers were filmed. For a moment, it seemed that she wavered; she lifted her own hand, and pressed it lightly against his, seeking either warmth or comfort. Then at last, she said, "Don't lie to me, Stephen. I have not lied to you." But her voice was softer than the words she spoke.

Stephen released a breath he did not know, until that moment, he was holding. He felt weak, as if her answer were not the one he had expected—or, rather, hoped for.

"It's the 'farewells' that I hate the most. Until I've said them, I can pretend that everything is, or will be, fine. But once you've gone, I can do nothing but wait."

"Should I have left you with the Hunter?"

"No." Her eyes were watery again; she looked away. "Because if I don't grasp the chance to say farewell, I might never have it again. This is the Hunter's land," she added bitterly. She bowed her head a moment. When she raised it, her expression was once again calm. "Shall we go? I didn't mean to keep you waiting."

Zareth Kahn was impatient to be off. Although still fatigued, his face was less hollowed, less dark; his eyes darted back and forth, as if he were trying to make sure he missed nothing, not even the most trivial of details.

The horses, saddled, were restive; the villagers—those that had the time—gathered in a quiet ring outside of the manor. They did not offer Zareth Kahn any friendliness, and for his part, he did not demand it.

"Are we ready to take our leave?" he asked, for perhaps the fourth time.

"We will be, momentarily," Stephen answered. "Lady Elseth said she'd something she wanted us to take to the King's City. She's gone to her rooms for it; she'll be down shortly."

"I suppose it won't wait?" The mage drummed his fingers against his leg.

Stephen watched, out of the corner of his eyes. It was hard to imagine that this slim, almost nervous man was the same one who had questioned them all two nights past. "It will only be a few more minutes," he said.

The mage nodded, and began to pace.

Gilliam, Lord Elseth, might have been annoyed at the mage's insistence—but he had his hands full. While the strange girl had, in the end, consented to ride within the confines of a carriage, she made it quite clear that she wanted nothing to do with horseback. Her incredulity at being asked to do so still made itself felt.

He was determined to try, but equally determined not to force the issue. Because, as Stephen said, she wasn't one of his dogs. His word was not—could not be—her law. He tried to tell himself this as he felt her press her disobedience. As he felt her test him, in a way that only the dogs ever did.

"Gilliam?"

"She won't ride," he said, the words clipped and uneven.

"Then let her walk. She'll change her mind." Stephen turned to face the girl, who was already half out of the tunic and breeches they'd managed to dress her in. "Then again, perhaps she won't. We aren't on the message relay," he added. "It won't make a difference."

Gilliam nodded curtly. He did not want to speak; the words would have added nothing. But he glowered at the girl more effectively than he could have shouted.

Stephen cringed. The girl did not. The mage politely inquired whether or not they could leave. And the manor door opened quietly.

It was the door that everyone looked to. Lady Elseth stood framed by it. Almost casually, she threw one bag to the ground; the other, she carried over her shoulder. Gone was even the practical dress of the morning; she wore dark pants, a loose, cream-colored shirt, and a large woolen vest. A hat covered and contained her hair, and on her feet she wore boots of thick leather.

"Mother?" Gilliam asked, contest with the recalcitrant girl forgotten.

"Yes?" She tilted her head to one side, raising a brow. One of the villagers ran up the stairs, and very carefully relieved Lady Elseth of her burden. "To the horse," she said, and he nodded.

Maribelle, quiet until that moment, suddenly seemed to appear from nowhere. "Mother?" In the word was the same question that Gilliam had asked, but without his harsh incredulity.

"Yes," Elsa said softly, answering the unasked question. "And I trust the keeping of our responsibility to you, Maribelle. You are old enough, and learned enough; my people will follow your commands."

Maribelle's forehead creased; watching her, Lady Elseth knew that those lines would one day become etched in her smooth brow. But in front of the villagers, she had the sense not to argue with her mother.

It was a cheat, of course. Elsabet had never had any intention of allowing her youngest the room or the space to argue with her sudden decision. She acknowledged it quietly when she hugged her daughter.

Maribelle said only, "Do you have to go?" But it was not the question of a child; it was the ambivalence of someone who had entered the twilight between childhood and adulthood, and stood on that line, for an instant, almost understanding all of the emotions of either.

"I have to go," Elsa whispered. "It's my duty and my right as Lady Elseth." Still, she felt oddly weak; her stomach was clenching, and her head felt a little too light. "No," she added, "that's not all of the truth. I—I have to be there. I have had to wait through so many Sacred Hunts." She swallowed, her voice tight and heavy. "But it isn't my duty to wait through this. They're my sons, Maribelle."

"And sons are always the most important," Maribelle said, her voice a whisper too, but a very, very flat one.

Lady Elseth felt her daughter's words as a blow. She held more tightly to Maribelle's shoulders. "No," she said, knowing that Maribelle would understand it one day, but not this one. "Sons are always the ones who die."

Her youngest surprised her. She returned the tight warmth of her mother's hug; held her longer than she should have in so public a circumstance.

"I wouldn't go," her mother said, again in the softest of whispers, "if I couldn't trust you here."

"I don't want them to die either," her daughter replied. And that was her apology. She pulled away, her clear eyes wide, her chin tilted, her shoulders squared. She was dressed to her station in a deep blue frock, and looked more the Lady than her mother, although no one who knew them would have mistaken the station of either. She curtsied, low, and held that gesture. "I will watch over Elseth in your stead, Lady." Her voice was strong, young, and rather loud.

"Thank you," Elsabet said. "You do our line proud." Then she looked at her still silent companions. "Well, gentlemen? Shall we ride? Or shall we rather gawk all day?"

Stephen shook his head in wonder, and then began to laugh. His body shaking, he caught the reins of his horse, and led it forward for his mother's use. Gilliam, still gaping, was nudged in passing.

"Yes, Lady Elseth. We ride." But the mage looked singularly less amused than Stephen did.

* * *

It shouldn't have been a grueling trip; it was. Zareth Kahn, himself exhausted and barely fit for the rigors of saddle, pressed the party hard. Lady Elseth accepted this prompting mildly, even docilely, Stephen and Gilliam accepted it gracelessly. But they did ride.

The girl, almost tireless, kept both feet on the ground, and circled Gilliam's horse whenever he paused. Still, she was quiet and caused little difficulty, perhaps understanding that there was urgency in their journey.

So it was that they came at last to the gates of the King's City, travel-worn, tired, and very much in need of sleep and bathing.

Stephen had thought to stay in an inn, but Zareth Kahn would not hear of it, and in the end they came to the grand halls of the Order of Knowledge, leading tired horses and a wild girl who never seemed to feel the exertion.

They were not an impressive delegation. Only Lady Elseth seemed to remember her bearing, although her clothing was not suitable for an embassy. She made certain that the horses were tended to, and quietly whispered a prayer of thanks to the Hunter—for Gilliam, pressed to move quickly, had elected to leave his dogs behind. The Order, of course, had no kennels for their keeping, as any normal inn would have.

Zareth Kahn, on the other hand, perked up almost the moment his feet crossed the grand threshold into the towering hall. Lady Elseth could well understand why. Her breath stopped a moment as she arched her neck back. Her eyes rose up, and up again, until they rested upon the very peak of the ceiling's stone arches. They were unadorned, but grand in their simplicity; a shout could be caught and echoed forever without losing any of its strength, or so she thought.

Stephen's eyes never reached the ceiling. He took in the rich red and gold of the carpeted stairs, glanced at the deep, dark wood that formed railings and borders, and then lighted upon the walls themselves.

They were not plain, although no tapestries or frescoes lined them. Where a statue or two was common in any such building, and an alcove dedicated to either a God or a relative should have been in evidence, these halls had neither. Instead, in row upon row, they had heavy, perfect shelves, with beveled glass in leaden frames, and ladders on wheels to walkways that rose four stories. And in each of these shelves, there were books.

Those books held voices, all silent now, that nonetheless called to him. The silence, the hush in the halls through which people could be seen moving, made perfect sense. This was a library that not even the King could boast. He reached out, pressed his fingers against the glass, and forgot about the complaints of a long and arduous journey.

"It is not so grand," Zareth Kahn said, his voice soft. "Our library in Essalieyan is by far superior." But he smiled almost fondly. "There is a library of older and more delicate works farther down the hall; it is the grandest of all of our rooms."

Stephen nodded, wordless. It made sense that the Order of Knowledge would have such a collection; it even made sense that mages would. Books, after all, were a hint of magic in Stephen's life.

"Wonderful," Gilliam snorted. "Do you have kitchens as well?"

As one person, they both turned, and their faces bore very similar expressions. Zareth Kahn recovered first. "Yes," he replied shortly. "We have kitchens. We also have rooms and wings for visiting ... dignitaries. If you follow me, I'll see that your needs are attended to. Forgive me for forgetting the hospitality of the Order."

He began to walk the halls briskly, leaving their wonder to Stephen. Stephen's frown deepened, aimed as it was at the spot between Gilliam's shoulder blades.

The rooms they were given were grand, even by noble standards. They were both larger and better equipped than the rooms in the King's castle and on his grounds, in which the Hunter Lords lived until the Sacred Hunt. The ceilings, tall, were not arched; they were flat, and crossed by magnificent beams. There were paintings hung above the fireplaces that bore artist's signatures that even Gilliam could recognize. Attached to each sleeping cham-

ber was a small, simple room with a stylized, but serviceable altar for votive offerings, prayer, and meditation. The
Order had taken pains to ensure that these altars could be
used by worshipers of many different faiths, although it
was equally obvious that the altars themselves saw little
use.

There was a sitting room, a small parlor, and a large
study. The study was equipped with shelves, although
these were empty, and two desks, either of which dwarfed
any that the Elseth Manor claimed. It was clear that who-
ever visited these chambers came to both work and live.

"Do these rooms meet your approval?"

"Indeed," Lady Elseth replied, before either Stephen or
Gilliam could speak. "They do. If this is the hospitality of
the Order, Zareth Kahn, than we of Elseth are deeply
grateful."

"Will you require anything? I shall send up servants
and water for the baths, unless you would prefer to use
the more public ones."

She raised a brow. "No, the small ones will do."

He nodded. "When would it please you to dine?"

"After our baths, I think." She lifted a hand to forestall
Gilliam, and caught him in mid-word. "Is there a hall for
the Order, or will we dine in our rooms?"

He hesitated a moment, and then bowed. "If it would
not trouble you, Lady, I would prefer that you remained
in your rooms until I have had time to confer with my
colleagues."

Her shoulders relaxed. "It would be no trouble at all."
Then she smiled, and although she looked weary, her
smile was completely genuine—the first such one with
which she had graced the mage. "My thanks."

". . . and that," Zareth Kahn said, sinking to rest in his
chair, "is the whole of it, Zoraban."

The light in the room was low; although it was full day,
and Zoraban's chambers had windows aplenty, the curtains had been drawn. They were a subtle, soft weave that
allowed a whisper of light, no more, to pass through, but
they were also magical in nature—a gift of creation from
the Order in the capital of Essalieyan. What was spoken

in these rooms when the curtains were drawn would be caught by no magical eavesdroppers, should any try to listen.

Zoraban nodded softly, and even in the poor light, the pale twinkle of his golden eyes was clear. He wore his age like a mantle, letting it suggest both wisdom and the power of gathered knowledge. It had been so for fifteen years, and if any thought it suspicious that Zoraban had not noticeably aged in those fifteen, they were wise enough not to voice their doubts. His long white hair gleamed softly, a halo around his slender features. His beard, thick and heavy, fell like milk into his lap.

Zareth Kahn raised his head idly, after minutes had passed in silence. Zoraban was not the most powerful of the mages that the Breodanir Order boasted—but he was easily the most learned of their number, and for that reason, held the seat of the Order. None had tried to gainsay him. After all, rare indeed was a god-born child of Teos, God of Knowledge—and when Zoraban had proved himself such a one, the Order had all but begged to receive him.

What are you thinking, Zoraban? What do you know that you've not seen fit to share with us?

As if he could hear the thoughts—and at times, Zoraban was uncannily, uncomfortably perceptive—the Master of the Order met Zareth Kahn's ringed eyes. Against all odds, the Teos-born man smiled; his face lit up with a deep, quiet joy.

"Have they eaten?"

"Pardon?" It was not the question he had expected.

"Have your companions eaten? Would they be willing to speak now, at my request?"

Almost, he said yes—but then he remembered two things. The first was the sour expression of Lord Elseth, and the second, that only Lord Elseth seemed to be able to communicate with the strange girl. Still, one did not easily say no to the Master of the Order. Zareth Kahn reflected on the wisdom of this, weighing the one against the other, before he sighed regretfully. "No, Zoraban. They will eat soon, and if you will it, I will bring them to your chambers the moment they have retired from their table."

Zoraban raised a frosted brow almost airily. "I see," he said, his words dry. "Then I will wait here in reposed patience." He smiled again. "There are answers here, Zareth—I can almost taste them."

"Answers?" Zareth Kahn asked mildly.

"To the questions the Gods ask," Zoraban replied. "Not to the questions of impertinent mages, even be they as exalted as to reach the second circle."

It was a matter of ease and custom to acknowledge a graceful defeat when the opponent was Zoraban; Zareth Kahn inclined his head elegantly. But his curiosity was piqued; it burned and flared to a life that hovered above his state of exhaustion, waiting. "If it won't trouble you, I will also sup quickly." He rose, without waiting a reply. In such a fey mood, Zoraban was unlikely to find a reason to protest.

Stephen found the very spartan simplicity of Zoraban's rooms almost shocking. Unlike almost every other inch of the sprawling order, it was unadorned by either paintings, shelves, or carpets. The floor was constructed of simple, well-oiled wooden planks, and the desk against the wall was small. It had two drawers, one on either side of the empty chair, and an inkstand that appeared to be empty.

There was a fire grate, but no mantle, and the only piece of finery in evidence anywhere was the expanse of draperies against the west wall. The drapes were closed and hung in a rippling cascade of oddly colored material; Stephen didn't like them, but he couldn't say why. Still, if not for those, he might have thought they'd been tricked into entering a confinement cell.

Zoraban did not seem to notice the shock of his visitors. "I bid you welcome to the Order of Knowledge," he said, rising. He wore simple robes, but dark ones; they were unbelted, and fell to his feet in a clean full-circle drape as he bowed, quite low. "I am Zoraban, Master here."

Lady Elseth, attired in a dress both simple and of obvious quality, returned his bow in kind; she knew that he was not, originally, of Breodanir, and left behind the formal curtsy that she would have otherwise offered. She was bathed and fed, a much renewed person, and as she rose, it was hard to imagine that she had been forced to the capital at such a harrowing pace.

"I am Elsabet, Lady Elseth," she said softly. "This is Gilliam, Lord Elseth, and his huntbrother, Stephen of Elseth. The girl is unfortunately afflicted and has been unable to give us her name."

"So I've heard," Zoraban replied. "But, please, those of you who will, be seated." He gestured to the walls, where four chairs were unceremoniously placed. The chairs, unlike the rest of the chamber, were finely ornamented; the hardwood of the arms and legs were worked with carvings and symbols, and laced liberally with gold.

Even Lady Elseth raised an eyebrow in question as she accepted the mage's offer.

"Bring the chairs in closer if you prefer; I don't usually have this many guests in my rooms, so I had the chairs brought and left to the side. I should have placed them more hospitably."

Lady Elseth was first to comply, although Zareth Kahn went to her aid; the chairs were heavy and not easily carried. Stephen followed his Lady's lead, and at length, so did Gilliam.

The girl sat at his feet, resting her chin on his knee. He stiffened, and she lifted her face, her expression almost a parody of hurt. Gilliam looked up then, at Stephen, as if for permission.

Stephen grimaced and then nodded quickly. He watched the girl's head settle back into Gilliam's knees, and after a moment, saw Gilliam slowly stroke her hair.

"Why have you come?" the Master of the Order asked suddenly. He rose, as if he had no need of a chair, but stayed his ground, surveying them all from the advantage of his height. And he was in truth tall, if not in seeming; the lamps at his back cast a long shadow, and the windows were allowed no chance to provide light. For a moment, light at his back and perfect, ivory hair against the black background of his robes, Zoraban seemed the maker-born image of a God.

Stephen drew breath sharply. Golden eyes seemed to flare, like the sun, in the pale face of the Master of the Order. At once, the Elseth huntbrother bowed his head.

The man laughed suddenly, and the shadows resumed their normal, everyday dimensions. "Yes, I'm of the god-born," he said. "Who else could hope to keep order within this Order of mages and knowledge-seekers?" Still, it was obvious that the chuckle was a pleased one, and although the fleeting aura of otherness vanished with the laugh, Zoraban did not choose to take his seat again.

"We want answers," Gilliam said abruptly. "We wouldn't have come had your mage not insisted."

Zoraban raised an eyebrow. "I would have known you as Hunter Lord with no introduction." His voice was grave. "But perhaps you will be glad of your journey, Lord Elseth. For I see that Zareth Kahn was correct in his appraisal. At your feet sits one god-born."

The girl looked up then, shaking her hair free of Gilliam's fingers. She met the mage's golden eyes with her dark ones, and then smiled and bobbed her head up and down, as if in greeting. Or agreement.

"Gil?" Stephen's eye were wide.

So were his Hunter's. "Yes," he said, half-whisper, half-word. "She says, yes." And he, too, looked up to meet the eyes of the god-born mage. He put a hand on the girl's shoulder, as if to draw her back—then realized what he was doing, and even had the grace to blush.

"The god-born can speak to the god-born," Zoraban said, his eyes gentle. "No matter what their language, no matter who their parents. But I have never seen such eyes on one so blessed—or cursed—among our number. Come, girl."

The girl rose and walked the length of the floor to stand before Zoraban. But she did turn—once—to glance back at Gilliam.

There were so many questions that Stephen wanted to ask—but as the mage lifted both of his hands and gently cupped the girl's upturned face, he forgot them. He could not speak; there was something about the scene that felt almost too private to watch. Yet it was compelling, magical. For a moment, the bright edge of mystery pervaded the room, and all of time seemed to whirl around the two who stood with the blood of the Gods in their veins, without ever eclipsing them.

The mage's eyes glowed; gold turned to sunlight, bright and crackling. The girl's face was turned away from them; they could not see her reaction, but she did not move or pull away.

"Yes," Zoraban said, in a voice too deep and too low for a human throat, "you are of the god-born. But I do not know your parent." He let his hands drop, slowly, and raised his head to face the spectators until now forgotten. "I will walk in the half-world for you—and for my own curiosity. I will call my father. Will you wait?"

Zareth Kahn's eyes widened in obvious surprise; Stephen, Gilliam, and Elsabet did no more than nod. What else could they do but wait? They had come this far seeking answers.

"He has only done this one other time," Zareth Kahn whispered, for Stephen's ears alone. "You are honored." Then he, too, fell silent, as Zoraban lowered his hands completely, until the long black sleeves melded with the drape of robes and his fingers curved loosely. His face, he lifted to some point beyond the ceiling, searching upward, and up again, as if the heavens themselves were visible to the golden aurora of his gaze. His lips parted, his beard rustled as if at wind.

The air before him began to sparkle; clouds rolled in, heavy and thick, like low-lying mist on the moors.

"Stand your ground; stay your place."

Stephen heard Zareth Kahn's command as if from a distance. He gripped the arms of his chair and looked rigidly down as the ground gave way to clouds and a lattice of darkness and light such as he had never dreamed.

"Gil!" He shouted, as he felt his brother begin to rise. "Stay seated. The half-world is not for us." He pressed his bond with his brother with more force than he had ever done; he could hear the distant screech of wood against wood as Gilliam sat back, hard.

"Trust him. He . . . has forgotten himself in his call. Let me explain. The half-world will open easily for the god-born—they speak with their parents in ways that normal mortals cannot. But humans were not meant to meet with Gods, and without a sure and certain guide, they cannot enter the realm. If they enter it, they can be lost until a God sees fit to return them—but no God can compel them there," Zareth Kahn said again, his tone calmer, his words slower. "The half-world will not consume us if we stay in our place. Lady?"

"I am . . . here. This is interesting, Zareth." Her voice was dry, with just the edge of a quiver. "What is this patchwork on the ground?"

"What do you see?" the mage replied.

"I see the golds and yellows of the harvest," she answered, measured, calm. "I see the shadows of the villagers in the fields; I see the foot of the seat of judgment. I see . . . I see my children—all of our children. The winter. It moves."

"What else?"

But she had fallen silent, and did not answer further.

"I don't see it," Gilliam said. "I see the hunt. I see stag and bear and boar; I see wolf and fox and hound. I see the spear and the sword and the bow. And Stephen."

"Stephen?" Zareth Kahn said softly.

"What do you see?" Stephen asked.

The mage laughed. "I see wind and rain and fire. I see the earth buckling, the heavens opening. I see books and lore and even a little death. More, but you wouldn't understand it. You?"

"I see darkness and light," Stephen replied.

"What?"

"Darkness, light—like the clouds here."

The mage was silent; his thought made the air heavy. "Stephen," he said at last, in a tone that was devoid of expression. "You are rare. What the half-world shows, no one fully understands—but not even I see it as it is; I see it as my hopes, my life, my dreams, my fears—but it is always connected with the every day."

"Earthquakes happen every day, do they?" Stephen shot back. But he shivered. And then he felt it: the presence of God. It crept into his body slowly; started as a tingle, the vaguest hint of something familiar that teases the memory. It did not stop there. Instead, it grew stronger, brighter; the clouds at his feet closed over the lattice until there was mist, no more.

Still, he felt it. And as it grew more persistent, he found himself moving, as if to escape, all of his warnings to Gilliam forgotten. First one foot, then the other, fell firmly against what had been planked oak, and then his hands left the confines of his armrests.

Unanchored, and alone, he stood in the mists of the half-world. He could not even hear Gilliam's shout—but he felt it clearly along their bond. It was comforting to know that not even this place where man and God might meet could sever what they had made together.

He sent his peace back to Gilliam. *Stay, Gil. I'm safe.* Then he began to walk forward. He thought he might walk forever, lost. Thought, without the guidance of Zoraban, that he might pay for his foolishness the way that the fools in the children's stories that Lady Elseth told always did.

But if he had to walk, he did not walk alone.

Gilliam, Lord Elseth, appeared beside him, a shadow with substance in a strange world that seemed to have none.

"Gil! I told you to stay!"

Gilliam smiled grimly, and punched his huntbrother, hard, in the shoulder.

Stephen laughed and offered no further demur; what he had said and what he felt were two very different things, and Gilliam rarely paid attention to the said thing when the felt thing beckoned.

"Where are we?" Gilliam said, looking around.

"In the half-world," someone answered. The ground, if ground it was, rumbled and buckled slightly. They both looked up, and up again, following the strange echo of the voice.

And thus is was that the Elseth Hunter Lord and his huntbrother first met a God in the half-world.

CHAPTER TWENTY-ONE

Gilliam saw a slightly bent old man, leaning against a smooth, dark staff with one hand, while in the other he carried a heavy tome with a thick brass latch and two cracked leather covers. He wore robes, those dark and gray ones that the Priests of the Hunter often wore, and his head, hands, and throat were unadorned. His hair, long and white, fell past his shoulders, gathering in the hollows of his stooped shoulders, and a beard trailed into the mist.

But his eyes were not gold, not any living color; they had a depth to them that eyes should not have. Were it not for the towering height of the God, Gilliam might have mistaken him for Zoraban, Master of the Order.

Stephen saw differently.

Age was a thing for mortals, and this tall, inscrutable Lord of the Heavens bore no such taint. He wore robes, yes, long and fine, but they had no colors and all colors as they shimmered to the unseen ground. His perfect forehead was cut by a circlet of light; his face was smooth, his hair drawn tightly, completely back. In Stephen's vision, the staff was no staff, but rather a fine and perfect blade, edged along both sides, pointed into rising fog. But he carried a book, and in it, Stephen was certain that the knowledge of the cosmos was writ.

He met the God's eyes for a second, no more, and then looked away. He did not trust the ground beneath his feet, and so bowed instead of dropping to one knee in deference.

"You are not the ones who called me," the god said, his voice filling their ears, although it was mild, even soft.

"No, Lord," Stephen said. His voice was quiet as the God's was loud.

"Then follow," the God replied. "We are close to the one that did." He raised a delicate brow and looked down his straight, slender nose. "You walked without him."

To that, there was no answer. Stephen nodded.

"Brave," was the only reply. The God began to walk, and as he did, the mist cleared behind him, forming a path wide enough for two men to walk abreast. In grateful silence, the Hunter and the huntbrother did just that.

They did not have long to walk; ahead, standing on what appeared to be a little hill or groundsheet, stood Zoraban; at his side stood the girl.

"Lord," Zoraban said, his voice oddly resonant.

"Zoraban." To Stephen's surprise, the God bowed low. "It is good to see you again so soon. Why have you called me?"

"To ask the right question," the mage replied gravely. He bowed as well, although there was nothing as majestic or grand in his gesture. Then he straightened, and his eyes widened. "Lord Elseth, Stephen."

"I found them wandering the mists," the God said. "Will you take them in?" The words were formal, almost ritualistic.

"I will, as my responsibility," Zoraban replied.

"Then they are your care." He looked down and then lifted the arm that held the sword. "Go and stand beside him." Although there was no light above, or anywhere in sight, the blade cast a cutting shadow.

They reached the side of the mage, chastened but unbowed. "You will let me speak," Zoraban said. They nodded, and Gilliam didn't even show rancor at the severity of the tone. "Teos, it is your light and your labor that has granted man vision beyond the seen. To you, all knowledge is eventually brought, and from you, the desire for knowledge is kindled and burns yet.

"I come to you with information; it is my hope, my supplication, that that information will return to me as understanding, if you will it.

"And if you do not will it, Lord, I will be content, and

I will continue to seek information in both your name and my own."

Gilliam rolled his eyes. "Why can't he just say 'I've got a question?' "

Stephen planted his elbow sharply between the two ribs his reach was most familiar with. He did not speak his disapproval, for fear of interrupting either Zoraban or Teos, the Lord of Knowledge—but he sent it sizzling along their bond.

The girl raised her head and looked back at Gilliam while the mage continued to intone the prologue that the Hunter Lord found of such little interest. Then, at last, Zoraban stopped.

Teos, meditative, looked down upon the four with his endless eyes. Then, if possible, the corners of his lips turned up as if in a smile. "Yes," he said softly, "you may present your case and ask your question." The mists curled up around him, becoming thicker and more dense. They took on shape and form, like water hardening to ice, until they at last held the appearance of a huge, if simple, throne. The god sat, laying his sword across his legs, and his book across the sword.

"This is an echo," Zoraban whispered, "of all that he is in the heavens." Golden eyes met endless ones without so much as flinching. If there was affection between the immortal and his son, it was not obvious, not noticeable.

"My lord, I bring you a mystery. This woman."

Teos studied the girl for a moment, and then inclined his head. Unlike a human monarch, he was not at all distressed by the state of her clothing, hair, or skin; these things rarely interested the Gods.

"She is god-born, Lord—but I do not know the God who was her parent, mother or father."

"Her place of birth?"

"She does not know it in a manner that I can repeat to you." He paused. "And she does not speak."

"I see." The God lifted a hand. "Come, girl." And on those two words, his voice changed. For a moment, it was indistinct, not a single voice, but a multitude of voices—high, low, deep, thin—all blended into a precise harmony of sound. Each syllable held the power and the mystery of command.

Stephen understood then that the bardic voice was an echo of the voice of the Gods. He was not certain that, had he wished it, he could have disobeyed Teos. The girl did not, but she did not seem troubled or even awed by the presence of the deity. The mists moved and parted at her feet; she traced a path cleanly and quickly, raising her face as she approached.

Teos reached down for her, and placed one hand upon her upturned head. Light lanced out from his fingertips, crackling in the silence.

"Lord Elseth," Zoraban said, his voice even, "stay your ground. She is not harmed."

But Gilliam had made no move, nor would he. Although he did not understand why, the girl was not afraid; had the God's magic harmed her in any way, he would have known it the moment she felt any pain. Still, his breath was tight and loudly drawn between clenched teeth.

Stephen did not even look at his Hunter; his eyes were drawn and bound to the hand of the God, the eyes of the God, the face of the God. Even the girl, straight and supple, with no taint of fear or awe, and therefore none of mortality, was barely a flicker in the field of his vision. He did not know that he held his breath until he was forced to expel it, and even then, he would not look away. He did not know why.

The God looked up. "She is god-born," he said, his voice once again a storm of voices. "But her mortal parent was no human."

"Ah," Zoraban said. "Which of the Gods was she born of?"

Teos' brow furrowed. Minutes passed; his eyes flickered gray and then flashed light, the essence of storm. "The Hunter God."

Gilliam closed his eyes and nodded. Stephen dropped to one knee; the mist rose to his chest. Only Zoraban dared to speak, and the word held only incredulity. "WHAT?"

"The God of the Breodani."

"But—but, Lord," Zoraban sputtered. "There *is* no Hunter God!"

"So we thought," Teos replied, while both Gilliam and Stephen gave way in turn to incredulity, if for very different reasons. "So *I* thought. But she is that, Zoraban." The God smiled suddenly, and the smile was a terrible, sudden change. "Ask the right question, my son."

"What do you mean, there is no Hunter God?" It was Stephen who asked the question, and he didn't care if it was "right" or not.

"Not a single Lord of Heaven has ever seen or met this God that Breodanir claims as its own," Zoraban answered tightly. "Not a single one of the so-called Hunter-born, *not one*, has ever manifested any signs of the god-born. Breodanir is a mystery to the Order—why else do you think so large a group would live in your King's City, away from the heart of Essalieyan, and the Order proper? But we have studied for years, and received no answers, found no records.

"Until now."

"There were answers," someone said. Stephen was almost shocked to find that the words were his own. "I have dreamt of them. Three times."

Very slowly, the God's gaze left the mystery of the girl and came to rest upon Stephen's face. Stephen tried to look away. "Three times, Stephen of Elseth? Tell me of your dreams, then. I would hear them."

"And may I then ask a question?"

"You are bold, but I am curious. Yes; you may ask."

Very quietly, Stephen began to tell the God of the dream that, three times, had troubled his sleep. He spoke of darkness, and as he did, the mists shifted, the ground rocked. He spoke of the destruction of the temple, the killing of the Priests, and the appearance, each of the three times, of Evayne.

"Evayne?" Teos said, lifting a hand.

"It was what she named herself," Stephen answered.

"You are wyrded."

Stephen nodded. "But upon each of these occasions, I found this, and winded it. And the Hunter's Death came."

So saying, Stephen reached into his jacket, and very carefully pulled out the Hunter's horn.

In the half-world, it crackled with light and energy. Stephen nearly dropped it as it outlined his hand with its aura of power.

"Will you wind it for me now?" Teos asked softly.

Stephen lifted the horn to his lips at the command inherent in the God's request. But before his lips made contact with the mouthpiece, the girl shrieked. His hands froze in midair.

For in that shriek, he heard two words: *Not yet.*

Eyes wide, he met the girl's agonized stare, and saw what he had never seen in her eyes: A human sentience, and a very human fear.

"I see," the God said. "Very well, put it aside, Stephen of Elseth. Guard it well. It is your answer."

"It's what the followers of Allasakar seek."

Teos lifted his fair face; the lines of his lips tightened; his pallor grew dark, and his eyes, darker still. "Why do you speak that name in my presence?"

"Because," Stephen replied, "Zareth Kahn, a member of your Order, recognized the pendant that only Priests of the Dark God wear. Or so he named it."

"I see." Teos' face became calm once again. "And yes. I do not know what credence to lend your dreams; they are Mystery given, and not even the Gods," here he frowned delicately, "may know Mystery's plans."

"Mystery?"

"He is called the Shadowed One in the East, the Unnamed One in the North; to the West, he is called Teiaramu, and in a time long past, he was called the God or the Guardian of Man. We of his brethren call him Mystery, and not even the Mother claims to know his purpose. But his wyrd may have shown you a truth. The darkness hunts that artifact." The God fell silent a moment, but lifted his hand for peace; it was clear that he had not yet finished. His eyes grew gray, and more dangerous, his brow furrowed. "Yes," he said at last, although it was a reply to none of the four. "We must trust you with this information. Hold.

"The Lord of the Darkness is not in his seat in the Hells."

"Not in his seat? Is he in the half-world?" Again, Stephen surprised himself, for the God was obviously used to a different ritual when receiving the questions of the merely mortal.

"No, Stephen of Elseth. This is what troubles us."

"Then where?"

"We do not know. No, do not fear that. The Covenant of God of Man forbids the mortal lands to the Gods. But I fear that his absence is a danger to all."

"Covenant of God of Man?" Stephen's eyes narrowed. Something about those words felt familiar; he wondered if, in one or the other of the books he had read as a child, he had touched upon this covenant, this agreement.

And then Zoraban suddenly turned, his face pale, his hands clenched tight in fists. "Stephen," he said, his voice low and urgent. "That pendant. The one you said Zareth Kahn recognized. What became of it?"

Stephen shrugged. "We brought it with us. Lady Elseth is its keeper; she has it for your inspection."

Zoraban spoke in a language that Stephen did not recognize, and then met the eyes of his parent. "My lord, Stephen's question to you, and my own, must remain unasked for this evening."

"Understood," Teos said, rising. The throne vanished as both of his feet touched the ground once more. "But what I have allowed, I will still grant." Before either of them could move, he lifted his sword and swiftly brought it down upon Stephen's shoulder. Stephen cried out as the flat of the blade pressed against his jacket.

A net of color sprang to life around him; the world spun, the mists grabbed at his ankles. He gave a strangled cry as he felt the Sword of Knowledge pass *through* him.

"Heed me, Stephen of Elseth. Although you are rash and impetuous, you have of me one question to ask, and I will answer it to the best of my ability. But you cannot ask it now; indeed, you cannot ask it at all if you travel to the halls of judgment. The darkness is gathering.

"But if you have the time, or the need, or the right question, you will be able to call as if you were, in blood,

my own son. And I grant you the gift of vision in your
fight against a most ancient enemy, even if you do not yet
understand what it entails.

"Now, go. *GO!*"

Zoraban lifted his arms, and the mist began to flee him,
almost scurrying in its sudden roll away from the swell at
his feet. The girl scampered forward to join him, and held
fast to the hem of his sleeve. The sky, if sky it was, darkened and grew indistinct and hazy.

Zoraban's face grew troubled. He cast his hands wide,
curling his fingers into his palms as if grasping at something invisible.

"What is it?" Stephen asked, raising his voice to be
heard, although there was no other sound.

"I don't know," Zoraban said. He motioned for silence,
his lips growing thin as the seconds passed.

And then, the mists exploded outward, fraying into air
and nothingness. Above them, instead of endless gray,
was a flat, stone ceiling; around them were those fine,
well crafted chairs. Lady Elseth sat slightly forward in
hers, and Zareth Kahn was likewise tense.

"Stephen, Gilliam!" She relaxed.

Zareth Kahn did not.

Without pause to greet them, Zoraban raced across the
room and stopped only when he towered over Lady
Elseth. "Lady, you carried a pendant with you to the
King's City. Where is it?"

Her brows furrowed, and her eyes widened as she
glanced at his face; his tone was not one she was used to
hearing. But it was clear that worry drove him. "I have it
with me," she replied, and sank her hands into the folds
of her skirt. "Here."

Zoraban stared at the pendant as if transfixed, and then
his eyes caught fire. Burning with the heat of liquid gold,
they flared so brightly that all in the room saw it.

The obsidian that formed the pendant's heart began to
melt. Lady Elseth gave a cry and dropped the chain, but
it was not pain that moved her; the platinum remained
cool against her fingers. "What are you doing?"

"Destroying a beacon," the mage replied gravely. "I
was careless; I was too absorbed with your question and

not with your plight. I pray that I've not been too slow to act." He drew his hand across his brow.

The door to his chambers buckled.

The wood warped in, as if some strange force had turned it to a thick, heavy liquid. For a moment, a fist far too large for a human hand could be seen pressing against the fabric that the door had become.

"Lady's frown," Zareth Kahn whispered. He rose, toppling his chair, and gripped the medallion of the Order in his right hand. His left weaved a complicated pattern in the air, his fingers deft, deliberate.

Zoraban joined him, although he wore no medallion.

Gilliam and Stephen rose as well, unsheathing their swords and waiting. Their movements were so dissimilar it was hard to see that the same hand had trained them, for Stephen was graceful, economical, and elegant; Gilliam wrenched his sword free with so much force, he stumbled back a step. But they acted in unison.

Even the girl fell to the ground in a low crouch, a feral growl in her throat.

"We—have the door." Zareth Kahn spoke through gritted teeth. "Lady, you might wish to move to the far wall."

Lady Elseth rose and drew a dagger. "If you have the door, it shouldn't be a—"

The stones around the door suddenly cracked. An unseen hand pushed against a part of the wall, hard; it fell forward into the room. Shadow, although there was no light to cast it, began to spill in through the hole.

"I see," Lady Elseth said. She moved. Quickly.

Something stepped into the hole in the wall. The shadows fell away from her, settling around her knees as if in homage. All that remained lingered against her body, supple, living raiment. Her hair was darker than the shadows, her eyes completely black. But her skin was pale and perfect, her chin a delicate point, her lips, unlined and full. She was not tall, yet even so there was nothing diminutive about her.

Before anyone could react, she lifted her hands, and the walls that framed her melted away, joining the darkness in velvet silence. Only the door, crackling blue, remained standing beside her, and it was not a fit companion.

"Zoraban," she said, inclining her head gently. "You are known for your wisdom and your learning, even in my circles." She smiled, and although there was no light upon her, her teeth glinted. "I bid you show it now. We have no interest in your Order, or any of your business. We want only the girl and her two companions."

"I'm afraid I will have to disappoint you," Zoraban replied. His eyes flashed, the rippling of almost liquid gold, and he added, "Giver of gentle death. Succubus."

A perfect brow rose in a perfect line, and she inclined her head in approval. "But perhaps, Zoraban, that choice should not be yours." She looked at Stephen, and her smile deepened, becoming at once full and soft.

Although only her face moved, Stephen felt a sudden lurch; he was at the core of her attention, her focus; everyone else in the room seemed to vanish. The shadows that curled around her feet and slid up her calves no longer seemed menacing; they were velvet, they were a midnight of promise and mystery. She stood at their heart, waiting. He knew then that he had never seen—and would never see again—so beautiful a woman.

His lips moved; he shook his head, as if in denial, but the sibilance of the single syllable shook the air. He knew, then, that he must look away; knew it, but could not bring himself to lose sight of her face, her eyes.

"Stephen!"

Lady Elseth's voice came to him at a great distance; he stopped walking, aware then that he did so, but did not look back. The woman of the shadows raised one hand, palm up, and then raised her second, cupping them together as if she held something precious. He wanted to lower his face into those hands and rest there.

At his side, he felt a sudden flare of magic; the tingling, the uncomfortable ache, passed quickly, melting into the distance, just as Lady Elseth's voice had.

"Stephen!"

It was a male voice this time—one he did not recognize. Distracted, he brushed it aside, lifting his hand in a gesture of annoyed impatience. He was almost there.

* * *

"Do something!" Lady Elseth said, her voice shaking. Mist left her lips; the tower was full of Winter night air, although the season would not come for months.

Zareth Kahn raised his hands in gesture, and once again, a crackle of blue light snapped against Stephen's side, only to be swallowed by the darkness.

"Zareth," Zoraban said. "Leave it be. She has called, and he has come."

"What?" The outrage in the younger mage's voice was unconcealed.

"The lore of the summoned," Zoraban continued, his eyes glinting. "He has ceded some part of himself to her keeping. Only he can disentangle it."

Zareth Kahn turned his attention upon the Master of the Order. Something passed between them then, and the younger mage bowed his dark head. "As you will it, Master," he said, but each word scraped against his throat.

"Gilliam?" Elsabet said, turning away from the mages.

"I can't," Gilliam whispered, his face pale, his sword shaking. "I can't reach him."

The shadows in the room grew thicker at the base of the wall, but they came up against a barrier a mere foot away. If Zareth Kahn and Zoraban were powerless to act in Stephen's defense, they nonetheless had power. They used it now.

Light limned the walls not shadow-claimed, sealing out the darkness, sealing in what little warmth remained. It flared, brilliant and harsh, as it sought to take the walls and failed.

"There are others," Zareth Kahn said softly.

"Are there? My power does not see them. How many?"

"Only one."

Zoraban sagged against the nearest wall. "Its shape?"

The younger man's brow creased as he concentrated. "I do not know it," he said at last. "But this is its echo." And he gestured, drawing light into a spiral that began to twist, ever faster, in the air before him. Like water draining into a deep hole, it swirled faster, and faster still, but instead of vanishing, it took shape; something hard and strange. It had arms and legs, and a head of sorts, but these were obscured by the spines that covered its body.

Even its round, flat face was ridged with small, precise blades. Where fingers might have been, there were daggers or small swords.

"A blade-demon," Zoraban said, and closed his eyes. "What does it do?"

"Nothing. I assume it's waiting."

"Don't. Guard the walls well, if you've the power for it. Mine is spent." He turned wearily and offered Lady Elseth a pained smile. "It's not easy to enter the half-world," he said, and that was all the explanation he offered.

"Come, Stephen. Rest. If you serve me, I will protect you; if you surrender unto me all things that I claim, I will even give you a measure of peace. Come." She had not moved from her place in the wall, but now the shadow framed her, clothing that had almost, but not quite, fallen aside. He felt it, thick and cold, at his feet.

Run, run, huntbrother.

He was trying to. She was close. But each step was harder to take; he had almost forgotten the feel of his feet as they moved, one in front of the other, like leaden, awkward things.

But her hands were close. Only a foot more, an inch more.

Run!

Yes. He drifted into the shadows; felt them sting him with their icy, invisible teeth. He didn't care. Very gently, and with infinite satisfaction, he rested his chin in the cup of her palms.

"Very good," she said, and her voice was a benediction that kept the cold at bay. She shifted her fingers, tracing his chin softly and gently with the sharp edges of her hands. Then, still holding his face, she lifted her left hand. Blood—where had it come from?—trickled down her forefinger.

"Shall you serve me? I am Sor na Shannen. I will be your master."

He tried to nod, but he could not move his head; tried to speak, but found his tongue heavy and swollen. There was only Sor na Shannen. There was only her.

And her smile, beatific, languorous, was the most beautiful thing in the world. She brought her finger down upon his forehead and began to trace a sigil there, with his blood as bond.

He heard her scream.

He screamed as well as a golden flash of light struck his face and sent him hurtling back across the room.

"It's not possible!" The demon shouted, lifting her arms in fury. She snarled, and for a moment, although she was still beautiful in a way that only immortals can be, the glamour, with all its heavy sensuality, was gone. *"Oath-bound!"*

Zoraban's eyes widened and he turned to stare at Stephen's crumpled body. "Oath-bound?" His voice was a whisper. "That's it!" And his eyes were like the sun suddenly stripped of clouds by a strong wind; they shone bright, completely eclipsing all memory of gray or night.

They were the last words that he ever spoke.

For although Sor na Shannen was succubus, she had not raised her arms for show; shadow limned them suddenly, and with shadow came an arc of icy blue. Magepower, focused and tightly drawn, flared from her hands, thrown like expertly wielded daggers that left a bright trail across the air.

They took the Master of the Order in the eyes.

Stephen rose in time to hear Zoraban's electric scream. He shook his head, clutching at his ears as if to halt the flow of noise.

Stephen!

Gilliam's voice, carried by bond and urgency, jerked Stephen to the side as the walls shattered. Chunks of stone crashed to the floor; shards, thin and hard, embedded themselves into the wood. Stephen looked up and saw nightmare standing beside the woman who had almost been his death. He saw her clearly; she was still strikingly beautiful, still unearthly in her glory. But her glory was shadow and darkness, and in three dreams he had seen what these forces, twinned, had wrought.

At her side was a creature that not even Stephen could

mistake for anything other than demon-kin. It was tall, and covered in what appeared to be shadow-tipped blades. Frantic, Stephen reached for his sword—and then saw it. It lay, only yards away, at the feet of Sor na Shannen; already shadow was rolling over it like mist in the lowlands. He could not remember dropping it, and as the blade-demon tensed to leap, he stopped trying.

It was almost unthinkable that something so large could move so quickly or so gracefully. But the demon-kin were not bound by the laws and the forms of the mortal; Stephen felt his jacket, shirt, and skin give way to three steel tines as they whistled past, brushing his back. He clamped down on a cry and reached for his dagger, staggering and turning on the same pivot.

The shortest of the creature's fingers, if fingers they could be called, were double the length of Stephen's dagger; as the demon flexed his hands, those blades rippled, incredibly supple although they must have been heavy. It leaped, Stephen dodged—and this time, the blades pierced his left shoulder.

Someone screamed in the distance. The demon stiffened before it could leap again, and then threw both of its arms back, exposing its chest. Stephen found no opening there, no way to attack—his dagger did not have the reach of the blades that bristled, more effective than plate armor, across the creature's midsection.

He threw himself back as the arms came round again, reaching for him. Blood glistened on the blades that were fingers, and Stephen wasn't sure whether or not it was his. He fell to the ground as the creature drove its fist through the wall. Rolled, as it kicked out, attempting to separate Stephen's head from his shoulders.

Zareth Kahn's forehead was beaded with sweat and human endeavor. His dark eyes were narrowed; the muscles along his thin jaw could be counted as they stood out in relief. He knew the "Givers of gentle death," or knew of them, better than any of the order here would have guessed.

And he knew that this one, this Sor na Shannen, was no ordinary succubus. Her ability to wield magic, her un-

canny threading of shadows and blue mage-fire, even the
demon-lords did not always possess.

He had not acted in time to save Zoraban, and later—if
there was one—he would mourn. He pressed his barriers,
hard. They shimmered as he struggled to make them
solid, more sure. Light crackled, describing their surface;
shadows huddled, deeper and darker with each passing
second, just at their edge. But through both of these, the
light and the dark, he could see her eyes clearly.

A scream cut the air; he ignored it. If the blade-demon
came for him, he would have no choice but death; he dare
not let these barriers down for even a second. Where had
she learned such power?

Lady Elseth was stiff against the wall; she made no
move to aid either of her two sons, although she had traveled here to protect them. She saw the folly of that now.
Her dagger, clutched tightly in white fingers, trembled
against her skirts.

She had never looked at a death so certain, so close.
Is this what you send for our sons? She mouthed the
words, eyes turned up to the heavens that the roof cut
from view. *Is this your Death, oh, Lord?*

But no; this creature, whatever it was, was not
natural—and it was obviously under the control, or command, of the woman in the wall.

Biting her lip, Elsabet lifted her arm, trying to look like
stone, like wall, like anything that was beneath notice. All
ladies were taught some weapon-skill. Hers had been
dagger. Very carefully, she reversed her grip, seeking balance, narrowing her eyes as she tried to get the best possible view of her target. She hesitated a moment. If she
threw this, she would have no weapon, no method of defense at all.

But if she did not try . . .

The dagger sailed, bolstered by the force of her throw.
She bit her lip and froze in place, forgetting even to
breathe. The demon didn't seem to notice her.

Until the blade was a foot away, maybe two. A hand
shot up, so quickly that its movement was invisible. The
dagger changed trajectory in mid-flight. The shadows that

pressed Zareth Kahn back faltered; the blade gathered momentum and speed.

It found its target, but it was not the target that Lady Elseth had intended. Horrified, she watched it strike and sink into Zareth Kahn's shoulder.

CHAPTER TWENTY-TWO

In all of the fight, the wild girl had been forgotten. Certainly Stephen did not notice her; nor did Elsabet or Zareth Kahn as the barriers he had so carefully built faltered for a crucial second. And her master, Lord Elseth, lay where he had fallen when the blade-demon had thrown his arms back in a wide, deadly circle.

He was still alive.

She would have known of his death. But his thoughts were gone from her; they had fled into patterns of pain so alien that she lost the ability to follow.

It was the only ability she lost. She crawled along the ground, nuzzling his neck with her nose, her cheek. He stirred, but he did not move or speak. The scent of his blood filled her nostrils.

She rose, leaving the floor, and planted a foot on either side of her master's prone body. She felt his consciousness flicker, and then felt it gutter as his breathing slowed.

What she did next, only she understood. And she knew that Gilliam, had he been conscious, or even sleeping, would have prevented it—without ever being aware that he did so. He could not do it now. No one could.

She began to change. Her hair, wild and tangled, stretched down in a sudden flash of brown; it widened, lengthened, and grew thick and hard. Then, in the pale crackle of the blue-light that was the contest of two mages, it became iridescent. Scaly. Her nose widened and lengthened, her jaw grew, and grew again in a sudden lurch. Her shoulders doubled in width, her arms and legs became larger, more muscular. Where there had been fingers and broken, dirty nails, there were claws of gold.

Where there had been flat teeth, with canines perhaps a little too sharp, there were fangs and the jaws of death.

She roared, and the tower shook.

She roared again, and the blade-demon spun, heavy and certain in movement, its quarry momentarily forgotten. Even Sor na Shannen was surprised enough to falter in her attack.

Zareth Kahn, struggling against pain, did not; he could no longer afford to let anything come between him and his concentration. He heard Sor na Shannen's frustrated curse with great satisfaction. Hands touched his shoulder, his side. He did not acknowledge them at all, but he knew that they belonged to Lady Elseth. She could not help, of course, but if she remained close to him, so much the better; his circle of protection had become exceedingly small and was unlikely to widen again.

Bleeding, dazed, his sight obscured by the blood that would not stop dripping into his eyes, Stephen of Elseth looked up, transfixed. The blade-demon had been a thing of nightmare. The creature that challenged it was a much more personal dread. He recognized its shape, its form; recognized its size and the death of its claws and fangs. Three times he had dreamed it, and once he had passed beneath its banner in the halls of the king.

He knew what must be done. He was certain of it. Fumbling, he reached for his belt, his inner pocket. His hands trembled as they closed around the horn that the girl had given him.

The girl.

He opened his mouth, but no sound came out. Shuddering, he tightened his grip upon bone and silver.

No—not now, not yet! This is not the death that you dreamed, Stephen of Elseth. Heed me.

He hesitated, and then shook his head; the words were a buzzing at his ears, and with a little effort, he hoped to drive them away. The time for action was—

Now. The beast lunged, jaws wide and snapping; the blade-demon countered with a strike. But those long, fine, deadly tines that pierced cloth and flesh with such grace and ease, met resistance in the hide of the beast; the force of the demon's lunge was enough to score scale, perhaps tickle flesh. No more.

Then the demon opened its mouth, and for the first time in the darkened, broken room, its voice was heard. It spoke with shadow in harsh, guttural syllables. Stephen did not understand them; he didn't want to. Transfixed, he held to the horn without pulling it from his jacket.

The beast snapped at air again; the demon was slightly faster, slightly smaller. It could not roll, but somehow, through some undulation that such a creature should have been unable to perform, it managed to drive a fist up and under the beast's belly.

There was pain in the answering roar—but Stephen barely understood it. For in the wake of the demon's attack, he could see what lay, unmoving, beneath the bulk of the beast. Gilliam.

Later, he would not understand what he did, or why; he could not have explained why the horn and the sounding of it became for a moment only dream. He moved along the wall, circling the blade-demon's heaving back, cringing just out of reach of those blades and those hands.

Gilliam!

There was no answer.

If a heart could be stopped and its body still live, Stephen would have had no heart. The shadows became cold and complete, and against them he sheltered only his fear. *Gil—Gil, are you alive?* Again, there was no reply.

He took a breath; it was heavy with dust and shadow. He scrambled across the ground, with an eye to the blade-demon's feet. He traveled near the wall, as far from Sor na Shannen as he could be in the small room.

Small? There were only two people in the room. Even the monsters, these living nightmares brought to life by magics and gods and the dreams of minds not mortal, had become as the shadows: dangerous, death-giving, and not quite real. The blood that still ran the course of his face, and the wounds that burned at back and arms, didn't change this.

There was Gilliam. There was Stephen.

He tried to speak, but he had no voice; tried to push the bond that had been theirs since he became of Elseth. Instead of Gilliam's answering voice, he heard William of Valentin. Saw Bryan, dead and lost. Saw Norn, lowered into a waiting grave, before Elsabet's cold, stony silence.

He crawled, and the ruptured wood beneath his fingers reminded him of Soredon of Elseth. Hunter Lord. Dead. Stephen was no longer twenty-two; he was eight—and without Gilliam of Elseth he had no life; he was empty.

Stephen was afraid. But he moved.

Gilliam, damn you, answer me! Are you dead?

But no, no, he couldn't be dead. Surely Stephen would know if he were dead; he would feel it. *GILLIAM!*

Splinters cut his wrists; sharp, small bits of rock dug into his skin. He crawled. Blood touched his eyes, but he let it run. He didn't want to lose sight of Gilliam and the shadow that lay across his back. If he could see his face, even his face, it would help.

But his face was buried against the floor.

Two feet. Three feet. Above him, as if in the heavens, this clash of beast and demon, two titans in a battle that Stephen wanted no place or part in. Four feet. Five. He could not look up now, although the feet of the beast, like the feet of the great, jeweled dragons that were myth and legend, had not left their perch on either side of his Hunter Lord. Gilliam was her—it's—treasure. But he was more than that to Stephen. Not master, as he was to the girl, and not lover, as Cynthia was to Stephen, but brother.

Huntbrother.

The tenth foot. The last inch. Stephen reached out with the tips of his fingers and touched Gilliam's hand. A shock rippled up his arm, lending him strength.

He prayed that the beast would continue its fight without looking down, but even had it done so, he would not have let go. He inched forward, and forward again, until his grip on Gilliam's hand was as solid as he could make it. Then he inched up the slack arm. Taking a breath to steady himself, planting his knees against the ground as a brace, Stephen *pulled.*

Gilliam had always been the heavier of the two, but Stephen had never felt it as a solid truth until now. He pulled again, harder, gained more height as he was forced to find leverage. He cried out loudly, furiously—and silently to any person in the room that was not Gilliam of Elseth. But he did not let go.

And the beast did not stop him. Instead, although Stephen barely realized it, it moved to interpose its body fully between the blade-demon and the Elseth Lord and huntbrother, as Stephen at last managed to drag Gilliam away from the fight, and to the safety of the farthest wall.

He did not know what Gilliam's injuries were. Could not tell if his limbs or ribs were broken, if his vital organs had been pierced. Blood was everywhere along Gilliam's chest, arms, and legs. Stephen tried to think, but he could not; all he could do was pull Gilliam close and hold him, tightly as William had held Bryan's body on the green before the altar.

Elsabet saw them at last, huddled against the rock of the wall that faced the demon, the shadow, and Sor na Shannen. Her face, already white, could pale no further, and she had no breath for words. She began to move, and Zareth Kahn caught her arm, restraining her.

"Don't break the circle, Lady," he said, his voice tight. "I cannot protect you."

But what of my sons? She wanted to shout it; she didn't. The fingers that dug into her arm were solid, strong. As she hesitated, he grunted. The barriers that lit the room gave ground, closing more tightly around them. Zareth Kahn cursed, unmindful of manners and propriety. She cursed with him, but silently, silently.

The barriers fell back again, bowing to the greater pressure of the less-exhausted mage. All of her life, Elsabet had known of magic, and magic's existence—but it had been as real as any God save the Hunter God. It would never be so comfortably distant again.

Zareth Kahn turned to her. She could see the dark circles beneath his narrowed eyes. The line of his jaw was thin and tense; his dark hair clung to his face in damp, thin curls. "I'm sorry, Lady," he whispered.

She had no weapon with which to aid him. Although her dagger was within easy reach, she did not dare to pull it from its sheath of flesh, and had she done so, she wouldn't have thrown it again. That had cost them much; perhaps this battle itself.

So she did what any intelligent person would have done in her place. She prayed.

First, to the Hunter God, that merciless scion of death and fertility that had so marked her land and her people; that had succored those in her care while destroying the two men who had become entwined with each root of her strength. Her eyes were drawn by the flash of blades and scales; by the roar of a beast and the dissonant syllables of a demon. Perhaps He had already answered a prayer that had not yet formed; it was not enough. Without pause, she continued, one hand now near-burrowed into Zareth Kahn's shoulder, one pressed firmly against her lips. She prayed to the Mother, for she knew of the Mother's mercy; she begged Luck to turn a smile upon them; she pleaded with Justice to intervene.

She was good at prayer; she had prayed just so, once a year, for all of her adult life—and for much of her childhood as well, a shadow at her mother's side. She knew how to draw strength from pleas; knew how to lose her fears, for a moment, in their intensity, although fear was the base of her whispers by the altar-side. And she knew that though the fiercest of prayers remain unanswered, the time taken to utter them gave her the space in which to find the dignity to face all travails as the noble Lady that she was.

But this one time, she was wrong.

Mercifully, gloriously wrong.

There was the sharp song of a crackle, and above them all, human, demon, and god-born beast, the fierce blue of cloudless sky destroyed the darkness of shadow. It was so total, so complete in its presence, that Elsabet of Elseth only recognized it as mage-light when it began to shimmer.

"The Order!" Zareth Kahn whispered, as his eyes began to shine. "The Order is here!" Hope gave him strength, and with a great sweep of his uninjured arm, he strengthened his barrier, pushing it in one great jolt to the foot of the wall. There, illuminated briefly by a power that was not hers, Sor na Shannen's face was a study in dismay. And then, the shadows roiled about her feet, drawing up and ever up, until she was consumed by them.

Zareth Kahn cursed and surged forward, only to be halted by Elsabet's strong grip. The tines of the blade-demon whistled past, an inch from his chest. "She escapes!" he shouted.

Light struck the shadows, hard; it was not the multi-layered wall that Zareth Kahn had built, but rather the thick, sudden blast of lightning. Rock sprayed up in answer to that strike. The shadows cleared as if by gust of strong wind, and beyond them, for the first time since the hole in the wall had been made, Elsabet could see the halls, and the stairs, beyond. They were full now; men and women in the robes of the Order—and some perhaps less formally clad, stood arrayed there, arms held out, hands twisting in an incredibly complicated dance.

Zareth Kahn could see this as well, but he did not let his barriers drop. Instead, he pulled in just the smallest filament of their power, draining the light above him at their unspoken consent.

"The blade-demon," he said, his voice quiet, although the words resounded like a shout in Elsabet's ears, "must be destroyed. The beast that fights it must not."

The sky of their magic began to twist in a spiral of blue and crackling white, a pool being slowly stirred. It gained momentum, moving more quickly with each turn, each spin, until it was dizzying to gaze upon.

And then, in a sudden surge, it came *down,* funneled by the will of the mages of the Order. The blade-demon, arms extended, body rippling in mid-leap, was struck. It screamed and froze. The light intensified until it could not be gazed upon by any of the untrained; eyes watering and narrowed, Elsabet looked away.

But she heard its cries, smelled the charring of demon flesh. And she heard one other cry, wordless, that she recognized: Stephen's voice. Her heart froze, and all danger, all magic, all unnatural combat, was forgotten in that instant. Wheeling, she let go of Zareth Kahn's arm and stumbled toward the wall. Her eyes still watered, and only the glow of the mage-light penetrated the darkness that same light had left her for vision. But she knew where the cry had come from. Knew what it must mean.

"Stephen!"

He didn't answer; she didn't expect him to, although she had hoped that he might. Her fingers trailed against cool stone as she groped along the wall. Her sight began to clear, and as it did, she saw someone huddled against the floor, rocking under the weight of an unwieldy burden. She dropped to her knees as she approached; felt the crisp fabric of her crinoline brush against her legs.

"Stephen?" Her voice was a whisper now.

He looked up. "We won," he said, whispering as well. But his arms were tight, and had her vision been just a little clearer, she would have seen that his fingers were white and shaking.

"Yes," she said gently. Her eyes clouded, but this time there was no magic to blame. "Gilliam?" She reached out, slowly, and touched her son's still face. "Gil?"

"He won't answer," Stephen said, his voice as flat as his eyes. But he allowed her to touch his Hunter, and she found, against the side of his neck, the thing that she sought.

"Stephen—he's still alive."

Stephen looked at her blankly.

"You can carry him, but we have to see a doctor or a healer. Quickly. He's—he's still here."

"But he won't answer."

"I don't know if he can. Are you so certain that he's dead?"

Stephen looked down at the blood that was set and sticky, no longer sure that it was Gilliam's and not his own. "I don't know."

"Then he *is* alive," she replied, standing. "You would know if he were not, Stephen. There wouldn't be any question, any doubt. Now, come!" She straightened her shoulders, and the tilt of her chin held the power of long years of authority. She did not expect to be disobeyed, and Stephen, exhausted by loss of blood and near-frantic worry, responded automatically, and although he lifted Gilliam at Lady Elseth's command, the weight he carried was diminished by the force, the absolute surety, of her words.

It was the beast that stopped him, swinging the wide trunk of its neck forward. Its eyes were dark, almost entirely black, but as it studied Stephen, he felt the last of his fear drain away. If this was the Hunter's Death, he had labored years under a nightmare that would not become reality.

It snuffled a little, and then brushed its snout against Gilliam's chest.

"We have to go," Stephen said softly. "To take care of your master."

The gleaming, iridescent head bobbed uncertainly to one side, its eyes flickering in the darkness, even as the last of the shadow faded. It turned, suddenly and swiftly, although so large a creature should have been slower, more cumbersome in movement.

Stephen followed its gaze as it surveyed the ruined wall, and the men and women that seemed to go on past torches and lamplight down the winding staircase. "It's over," he said, equally softly.

The beast growled; the air around Stephen's ears buzzed with the sound of that throaty voice. And then, before Stephen's eyes, it began to change. He watched in wonder, and almost in terror, as the scales seemed to dwindle and gather in a cowl around its neck. It lifted its forepaws from the ground, and reared up on its hind legs, and the golden claws, now rimmed with darkness that might have been demon-blood, became flat, dull, and smaller. The jaw shrank, the head altered, and in a minute a naked, dirty girl stood before him, her head still cocked in an odd, questioning angle.

For the first time, Stephen felt no resentment and no unease as he gazed upon her. Her body was small, almost delicate, and were it not for dirt, and one or two long scratches, it would have been perfect, if a little boyish. Her hair was still a messy tangle, but its deep brown-black framed her silent face. She opened her mouth, and spoke.

In a whine.

He nodded, although he did not understand what she

said, and began to walk, quickly now, as urgency grew, toward the open wall and the magicked door, still closed, that stood in its frame.

Before he reached it, the mages made way, and two women stepped out of the gathered, silent crowd into what remained of the Master's study. Stephen was the only person present who recognized both of them. He would have bowed, but that would have meant letting go of Gilliam.

Evayne, the mysterious woman of the wyrd and the night of demons, came first. Her dark blue cloak was draped around her, like the shadows had been around Sor na Shannen, but her cowl rested along her shoulders, and the blackness of her hair, drawn back, still framed her white face, her violet eyes.

At her side, lips pressed into a thin line, and eyes circled by weariness, stood Vivienne, the Priestess of the Mother. She was dressed in brown and gold and white, and her hands, as she lifted them, palm up, were steady.

"Lady," Stephen whispered. He took three steps, and stopped when he reached her side.

Her dark eyes widened. "Lay him down at once," she said, her voice almost harsh.

He did, but gently, placing Gilliam of Elseth at the feet of the Priestess. White, ringed hands touched Gilliam's neck carefully, and then moved out to span his chest. "You were right," she said, speaking over her shoulder to the woman in midnight blue who had not moved or spoken. "And I apologize for the harshness of my temper. He would not have survived the journey to the temple. Do not move him further, Stephen of Elseth. I have him now, and I will help as I am able."

Stephen nodded, and knelt by her side.

"I should have known," Vivienne added, in her slightly sharp tone, "that it would be one or the other of you. The night had that darkness about it. Breathe easy, hunt-brother. If he can be saved at all, I will save him."

He recognized a dismissal when he heard it and made to rise. The girl did not, and one other came to kneel at the Priestess' feet. It was Lady Elseth.

* * *

This is the first time, she thought, head bowed, body stiff with control, *that you have answered my prayers.* She wanted to cry now, for the first time in years, but dignity and station forbade it. She could almost feel the warmth and heat that radiated from the Vivienne's hands, and she was grateful for it, although she longed to touch her son and feel for herself the strength of his pulse, the beat of his heart, the tickle of his breath.

She knew better than to interfere with the healer's communion, and clasped her hands in her lap instead. She was not going to lose her son this night. She let that sink in, let herself believe it. Glancing up, she saw the eyes of the strange woman who had led the Priestess in. They were fixed upon Vivienne and Gilliam with such intensity that Elsabet could not help but notice it.

There was something odd about the stare, though; something strange about the woman. She was, to look at her, very young—no older than Maribelle, and perhaps younger—but her face was hard, emotionless, and her lips were drawn in a line that held no mirth, nor ever seemed likely to.

Then she turned, ever so slightly, and met Lady Elseth's gaze. They locked eyes, and for a second Elsabet caught a glimpse of something younger in the woman's face. A hint of wistful envy. Before she could even name it, it was gone, and the ice was back in place.

"Lady Elseth," the woman said, and bowed. "I am Evayne."

"Zoraban is dead," Zareth Kahn said flatly, wincing as the dagger was at last pulled from his shoulder. He felt the warmth of blood and the sting of the cut; it was deep.

The older man who attended him nodded grimly, although it had not been a question. "We know. Sela attends his body now, with Jareme. Sit *still,* Zar. You only make it worse, and I fear that the Priestess will have neither the time or the energy to attend to you."

"She wouldn't have had to," the mage said, clenching his teeth and attempting to sit still, as Elodra so quaintly put it, "had you deigned to notice the shadow-magic and arrive less tardily."

Elodra raised a frosted brow, and tugged tightly at the bandages he manipulated by hand. His was a slender, almost arch face. "Zareth," he said softly.

Zareth Kahn flushed heavily and looked away. "You didn't deserve that," he conceded.

"We didn't feel the shadow-magic," Elodra said. "Until we came to the tower's height itself." He knotted the bandage and then examined it more closely. Satisfied, he stepped back. "Is this to do with Krysanthos?"

"I don't know. He wasn't here, if that's what you're asking, and I didn't feel his signature." Free from Elodra's fussing—it was something that Elodra did well, and did constantly, which was why he also handled most of the Order's financial dealings—Zareth Kahn flexed his shoulder, winced, and then sagged. "But if you didn't—"

"The woman," Elodra replied, turning his gaze upon the diminutive figure who stood in the isolation of her midnight-blue robes and her unearthly strangeness. "She came, with the Priestess of the Mother, and bade us hurry for the sake of your lives. I started up on my own, but she insisted that we gather the brethren before we made our ascent." Elodra shivered. "I well understand why, now."

Zareth Kahn nodded, and then slid his hands over his face. It was safe, now, to shudder; to feel pain and the hint of a loss that the Order might never fully recover from. And in scant days, perhaps hours, he would also begin to question, to dissect, to understand, treating the events of this night as all things, in the end, were treated by the Order of Knowledge.

But here and now, his mage-power guttered, and the chill already beginning to set his teeth on edge, he had only questions with no depth and no force behind them. Shivers turned to shudders; he curled into the floor, bringing his knees to his chest.

Elodra was at his side at once, offering help. No, not offering, not precisely. Few indeed were the mage-born who resisted any of Elodra's assistance for long. And one caught by mage-fever had less chance than most. Almost docile, the second-circle mage allowed himself to be pulled to his feet, braced, and led out of the ruins of the tower.

Although Gilliam's injuries were healed, he had suffered much blood loss, and over his loud objections, was taken by mages out of the tower's rooms. The girl accompanied him, circling his carriers in an odd hop and jump step, and Lady Elseth walked, shivering and pale, at the side of his stretcher. Vivienne, Priestess of the Mother, was wan and pale. Only with the Hunter-born and their brothers was the cost of the healing—physically and emotionally—so one-sided. She was glad of it, or she would be, later.

But Stephen remained in the room until the last of the stragglers had left it. Then, and only then, he bowed once, deeply, to Evayne.

Evayne's smile was a bitter one. "Stephen of Elseth," she said, her voice soft and alien. Where, in the dreams, she had been power and mystery, in this room, at this moment, her words were no different in strength than the words any woman might speak. In such a situation. Indeed, perhaps because his vision of her had been the object of fear and confusion for so long, he found her almost disappointing.

"Evayne," Stephen said, stepping forward. "Twice now you've saved our lives. I should thank you for it."

The smile became more edged, the eyes colder— violets hit by a sudden, deadly frost. "But you won't, Elseth huntbrother."

The vehemence in the words took Stephen by surprise; he stepped back a pace, although she had not so much as lifted a hand. Then, before he could speak, she passed a hand over her eyes. The folds of her robes changed and fell as she moved, and he thought of shadow again. Natural shadow, of the kind that occurred only upon the clearest of nights, with the moon in her glory.

"I am sorry," she whispered, as her hand fell away over shut lids. "That wasn't necessary. I have never been good at beginnings, Stephen. Let us try this again."

He nodded, although he didn't understand. "This isn't the beginning," he said tentatively.

"No," she replied. "And, yes. I will not leave you when sleep does, and I will not leave you to flee. You have questions, and I carry news; we will share these together before I depart." She shivered again and seemed to shrink inward.

Stephen moved slowly forward, and held out his arm as stiff support. He looked down at his sleeve, wondering why it was so dark, when it had become so, and whether or not the shadows of her fingers would pass through his forearm instead of resting there.

"Don't." Once again, she was ice as she pulled back, staring at his proffered arm as if it were a sword. "I am not so weak, or so old, to require your aid."

"You don't have to be weak or old to be weary," Stephen said, but he stepped back and lowered his hands to his side. "Evayne." His voice was soft. "If you do not wish help, I won't offer it again."

She shook her head, looking down at her feet in silence, as if suddenly aware of her poor manners—if manners and the politenesses of society could be an issue in the ruined tower of a dead mage. "You have questions to ask me. Why don't you ask them now?"

"The questions I have I can't ask without Gilliam."

"No?"

"No. He is my Lord, as you are my wyrd."

"Don't," she said again, but less sharply. She lifted a hand as if in surrender.

"Come," he was gentle, as if he spoke soothing nonsense to a wild creature that stood petrified just out of reach. "It's dark here. There will be light in the morning, and perhaps we both need it."

"Before the morning, there's always the dreaming," she said, and then bit her lip. Her teeth trembled there for a moment, and then her expression flowed into a still, stately mask; she looked older, more regal—a thing of vision or wyrd. "Lead the way, then, Stephen of Elseth."

He did, although he had to force himself not to offer her his arm again. He stepped carefully over rubble and dust, lifting his hand to cover his head as he passed below the edge of the ruined wall closest to the ceiling.

Evayne watched him go.

Why, she thought to herself, for she was very, very weary, *can you never choose someone I can hate?*

There was no answer, of course, and she expected none as she followed Stephen's awkward gait. But she prayed as she walked, that he would be the last.

She knew that this, too, would not be answered.

CHAPTER TWENTY-THREE

Evayne did not disappear with the troubled dreams of the short night. By the time that dawn had cleared the remnants of darkness from the sky, she was awake and waiting.

Or so it appeared to Stephen of Elseth, as he entered the long hall that served as both study and library to the wing of the building that only the mages were called to. He saw her by the large arch of a window, as the sun streamed in through pale yellow panes of thick, perfect glass. She stood, facing out into the gardens, positioned beneath the peak of the window's height. The sun cast her shadow in a thin dark line against the empty tables at her back.

"That's her?" Gilliam said quietly, catching Stephen's attention.

"Yes."

"She doesn't look the same as she did when she saved us from the demon-kin."

"No," Stephen replied, as he began to move again. Still, it comforted him to hear it—because until Gilliam had spoken those words, in this place, he had not remembered it. A shadow lifted, perhaps a hint of the doubt that Stephen had not even felt strongly enough to place into words. "Sit still, Gil."

But Gilliam, not used to this odd contraption of a chair and wheels, could not. The girl who walked on his other side suddenly reached down and butted her head into his shoulder playfully.

"And keep your arms away from your sides."

"Yes, Priestess," Gilliam replied smartly. He cursed when Stephen whacked him suddenly on the top of the head. "Stephen," he began, as he grabbed the girl's arm before she could retaliate on his behalf.

"Gilliam," his huntbrother countered. "This is not the time or place. We've come to speak with—"

"Me." And the dark-robed figure at the windows turned.

She was hard to look at; the sun at her back made a shadow of her, a figure of darkness. Stephen could make out the outline of her chin and brow; he could see the light pass through stray strands of her hair, so he knew her hood was back and at her shoulders. But her hands were at her sides, and she was so perfectly still she could almost have been a dark statue, an ornament in a library for scholars and students, to be remarked upon and then forgotten as part of the daily surroundings.

"I am here," she said quietly, "and I have much to tell you both." She stepped into the room, away from the frame of blinding light that kept her obscured. "Shall we start?" She lifted a hand and curved her fingers gently in summons.

"We should wait for Lady Elseth and Zareth Kahn," Stephen replied, rolling Gilliam, with a grunt, over the edge of the carpet. "The Priestess will be here, too, I think. She's been tending Gilliam, but says she hasn't recovered enough to finish until this eve."

Evayne continued to walk toward them, and as Stephen's eyes grew used to the normal light of the room, he froze. For although her face was familiar, she was not the same woman who he had tried to comfort the evening before.

No, her chin was harsher, more defined, and her brow was lined; her eyes, although still violet, were lined as well. She walked, and carried herself, as Lady Elseth did, and would do in the future—as a woman who wears age and wisdom as tokens of power.

He recovered quickly, although the words did not return as easily as they might have. Instead, he busied himself, arranging Gilliam's chair at Evayne's dark side.

"None of your companions will arrive," this Evayne replied, with just a hint of bitter amusement to turn her lips at the corners.

"None?" It was said quickly; harshly. Stephen frowned as he met Evayne's eyes directly for the first time that day.

"No, Stephen of Elseth," she said, dropping her smile and her voice, "but not because I have magicked them or caused them any harm."

He had the grace to blush, and she, to look away.

"Go," she said, "and look outside for only a moment. You will understand, then, as much as I can explain to you. Do not ask me questions about what you see, Stephen. Even if I wished it, I could not answer them."

Reluctantly, he let go of Gilliam's strange chair and turned to the window that towered above him, stretching for the ceiling and the sky. The girl, as ever, stayed at Gilliam's side; Stephen might not have left his Lord otherwise. But whatever it was that Evayne thought he might see escaped his notice, and he almost turned away in disappointment.

The sky was blue and lightly clouded. The grass was perfectly cut, and rolled into distinct, velvet flatness—even around the base of the trees that topped the building's height by many, many feet. Flowers, in precise rows, grew against the base of the walls, gates, and walkways. Small animals, with more temerity than wit, ran across the green, and birds of all sizes cut across the air between ground, tree, and fountain.

And then he knew what the subtle strangeness was; knew why Evayne thought that none, after he and Gilliam, would arrive. One of those birds was frozen in the air, iridescent wings stretched wide, feet forming an outward strut inches away from the nearest fountain's ledge. It did not land; it did not move. As he shifted his focus, he saw that nothing did.

Not even breeze disturbed the Order's garden.

He turned slowly to face her and noted that she did not squint into the sunlight. But her face, with sun to light it, was still as pale as it had been last night, her eyes still as brilliant.

"I . . . understand." He bowed.

"Good. Explain it to me," Gilliam said. He shifted in

the chair, winced, and settled back into his former position.

"I think—I think that time doesn't turn outside."

"Very good, Stephen. But within this room, it does, and we have little of it. This is costly, even if necessary, and I cannot hold it long; the world here is already too hectic and too busy."

He wanted to ask her why she needed to perform this magic, if magic it was, at all. Why not just speak with Zareth Kahn and Lady Elseth and the Mother's Priestess? He did not ask; her glance strayed.

"Hello, wild one," Evayne said quietly. She held out one hand, and after a moment, the wild girl—Gilliam's only packmate in residence—stepped forward almost timidly. "You found them, I see." Although the girl wore a simple shift—one loose enough not to be immediately discarded—she was hardly decent. Evayne, if she noted this at all, did not remark upon it.

The girl opened her mouth in a whine and bark.

"You are well. Don't worry; we will not fail."

"You—you know her?"

Evayne nodded. "I do now." She turned away from the girl. "And I know you, Stephen, quite well. I apologize if I confused you last night. It was—the first time I'd met you, and I am not good at first meetings, even though many years have passed," She raised a hand, looked at it carefully, and then let it drop.

"Years?"

"It hasn't been years yet, has it?" she said, almost to herself. "No, never mind it. As I said, I cannot hold us above Time forever; already I tire."

"Who are you?" Stephen asked softly.

"Evayne."

Exasperated, he opened his mouth; she raised a hand and gently swatted his words away, as if they were insects.

"You said, last night, that you would answer our questions," he said, undeterred by her cool gesture. His arms, clothed in the velvet that told his station, he crossed against his chest. Gilliam recognized the look on Stephen's face.

"I was young then, Stephen. If you prefer to think so, call me liar. But I am not what I was, and I cannot answer the questions that I know you will ask."

"Time?" he asked, but it was almost a sneer, he was so frustrated.

Her face lost the last of its warmth, and there had been little enough of it. "Would you become as I, Stephen of Elseth?" Her shoulders fell back, and her chin, proud and harsh, came up. "Would you walk a separate path, a separate time, from any other?"

He didn't understand the question.

"Tomorrow," she said, "you will wake and your Hunter will wake; you will go and breakfast and speak of the things that concern you, the worries you share.

"Next year, you will marry the woman you choose—should you choose—and you will eventually father children. You will watch them grow, and you will love them as you are able, regardless of how they change. You will understand them because you will have had the time to share, the time to form the bond.

"Tomorrow," her voice grew cooler, but softer, and her eyes became eerie in their remoteness, "I will wake to the clamor of war on a distant plain. People that I have not yet met will die there—and perhaps ten years from now I will have seen enough of them to mourn their passing in some human fashion.

"For I have walked away from Time's path, and forged a path of my own. None can walk it, Stephen; none can follow it with me.

"If you ask me questions, perhaps I will prove too weak to turn them aside, and you may find yourself above Time's path—and quite alone."

He did not doubt the threat, but doubted the weakness; in her voice there was ice, and that ice was not brittle.

"I'm sorry," she said suddenly, although she did not sound at all contrite. "There is no time. Let me tell you what I must. Come, child, sit—either at my feet or at your master's. Do not distract him until I have finished."

The wild girl tilted a head until her ear was almost level with her shoulder. Then she nodded, which looked even more peculiar, and folded up into a quiet little ball at Gilliam's feet.

Without further preamble, Evayne said, "You must leave Breodanir and travel to Essalieyan."

Gilliam's eyes narrowed.

"Essalieyan is the heart of the world," Evayne continued, serene now. "In it, there is much knowledge, much that is old, much that is wise or powerful. It is there you must find what you seek."

"What do we 'seek'? Why in the Hells would we travel to Essalieyan?" To say that Gilliam growled would have been inaccurate, but he did convey the sense of a growl by the curl of his lip and the lowering of his head.

"Because in Essalieyan, Lord Elseth, you will find a cure for the ailments of your companion."

Involuntarily, Gilliam looked down at the brown—and for the moment, untangled—hair of the wild girl. He had not yet named her, and although he felt, no, knew her to be of his pack, he could not bring himself to do so. He reached down and stroked her fine hair. Answers. Essalieyan.

Prejudice, for no one from Breodanir could ever forget the damage done by foreign nonbelievers, hope, and fear struggled within him. It was Stephen who spoke next, and he spoke to break the silence, after contemplating her directive.

"Lady, you ask much without explanation."

"Yes," she said, bowing her head. Her brow wrinkled; she massaged it gently with her fingertips. "Stephen, you will be free from your wyrd only in Essalieyan. The demon-kin will hunt you, and only in Essalieyan is there any hope of refuge."

"Why will they hunt me? What do they seek?"

Silence answered him, silence and the remote chill of her expression. She watched his face; he felt her eyes, unblinking, scrape across his brow. His skin tingled as if he had endured a great cold before entering warmth. *Essalieyan.* It was a whisper of a word, a youthful dream, a story. He looked down and met Gilliam's eyes. Gilliam nodded. "Evayne, Lady, what you offer us, we accept. We will travel, if possible, to Essalieyan. Shall we venture to the capital, Averalaan?"

"Yes," she answered softly. Then, her eyes narrowed as if the light from the window had grown too intense. "But you must leave at once."

"At once? Impossible."

"Is it so?"

Stephen looked away. He had known, somehow, that she would ask them to leave immediately; he had his answer prepared. "We cannot make the trek and be guaranteed to return in time for the Sacred Hunt; it's a journey of two or three months. We will have to wait until the Hunt is called before we take our leave, or we lose our lands, our titles, and our people."

"If you wait for the Hunt," Evayne said, turning her back upon him, "you doom Breodanir."

Silence reigned in the wake of her words. The words themselves seemed to reverberate with a life of their own; they had a truth to them that Evayne was conduit for, no more.

"Will you go? I cannot travel with you," she added, a little bitterly, "but I will see you on the road, and in the city itself."

Stephen looked back at his Hunter.

Gilliam was silent, almost brooding. For it was Gilliam who held the title and the lands that were forfeit if they did not return in time to Hunt at the King's—and the God's—call. "Could we make it?" he asked, his voice a whisper.

"If traveling conditions are good; if there are no bandits and no problems in the free towns; if the mountain pass is not heavy with snow—don't forget, it's late enough in the season. That would leave us with scant weeks, maybe two in total, in the city of the Twin Kings before we had to retreat. And once again, we depend on perfect conditions of travel if we are to return to the King's City, and the Sacred Hunt."

"And how long will this thing take?" Gilliam said, speaking directly to Evayne's dark back. She turned slowly, glancing over her shoulder, showing the perfect profile of her face.

"I do not know."

"And what exactly must we do?" Gilliam said, bringing his hands down hard on the armrests of his chair.

"I am not certain; I can't see it clearly."

"That's what I thought." He was silent again. Almost brooding. Stephen felt his Hunter's anger and his fear, his hope and his unease, as they braided themselves around the bond that he and Gilliam shared. And then, almost at once, they went slack as Gil raised his head, and his voice, again.

"Evayne."

"Yes?"

"What is her name?"

The question was unexpected, even to Evayne, who stared a moment in confusion before she realized who Gilliam was speaking of. Then a smile shadowed her face for the briefest of instants. "Her name is Espere."

The wild girl, so named, suddenly raised her head and barked. If she had had a tail, Stephen was sure it would be thumping away at the carpet.

Gilliam started to stand, which galvanized his huntbrother into action. That action, unfortunately, was to offer an arm as support, rather than to force an errant Hunter back to his seat. Gilliam would stand, and Stephen, knowing that this was not a point that he could win without a protracted and public argument, gave in gracefully.

"Evayne, mage, or whatever you are, we will go to the city. With Espere."

At this, Evayne laughed, although the laugh was a gentle one. Then the laughter faded, and she turned to face them both, fully. "He chose Espere's protectors well, when he sent her to you. Listen, both of you. Listen well. What I speak here will not be repeated." Her arms, she raised to either side; stiff and dark-robed, she became a mortal cross. Her eyes, violet, became darker still, irises spreading across the whites until nothing human remained.

When she spoke, her voice was a chorus.

Just as Teos' voice had been.

"The Covenant has been broken in spirit; the portals

*are open; the Gods are bound. Go forth to the Light of
the World, and find the Darkness. Keep your oath; fulfil
your promise. The road must be taken, or the Shining City
will rise anew."*

"What oath?" Stephen shouted, for the voices were a
storm; even when the words had finished, the air was
heavy with their texture. Pain and peace, age and youth,
love and hatred called out through Evayne's lips, and then
lingered a moment in her eyes. *"What oath?"* His words
were heavy; sharp. The Shining City was a thing of
legend—and a legend so fell and so dark that in the end,
it claimed Morrel's life at the dawn of time.

Violet eyes cleared as Evayne lowered her arms; she
had offered him no answer. "I thank you both," she said
softly, her voice once again her own. "But I must travel
now." Speaking had diminished her somehow.

"That was a God's voice," Stephen said.

"Yes. I am your wyrd, Stephen. You know which God
speaks through me. And if you do not, I cannot speak of
it. I must leave."

"What in the Hells did it mean? What oath are we supposed to keep? What is the darkness and what is the
light?"

"I don't know." Bitterness returned to her face. "I only
know from my own experience that my advice to you is
sound—you must go to Essalieyan." When his eyes narrowed, she added, "I am no more god than you, Stephen
of Elseth. Do you think that my God will grant me permission to enter his counsels, any more than yours does?"
She turned, then, and began to walk away.

"Wait!" Stephen said, swiftly following her. He caught
her shoulder in a tight grip, and she drew herself up to
her full height. She did not pull away, but instead pivoted
to face him.

"Yes?"

"Last night—last night you . . ." He didn't know what
he wanted to say, and looked away from the pale violet of
her steady glance. "Did you know, last night, what would
happen to us? What we would choose?"

Her brows drew together into a peppered line; the
wrinkles there deepened enough that it was clear what ex-

pression had formed them. "Yes," she answered at last, as if the words had been dragged from her. "But I did not know that now you would ask me of it. I was bitter in my youth," she added, and her lips turned up in a simile of a smile, and of wisdom. Neither reached her eyes. He saw her age clearly, but more clearly saw the weakness and the fear that he associated with only the very youthful.

"And not now?" He pressed her.

"I don't know. Am I?" Before he could answer, she reached up and touched his cheek, trailing its hollow with her fingers until they trembled off the line of his jaw. As he opened his mouth in shock, she withdrew her hand. There was an intimacy, a knowledge, a familiarity in her touch that Stephen was afraid of. She started to speak, and then shook her head and pulled away. He did not stop her.

But she turned again as she reached the door. "Time will start the moment I leave."

Gilliam, Lord Elseth, Stephen of Elseth, and the newly named Espere, watched her with wide, unblinking eyes.

It was to Stephen that she spoke, and the next words were so odd they were almost incomprehensible, although they were simple and plain.

"Stephen—when I was young, you were kind to me. Will you—can you—" she looked away. Drew herself up. Smiled ruefully, and shook her head. "We will meet again, you and I. Be as merciful as you can."

"She's gone," Stephen said quietly when Zareth Kahn pushed the door open and lightly stepped into the room. The scene that greeted his eyes was almost cozy; wood burned in the curtained fireplace in the room's northernmost wall, and around it, Gilliam and the wild girl sat, eyes drawn to the flame, attention absorbed by what they saw flickering in its heart.

It was late enough in the season to be chilly here, but the mages rarely burned wood at this time; they chose instead to don heavier robes and save the heat for more dire need. Zareth Kahn opened his mouth to mention this, then shut it again on the words.

Gilliam was quiet and pale, and the girl, not touching

her Lord, but still by his side, even more so. Were it not for the windows, with their open view of birds and greenery, he might have thought it winter.

He cleared his throat, but before he could speak, the door at his back opened rather awkwardly. Navigating its wide, heavy swing, he stepped quickly out of the way as Lady Elseth entered the room.

She was severely dressed in heavy wool skirts and a rather stiff jacket; it was as if she, too, felt the cold here. "Well?" she said quietly, as all eyes turned to face her.

"Evayne is gone," Stephen replied.

Lady Elseth nodded mildly, as if to say that she had expected as much. She walked over to her sitting son and inspected his ribs with all the nonchalance of a worried mother. "What did she have to say?" she asked in a casual tone of voice that fooled no one.

"We're to travel," Gilliam replied, leaving off the preamble that would have been Stephen's opening, "to Essalieyan and the city of Averalaan. We leave within the week."

Lady Elseth had twice undertaken that trek on matters of commerce and trade before Gilliam's father had passed away and the duties of the Elseth demesne demanded her attention and her presence. It took her less than a minute to pale. Her eyes grew round and her hands fell to her sides as her fingers began to curl into the heavy, thick wool of her skirts. But her voice didn't waver. "Why?"

"I don't know," Gilliam said, and looked to Stephen's back.

"What did she say?" Zareth Kahn stepped between Lady Elseth and her adopted son. "What did Evayne say?"

"That Breodanir will fall if we fail to leave." Stephen stared into the fire, seeing in the flames neither warmth nor comfort. "I believe her," he added softly.

"Does she know what this may mean to Elseth?" Elsabet's eyes narrowed as she waited for the answer.

"She knows."

"And you know it," Lady Elseth said. "Very well." She swallowed and then pulled her hands from their nervous dance. "A week is not long enough to see to all of your needs. But—"

"It has to be long enough," Stephen said, and turned then to face her. His eyes were ringed, his face pale.

"This has to do with the . . . the demons, doesn't it?"

"What else can it possibly be?"

"Stephen." Gilliam, hand on either wheel, rolled his chair forward until he could touch his huntbrother's hand. "We faced them last night, and we won."

Stephen nodded, but it was clear that he took no strength from his Hunter's words. He was afraid. Time had begun, as Evayne had promised, the moment she left the room. Time turned; the birds touched branches and left the ground, the wind bobbed in leaves, teasing them away from their trees.

The shadows grew darker, although the sun was bright. The Hunter's Horn hung, heavy, at his side. He had the uncanny sense that if he left this city, this kingdom, he would never return to it again.

And everything that he loved was in Breodanir.

"Lady," he said, and bowed to the woman who was his mother. "We will have two weeks in the city of the Twin Kings to see to our task."

"What is your task?" the mage asked, crossing his heavily clad arms, daring to interrupt their discourse. Stephen had expected that Zareth Kahn would be irritated, but instead the mage seemed peculiarly intense and intent. His thin face, shadowed by lack of sleep, looked sharp—the edge of a personality, honed and pressed a little too close for comfort.

"Find the Light of the World. Find its darkness. Keep our oath."

"In other words," the mage replied, "you haven't the barest of notions." He shook his long dark hair, and his eyes became very bright. "But I may have, at the end of this week. With your leave, Lord Elseth, Stephen, I will travel with you at the end of the week—at least as far as Corason."

Stephen had never thought to be grateful for the company of a mage—especially not one who had attempted to force words from him by dint of a spell. He was grateful now. "She said—she said one other thing," he told Zareth Kahn in the quiet of the library.

"And that?"

"We must stop the Shining City from coming again."

"The Shining—"

Silence.

Elsabet watched as her two sons left the King's City. She knew that they would stop in the Elseth demesne; Gilliam would not be parted for months on end from all of his dogs, and had elected—against the quiet, restrained objections of Zareth Kahn—to take six of his dogs on the road with them.

The girl—Espere, he had called her; she wondered if he knew what it meant—still walked, pranced really, by the side of Gilliam's horse. She could not be forced to mount, but Gilliam insisted that this would not slow their progress. She did not believe him. Still, she had no choice but to believe Stephen when he solemnly backed his Hunter's word.

Time, she had told the more serious and studious of her sons, *is everything now. You have two and a half months, Stephen—don't tarry.*

If the Hunter's Death was a loss that every mother feared, Hunter's Disgrace was a life that they feared more. The Sacred Hunt would be called, and if her sons failed in their oaths ... She clutched the locket at her throat as tightly as she dared and exhaled. There was no greater crime in all of Breodanir.

Then, squaring her shoulders and drawing her long, woolen overshawl tightly about her body, Lady Elseth began her short trek back to her rooms in the Order of Knowledge. She would have liked to travel with her sons; she was not certain when she would see them again, or in what circumstances.

But she had much to do; letters to write to Ladies Morganson and Faergif, a Queen to make a plea before, and a number of different Priests to see. She could not travel with her sons, but she could help them best without ever leaving the King's City.

* * *

Smoke was in the air; there was fire, dust, and the smell of rotting flesh. The sun had come and gone, but there had been too many casualties for the victorious troops to deal with all at once. In the morning, the rest of the bodies would be gathered and buried. Or burned.

Evayne began her quiet search in the darkness. She did not know yet when she was; nor did she know where. She did not know what battle this was, between what armies, over what disagreement. In the shadows and the muted hub of campfires in the distance, the banners hung like slack shadows against their poles, withholding all information. She had hoped, just for a moment, that this would be the end; the point at which, briefly, her path and the path of the rest of the world would finally coincide in a solid way, a meaningful way.

But that was the end of it; she knew it. And this was not the time. There was too much left to do. Who?

She traveled by mage-light and masked her coming; hid the sounds of her retching when the smell or the sight of the not quite dead overpowered her. Drawing the folds of her robes well above her knees, she continued to search. Who?

And then she saw the dirty thatch of long blond hair; curls crushed into shoulders and dirt and a tangle of arms. Her breath was sharp; she was never certain—never—that this time would not be the one in which she would find him dead. He alone, of all of her servants—her victims, as she had once called them in her youth—she had no ending for; no death, no finish. She did not understand Time, or his working, and he didn't understand her motions; they existed, uneasy, as allies of the unnamed God that they both served.

She knelt; felt someone's chest give beneath her left knee. Shuddering, she brushed the heavy, wet hair away from a face. His face. She looked at the lines of it, thinking, *we are almost in the same time*. Then, carefully, she dabbed the dried blood at the corners of his mouth.

He stirred. "Is it you?"

"Yes," she replied, cradling his head against her chest as she summoned her power. "Where are we?"

He shook his head, and struggled to sit up; grimaced in pain, but did not leave off his attempt.

"Kallandras," she said, more urgently. "Where are we?"

"I will not tell you," he replied, his breath a wheeze. "It hurts me; it will hurt you, no matter when you come from." He coughed; she lifted a hand and danced his noise away with her fingers and a little spark of blue-light. "Come, help me away."

She nodded in the darkness, brushed the top of his head with the tip of her chin. He froze, and she blushed and pulled away. She blushed—at her age, with so much death and darkness behind her.

But he was gentle, at this age, where he had been cruel in his youth; his anger was softened, although his lined eyes spoke of loss and a yearning which nothing could ever fulfill. No, not nothing. She grimaced as she thought of the Kovaschaii. Stiffened.

"Evayne," he said, and caught her arm. "Not here. I know now that we made the right choice."

She nodded and drew herself up. "To safety, then. I cannot stay."

"No," he whispered. "And I cannot leave." He caught her hand in his, let her support his weight with her shoulder, and followed her lead from the field of death.

And she remembered the first time she had met him at this age—she had been much, much younger then. And he had been almost kind.

"Where were you?" he asked, after they had passed through a circle of trees and over a wide lake, their feet never touching the ground in the moonlight, their bodies casting no shadows.

"I was with Stephen. Of Elseth."

"Ah." He put an arm around her waist, and drew her closer, offering her silence without the pain of words.

There was no light in this darkness. Even the brightest of magical light guttered like a tired torch when it crossed this threshhold. There was shadow, thick and heavy, and then there was a cold, cold night.

But Sor na Shannen needed no pathetic mortal light,

magical or no, to see into the depths of this growing chill. She stayed at the edge of the arena, and knelt low, brushing perfect marble with strands of her hair. Her head, she pressed into the floor, as countless numbers of humans had done before her.

But there was no blade above her neck, and no punishment to follow at the hands of a Priest. There was only the demon and the Gate.

She could still see the gilt-edged marble that had, mere months ago, been solid floor. She could read the words and phrases written there by mages who understood only a small portion of their meaning. Such words, the Gods might have spoken when they had dwelled, aeons past, upon the mortal plane. None spoke them now, not even Sor na Shannen.

She waited in the heavy silence before she dared to raise her head.

"My Lord," she whispered, when she deemed it safe, "your enemies become aware. The daughter of the Unnamed one has entered the field, and I do not believe she will leave it."

In the very center of the complicated pattern that was woven out of strands of silver, veins of gold, folds of marble, there was a motion that was barely strong enough to be noticed. But she felt its power as the darkness thickened and grew even more chill.

Demon-kin do not feel the cold, but Sor na Shannen shivered.

"I hear your will," she answered softly. "The mages who serve us will be summoned to your temple, Lord. We will work more quickly, more urgently. I have my spies in the land of your enemy."

She rose, her lips thin and taut as she pressed them together. Here, she wore no glamour, and called no power. For although the God was not present—not yet—the portal that had taken over a decade to bring to life served as an adequate conduit for his power.

She had no illusions. She was alive because he needed her to be alive. And she had enough time to prove herself before he arrived to once again walk the world in the fullness of his Night and the glory of his Shadow. Nothing else would go wrong. Nothing else could.

After all, the Horn of the Hunter—and at this, just a hint of delicate fang was shown to air—had not been found, or used, by any of the Hunter's followers.

"In months, My Lord, the gate will be open. The barriers will be breached. And you will be the only God who may walk upon the face of the world.

"Those who have not chosen, no matter how bright their souls, will be yours."

Melanie Rawn

EXILES

☐ **THE RUINS OF AMBRAI: Book 1** UE2668—$5.99
☐ **THE RUINS OF AMBRAI: Book 1** (hardcover) UE2619—$20.95

Three Mageborn sisters bound together by ties of their ancient
Blood Line are forced to take their stands on opposing sides
of a conflict between two powerful schools of magic. Together,
the sisters will fight their own private war, and the victors will
determine whether or not the Wild Magic and the Wraithen-
beasts are once again loosed to wreak havoc upon their world.

THE DRAGON PRINCE NOVELS

☐ **DRAGON PRINCE : Book 1** UE2450—$6.99
☐ **THE STAR SCROLL: Book 2** UE2349—$6.99
☐ **SUNRUNNER'S FIRE: Book 3** UE2403—$5.99

THE DRAGON STAR NOVELS

☐ **STRONGHOLD: Book 1** UE2482—$5.99
☐ **STRONGHOLD: Book 1** (hardcover) UE2440—$21.95
☐ **THE DRAGON TOKEN: Book 2** UE2542—$5.99
☐ **SKYBOWL: Book 3** UE2595—$5.99
☐ **SKYBOWL: Book 3** (hardcover) UE2541—$22.00

Tanya Huff

Mickey Zucker Reichert

Jennifer Roberson

<u>THE NOVELS OF TIGER AND DEL</u>

☐ SWORD-DANCER   UE2376—$5.50
☐ SWORD-SINGER   UE2295—$4.99
☐ SWORD-MAKER   UE2379—$5.99
☐ SWORD-BREAKER   UE2476—$5.99

<u>CHRONICLES OF THE CHEYSULI</u>

☐ SHAPECHANGERS: Book 1   UE2140—$4.99
☐ THE SONG OF HOMANA: Book 2   UE2317—$4.99
☐ LEGACY OF THE SWORD: Book 3   UE2316—$4.99
☐ TRACK OF THE WHITE WOLF: Book 4   UE2193—$4.99
☐ A PRIDE OF PRINCES: Book 5   UE2261—$5.99
☐ DAUGHTER OF THE LION: Book 6   UE2324—$4.99
☐ FLIGHT OF THE RAVEN: Book 7   UE2422—$4.99
☐ A TAPESTRY OF LIONS: Book 8   UE2524—$5.99

OTHER

☐ RETURN TO AVALON   UE2679—$5.99
Edited by Jennifer Roberson.
A tribute anthology to author Marion Zimmer Bradley, with contributions by Jennifer Roberson, Melanie Rawn, Charles De-Lint, Andre Norton, C.J. Cherryh, and others.

GAYLE GREENO

☐ **THE GHATTI'S TALE:**
  Book 1—Finders, Seekers UE2550—$5.99
The Seekers Veritas, an organization of truth-finders composed of Bondmate pairs—one human, one a telepathic, cat-like ghatti—is under attack. And the key to defeating this deadly foe is locked in one human's mind behind barriers even her ghatta has never been able to break.

☐ **MINDSPEAKER'S CALL**
  The Ghatti's Tale: Book 2 UE2579—$5.99
Someone seems bent on creating dissension between Canderis and the neighboring kingdom of Marchmont. And even the truth-reading skill of the Seekers Veritas may not be enough to unravel the twisted threads of a conspiracy that could see the two lands caught in a devastating war . . .

☐ **EXILES' RETURN**
  The Ghatti's Tale: Book 3 UE2655—$5.99
Seeker Doyce is about to embark on a far different path—a ghatti-led journey into the past. For as a new vigilante-led reign of terror threatens the lives of Seekers and Resonants alike, the secrets of that long-ago time when the first Seeker-ghatti Bond was formed may hold the only hope for their future . . .